To my frien
From autho
Reid [illegible]

A Miner's Story

By

Reid Youngberg

My story is dedicated to Wilfred Jean Batiste Laberge

(Some called him 'Bill Lebarge')

One of the best miners of my acquaintance

Artist of the cover picture is Beth Coulas

A Miner's Story – Chapter 1

The shrill whistle blew as the steamer pulled the train around a bend in the line, edging the rocky shore of the placid Precambrian lake. It was a warm day in late May, 1957; the antiquated C.N. coach with its windows stuck shut was stifling. A tall gaunt figure of a man slouched in one of the stiff upright seats. He sat alone next to the soot-streaked window, his elbow on the armrest, his jaw against his hand. He stared vacantly out the window as the lakes, rock hills, muskeg, and bush of the Precambrian Shield rolled by. He wore faded grey khaki shirt and pants, with an old set of canvas runners for footwear. He had on the seat beside him two kit bags of medium size. One was fairly full, the other about half filled. The bags were as faded and worn as his clothes. His complexion was sallow, his eyes a little bloodshot, with a yellowish tinge. His face bore a sullen, bored expression. His brown hair, in need of a cut, receded at the temples and was combed straight back, the excess matted against the back of the seat. His left hand, which rested on his lap, was trembling slightly.

There were not a lot of other people in that coach. A young Indian couple with a small child sat in the seat ahead of him. The little girl could barely see over the back of the seat standing up. The man grinned as she ducked her head shyly, giggling, and then came back up slowly, batting her big brown eyes at the man, until her mother pulled her back, scolding her in Ojibwa. A big heavily muscled man sat behind him; a curly haired blonde man, fair-complexioned, perhaps in his late twenties. He was in jeans and a brown suede leather jacket fringed in leather. On his feet he wore a new pair of high top Kodiaks, laced half ways up. He was a tidy man, relaxed, enjoying the ride. His packsack lay on the empty seat in front of him. There may have been half a dozen others in the coach.

An asthmatic Newsie entered the coach announcing his wares which were placed on a tray hung from a strap around his neck and resting on his paunch. "Coke, candy bar, chip, chip." The Newsie wheezed as he waddled down the aisle then noisily sucked in air. "Coke, candy bar, chip, chip, chip"

"How much for a coke?'' the man in Khaki asked.

"Fifteen cents."

"I got twelve," he offered hopefully.

"No, sorry....coke, candy bar, chip, chip, chip," he continued.

"I buy it you coke, mister," a voice from behind spoke out. The big blonde fellow got up and dropped thirty cents on the newsie's tray. He took two of the cokes from the newsie, and taking the seat across from the man in khaki, offered him one, sticking out his hand.

"Name Toivo. Toivo Maki."

"Wilf Baker," accepting the offer and the two men shook.

"You've got a good hand," Wilf went on, feeling Toivo's grip.

"I cut pulp," Toivo explained, then added, "I Finlander."

"I thought so," said Wilf. He couldn't help grinning. He took a pull on his coke, almost draining the little six ounce bottle. Toivo watched, impressed. He couldn't help grinning either.

"You got good hand, too. What you do?"

"I'm a miner...an underground miner."

"You work?"

"No, hoping to get on at Steep Rock. I heard they're hiring." He finished his coke and belched.

"Thanks," he said, laying the empty bottle on the seat.

"You get it yob no 'roblem."

"Hope so. You wouldn't have a smoke, partner, would you?"

Toivo pulled out a package of Players, gave one to Wilf, and took one for him. He saw the gleam in Wilf's eye as it fell on the cigarette.

"Got no light, partner....just got the habit...."

"No 'roblem, Wilf," he said, holding out a match. He noticed Wilf's hands shaking as he accepted a light, and watched him as he drew deeply on it as he leaned back in his seat.

"Good, eh?

"That's for sure, Toivo....that for sure."

Toivo looked around the coach discreetly, and then pulled a mickey of rye from inside his jacket. "You want it 'rink, Wilf?"

Wilf's eyes rolled onto the bottle. "Yeah...," was all he could manage.

Toivo removed the cap. It was a fresh bottle. He took a good swallow, and passed it to Wilf, saying, *"Kippis."* Wilf had drunk with Finns; he knew their solemn toast, Kippis. Having said the word, he upended the bottle to his mouth and let the contents pour down his throat. Toivo watched, impressed, as the bubbles of air rolled up the neck of the bottle, displacing the whiskey. At last Wilf put it down, letting out a very satisfied gasp. He passed the remainder of the bottle back to Toivo; apologizing and somewhat embarrassed that most of the bottle was gone.

"No 'roblem," assured Toivo, "I was 'tink you tirsty." He raised the bottle one more time in a gesture to fellowship. *"Kippis"* he said. He emptied the bottle and put it back in his jacket, again careful to look around. "Feel better now, Wilf, eh?" he went on.

"That's for sure Toivo," he replied, smiling....."That's for damn sure!"

Toivo stuck out his hand again, and they shook. He noticed Wilf's shakes were gone. He offered another cigarette and they both lit up again. The train was slowing down now. The conductor entered the coach, announcing Kashabowie, a ten minute stop. The train ground to a halt.

Kashabowie wasn't much. From the train window Wilf could see a general store and part of a street with a few houses and shacks, one with a rag stuffed in a broken window. The train had come to a complete halt now and the Indian family got off. "Not much of a place," he thought.

"'Rappers," (trappers), said Toivo, seemingly reading his mind.

"'Board," bawled the conductor, and the train jerked into motion. Wilf was nicely feeling the effects of the whiskey now. Not enough to get drunk.....if he could only drink like that...it sure hit the spot. The pain of his last drunk was gone. His nerves were settled.....he felt good...relaxed.....O.K. His eyes closed slowly....then he caught himself and jerked awake. Toivo had gone back to his seat. He let himself sleep. God, he was tired. He was awakened a little later by Toivo shaking his shoulder. Toivo was standing in the aisle with his packsack on his back. He looked up to see Toivo handing him a five dollar bill.

"I go, now, Vilf. I home ....Sapawe."

Wilf stood, up accepting the five dollars, and shook his hand once more. "You sure helped me out, Toivo. Hope I catch up to you sometime."

"No 'roblem, Vilf. Ve see you again. Good luck my 'riend." He returned Wilf's handshake and left the coach. It was getting dusk as Wilf watched him stepping onto the platform. A Native woman and a little girl came to meet him. The woman kissed him on the mouth while the little girl hugged him as they started for home. Wilf was near tears, watching them head down the gravel road from the siding. "There's a family," he thought.

He felt disgust and self loathing that he had come to such a place again.... flat broke, hungover, and homeless. This wasn't the first time. It had to be the last. "Pretty decent guy", he thought, "I gotta get back to him."

The train was pulling out now, and he could just see their backs now, disappearing down the little gravel road, Toivo with his packsack on his back, his lady at his side, his little girl holding his hand. "They got themselves a life," he thought.

Atikokan was the next stop. It was dark when the train pulled up. "Atikokan," the conductor bawled out, "twenty minute stop....."

Wilf gathered up his two kits, hanging the heavier one by its strap on his shoulder. In that one he had his mining gear. The other, much lighter and loosely packed, contained his remaining clothing....a pair of rubber boots, a few pairs of socks, shorts, two sets of long grey woolen underwear, an extra pair of faded khaki shirt and pants, a navy blue wool toque, his shaving gear, and a red and black checked mackinaw shirt. He wrapped his hand around the neck of the lighter bag and swung it over his back. Letting the bag hang over the same shoulder as the other, he made his way off the coach.

Stepping down to the station platform, he could feel the coolness of the evening coming on. It was getting dusk. He checked his 'big ben' pocket watch. It was five before nine. There were people milling about the platform, some getting on, some getting off, some were there to meet them or see them off, and some just spectators. Wilf's attention was on his stomach. He was starved.

Looking down to the end of the platform, past the maroon coloured CN station house, was a white building, almost equal in size to the station house, showing the sign "BEANERY". 'Good enough', he thought and headed straight for it. Getting through the door, he looked around at the dining area. It was a spacious room, with a few chrome tables and chairs against the far wall across from the entrance. Other than that, the main seating arrangement was around a large horseshoe-shaped counter surrounded by chrome stools.

The kitchen was separated from the dining area by a wall, which had an entrance coming through into the middle of the horseshoe, and an order window slightly to the right of it. To the right of the window, the counter came right up to the wall. The other end of the counter left a four foot gap so the waiter could access the tables.

There were a few people sitting around a couple of the tables, and half a dozen spread out around the counter. The waiter was a stout, tall man with a double chin and a heavy, dark moustache. He was dressed in whites, a white apron, and a boat shaped white hat. Wilf set his gear down at the foot the counter, taking a stool two over from the nearest customer. The waiter approached him, handing him a menu, asking as he did so..."cof-fee?" Wilf nodded, taking the menu, and the accent. *"Oui, m'sieur, s'il vous plait," (Yes sir, please),* he answered. The waiter smiled, obviously pleased, showing a gold tooth between his thick lips. Wilf couldn't help grinning.

The waiter returned with the coffee. *"Parle Francais, eh?" (You speak French, eh?)*

"Un 'tit peu, ouais," (a little bit, yup,) he came back, and then continued in English, "I'll have the cheeseburger deluxe, please". The waiter answered in French with *'pas'd probleme', (no problem)* as he placed the order at the order window, shouting through it to the cook, "cheeseburger deluxe, Marie, *et fait ca une bonne, OK (and make it a good one, OK)".* She appeared briefly at the window, sizing up the request. The waiter pointed to Wilf. She nodded approval. She was a pleasant looking woman, even bigger than the waiter. She went to her grill to fill the order.

"I am Jean Guy, my friend....Jean Guy Trembley," he said, sticking out a large hand.

"Wilf Baker".

"Dis my place, Wilf. Dat my wife, Marie. She not speak de good English yet," he explained.

"Takes time, Jean Guy."

"Mais oui, ce prend de temps" (Oh yes, it takes time), he said, reverting to French, and then as if correcting himself, went on, "Yes, it takes time." He refilled Wilf cup, and then went around to the other customers with the pot. By the time he came back, Wilf's order was on the window

Wilf was pleased to see a thick cheeseburger beside a generous pile of French fries, and Jean Guy was pleased to see the gleam in Wilf's eyes as he beheld the feast, the likes of which he'd not know in a few days. *"Bon appetit, mon ami," (Good appetite, my friend),* he said, gently placing the inverted bill by Wilf's plate. Wilf looked up, his mouth already, full, and gave Jean Guy an emphatic thumbs-up. Jean Guy smiled at this, and as he moved away, Wilf lifted the bill for a look. It was eighty five cents. He fairly inhaled his food. Jean Guy had another coffee waiting for him as he got the last of his chips down. He drank it and went to the till with his bill. Jean Guy gave him $4.50 change. Wilf looked at the change and then Jean Guy, puzzled.

"You can find a room across the street for $4.50," Jean Guy explained.

"Thanks..." was all Wilf could manage.

"No probleme, mon ami, pas'd probleme pentoute. A la prochaine fois," (No problem, my friend, no problem at all. Until the next time), he said with a wave.

"Merci beaucoup, Jean Guy....a la prochaine fois" (Thanks a lot, Jean Guy. Until the next time), he replied, almost choked, and left. It was quite dark now, as he stepped out into the night. He walked past the end of the beanery and looked across the street and saw the building Jean Guy was referring to The Atikokan Hotel. He started over, feeling his money. With his nerves eased, and a full stomach, sleep would hit the spot now. "On the other hand," he thought, feeling his money....." a beer would sure hit the spot now....a guy could sleep outside in this weather". ...he'd done that before.

He walked past the lobby entrance a little ways, to the barroom doors and stared through the window of the barroom door. 'There's money in this town,' he thought, taking in the scene. The room was packed like any bar in any mining boomtown, full of noisy drunken miners, everybody talking.....nobody listening much. Wilf could hear the din through the doors. His mouth was starting to water. 'Yeah,' he thought, 'I'll go in and have a couple....see what's going on.' He could see people he knew .... Pete Hendricks, Art Crofton, and Bud Neilson were at one table with a couple of other guys he didn't know. None of them could be counted on for a touch....but what would he have to lose?

A Miner's Story – Chapter 1

He was almost ready to push through the door. He had it half open, when the stale smell of smoke and spilled beer hit him. His mouth watered, and the thought of having a beer was irresistible. Just then he saw him! It Vince Jamieson coming to join them at the table, just on his way back from the can. It was the same old Vince; black hair, thick, uncombed and in need of a cut...three or four days stubble on his jaw, beneath a heavy black moustache. He was a big man, tall and barrel-chested. His shirt, like always, was open halfway down, exposing a thick, hairy chest. His sleeves were rolled up halfway to the elbow. He wore jeans held up by a broad studded belt, cinched up below a beer-belly just nicely getting started. And on his feet, as always, we're the inevitable Kodiaks.

He hated Vince. It still grated on Wilf the obnoxious amusement Vince felt at Wilf losing his job at Cochenour, a gold mine in Red lake. Wilf had come back to work too late from a drunk once too often to find his time already made out. Wilf could hear Vince's unmistakable laugh right across the mine Dry; raucous and piercing in unrestrained glee, he laughed uproariously as Wilf was packing his diggers (diggers being his mining gear) into his kitbag to leave the mine for the last time. "Happy trails, haywire," Vince shouted at Wilf as he left adding insult to injury. Vince pulled up an empty chair joining the group at the table and Wilf stopped dead in his tracks. 'So much for saying 'hello', he thought, and then he heard a voice behind him...

"Are you coming or going?"

He turned, about move out the man's way. "Not sure lately..." Wilf started to say when his mouth fell open. It was Stan Rooster, grinning, punching him on the shoulder and sticking out his hand. "How's it going haywire? You working or performing?"

Wilf shook the extended hand. "Not much of either lately. Sure good to see you, Stan....but did you have to break my shoulder?"

Stan was tall and strong .There was no beer-belly on him. A handsome man of dark complexion with a full head of black hair combed straight back. He was a half-breed Ojibwa Indian. In jeans and a t-shirt, he showed muscular arms, and a thick neck which came out in muscle down to his shoulders. He was one of the strongest men Stan had ever met.

Wilf once seen him straighten out a brand-new horseshoe over an argument in a game of horseshoes at the 1st of July games between the local gold mines at Red Lake. Stan and Wilf were partners in a track drift at the Cochenour Mine at the time. (A drift is a flat tunnel in an underground mine). Dickenson, Campbell, H.G. Young, Madsen, and Mackenzie Island were all mines in the competition. In the end it had come down to a match between a big Swede named Ole Svenson, who spoke with a thick accent representing the Dickenson Mine and Stan who was there for Cochenour. Stan finished with a double ringer, and to anyone present was the obvious winner. Ole, who been drinking a lot of beer throughout the event didn't agree with that.

Ole stood in Stan's face, reeking of beer. "You no vin." he said. "You yust good for yerk it off." Ole continued by pushing against Stan's chest. Stan didn't say a word, picked up a horseshoe and gripped it with both hands. He held it in front of the Swede's face and straightened it with seemingly no great effort. The Swede's jaw dropped like a loose hinge and his eyes looked like saucers.

"O.K.....you vin," Ole said finally and stuck out his hand. Stan shook the Swede's hand and there was a loud cheer from the crowd who were all well into their beer. Wilf was laughing. It was a lovely, warm summer day. Funny thing about Stan.....he didn't drink.

"Looked like you were headin' in for a beer, Wilf...."

"Well, I was..." Wilf said, looking through the window. "But..." His voice trailed off.

Stan took the problem in at a glance. "Still got a hard on for Jamieson, eh?"

"Yeah, I owe that prick... it's not the time just now," Wilf responded

"Wilf, don't even bother. He's a bag of shit with a big mouth. You're better than that, Wilf. I found him changing right next to me in the Dry my first day at Steep Rock. He says to me, 'Who let you off the reserve?' Then he laughs in my face, wheezing and spitting all over me." Stan recounted.

"You let him get away with that?"

"Well, no. I popped him one in the gut, and he sat down on the bench, real quiet-like. He didn't have much to say after that. Vince Jamieson was never good enough to make that kind of talk. He's just an asshole with a big mouth,"

"Sure is," confirmed Wilf

Stan pulled him away from the door. "Come on, Wilf, let's get us a coffee." They left the hotel by the railway and Stan lead the way toward Main Street, Atikokan. It was a little past ten, still comfortably warm. Stan had pretty well sized up Wilf's situation.

"Just got in, eh Wilf?"

"Yeah, just off the train."

"No place yet, eh?"

"No. I had the price of a room at that hotel...." said Wilf.

"... and not too much more by the looks of you..."

"No, not too stakey...." Wilf confirmed.

"I figured so. I doubt you'd get a room in the Atikokan, Wilf. This town is full. You can't find a place unless you get real lucky."

"Could always camp out for the night."

"Cops will have you right back on the train, Wilf." They were on to Main Street now, facing a fairly large flat roofed two story rooming house done in imitation red brick siding. Stan stopped here and said "That's where I stay, Wilf. (There was a small sign over the door, saying Cross' Rooming House). I think I can help you out, Wilf. Here's the deal. I leave for work in an hour, and I'll be graveyard shift for the rest of the week. I'll speak to Sadie (Cross), if you can use my bed while I'm on shift ......" Wilf was nodding, hopefully. "But Wilf....no drinking, right."

Wilf shook his head almost speechless. "No", was all he could manage.

"O.K...." said Stan, ringing the doorbell. "We'll see what Sadie has to say."

The door opened, and a pleasant looking tall brunette appeared at the door. Wilf judged her to be in her mid forties.

"Hi Sadie," said Stan. "Hope I'm not calling too late. This here's my friend Wilf Baker; he just got in....needs a place. I know you're full up, Sadie, but do you think there might be any rooms coming up?"

Sadie looked Wilf up and down as he did his best at looking bland. After a moment she said, "Maybe at the end of the week, I think there could be a vacancy. That brings us to the end of the month. There's one young fellow a little too haywire to my liking I might like to see go……maybe get back to me by Friday, and we'll see how we stand."

"Sure thing, Sadie. In the meantime, I'm working Graveyards for the week, so would it be all right for Wilf to use my bed while I'm at work?"

"Sure, that's fine with me. I don't mind if he don't." She smiled, and went back inside.

There were outside stairs coming up the left side of the building from the sidewalk to an unlocked entrance off an enclosed landing at the top of the stairs, which opened up to the upstairs of the building where the rented rooms were located. Wilf followed Stan up the stairs and through the entrance which opened into a hallway. He followed Stan down the hallway to the door of his room, which was the third one down on the right. On the way, they passed a room immediately across from the entrance, from which a loud, drunken conversation could be heard through the walls.

"That the one who might be leaving Stan?"

"Ya, I think that's the one."

At his own room now, he put his hand on the knob, and then turned and faced Wilf squarely. "Wilf," said looking him hard in the eye, "No drinking, right?" Before Wilf could agree, Stan continued, "You take a drink and the deals off."

"I hear you man, I won't touch a drop…" said Wilf.

"Good enough," said Stan," I won't mention it again."

Stan opened the door. "This is it my friend….home sweet home."

A Miner's Story – Chapter 2

Wilf took in the room in a glance. It was small, but big enough for a flop. There was a half-width bed against the left wall, a small writing table under the window beside the bed. There was also a dresser with a mirror to the right side of the room and a wooden armchair next to that, with a narrow closet on the left side, at the foot of the bed.

"Just throw your kit in the corner, there, Wilf," said Stan, picking up his lunch pail, "We'll go over to the restaurant for a coffee. I pick up my lunch for work there and then I walk over to the Steep Rock Hotel later to catch the bus to the mine. It's just a few blocks from the restaurant."

He locked the door, and gave Wilf the key. "I'll be back from work about 9:00 am. Wait for me at the restaurant. We'll have breakfast, and then I'll get you lined up for some work. We can get a spare key cut tomorrow."

The restaurant was across the street, and up one block. The neon sign saying 'Sinclair's' hung over the door. It was not a big restaurant, but it was busy. The booths were full, but there were a couple of stools available at the counter, and Stan and Wilf pounced on them, mindful of a few hopefuls standing by the door. The jukebox was going full tilt, and about half the customers were drunk, adding to the noise.

A waitress approached them, and said "What'll you have, Stan?" Wilf was struck by her good looks. She had dark brown hair, brown eyes, stood about 5'6" and full figured. She had a lovely smile, showing beautiful even white teeth. Wilf found it an effort not to stare at her.

"How 'bout a couple of coffees Serena?" Then handing her his lunch pail he said "and could you fill 'er up?"

"Sure thing Stan." as she handed them each a coffee.

"This here's my friend Wilf, Serena...just got to town."

"Nice to meet you, Wilf," Serena said, handing them their coffees.

"Likewise, Serena," Wilf said, trying to appear casual. Wilf was sure he was blushing. She looked at him a little longer, and smiled, then left with Stan's lunch pail.

"Not hard to look at, eh?" Stan commented, adding some cream to his coffee.

"No."

He offered Wilf a cigarette, and took one for himself, and lighting them he went on...."I think she's on her own".

"Don't hurt to dream I guess," said Wilf.

"No, sure don't."

They finished their coffee as Serena showed up with Stan's lunch. Stan gave her a quarter for a tip and thanked her.

"Well, off to the salt mines," Stan said, getting up.

"Don't work too hard," she said with her smile, and turning to Wilf said. "See you again". Wilf managed a nod.

Stan paid for their coffees at the till, and Wilf got a package of tobacco and some rolling papers. They stepped out into the night, under the light of the neon sign. "I catch the mine bus over by the Steep Rock Hotel," said Stan, "It's just a few blocks from here."

"Ya, you were saying. I'll walk over with you," said Wilf He walked with Stan to the Steep Rock Hotel. There was a group already there, a few of them Wilf knew from Red Lake. The bus pulled up shortly.

"See you in the morning, partner," said Stan, as he was climbing in.

"Sure thing. About nine eh?"

"Ya about nine at Sinclair's." The driver closed the door, and headed the bus off to the mine.

When Wilf got up to the room, he thought he'd clean up before bedding down for the night. It would feel good to be clean. He pulled a towel, a face cloth and a small shaving kit from one of the kit bags As he headed up the hall to the bathroom, he noticed the noise was still coming from the drunk's room, only it seemed now that one guy was doing all the talking. He didn't pay much attention.... just went on to the bathroom.

The bathroom was big enough. He'd hoped for a shower, but there was only a bathtub...an old timer at that; one of the old porcelain types, but it was a nice deep one.

"Good enough," he thought, putting in the plug, and turning on the taps, "It'll do just fine." He got undressed as the water was running, and then stood at the sink to shave. There was soap provided at the sink. He took his face cloth soaked in hot water, and pressed it to his face. As he began to rub the soap in to his beard, he realized he could still hear the drunk from down the hall, even over the noise of the water running full blast into the bathtub.

"This is not going to work," he thought as he finished shaving. The blade was a little dull, and he was a few days overdue with the shave, but he got it done, and it felt good now, as he wiped his face clean with the warm, wet cloth. He even noticed he was smiling at himself in the mirror. The tub was full now, so he shut off the taps, and eased himself into the hot water. God, it felt good! He just laid back and let himself enjoy a good soak for awhile. It had been some good few days since he'd done that.

After a little more such indulgence, he got on with the bath, and wiped the tub clean as it drained. There was a knock on the door as he was drying himself. "Just give me a minute," he said. The magic of the moment was a little shaken, but it felt good to be clean. He got dressed, and as he was picking up his towel and face cloth, the knock came again, this time harder. He picked up his shaving gear. He was getting annoyed now. He opened the door with his free hand, and one of the drunks, no doubt the conversationalist, stood blocking his exit, standing in the doorway, explaining "Need a piss partner." He was a tall man, maybe Wilf's height, if he was able to stand up straight. He wasn't though. He was pissed drunk. He looked to Wilf about twenty five going on forty, hair a mess, shirt half open, four or five days stubble on his face, his eyes, bloodshot and vacant.

Wilf had seen himself in the same shape, for months on end even, and not that long ago. He put his hand against the top of the drunk's chest, and gave him sharp, quick shove. The drunk fell over backwards, landing on his ass in the hallway.

"She's all yours," said Wilf, and climbing over him, he made his way to his room. He put his shaving kit on top of the dresser, and was just hanging the towel and face cloth over the arms of the armchair, when he could hear a loud drunken voice down the hall again. Apparently, the drunk had accomplished his mission in the bathroom, and was back in his room, back into his 'conversation'.

Wilf looked at his watch. It was passed midnight now. "This won't do," he thought. He went down the hallway to the drunk's room, and opened the door without bothering to knock. The drunk, who had been sitting on his bed, stood up now. The man he'd been talking to was passed out in the wooden armchair. Wilf understood now why the conversation had been one-sided. The drunk took a step towards Wilf. "Whaddaya want here?" he asked staring vacantly.

Wilf looked him in the face, and as he did so, reached up with right hand and squeezed the drunk's throat. He squeezed hard, until he could feel his grip wrap around the drunk's windpipe, and continued to squeeze until the drunk couldn't breathe. The drunk was speechless now. His face turned crimson, his eyes distended like golf balls, as he stared, helplessly at Wilf, who was beginning to feel the drunk's weight, as the man's knees weakened for lack of air. Wilf loosened his grip, and allowed the drunk to fall back onto his bed. Wilf then put his finger to his lips and winked at the drunk, who was desperately trying to suck in some air. He did manage to give Wilf a nod; the message had gotten through. Satisfied with that, Wilf closed the door, and went back to his room.

With things nicely quiet now, he smiled to himself, as he got undressed down to his shorts; then folding his shirt and pants over the back of the armchair, he placed his socks inside his running shoes, and turning off the light, he climbed into bed.

It was a narrow bed, but it sure felt good to be in one, after hanging out for the winter in Port Arthur's Cumberland Street. Port Arthur wasn't a big city. It was a about fifty some thousand people, but was a busy port. Port Arthur's twin city, Fort William had about the same population; they were jointly referred to as the Lakehead, since they were situated at the head of the Great Lakes. Port Arthur was at the far west end of Lake Superior, and was the farthest western port of all the Great Lakes. It had a number of grain elevators, it had paper mills, and it also had the docks for loading the lake freighters with the iron ore which came by rail from Steep Rock Iron Mines. The freighters would ship the iron ore to the steel mills in Sault Ste. Marie, and Hamilton. Last year, 1956, the mine had shipped 3,365,000 tons of iron ore through the docks of Port Arthur. Iron ore was at a premium that year @$23.00 a ton.

Despite a population of only 50,000, Port Arthur had a fully developed skid row. There were a number of vintage hotels, among them, the

Kimberley. Once a proud red brick building, it was showing its years. The bricks were now weathered and worn, the rooms were shabby, the hotel was old; the main floor was a bar the full size of the building, and it was always busy. If a guy wasn't too fussy, he could score a flop for thirty five dollars a month. And, oh yes...there were always a few hookers available, if you had the price.

Wilf had left his job in Cochenour, on a weekend's drunk, and never made it back to work. The Kimberley was where he ended up; a little stakey at first, but before long, flat broke, and finally taking a flop at the Kimbeley, waiting for his next pogy cheque. (Pogy is the slang term for unemployment insurance.) By the end of April his claim ran out, and he was out on the street. He got a small income tax return in May, and before he drank it up, he got himself a train ticket to Atikokan. He'd heard Steep Rock was hiring.

As he lay in bed waiting for sleep, he reflected on his day, and where it had brought him. He knew from the long trainloads of iron ore rolling into the docks Port Arthur daily, to be emptied into the waiting boats for shipment to the steel mills, that Atikokan was booming. He heard the talk in the bar from miners coming to town that Steep Rock had started as an open pit operation, but they were developing an underground now, and were looking for miners. He heard it was a good paying outfit, but there was no camp.

A camp made everything so simple, if there was one. You could hire on flat broke, and your worries were over. You had a room in the bunkhouse and meals in the kitchen, all for payroll deduction. Once you were hired, you were home free; just go to work, and wait for payday.

However, this was not the case. He knew if he was lucky enough to get on at Steep Rock, he would have to find his own accommodation. This would require money. As it was with him, on the booze, he hadn't thought this through or much else beyond pan-handling his next beer. He just knew he had to make a move, and had gotten on the train in Port Arthur, flat broke, and his last dollar went for his ticket. Well.....so far, so good, but he better not drink. He rolled over onto his left side, and went to sleep, awakening the next morning to a bright sunny day. The birds were singing, and the light poured through around the blind over the window. It took him a minute to realize where he was. He turned his head towards the clock on the table next to the bed. It was 7:15 am. He was surprised he'd slept so late, not that he didn't need it, but there was no hurry. Stan wouldn't arrive until nine. He had only to get dressed, brush his teeth, and maybe shave again (and that would be a little easier this time.)

He stretched, swung his feet onto the floor, and stretching again, stood up. He'd slept right through, not even getting up for a leak. He hadn't felt that good in months. No hangover, a good night's sleep, and, a good breakfast on the way; life was good. He reflected on that as he got dressed. How many times he'd cursed his drinking, and where it had taken him. It could be this good all the time, if he just didn't drink.

Stan knew him like a book. If he'd have stepped into the bar, when Stan met him at the door, there would have been no help there for Wilf. Stan was the best guy Wilf ever worked with. They worked partners in a track drift in Cochenour for a year and a half. Powerful and capable, Stan was as good a miner you could hope to meet. Good natured, he was a gentleman to work with, but not a guy you'd want to piss off. Wilf had seen him lose it once, and once was enough for the other guy. The guy was as big as Stan, but apparently not as tough. Ed Johnson had an obnoxious streak, and liked to needle Stan about his race. Stan ignored it for the most part, but one Saturday afternoon Stan was having a few beers in the Red Lake Inn, when in walks Ed. He stopped in front of Stan, who was sitting with Wilf and said," How's the Indian today, Stan." That was good enough for Stan. Wilf saw the look that came over Stan's face, and he knew what was coming.

"Why don't you come outside and I'll tell you about it," said Stan.

Ed got his look and tried to back pedal. "Hell, I was just being funny, Stan."

Stan ignored the conciliatory attempt. He was out of his chair like a jack-in-the-box, and grabbing Johnson's shoulder with his right hand, spun him facing the door, and then kicked him hard on the ass, yelling "OUTSIDE" so loud his voice could be heard out on the street. Ed stumbled ahead a few steps, but managed to catch himself without falling on his face. He hurried for the door now, but Stan was right on his tail. The side door came out into a stairwell that went up into the parking lot. Ed got through the door just ahead of Stan, and turned to swing at him with his right. Mistake! He didn't connect. Stan moved to the side and caught his wrist with his right hand, and then with both hands started twisting Ed's arm. Ed's face was soon pressed hard against the steps of the stairwell, his arm straight up behind him in Stan's iron grip. He was screaming in pain, "Let me go, let me go", as Wilf came through the door. Stan put his right foot against the back of Ed's head, and kept twisting. Wilf heard a popping sound, over the screams, coming from Ed's shoulder, and knew either the arm was broken, or the shoulder was dislocated.

Wilf tried to stop Stan, tried to pull him back. "He's done, Stan....he's had enough," but when saw Stan's eyes, as he turned and faced Wilf, he saw Stan as he'd never seen him. His eyes were glazed and transfixed, as though he was looking at something on the other side of Wilf's head, and Wilf could see that Stan wasn't done. Stan let go of Ed's arm now, and grabbing him by the shirt, shoved him against the side of the stairwell, and with Ed bent over backwards, began slapping his face, leaning into broad sweeping, open handed slaps, over and over, like a windmill, as hard and as fast as he could slap, a sharp cracking sound coming from every slap.

Finally Wilf forced his way between them, facing Stan. He could feel his power, sense his rage, and knew he was no match for him either. It was all he could do to hold back him for a second and get his attention.

"It's me Stan..... Wilf...he's done Stan....let him go."

Finally Stan relaxed. He stared blankly at Ed, who was crying pitifully now, supporting his right arm below the shoulder with his left hand. His face was a shapeless purple mass, with one eye swollen shut, the other half closed. He left town the next day, with his right arm in a sling, supporting his dislocated right shoulder.

Stan didn't go back in to finish his beer....in fact he never drank again. He wasn't a big drinker to begin with, but he felt badly about what he'd done, and knew he wouldn't have been there if he wasn't drinking. Wilf pulled the bed together, and headed for the bathroom with his shaving kit. His bladder was badly in need of relief by now, and he could feel a dump coming on. Shaving was easy this morning, even with a dull blade. As he was leaving, he came across Sadie Ross in the hallway. He stopped to greet her.

"Good morning Sadie".

"Good morning Wilf. Sleep OK?" she asked.

"Oh ya slept good."

"Basil didn't give you any trouble?" She gestured toward the drunk's room, now quiet.

"Oh no, ma'am. No trouble at all."

"Well, anyways, I think we'll have a spot for you by the weekend. He'll be leaving," she said.

"Well, that's good Sadie....I mean good you've got me a spot."

She grinned. "Yes, I guess it's all good."

Wilf locked the door, went down the stairs, and headed for the restaurant. It was a lovely May morning. The trees were in full leaf now, birds were singing, and by 8:30 am it was already warm. The air was fresh, and it felt good just to breathe. The restaurant wasn't so full at the moment. The breakfast gang from dayshift was gone to work, and the crew from the graveyard shift hadn't arrived yet. Wilf took a copy of the 'Atikokan Progress' from the rack, paid the ten cent at the till, and took one of the empty booths. He sat facing the door so Stan would see him when he walked in. A blonde, hefty waitress came over to him.

"What'll ya have?" she asked.

"Just a coffee for now...when my friend gets here we'll order breakfast," Wilf answered.

"Ok."

She came back with a coffee. Wilf rolled himself a smoke, lit it and got into his paper. He glanced at the headlines, something about a fatal car accident on the Lakehead highway, and then went to classified ads. Under employment opportunities there was a large ad from Steep Rock Irons Mines. "Needed...experienced underground miners. Bring references." 'That could be a problem,' he thought. Wilf was one of the best, but he hadn't always parted on good terms.

Just about then, Stan showed up asking "Sleep OK?"

"Slept good...good shift?" asked Wilf.

"Got'er in," replied Stan.

"Sadie figures she's got a place for me by the week's end."

"I'll go by and get you covered. Its fifty bucks a month," said Stan.

"I'd appreciate that, Stan. Payday stakes?"

"Payday stakes, Wilf."

The waitress came back with a coffee for Stan, and took their orders.

"Ham and eggs over easy with brown toast", said Stan.

Wilf said he'd have the same. "I see they're looking for miners," said Wilf, waving the paper before he put it down, "but with references," he added.

"That won't be a problem, Wilf. They've got a hiring place right here in town, below the Hydro building. I'll be your 'reference'....I'm pretty good with the super, Briggs. He's usually around in the mornings there lately. We'll go over after we eat. It's only a couple of blocks from here. If Briggs is there, you'll have no problem."

Over a couple more coffees each, they finished their breakfast. It had come with a generous amount of ham and home fries. The restaurant was full now, with the rest of the graveyard shift filling the place. "Good food does good business," thought Wilf, as they got up.

"I'll get this", said Stan, as they went to the till.

"Thanks Stan."

"No problem, Wilf."

The owner, Bill Harrison, stood at the till.

"Morning Stan," he said as he punched in the amount, and took his money. He gave back a dollar fifty from a five dollar bill. Stan kept a dollar and put the silver in the tip jar beside the till.

"This here's my friend Wilf, Bill...just new in town. I wonder if you'd run a tab for him for a month, till he gets started. I'll guarantee him, if you're good with that."

Bill looked at Wilf, and then stuck out his hand. "Bill Harrison," he said, simply.

"Wilf Baker," said Wilf shaking his hand. "And thank you."

"Thank your friend, Wilf....he all right."

They stepped out on the sidewalk. "Well partner, let's go and get you working," Stan said, and they headed for the Hydro building. Although the distance was short, they passed two women, both quite pregnant, and one of them pushing a baby carriage. Wilf made a comment and Stan answered that a few years previous, Atikokan had the highest birthrate in the country. "That's how it is in a boomtown, Wilf."

"I see that."

They were soon at the hiring hall. There were eight or nine men in a lineup approaching a counter, and a few others filling out applications at a table toward the back of the room.

"I don't see Briggs here this morning. Maybe just get in line for now, I'll wait around."

"No need for that, Stan, I should be OK now."

"No, I'll wait." He took one of the chairs available along the left wall of the room, opposite the counter. Before the line moved up two places, a heavy man with receding brown curly hair, and graying temples stepped out of an office in back of the front counter. He came over beside the personal man at the counter and said something to him so quietly that Stan couldn't hear. He was obviously in charge. He looked up as just about then as Stan was getting out of his chair, making eye contact with him, and grinned.

"I thought we already hired you, Stan," he said

"You did....I'm here for my friend," said Stan.

"Where's your friend?"

"At the end of the line," said Stan.

"Hell, bring him in." He lifted the hinged section of the counter, and waved the two of them into his back office. There were some puzzled looks from the line up, which were ignored and some subdued expression of exasperation from the personnel man which also went unnoticed, as Stan and Wilf followed the man, who had to be Briggs, Wilf was sure, into the back room. They closed the door behind them.

"So who's your friend here? ...I'm Bill Briggs., he said, sticking out his hand.

"Wilf Baker," said Wilf shaking his hand.

"Pleased to meet you Wilf," said Bill. As Wilf nodded in agreement, Bill gestured them to sit as he took his own seat on the swivel chair behind the desk. "So you're a miner, Wilf?" he went on. Wilf nodded. "And where do you know Stan from?"

"Cochenour….we drove a drift together."(A drift is an underground tunnel.)

"How big?"

"It was an 8 by 8. Two man crew. We'd pull an eight foot round every shift", said Wilf.

"Muck out, drill off, and blast?"

"Yep, we'd make a cycle every shift."

"How 'bout timber?"

Wilf answered, "No…we didn't need to….it was good ground in Cochenour." (Ground refers to the rock content as being soft or hard.)

"Sometimes we hit some bad ground and we'd have to stick in a few rock bolts, but we'd still make our round," continued Wilf.

"How long you work with Stan?" Bill asked.

"Close to a year and a half," said Wilf. Bill looked at Stan, and Stan nodded.

"Well OK, Wilf. If you could cut'er with Stan Rooster, that's good enough for me," said Bill. We're having a hard time getting good men here. Elliot Lake seems to be getting them all. We've taken a bunch of coal miners from Springhill, Nova Scotia here, but they're not hardrock miners. Some of them turn out all right, but they don't know much when they get here. Lot of guys here are green as grass. We have to take them 'cause it's hard to get good men. A man like you is good to find. You can go right to work….don't need to be trained or anything."

Bill leaned ahead on his chair. "I'll tell you what Wilf….you do want a job, right?" Wilf nodded, trying hard not to betray too much enthusiasm.

"Yes, as I was saying, Wilf, we could definitely use a man like you. How soon can you start?"

"Today… tomorrow… soon as you like," said Wilf.

"Well there are a few things we need to look at." Wilf felt his heart skip a beat. "Nothing much… just the usual. Is your chest X ray still good?"

"No, it's run out a couple of months ago."

"Well, we've got to take care of that." Bill filled out at requisition slip and handed it to Wilf. "You take this up to the hospital, and get your chest X ray, then go to the clinic and they'll give you a medical. When you're all done with that, you can catch a bus in front of the Steep Rock Hotel, about 2:45. That's the one for the afternoon shift crew going to work. You'll need to pass an idiot test in the mine. I'll let them know you're coming. You might as well take your gear out with you and get yourself a hook, 'cause I'm sure you'll pass that foolish test. The office is in the same building as the head frame, so you should be able to get through it all in time to catch the day shift bus back at 4:30. You can start day shift tomorrow, if you get 'er all done."

Wilf and Stan stood up together, and Bill stood up sticking out his hand to Wilf once more. "Good to meet to you, Wilf....we'll see you soon."

"For sure, Bill. Thank you." They went past the growing line of hopefuls, and stepped back out into the day.

"Boy, he sure must like you Stan."

"Bill's all right, Wilf. If Bill likes you, you've got no problem"

"I see that", said Wilf.

"Well, I gotta get me some sleep partner," said Stan, "We better get us a key cut first."

There was a hardware store on corner of the block and they went in and got the extra key cut. Then Stan gave him directions how to find the hospital and the clinic. Having done that, he handed Wilf a twenty dollar bill. "A little walking around money for you, partner," he concluded. Wilf accepted the bill, almost choked. One place he wouldn't be walking around was inside another pub.

A Miner's Story – Chapter 3

Wilf found his way to the hospital, from the directions Stan had given him. He went South of Main St. a few blocks, until he came onto a crescent shaped boulevard. Annual chest X-rays were required for miners in Ontario to check for the presence of silicosis, a condition indicating the presence of accumulated dust in the lungs. Someone in this condition was commonly said to be 'dusted'. This chest X-ray was rightly the next thing to do.

About half way around the curve of the crescent, he came to a wide footpath that Stan had mentioned led to a footbridge crossing the Atikokan River. On the other side of the bridge a path to the left went up an embankment to arrive at an intersection of three streets coming together, one of which was Hematite Avenue. Stan had told him he would find the hospital near the end of Hematite.

As he approached the hospital, he was struck by how good it felt to be clean, well rested, well fed and to be breathing fresh air on such a beautiful spring morning. He would put the drinking behind him. Life was giving him a break, and he would make it good. He felt a determination he hadn't known for some few years now, since the drinking had taken hold of him.

A farm boy, he'd found his first mining job with Inco (International Nickle Company) at the Levack Mine in Sudbury. He was seventeen, and lied he was eighteen, as eighteen was the required age to work underground. Lying his age wasn't a problem, as he was already a big man, and the mine was short of help. Inco liked to hire green men, and train them themselves. It was a good place to start. It was a good place to start drinking as well. As he entered the hospital, he thought about that. "A man would have to be crazy to pay good money to make himself sick", he thought.

The hospital had the familiar antiseptic smell to it. Near the entrance to the right, was the front office and reception. He stopped at the counter, and the woman behind a desk got up and came over.

"Can I help you?" she asked.

"Yes, I'm Wilf Baker ....I need to get a chest X-ray for Steep Rock..."

"Oh yes, Mr. Baker, we're expecting you. X-ray is down the hall, and to the right. Just go ahead in."

It had been awhile since anyone had called him mister, he reflected. He found the X-ray room. The attendant, a young female technician, had him strip to the waist and stand in front of the screen while she took the X-ray. "OK, Mr. Baker, you may get dressed now….we're all done here"

He put his shirt back on and headed back into town the way he'd come...back across the footbridge, and around the boulevard, which straightened out to become Mark Street. On the left side of the street, he spotted the clinic, a plain one story building by itself. He went in by the front door. Inside the clinic there were half a dozen or so in the waiting room. He approached the receptionist and told her his name.

"Oh yes Mr. Baker, Dr Grayson will see you shortly...just have a seat."

He picked up a magazine from a pile of and sat down, and waited his turn. The man seated near him made an effort to chat him up. "New in town?" he began.

"Yup isn't everyone?" Wilf came back. The man nodded agreement. To Wilf's relief he was called next

The attending nurse led him down the hallway and sat him down in a room. Soon after, a balding man of about forty entered the room. He greeted Wilf, sticking out his hand. "Hi, I'm Dr. Grayson."

"Pleased to meet you doctor," Wilf said starting to stand.

"No, just relax, no need to stand." He wrapped the blood pressure monitor around Wilf's bicep and pumped it up. "A little on the high side...have you been sleeping all right?"

"Well, I won't lie to you doc….I'm just coming off a drunk, and I hope it's my last."

Wilf thought that he was hearing someone else talking. He could hardly believe he'd just said that. He thought he'd might have blown it, and wondered what the hell he could have been thinking to have said what he just said.

"Well that's the kind of talk I like to hear, Wilf." the doctor said checking his ears. He said nothing more on that put his stethoscope to his chest, got him to cough and then had him look at the eye chart. Wilf eyesight was 20-20. Finally he asked, "So you think you'd like to stay sober, do you?"

"I sure do." Wilf answered.

A Miner's Story – Chapter 3

"Well outside of your blood pressure, I'd say you're in pretty good health. I'm going to pass you on this but I'd like you to come back and see me in a couple of weeks. We'll check your blood pressure again, ok? Just stop at reception on the way out, and Marge will book you an appointment."

"Ok, Dr. Grayson, I'll see you in two weeks."

Wilf felt like a kid let out of school. On to the mine now! He went back to the rooming house. With the stealth of a cat, he opened the door to Stan's room, and retrieved the kit bag with his mining gear. Stan was sleeping soundly. He closed the door quietly, locked it again, and then headed for the Steep Rock Hotel to meet the afternoon shift bus. He checked his watch. He made it in good time.

There were a dozen or so in front of the hotel waiting for the bus to take them to work. The bus made a couple of more stops on its way out of town. By this time it was quite full, but no one had to stand. The bus arrived at the mine about fifteen minutes later. Wilf was struck by the red iron ore dust which seemed to be on everything. Except for a few vehicles in the parking lot, which had been recently washed, most of the vehicles were coated in the red dust. It was everywhere, and on everything. The roadways around the shop area were red. The buildings were red. The mine vehicles were yellow but mostly showing red. Wilf had worked for a number of mining companies, but had never seen the likes of this iron ore dust to dirty and cover so much of everything.

The bus pulled up and came to a stop near the headframe. For Steep Rock Iron Mines, the headframe was a large structure that not only housed the mine shaft and the hoist room for the cage servicing the mine, but also contained the 'dry' for the miners, as well as the office where Wilf needed to go to take his IQ test in order to get signed on.

As the bus emptied Wilf stood in the aisle, with his kit bag slung over his shoulder, then followed the others off the bus and into the dry. It was the place where the miners would change from their street clothes to their 'diggers'(mining gear) and vice versa later after their shower at the shift's end. Once into the dry itself, he saw a man over to one side putting away a push broom. He was sure it would be the dry attendant so he approached him, as the attendant would be the one to delegate hooks and lockers to new hires.

"Hi, I'm just getting started here," Wilf said. "You'd be in charge here?"

"Well, I try keep things clean anyways," the attendant replied, grinning, somewhat amused by the importance Wilf gave him. He was a graying man who looked about mid fifties but looked younger by his manner. "Name's Morris Waranuk," he went on.

"Wilf Baker." Shaking his hand, he continued "I'll need a hook if you can help me."

"I can take care of that for you. Got your hiring slip?"

"No, not yet. I gotta go to the office...take some kind of test, I guess, and then I'll get my paperwork."

"Oh yes... the idiot test. You should be doing that first, but I'm sure you'll make out OK. I'm going to go ahead and get you set up." He liked Wilf, plain to see. "Let me just see what we've got." He went into a small cubicle of an office and checked his roster.

"I can give you #146, if that works for you..."

"Sure... whatever. How many miners you got here?"

"There are 100 miners on each shift...and they're running four shifts here.

"Four shifts?"

"Ya... they call it a swing shift; six days on, two off... so you always got three shifts working and one crew on days off. They're running the underground steady, seven days a week, 24 hours a day. It's a continuous operation. Just follow me, and I'll show you your hook." Wilf followed him to a place, across an aisle and up a couple of rows. "There you go, sir...that'll get you going. There's your locker for your clean clothes, right there. Got a lock?"

"Not with me but I'll bring one. Thanks, man....I'm OK, now."

The crew coming in was out of their street clothes by now, and most of them were all ready into their diggers. In spite of the number of men, the Dry was spacious enough that it was not crowded. Wilf saw some that he knew, but wasn't there to visit. He got the odd nod here and there, as he hung his gear. The 'hook' was a treble sort of gang hook fixed to the bottom of a pail, which came down from the ceiling by a rope over a pulley affixed to the ceiling. The rope was dead-ended to his locker. Once he had his gear on the hook, he pulled it up to near the ceiling, and hooked the ring on the rope to the bar which ran along the benches opposite the row of lockers.

Once done, he found his way to the office area, upstairs in the headframe, above the dry. There was a reception wicket at the head of the stairwell, with an entrance door to the right of it. A young woman got up from her desk and came to the wicket. "Can I help you?" she asked.

"I'm Wilf Baker. I'm a new hire...I'm supposed to be taking some kind of a test."

"Oh, yes...please come in. I'll get you set up."

She opened the door for him, and led him past a couple of men bent over a drafting board. There were a few others at their desks. She led Wilf into a private room and sat him down at a desk, putting the test in front of him. "Take as much time as you need", she said, giving him a pencil, and a pin. "For part of the test, you'll use the pin to punch holes". She left him to it.

The test, Wilf was soon to discover, was pretty simple. He had to smile at some of the questions....'which would be heavier... a pound of feathers or a pound of lead?' Or 'would your mother's sister be your brother's aunt.' Some were more difficult, like how much is 14 divided by 2 plus 17. Wilf was finished in half an hour. He brought back to the receptionist. She looked a little surprised. "You finished already? Just take a seat while I check this out. It won't take too long."

He watched her going over the test. She super-imposed a plastic template which had holes in it to correspond with the correct answers over the test sheets. She was right. It didn't take long.

"You did very well, Mr. Baker. We're not at liberty to tell you exactly what you got, but you passed with no problem. On condition the test went well, they had you down for dayshift, so if you're OK with that, you could even start tomorrow morning."

"The sooner the better for me."

"Well then, I guess we're all done here."

"Thanks...see you, then"

"Bye, now."

Wilf went back down the stairs and through the Dry to catch the bus back to town. Dayshift had already come up. Most were showered and dressed, but a good number were still in the Dry. "Good enough," he thought, "the bus hasn't left." He was almost to the exit door when he heard a familiar voice.

"Well, look what the cat dragged in....must be hard up for help around here."

He turned. It was Vince Jamieson. "I see what you mean," Wilf came back, ignored the offer of a handshake He just stood facing him, looking him up and down, with his hands in his pockets. Vince seemed to take no offence and broke into that raucous, piercing laugh that Wilf had come to loathe. Wilf turned and walked away.

The bus was only starting to fill, so there were plenty of seats to choose from, but Wilf spotted Andy Anderson, who he knew from Sudbury, and sat beside Andy. He wanted to say hello, and thought he'd sit with Andy, rather than sit alone, and possibly have Vince join him.

"Mining iron ore these days, are you Andy?" he opened up.

"Yeah... how yuh doing Wilf?"

Wilf shook his offered hand. "Well, so far, so good, Andy. Just got signed on, and got my gear on the hook. How you been, anyways....long time no see.

"Ya, it's been awhile, Wilf."

"Like it here?"

"Money's OK....soft ground though...in the ore body that is. It's good solid ground where I am though. I'm driving the footwall drift on 900. Those cross-cuts they're driving on the 700 level go right through the ore body, and that is soft ground. You'd think iron ore would be hard, but it's not. They have to put steel sets every four feet lagged tight to the back and all the way in those crosscuts. The hanging wall and foot wall drifts were driven in solid ground but the crosscuts run from the foot wall to the hanging right through the ore body in between."

The last of the dayshift had boarded by now, and to Wilf's relief, Vince had taken a seat near the front. "With four shift's going, why did they have to put me on his shift," he thought.

The bus was soon into town. It made a couple of stops along the way, and then came a stop opposite the Steep Rock Hotel, where he'd gotten on. He was pleased to see Vince had gotten off at the previous stop. Andy had gotten off there too. This last stop emptied the bus, and Wilf got off with the rest of them. He looked at his pocket watch, and it was a quarter to five. He didn't want go straight to the room, in case Stan was still sleeping, so he went back to Sinclair's for a coffee. The restaurant was filling up from Dayshift, so Wilf just took a stool at the counter.

He was delighted to see Serena on the floor. She waved to him from the coffee maker, and held up a pot. He nodded, and had to smile back at her smile. She poured him a coffee, and brought it over. "Anything else, Wilf?"

"Not just yet, Serena. I'll wait for Stan."

"He'll be along. He's usually in about 5:30. Remembered my name, eh?"

"Couldn't forget that." He knew he was blushing. He was pleased she remembered his. She smiled at this and kept going. The place was getting busy now. He rolled a cigarette and lit it, and inhaling deeply, he let it out slowly. With things out of the way for the moment, it hit the spot. He was nicely finished his cigarette and coffee, and Serena came by with the pot. He pushed his cup towards her, and she gave him a refill.

"Thanks," he said, and just about then, Stan entered the restaurant. There was an empty stool next to Wilf, and Stan took it. Serena brought him a coffee, and he thanked her.

"Well, how'd it go, partner?" he began with Wilf.

""Good....yep...got'er all done. I'm all signed up, and got my gear on the hook. I start dayshift tomorrow," said Wilf.

"Boy no flies on you eh?"

"No use wasting time," said Wilf rolling another smoke feeling quite pleased with him.

"Well good for you, Wilf. Sadie came and spoke to me, by the way. You're good for the room tomorrow. She gave that haywire his notice. I've already got her paid."

"Thanks Stan. Thanks a lot."

"No problem, partner."

About the time Stan finished his second coffee a booth came available, and they took it. Serena came by with menus, but Stan interrupted, saying, "Let's have us a steak, partner. We got something to celebrate here." Wilf was quite agreeable to that. Serena held her order pad against the menus.

"I'd like mine a medium rare, Serena....lots of mushrooms OK. No gravy on the chips. I like vinegar."

She wrote it down...."and how 'bout you Wilf," she asked.

"I'll have the same, Serena." She smiled, wrote it all down. "More coffee?"

"Sure... maybe one more to finish us off."

As she filled theirs cups, Stan offered Wilf a cigarette. "Have a tailor made partner." Will accepted and they lit up and sat back with their coffee.

"I sure hope I don't get stuck partnered with that fucking Jamieson," Wilf broke in.

"Run into him again, eh?" Stan found this amusing.

"Yeah...he was in the Dry when I was leaving to catch the bus. I'd like to pound his face in, but what can I do?"

"Nothing...you did the right thing....nothing. You'd get fired before you even get started. Don't be giving that foolish bastard as much as a thought. He's just a bag of shit with a big mouth."

Wilf admired Stan's ability to ignore Vince Jamieson, but he couldn't. Vince had seen Wilf at his worst, and loved to rub his nose in it. "Taking a break from Cumberland Street, are you, Wilf?" Then that raucous, piercing laugh, like some kid, pulling the wings off a grasshopper. One day Wilf would settle the score...he'd wait for his time...and it would come.

A Miner's Story – Chapter 4

Wilf took the dayshift bus to the mine the following morning. When it arrived at the mine, he followed the crowd from the bus into the dry, found his way to his hook, and got undressed, hanging up his street clothes in his locker. Then dropping his hook, he got into his mining gear. His heavy long woolen underwear was a little worn, but still intact. He put on his faded grey khaki pants and shirt with metal snaps, two long pairs of grey wool socks, and then pulled on his ankle tight steel-toed muck boots. Dressed now, he stood up, put on his weathered hard-hat, and his lamp belt on which he hung his 12 inch crescent sheathed in a holster he'd made from a short chunk of air hose.

All miners packed the 12 inch crescent. The jaw was removed to have an extra tooth ground into it and then replaced with a drop of weld to cover the shaft of the spurl, so the wrench would never fall apart. Thus altered the wrench could open wide enough to fit the air and water hose connections. Wilf also had a three quarter inch nut welded to the heel of his wrench which could serve as a hammer. The ring at the end of the handle was a 7/8th socket which nicely fit the nuts on the four inch Victaulic clamps, or the shank of a stuck drill steel.

With his black Diamond slickers hanging from his shoulder by the straps, the slicker coat slung over his shoulder, he followed the others and found his way to the shifter's wicket. ('Shifter' was a common term for the shift boss) There were five wickets in all. There were two production shift bosses, two for development, and the last wicket was 'safety', which was where Wilf had been told to queue up for his induction tour.

He found himself in line with six other men. Only one other had used mining gear. He didn't know him, but he'd seen him around Red Lake. The other five had shiny new boots, hard hats and belts... no doubt green recruits. The miners from around the other wickets gradually melted away as the men got their work sheets, and took the stairs down to the shaft house to catch the cage to their levels.

Finally a face appeared at the safety wicket, a slim man of medium height, and thinning hair. His lamp dangled loose from its cord hung over his neck.

"Hi guys", he opened with. "I'm Vern Green, the Safety Super here, and I'll be taking you boys around for your first shift. Could I get your names please?" One by one they gave their names and Vern checked them off. Once done, he came around through the door of the shifters room, and led them down a short hallway into a small projection room. There were some chairs arranged in two rows facing a screen, and a projector set up behind the rows with a reel of film mounted and ready to roll.

Vern started with "Grab a seat, boys. I'll show you a short film on what we do here." He began running the film commenting as it played. "The method we're using is called Block Cave. The Errington pit couldn't go any deeper as it pinched out at a depth of 400′ so we've gone in on the 700′ level underground. We're going to continue mining the ore body from underneath it."

As Wilf took it all in, he could plainly see it was a method he'd never heard of. The main production level was on 700′ and the development on that level was mostly done. The ore body was 400′ wide and well over a mile long. The hanging and foot wall drifts were already driven through the hard ground on either side of the orebody. Most of the cross cuts had been driven through the ore body at 200′ intervals connecting the hanging wall and foot wall drifts. At right angles to, and just above the cross cuts were the scran drifts. These were at 50′ intervals driven to 100′ lengths. Their mill holes right above the cross cut were set up so the slusher man could rake the iron ore coming out the boxholes into the scrans right into the train below. The boxholes were driven up from the sides of the scran alternating sides every twenty feet down the length of the scran from the millhole to the tail block at the far end of the scran.

The boxholes were first started from a 6′ round taken flat straight in from the side of the scran drift. Then two 6′ rounds went up at fifty degrees away from the scran off the back of these rounds cut in from the scrans. A third round was drilled off but not blasted. This round was 'coned out' by drilling slash holes fanned in all directions of the sides of the round like an umbrella.

When the cones were blasted out it was calculated that the fractures would connect from boxhole to boxhole. With the softness of the ore body, it would entirely cave into the pit bottom right up to 300′ above. It could all then be pulled out through the scrans into the trains below. In short, that was the Block Cave method on mining.

When the film ran out, the lights came on. "Well boys," said Vern rewinding the film. "That gives you some idea. Now let's get ourselves some lamps and go down there and have a look." He looked at Wilf's slickers. "You won't need those today partner." Wilf was slightly amused while looking at a thin balding man with glasses calling him partner. But then, everybody was partner. He was happy to put the slickers back on his hook.

Vern read out their lamp numbers from his sheet. "Now remember your lamp number guys because if you're here twenty years from now, you're going to have the same lamp." He showed them to the lamp rack. They all took their respective lamps, strapped the batteries to their miner's belt and clipped the lamp at the end of the lamp cord to the bracket on their hardhats.

Vern led them down the stairs to the shaft house and rang for the 'cage'. (Cage is the word for the elevator for a mine shaft.) The cage came to surface within minutes. The cagetender rang three bells and when the hoistman answered with three bells, the door swung open and Wilf got on board with the newcomers and Vern. It was the biggest cage Wilf had seen since he'd worked for Inco in Sudbury. It was long and wide; big enough to accommodate a ten ton Grambie muck car if necessary. A set of rails ran up its middle which corresponded with the tracks that met the cage in the shaft house and the tracks in the stations.

The cagetender slammed the door shut, rang three bells and the hoistman answered with three. Then the cagetender rang 2-3 for the level and the hoistman answered 2-3. The cagetender rang two bells....going down. The hoistman answered with two dropping the cage to the 700' level in less than two minutes. Then the cagetender rang the three bells to signal the proper arrival at the level to the hoistman who acknowledged with three bells in return. The cagetender opened the cage door and swung opened the shaft door letting the crew off at the station. Having shut the two doors again, he rang 2-4; the hoistman answered 2-4, and then at 2 bells dropped the cage to the 900' level.

A Miner's Story – Chapter 4

As they got off the cage on the 700' level, Vern told the new recruits that the area immediately coming from the cage onto the level was called a station. The station on 700 was a long, wide area, cut out large enough to accommodate two parallel sets of tracks. The tracks converged into one set about ten feet from the front of the shaft door. They became one again at the other end of the station where the hanging wall drift began. On one side of the double track were parked a couple of two ton Hudson cars.

Vern explained that the Hudson cars were for cleaning up spills or mucking out the drift rounds on the 1100 level. Mucking was the process of digging up and loading the blasted rock or 'muck' into the Hudson muck cars. "The Hudsons are side dumping cars. A drift crew would have eight cars in their train for mucking out," he went on. "They haul the muck blasted from the drift rounds to the waste dump where it's dumped and ends up in a loading pocket. From there it's skipped to surface and later moved to a waste pile."

There was also a lengthy timber truck bearing some lengths of twenty foot 4" and 2" pipe, half a dozen twenty foot 40lb. rails, some ties and a keg of track spikes. Vern carried on "A Timber truck is a flat car used for moving timber, pipes or rails underground. The rails used by the drift crew on the 1100' level are 40 pound rails. 40 pound rail means 40 pounds per linear yard or three feet. In contrast, on the 700' level a heavier track is required to hold up against the weight of the trains hauling ore so only 85 pound rails are used. These are the same rails that the CN railroad (CNR) uses."

Toward the end of the side track a large Mancha Mule motor was parked on charge adjacent to the charger which stood against the station wall. The track which came to the shaft door was clear of any equipment. Vern led the group onward, explaining things as they went along. They left the station and proceeded down the hanging wall drift. The hanging wall drift was also the main haulage drift for the level. They walked a little ways and came to a switch. Vern went on that a switch consisted of the points used to alternate the direction of the track. The points were affixed to the 'frog' which is the juncture of a switch in a track drift. Vern said "A track drift is one which uses track for conveyance purposes." Wilf had a hard time not to laugh as he was quite sure that even a greenhorn would know a switch when he saw one and would know why the tracks were there.

At the switch there was another set of tracks branching to the right. Vern stated that this was the footwall drift which was used mainly as a service drift for the man-haul car and bringing in supplies to the headings. The hanging wall drift was for the mainline trammers hauling the ore from the scrans to the ore pass.

Continuing on, within a short time they came up to the ore pass. The train had just pulled up to dump. The motor, a big Mancha Mule, had a dozen 10 ton belly dump Grambie cars in tow heaped to the sides. Heavy 85 lb. 'used' rail from the CNR was laid over the ore pass since there was nothing directly below it. The cars would dump the ore through the slot between the rails directly over the ore pass, and then close automatically as the train pulled through. From there, the ore went through a jaw crusher, and then was moved by a conveyor up an inclined drift to the surface, where it was loaded into rail cars for shipment. In no more than twenty minutes, all 12 cars were emptied and the motor crew was on its way back for another load.

Vern had his group standing well back until the train crew was done and on its way. "Well boys, that's production," he said."I just wanted you to see that. We'll go back to the footwall drift, and follow that to the scrans. It's a little less hectic on the footwall side". They back tracked the short distance back to the switch, and headed up the footwall drift.

After a ways they came to another switch, with track going straight along the footwall, and tracks turning left towards the hanging wall. "This is number one Xcut (crosscut), guys. Let's go up, and I'll show you one of our producing scrans." He led the group up the crosscut.

The cross cuts were driven through the ore body which was unstable ground. Every four feet up the drift were steel sets for support. They were lagged and blocked tight to the back. Wilf noticed that even with that, some of the sets were taking weight and bent a little here and there from pressure.

Approaching the first scran they came upon two men. They had with them a smaller type battery motor hooked up to three 2 ton Hudson cars. In front of the cars was an Eimco 21 mucking machine (A mucking machine was often referred to as a 'mucker'; mucker could also refer to the operator of the mucking machine.)The mucking machine was derailed crossways in the drift; the front wheels off on the ditch side and the rear wheels off on the opposite side. The two men were attempting to get it back on the tracks with a track jack, but as they applied the jack, the machine would just spin and the chassis would stay where it was. The superintendent, Bill Briggs, just happened to be there, and was exasperated at their incompetence. He knew exactly what to do, but as a staff member he was not allowed to help. He saw Vern's group approaching, and seeing Wilf he brightened right up. "Can you help us out here, Wilf?" he asked.

Wilf sized it up in an instant. There was a five foot drawbar on the motor. He took that, and placing one end against the rocker of the mucker, the other end against a tie between the rails, he raised the bucket slowly. As it came up, the rocker came against the drawbar. The chassis lifted and spun as the machine started to center itself, nicely clearing the tracks. When the wheels were directly over the rails, he let the bucket down, and the back wheels fell neatly onto the tracks. He then raised the bucket to the dump position, thus locking the machine centered. Placing the drawbar in front of the mucker with one end against a tie and the other end flat against a bolt head on the inside of the machine on the opposite side where the wheels were off, he pushed gently on the traction lever. The front end swung upwards, and as the flange of the wheels cleared the tracks, he let it drop directly on to the rails. He did all this in a matter of a few minutes.

"How 'bout mucking a car for us Wilf?"

Wilf stepped up on the stand, and backing up the mucker, he dropped the bucket in the middle of the tracks, and pushed it ahead cleaning the tracks up to the spill below the mill hole. Then swinging and dropping the bucket first to one side, then the other, he cleaned both sides of the drift right up to the spill. That done, he started mucking, pushing the bucket into the spill and pulling it up full in one deft motion, then emptying it into the car in one clean jerk. In three minutes flat the two ton Hudson was nicely filled. He flashed his light at the motor man as a signal to switch him another empty, but when the motor man went to pull back, he found he wasn't hooked to the cars. Bill Briggs just shook his head. "You watch this guy," he said, pointing to Wilf, "he's a miner".

The motor man looked sheepish as he hooked the cars to the motor. Bill then turned to Wilf. "You come out tonight on graveyard. I'll get you partnered up with Stan Rooster in the drift on 1100. It's a wet one but the ground is good."

Without waiting for an answer, he turned and walked away. Vern took it all in quite speechless. Finally he said, "Let's have a look at the scran guys," and started up the manway.

Stan couldn't have been more pleased. Wilf had come back from his induction tour and found Stan having a shave."Like old times, partner", Stan said. Wilf was all smiles. "I'll let you finish up here", he said, watching Stan shear off his whiskers. "I'll see you in Sinclair's", said Stan.

Serena was on. She smiled at him as he came in and took a stool. She brought him a coffee and commented. "You're looking happy."

"Yeah, I got on at the mine. Start on graveyards tonight on Stan's shift."

"Good for you," Serena exclaimed putting his coffee down. "I'll get back to you." she continued taking the pot to make her rounds. Wilf nodded and rolled himself a cigarette. By the time he lit it, Stan appeared and a booth became available. As the two men settled into the booth, Serena showed up with Stan's coffee.

"Menus?" she asked.

"Not today princess....we're having steaks, and please don't cook mine too much," Stan said.

"Two days in row?" she asked. Stan nodded.

Wilf was stuck for words, but managed to say after a pause, "Same for me Serena." Wilf knew he was blushing. She smiled, and took the order to the cook.

"Steaks again?" he said, looking at Stan.

"You bet partner. This calls for a celebration."

The steaks were a perfect medium rare....two good sized T-bones.

"Sure hit the spot, Stan."

"And why not?" asked Stan. "You're going to need something in your stomach tonight. That drift is a wet one."

"That's what I hear," said Wilf.

"The water comes down from the pit and seeps in through the slips. Sometimes it's over my boots...good solid ground though...not like those guys on 700 in the ore zone. That's bad ground up there." (Slips are thin seams of mud running through the hard ground.)

"Yeah, I had a look at that on my tour. Lots of sets. Lots of cement. Still the ground keeps squeezing."

"There's a third man with us," Stan continued, "...old Gus McKinnon. A good man...he's the mucker. When we drill off, he takes the left side; I'm in the center, so you'll be on my right."

"Who am I replacing?" asked Wilf.

"That idiot Basil down the hall from me", said Stan, "...missed one shift too many."

"Lost his room, too, eh?"

"Well I guess he won't need one now," said Stan.

"Things are really panning out for Basil."

"Well, that's booze for you," said Stan. "It's the best cleaner in the world. It'll clean you out of everything".

Wilf made no comment. He knew the problem intimately. He was glad to be off that merry-go-round. Also glad to have his room.

To fill in the evening before shift, they went to a movie. The movie theater was right across the street from the rooming house. It was a new theater called the 'Park'. It was a good size, with a balcony for smokers. The movie playing was 'The Defiant Ones', with Tony Curtis and Sidney Poitier. It was about two escaped convicts manacled together. Wilf hadn't been to movie in years. Admission was a dollar; not much compared to a night in the bar. It was Stan's idea. Wilf had thoroughly enjoyed it.

"Go to many movies?" asked Wilf.

"Now and again...you?"

"First in quite awhile. That was a good idea Stan."

They went back to the restaurant for a coffee and to pick up their lunches for work. Serena was gone. The big blonde woman served them. They had a coffee and a couple of donuts, picked up their lunches, and headed off to catch their bus for the last graveyard shift.

"You'll be a little short on sleep," Stan commented.

"I'll be fine."

The bus showed up, and to Wilf's relief, he didn't have to be on the same shift as Vince Jamieson.

While Wilf changed into his diggers at the mine Dry, Vince sat in the bar of the Steep Rock hotel, holding court with his usual entourage ....Pete Hendricks, Art Crofton, Buddy Neilson, and a couple younger men, new to the mining industry, and much in awe of Vince Jamieson. As the cage came for Gus, Stan and Wilf right at midnight, last call was bawled out by the bartender to the pub full of noisy drunks in the Steep Rock Hotel.

Vince had been successfully twisting wrists with the two greenhorns, and so informed them bluntly that they would be paying for the last round (as a penalty for losing). They of course accepted his terms, and as the table was again filled with beer, they graciously paid. Vince didn't demean himself to thank them. As the last of the beer was drank, and the bartender flashed the lights off and on, simultaneously yelling 'closing time', Vince rose from his table, kicking back his chair and belching loudly. He honored his favorite of the group, Bud Neilson, with a handshake, and then headed to the can for one last leak before vacating the premises.

Entering the parking lot, a little wobbly, he found his way to his pickup, an orange 1950 International. He fumbled for a moment with his keys, and finding the right one, started it up. "That's a good girl," he said, as the engine fired dutifully. (He always spoke respectfully to his vehicle). Vince was a careful driver, even intoxicated, and found his way safely home.

Home was a small house in 'Lone Pine', an area on the edge of town leading onto the mine road. He shared the house with a woman, Margo Parker and her son Jimmy, age 13, a thin, nervous boy, who stuttered very badly. (Vince found this very amusing.) Margo was a very plain looking woman in her early thirties, a widow, whose husband never came back from the war. She had accepted Vince's proposition for cohabitation after a brief period of dating, more in the hopes of escaping the destitution of her existence, than of finding a soul mate. She worked as a cashier at a small neighborhood grocery store and before Vince came along, she and her son had lived a terribly simple life, barely able to eke out their existence. Vince did have his faults, she was well aware, (but nobody's perfect). At least now she had a man in her life.

Vince parked the truck in the driveway, and shutting off the engine, he gave the truck a gentle pat on the dash, as he extracted the key, saying, "Good girl, we made 'er home." Margo had left the porch light on for him. He opened the door and went quietly in. Margo was in bed, asleep, as he expected, snoring gently. In spite of her plain looking face, she was blessed with a substantial bust, which Vince enjoyed greatly, and she would oblige Vince by sleeping in only her panties. Jimmy was asleep in the other bedroom, a much smaller room.

Vince turned the light on the bathroom and viewed himself for a moment in the mirror. One could say he had a good face. His blue eyes were a little wide-set, and his teeth were a good white, perfectly even, and none were missing. He very proud of his teeth, and felt that a few days growth of his black whiskers plus his heavy black moustache showed his perfect white teeth to their best advantage.

He put a generous amount of toothpaste on his toothbrush, and brushed his teeth carefully and thoroughly, watching himself in the mirror with utmost solemnity. Once done, he rinsed his mouth with a strong mouthwash and then smiled at himself for a moment. As he did so, he stroked the stubble on his face, vaguely thinking of shaving, then decided to leave it another day or two...(it had only been a few days so far).

Shutting off the bathroom light, he slipped into Margo's bedroom, and without turning on the light, he undressed himself in the dark, laying his clothes carefully on a straight back chair in the corner of the room. Naked now, he crawled into bed beside Margo. Her back was to him, and she was sleeping soundly. He smiled indulgently, as he reached across her, taking a firm hold of her nearest breast. He grinned, as she awoke with a start, and then he rolled her onto her back, positioning her to accept the inevitable.

Vince continued his foreplay, squeezing both breasts simultaneously, sucking on her nipples alternately, biting on them enthusiastically, and groaning loudly in ecstasy. Margo was moaning audibly too, but not with pleasure. Done with fondling her breasts, Vince moved his hand down to her crotch stroking her mound methodically, and finally fingering her vagina with his mid finger to make sure it was wet. Satisfied that she was ready now, he rolled on top of her, and pushed his stiff, erect and eager penis into her opening, and fucked her. Before long, he came, and came strongly. He lay over her panting noisily until he caught his breath, then rolled over and went to sleep. Margo got up and took a bath, before returning to her bed.

Stan and Wilf got to their hooks in the Dry, got into their diggers and went over the lamp rack and got their lamps. Wilf followed Stan to the shifter's wicket and waited a little behind him. The shift boss at Stan's wicket was not a big man., maybe 5'6" or 5'7" at the most. He was dressed for work, but had his hard hat on the counter beside him, his lamp hanging from its cord around his neck. He looked fit enough. He looked up from his log book when he saw Stan. "Hello Stan. This is your new partner?"

"Yeah, this is Wilf."

"Hi Wilf, I'm Garth Young. Welcome to graveyard." He kind of grinned when he said it. Wilf knew right away that he liked him.

He turned back to Stan. "You're going into a clean face, Stan. The cross shift put in track. You'll need to put in air and water." (The face is the end of a drift upon which the next round is drilled and blasted in order to advance the length of the drift). Stan nodded, and then left the wicket. Wilf followed him down the stairs that lead to the shaft area. There were benches along the side of the shaft house for them to wait for the cage. A third man came and joined them, a big man of medium height. Thick through the chest and shoulders, he had his lampbelt cinched loosely underneath an overhanging paunch. The belt hung over his hips, which were proportionately smaller. His face was roundish, and already sweating. He sat beside Wilf, and Wilf could smell the beer.

"You're with Stan?" he asked. Wilf nodded. "Gus McKinnon", he went on, and stuck out his hand.

"Wilf Baker". He shook Gus' hand, eying him blandly. His hand was thick, and his grip was firm.

"I'm with Stan too. He lets me muck out." Stan grinned at this, looking away, and Gus was grinning as he said it, as though they shared a joke. Wilf could see they got along. "Good to meet you, Wilf."

Stan cut in, "He plays a good fiddle when he's in the mood." Wilf perked up at that. There was nothing he liked better than good fiddle music.

A Miner's Story – Chapter 5

As the cage came to the surface, the hoistman answered the cagetender's three bells and the cagetender rolled open the door. He called out "Eleven hundred!" and only eight miners got on board.

"Big cage for eight men," Wilf commented to Stan.

"There are almost a hundred men on 700' and 900' levels, mostly on the seven. All there are on 1100' are two drift crews and two raisemen." (The raisemen drove the raises, which were tunnels driven upwards from one level to the level above. They were usually 5'x6' I size, and went up on a 50 degree incline.)

The cage stopped at the level, the hoistman answered the cagetender's three bells, and the men stepped into the station. The cagetender closed the door again and rang 2-2, the hoistman answered 2-2. They rang one each, and the cage returned to surface.

The second drift crew had a clean face too. They took the first motor in line and not needing any track or pipe went straight up the drift to their heading. Stan took the second motor and moved it abreast of a pile of twenty foot 4" air pipe. Gus grabbed the end of one of the pipes and nodded to Wilf who immediately grabbed the other end. They laid the pipe on top of the motor. There were cleats welded along the edge of the motor's cover to prevent them from rolling off. Gus went to the pile of 2"water pipe, grabbed a twenty footer by himself and placed it on the motor beside the air pipe. He moved like a cat, for such a big man, and Wilf could see he was no slouch.

"Jump on," he said to Wilf, stepping up on the step welded to the back end of the motor. Wilf got on the other side.

"Clamps?" he asked.

"We've got clamps inside, Wilf."

The ditch on the left side was full with fast moving water....fairly clear and moving steadily toward the sump by the shaft.

"She's a wet one, eh?" Wilf commented.

"Yup...they keep a 2% grade here to keep that water moving. Wait till you see the face." They stopped at a switch leading to the right where the other drift crew had gone in. Gus threw it back in the direction of their heading. "I hope they don't get in our way when we're mucking out," Gus commented as he climbed back on the motor.

The objective in advancing a drift was to make a complete 'cycle' every shift. This involved drilling off and blasting an eight foot drift round and then mucking it out afterwards. In a 9' by 10' drift round this required 38 eight foot holes. A cycle completed with a round drilled and blasted with a good break and then mucked out would advance the drift another eight feet.

It was a line drive right to the face which wasn't all that far, maybe a quarter mile. There was a short drift splitting off to the left, not too far back from the face. At the end of the short drift eight two ton Hudson muck cars were parked ready for the mucking cycle. About twenty feet back from the face was an Eimco 21 mucking machine.

Stan took the motor straight up toward the face, and stopped right where the pipes ended. Gus immediately went back to the shut off valves and closed the air and water lines. He flashed his light at Stan who was by then at the headers. On Gus' signal, he opened the valves on the headers and bled the pipes. Gus then walked up with the 2" and 4" clamps, and took off the headers. As he did so Stan walked ahead and screwed a J-hook into a hole drilled in near the top corner of the right wall, twenty feet ahead of the last pipe, and hung a length of J hook chain from it.

Gus already had the gaskets in place on the end of the pipes. Stan took an end of the 4" pipe, and Wilf knew to grab the other end. They raised the pipe level with the air line. Stan wrapped the chain around his end and hooked it back into the J-hook, and Wilf held the other end flush with the end of air line so Gus could move the gasket over it, place the clamp, and bolt it together.

When the clamp was tight they did the same thing with the 2" water line. This time Stan used a length of haywire to hang the lighter water line below the air line. Gus went back to the shut off valves, blew out the air line and flushed out the water line, and when Stan flashed his light, Gus shut them both off. Wilf brought the headers up to Stan and held them in place, while Stan clamped them on. At the flash of Stan's light, Gus reopened the shut off valves and they were ready to go. The whole procedure took barely twenty minutes.

Wilf could see that Gus was an old-timer and a hi-baller that he knew his business. That big gut of his wasn't getting in the way.

"Looks like you've done this before," Wilf said.

"Yeah, once or twice." Gus always seemed to be smiling and always sweating. As he spoke he went for his jackleg which stood against the wall of the drift, a ways from the face. Stan and Wilf followed suit, each of them packing their machine to the face. Without another word spoken, they hooked up the air and water hoses to their machines, and went back for their drill steel, bits, and drill ladders. Once they had the bits on their steel, oil in the lubricators, and the ladders placed against the bucket of the mucker, they were ready to open up the air and water to the machines and start drilling. Just about then Garth showed up, making his rounds. Wilf and Stan lit up a smoke. Gus scooped himself out a fresh wad of Copenhagen, and stuffed it under his lip.

"All set up eh, boys," Garth broke in. "Well, I won't hold you up". He turned to leave.

It was Gus who spoke. "And what's your hurry Garth. Not feeling sociable?" Wilf could tell he was Nova Scotian as soon as he spoke, and that East Coast amiability hadn't missed Gus.

"Well I wouldn't want you boys to miss your round," Garth returned, warming up to the comment, "not by my interference anyways."

"And when did you ever see us miss a round, Garth?"

"Maybe once last year.....remember when the compressors quit?"

"Oh ya, right".

They talked a few more minutes, mostly about nothing relevant, and Garth went his way. Stan was grinning.

"Not a hard guy to like," said Wilf.

"No, Garth's all right."

"We do five back holes (topmost holes), five lifters (bottom holes), and three up the side.

We drop our corner backholes eight or nine inches to round the back a bit for strength." said Stan lifting his machine by the handle on its back end. He put his hip against the leg of the machine, and with his left hand, shoved a four foot steel into the chuck. "The rest of the round we drill like an eight by eight....just stretch it out a bit. We've been breaking Ok."

He'd directed his comments to Wilf. Gus already knew the score and had a four foot steel in his machine ready to drill the first lifter. Gus had already started on his first lifter. Wilf nodded and put a four into the chuck of his machine. The machines they were using were Atlas Copco 'Lions', a recent improvement in jacklegs. Wilf and Stan had been using Holman 'Silver Bullets' in the drift in Cochenour which were awkward and heavy with a cast iron machine and big steel leg. It took a strong man to handle the Silver Bullet, and an extra hand would have helped.

On the Copco Lion, the machine (the drill) was caste aluminum, and had an aluminum leg. The leg was retractable...and just by pushing a button on the back of the machine, it would suck the leg right back into the casing; release the button, and the pressure was back on the leg. It was well balanced and handled nicely. The 'machine' and the leg combined were called a jackleg. It was much faster drilling than the old Holman and weighed less than a hundred and fifty pounds. The Holman Silver Bullet was much heavier.

Wilf put the foot of the leg of his Copco into a rung of his ladder, put a four foot steel in his chuck, and collared his corner lifter. Gus was already starting on his inside lifter, next to Stan's center lifter. Once the lifters were drilled they 'flagged' them by putting in short pieces of broken drill steel in the collars of the holes to serve as a marker, as debris would slough from the face during the drilling off of the round and would end up covering the lifters.

The roar of the three machines prohibited any conversation, but none was necessary. These were three good miners who knew their business.

Wilf was right at home in the drift. He'd lucked out, getting on with Stan and Gus. He was amazed at how Gus could get down drilling those lifters with that big belly in front of him; that didn't seem to slow him down one bit. Stan had his center lifter drilled to eight feet now, and put a four foot steel in his chuck to start on his cut; Wilf immediately shut off his machine and took hold of Stan's steel to help him collar the cut. Stan brought the bit of his four foot steel against the center of the face. Wilf wrapped his hands around the steel and held it steady on the mark.

As Stan open up the throttle of his machine, chunks and grit flew from the face as his bit cut into the rock. Wilf continued with him until all six cut holes were collared, then went on to drilling his own side of the round. Stan was good to go now. He always drilled a perfect cut. He drilled his center hole of the top line the full eight feet, then pulled the eight foot steel back a few feet and used it to line up the rest of his cut holes. Putting the four foot steel back in his machine, he drilled the remaining holes in the cut to four feet, lining up on the eight, and then deepened the holes to eight feet. Stan was flawless in alignment. His holes never connected his holes. When he blasted his round, his cut always broke right to the bottom.

The ground was good on 1100; no worry of sticking your steel. Water oozed from tiny slips running through the face (little seams of mud), but the slips didn't grab the steel. It was good drilling. Wilf decided to go straight eights. When he finished his corner backhole he pulled the machine off the eight, leaving it out of the hole a few feet, put the foot of his leg onto the farthest rung of his ladder, and pulled his other eight into his chuck. Stan saw what he was up to and reached over to help collar his top side hole. Gus started doing the same. When Stan was done his cut he went with the eights. The three of them continued with straight eights, not bothering with the four footers.

Once they started going like that, it was nonstop. There were 38 holes to be drilled in total, four more than the regular 8 by 8 round, plus three of the holes in the cut to be reamed. Wilf loved it. He was in a pretty good sweat by now, not having worked in months, and only sober a few days, but he had hooked in with a good crew. Their machines went nonstop...they were a team....it went like clockwork. In just two and a half hours they were drilled off. Stan was last to finish. He had half a hole left to ream in his cut. He finished, ran his steel out, and shut off his machine.

"Smoke time,"he said. Stan and Wilf lit up a smoke, and Gus took on a fresh chew.

"You're Nova Scotian", began Wilf, looking at Gus.

"Yup, North Sydney, Cape Breton. How'd you guess?"

"You sound like East Coast..."

"And you're from the Ottawa Valley," said Gus. He knew the accent.

Wilf liked this. "And how'd you know that?" he asked

"Can smell the cowshit. Irish, eh?"

Wilf was quite pleased he thought so. "Half", he admitted, "My mother was French"

"Quebec side?"

"Yup...a tiny hole of a place called Corning, near Bryson".

"Bet you can step dance."

"Done that."

"We'll have to get you over the 'Hoot n' Holler Hall'. I play the fiddle there most Saturday nights."

"Maybe I'll do that".

Stan had finished his smoke. "Let's get going guys," he said, and shut off the air and water to the machines. Wilf and Gus bled the air out of machines and took off the hoses. When Stan came, the three of them packed the jacklegs back a good hundred feet from the face safe from the blast, and stood them up side by side against the left wall of the drift opposite the pipes. Gus backed the mucker a good piece back from the face. Once they had two of the air hoses, the three water hoses, the drill steel and the ladders well back from the face, the three of them were ready to start loading the round.

This was all done without a word spoken, with no time lost and no wrong moves. Gus hooked the remaining air hose to the blowpipe. Wilf took a shovel and scooped the bottom of the face clean, pulling back the cuttings and sloughed rock to clear it down to the lifters. As he removed the broken pieces of steel that marked the lifters, Gus blew out the lifters clean one by one with the blowpipe.

Stan was then already loading the cut. The cut holes were in the very center of the round and were the first holes blasted when they opened up the round. The level nipper had left them three cases of CIL 70% 1"x8" stick dynamite (commonly referred to as 'powder'), four rolls of tape fuse (ten fuses to a roll), and two boxes of Thermalite (which is a specific type of igniter cord used ignite fuses used for blasting). The tape fuses were ten feet long with a cap on one end. The cap was inserted into a stick of powder to make a 'primer' and pushed to the end of the blast hole. A slotted copper end was at the other end which was snapped onto the Thermalite. When lit, Thermalite burns at 20 seconds per foot eventually through the copper end of the fuses thus igniting them. The tape fuse burns at 40 seconds per foot and sets off the cap detonating the charge.

He'd also left them some spacers which were three quarter inch sticks of wood eight inches long. Spacers were sometimes used loading the cut in softer ground like limestone so as not to 'freeze' the cut. However, since they were in good solid granite, Stan didn't need them. Granite would 'burn good', so there was no need for spacers. He could load the cut solid, leaving about a foot collar, and tamp well all three blast holes in the cut. Once Gus and Wilf were done, and the round was loaded, Stan took one of the boxes of Thermalite and started to wire up the round. One box was enough. The extra box was safety measure, but Stan would always get it right the first time.

Each loaded hole was referred as a shot. Of the 38 holes drilled in a 9' x 10' drift round three holes were reamed and 35 holes were loaded and blasted. The Thermalite was marked at six inch intervals. Stan would measure out eight and a half feet from one corner lifter to the back hole in the opposite corner; then did the same with the other corner lifter and backhole. Backholes were the holes drilled at the very top of the round; lifters were the bottom holes. At the four foot mark coming from the top, he would make a knot well wrapped in extra Thermalite, joining the two stands in the middle in an X. From that center he would run a single strand, onto which he would connect first the cut blast holes and then the four cut helpers in a single sequence.

He hooked the rest of the holes in sequence, quickly snapping the copper ends of the fuses onto the Thermalite in order one by one, ending with the corner back holes and corner lifters. Because he had an extra six inches running to the lifters, this ensured the lifters would go last; this was sure to lift and loosen the muckpile, making it easier to muck. In a matter of minutes, Stan had the whole round wired, and Wilf and Gus by this time had everything put away. Gus was in the cockpit of the motor and Wilf was on the step on the back end of the motor, ready to go, so Stan lit the tail of the Thermalite.

Stan watched it burn until it ignited the fuses to the cut and helpers and the knot in the middle. Once the Thermalite was burning to the four corners of the round, he turned on the air header aimed at the face on full, yelling, '

FIRE', jumped on the motor, and Gus ran the three of them to the station on the motor. They stopped at the intersection where the drift split off to the other drift crew, to guard their blast, and count their shots. When the last of their shots went, they continued on their way to the station, where there was a bench to sit on and have their lunch, while the smoke cleared.

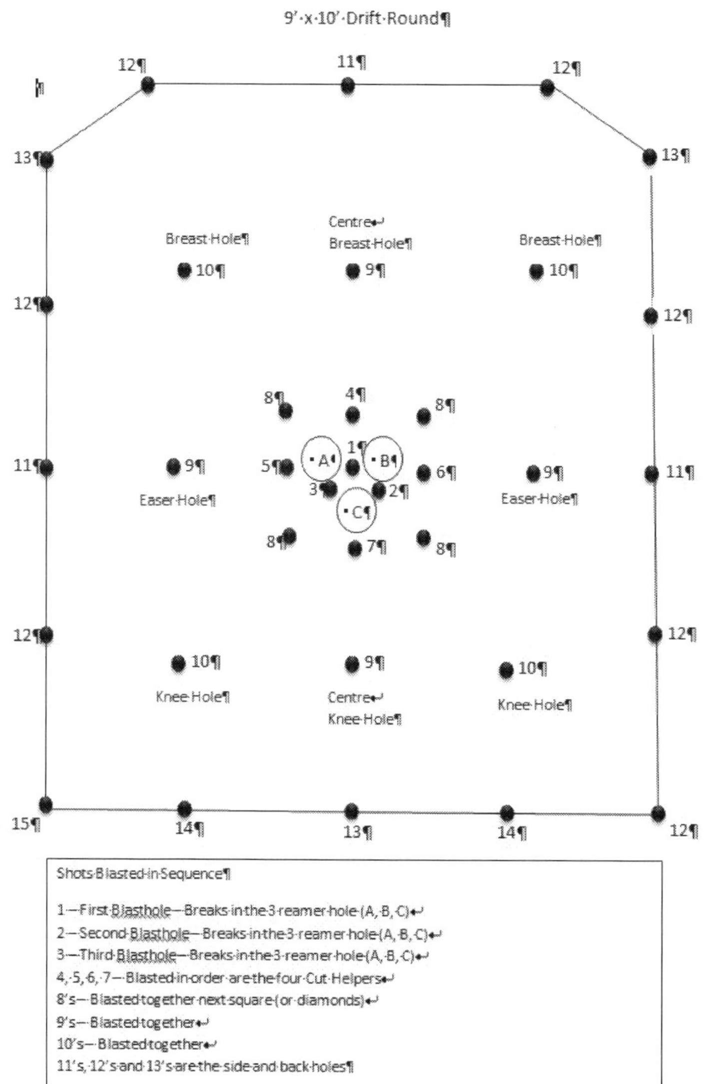

9' x 10' Drift Round
12
11
12
13
13
Breast Hole
Centre
Breast Hole
Breast Hole
10
9
10
12
12
8
4
8
1
A
B
11
9
5
6
9
11
3
2
Easer Hole
C
Easer Hole
8
7
8
12
12
10
9
10
Knee Hole
Centre
Knee Hole
Knee Hole
15
14
13
14
12
Shots Blasted in Sequence
1 – First Blasthole – Breaks in the 3 reamer hole (A, B, C)
2 – Second Blasthole – Breaks in the 3 reamer hole (A, B, C)
3 – Third Blasthole – Breaks in the 3 reamer hole (A, B, C)
4, 5, 6, 7 – Blasted in order are the four Cut Helpers
8's – Blasted together next square (or diamonds)
9's – Blasted together
10's – Blasted together
11's, 12's and 13's are the side and back holes

Gus seemed to be always the talker. Wilf quite liked the guy. He spoke to Wilf, pointing to Stan.

"So you know this guy before?"

"Oh ya. We were partners in the drift at Cochenour."

"I've been to Red Lake. Worked at Madsen, but that was after the war. I hear they got a road in there now."

"Yup. It's a gravel road, but it gets you there. So you play the fiddle, Gus."

"Sure do. Play with the best of them. I'll be playing this weekend at the Hoot n' Holler Hall, like I said; so come if you can make it. They set up a bar there, but some bring their own booze." He winked at Stan as he said that, who nodded, knowingly. "You like a drink, Wilf"

"Well I'm trying to quit, actually."

"Aw nothing to that. Done it hundreds of times."

Stan had to laugh, but Wilf knew what he was saying. Wilf hoped to stay quit...he just let that one go. Stan looked at his watch. "Should be able to breathe in there now," he said, getting up. He got into the cockpit of the motor, Gus and Wilf jumped on the tail end and they headed back to the face. It was still a little smoky a ways up but nothing too thick.

When they got to the switch at the layby for the cars, Stan stopped while Gus threw the switch into the layby. (A layby is a side drift off the mainline used for switching cars in the mucking out cycle; or for parking extra equipment not in use out of the way.) Then Stan pulled ahead, and Gus hooked him up to the string of Hudsons. As Stan pulled back over the switch again, Gus threw the switch back in the direction of the face. Stan moved the train up toward the face, stopping just behind the mucking machine with Gus riding the back end of the motor. Gus hopped off at the headers, and shut the air header off that was blowing fresh air toward the face. The air was clear at the face now, so he got on the stand of the mucking machine, and started cleaning up the scattered muck up to the muckpile.

Wilf grabbed the end of the water hose, and turning it on full, started washing down the scattered muck, and then the muckpile, being careful to stay out of Gus' way. He watched Gus go on the mucker, and he was good. He dropped the bucket to the tracks first, and ran it up to the muck pile, keeping the chain tight, and nosing into the muckpile, brought it up full. Stan pulled up with an empty car for him, and Gus hit the bucket lever hard, dumping squarely into the car.

Stan pulled back, as Gus moved back to clean up the sides. He swung the bucket to his side first, dropped it and pushed ahead, neatly cleaning the left side up to the muck pile. Stan moved up, allowing him to empty his bucket, then pulled back again, allowing Gus to clean the right side. Stan moved up again and stayed, as Gus was now into the muck pile.

Gus was smooth and he was fast. The car was neatly filled in a few minutes, with nothing spilled and no space wasted. As Stan pulled back to switch, Wilf left the water hose for Gus, and went back with train, switching cars for Stan.

Stan pulled the train back past the switch to the layby, and Wilf threw the switch and uncoupled the full car; then Stan gave it a shot with the motor, leaving it up the layby by itself. When Stan had pulled back past the switch again, Wilf threw the switch back toward the face. Wilf stayed at the switch now and did the switching, while Gus mucked, and washed down waiting for his next car. Each time Stan came back with a full car, Wilf would switch it into the layby, and hook it up with the other full ones. Before long, all eight cars were filled, and Wilf rode the tail end of the train to waste pass to dump the cars. Gus stayed behind, scaled a little, and having dug in a tie pushed the slide rails ahead to the muckpile.

The waste pass was open for use, when Stan pulled up with the train. He turned the valve to the air cylinder which raised the big sliding cover over the waste pass, then pulled ahead, until the last car was directly in front of the waste pass. Wilf pushed down with his foot on the release pedal on the side of the chassis, opposite the pass, simultaneously pushing hard and upwards with both hands on the top edge of the side of the car. The car tipped its load into the waste pass, its top edge slamming against the long steel plate in place to prevent the car from tipping right into the pass. It emptied completely, and Wilf pulled the car back upright.

One by one, Stan advanced the cars, and one by one Wilf dumped them. When the last car was dumped, Wilf hopped onto the back end of the motor, and went with Stan, as he headed the train back to the face. The other drift crew was parked at the switch to the other drift, waiting their turn as Stan and Wilf went by with a wave.

"Let's see if we can beat them back," said Stan.

When they got back, Gus was ready with a full bucket. The train was loaded in a little faster this time, and with the last car filled, Wilf rode out to the dump with Stan. Gus dug in the next tie, pushed the slide rails ahead, and took the scaling bar and began scaling whatever he could reach. He let the water hose run on the muckpile as he did so. He was getting closer to the face now, as a good half of the muckpile was gone. He could see their round was a clean break. No frozen ground and no bootlegs. They had a good cross shift. Their rounds always broke to the 'nuts'. (Bootlegs are the remnants of a blasted hole which didn't break to the end. For example, an eight foot drift round which only breaks six feet leaves two feet of bootleg).

The waste pass was free again when Stan and Wilf pulled in. The dumping went a little more quickly this time as Wilf and Stan were well coordinated now, and leaving they passed the other drift crew, again waiting at the switch. Stan gave them thumbs up as he rode by grinning generously. This grin was returned with a deadpan stare from the waiting crew.

Gus dumped a fresh bucket into the end car, as it came nicely to a stop against the back end of the mucker. On his second last car, Gus derailed his front wheels off to the far side of the tracks. He dumped his bucket; then dropping it to the tracks again, he immediately slammed it back up again, hard. The second it hit the back end of the mucker, the front wheels bounced up clear of the tracks, and at that precise instant, Gus, hanging onto the levers threw his weight back hard, jerking the front end towards himself, and dropping the front wheels nicely on the tracks, all done in seconds.

He was mucking again in less than a minute. Stan and Wilf took off to dump again and Gus dug in another tie, and pushed the slides ahead. He was able to reach right up to the face now with the scaling bar, and finish the scaling. There was very little loose....it was good ground; the cross shift kept their backholes in perfectly flat, keeping a nice even back. Stan and Wilf had dumped and were headed back to the face.

"We've only got about six more cars to go," said Stan, "we usually get 30 to 31 cars to a round."

On the way back they found the other crew derailed at the switch leading into their heading, right in the way of Stan's train. They got off their motor and walked up to them. The motor was crossways at the switch.

Stan greeted them. "Trouble boys?"

"Yup....the front wheels jumped right at the frog. Must have been a rock. Anyways we were moving pretty good, so the cars pushed against us and pushed the back end crossways."

"Well let's see what we can do," Stan said.

He went back and found a tie. "Let's see if we can sprag'er on, Wilf." (A sprag is a short piece of timber used to 'sprag' a derailed car or mucking machine back onto the track.) Wilf held the sprag against the flange on the back of the derailed motor and signaled Stan with his light to come ahead. Stan moved the train gently ahead until he felt it come against the butt of the tie which Wilf had aimed to connect just above the coupling. Stan paused for a moment until Wilf flashed him another light. Then carefully he pushed, raising and swinging the back end of the motor directly over the tracks. Wilf then flashed his light again so Stan backed off allowing the back wheels of the motor to fall neatly onto the tracks.

The motorman of the stricken motor uncoupled the cars and had enough traction with two wheels on the track to move the motor a few feet head of the cars. He and his partner attempted to sprag the front end of the motor on but succeeded only in lifting the battery.

"I think if we had a plank to come up on, it might jump on if we drag it over the switch," Wilf suggested. "We've got a chain on our motor if we can't move it on its own."

One of the derailed crew showed up with a piece of 2'' lagging. (Lagging is 4' slabs of 2" or 3" rough planking. They were normally placed from set to set against the back between the cap and the back or from post to post between the wall and the posts.)

The miner scraped away the ballast with the handle of his 12" crescent from in front of the derailed wheel that was on the outside of the track, and then jammed the butt end of the lagging against the wheel, laying it flush with the tracks toward the switch. Wilf had the chain in his hand, and by then had explained the plan to Stan. He hooked up the derailed motor to the last

Hudson in Stan's train with the chain, and gave Stan the light. Stan got the signal and tightened up the chain. Wilf gave Stan another flash, and Stan gently pulled the motor ahead.

It worked. As Stan pulled the motor ahead, the wheel came up onto the lagging giving the flange of the wheel the clearance it needed to jump onto the tracks. When the motor was pulled over the frog of the switch, the wheels were pulled in line, and dropped nicely onto the tracks. They hooked up to their cars, and backed their train out of Stan's way.

As they were going past, Stan called out, "Drive carefully, boys." The two from the other crew couldn't help smiling. On their way back to the heading Stan and Wilf came upon Gus, who was walking toward them up the drift, coming to check on them. Stan slowed down, and Gus jumped on the front end of the first car. He flashed his light, and Stan continued up to the face.

Wilf shook his head. "I hope he never falls off doing that."

"Just don't fall off, and don't get caught," said Stan.

At the 30th car, Gus had the round pretty well mucked out. Stan spotted the 7th car, and with a few more buckets, Gus was done. "About two bushels over thirty cars," he commented. Wilf always found him funny.

On an 8x8 eight foot round, neatly drilled, and broken to the nuts, Stan and Wilf used to get 24 cars to a round at Cochenour. Here they were taking eights, but 9x10, so it made on a good break about six more cars. Gus washed down the back and the face, while Wilf went out to the waste pass with Stan and emptied the train for the next shift. Gus had gone ahead and set up the three jacklegs, had the drill ladders in place against the bucket of the mucker, and had the grade chains ready to shoot line. Stan and Wilf returned with the empty train, and parked the empty cars in the layby, hooking them up to the one car that wasn't used.

"What took you so long," said Gus, quite pleased with himself.

Stan and Wilf came up, seeing it all set up for the cross-shift. "You're spoiling them rotten...they didn't leave us set up."He checked his watch, and said, "We still got twenty minutes....did you want to drill off too?"

"Naw," said Gus "gotta leave them something to do." He had the paint can in his hand. "Wouldn't hurt to give them grade."

Stan sighted the grade through the washers at the end of the grade chains. Gus marked center, and measured off the rest of the face. That done, the three men hopped on the motor, Stan driving, Wilf and Gus on the bumper, and headed for the station. They were there ahead of the other drift crew. The two raisemen had just blasted, and were already in the station. They were well ahead of the cage. The other drift crew showed up just as the cage came to the level, and the men got on board. The cagetender rang 2-2, the hoistman answered with 2-2, and the cage sped up the shaft to surface.

So ended Wilf's first shift with Stan and Gus, and his first days off were just started.

It was Friday morning, 8:00 am. They filed out of the cage, passed the lineup of the dayshift crew, waiting to go down. Among them was Vince Jamieson, whose head jerked when he saw Wilf. He made no comment, and Wilf looked past him like he wasn't there. Passing the lamp rack, Wilf put his battery on charge, followed the midnight crew into the Dry. Finding his hook, he hung up his diggers and then joined the others in the shower room.

It felt good getting back into his street clothes. He felt extremely blessed to be with two great partners Stan Rooster and Gus McKinnon. Unlike the production crews on 700, the development crews were on a five and two schedule, with weekends off. Although he was to work days, graveyards and afternoons (and in that order), there was only one cross shift in their heading. Marc Charbonneau, Kenny Nelson, and Amy Gaudet were the three miners on their cross shift. These men were top notch, a good crew to follow, and this was quite obvious to Wilf in the way he found the heading at the start of the shift. The hoses and gear were neatly pulled back from the blast. They'd made a perfect break on their round, leaving Stan's crew a nice, clean face to drill on. The new rails were stood perfectly on grade, and a good reminder was left to bring in needed pipe.

Wilf had done a good days work for the first time in many months, and was now about to have a place of his own. He dozed off on the way back to town, waking up back in town with a nudge from Stan.

"Wake up, old timer."

Stan grinned as Wilf's eyes popped open, like he didn't know where he was. "We're home," he said.

Wilf liked the sound of that word 'home'. They headed for Sadie's, who came to the door smiling.

"You boys go for breakfast," she said to Wilf. "I'll have your room ready when you come back."

As she was talking, Basil, apparently packed, was just passing in front of them, having come down the stairs on the far side of the building. He had his one kit bag over his right shoulder, and walked on passed them, eyes averted, without saying a word. He looked hungover and in need of a shave.

"Too bad he drinks," commented Sadie.

"My good luck," thought Wilf to himself. Wilf was good with that. They headed for Sinclair's. Wilf was pleased to see Serena on duty, who immediately poured them each a coffee.

"Good morning guys...hungry?"

"No need to ask," Stan said, "Ham and eggs over easy, brown toast, and lots of home fries." Wilf nodded, indicating the same. They took their coffee to a booth just vacated as Serena wiped off the table. She took on a very pleasing animation when she was working. Wilf could see she didn't mind work at all. They had a smoke with their first cup of coffee, waiting for their order. The restaurant was good with the food....two thick slices of good ham, lots of good home fries, good thick brown bread toast, and the eggs over easy, nicely done. They ate in silence, like hungry men, and once finished, lit up a smoke with their second coffee.

"Off to a good start, Wilf."

"Yup. So far, so good," said Stan.

" I noticed Jamieson's head kind of jerk when we were coming off shift," commented Wilf.

"Yeah... he'd be wondering how you got right onto development", replied Stan. "That would piss him off."

"Good. What's he doing?" Wilf asked.

"I think he's up on 700, driving those scrans. That ground is so soft there in places they have to drive them with chippers, to avoid blasting and caving them in. Even when they do drill and blast, they just use a V-cut and only 5' steel. The holes keep caving. They have to cement every foot of those scrans with rebar to keep them from caving."

"That'd be a good place for Vince," said Wilf.

"They had him on 1,100 for awhile, but he wasn't breaking his rounds so good."

"Sounds like Vince." Wilf had to smile.

"He was cross-shifting the other driftcrew, but they had him taken out. They said he was a hard worker, but not a very good one, said Stan "Always left them a mess...not breaking his rounds...over a foot of bootleg every round, sloppy drilling, back holes looking up, side holes looking out. Dave and Joe got fed up."

"That'd be Vince," said Wilf.

"He can sure sling the shit, though."

"You got that right," concluded Wilf.

Serena dropped the bill, and Stan grabbed it. "Let's go and see about your room, partner," he said, "...enough about Vince Jamieson."

Wilf didn't mind cutting up Vince, but it was time to move on to important things. Sadie had the key ready when they came by. It was a beautiful sunny morning, and was already getting warm. She handed Wilf the key.

"You're paid up till the end of June," she said.

"Thank you, Sadie," he said, accepting the key.

"Nice to have somebody sober," she went on.

He nodded, without comment. They went up to the room, which was between Stan's room and the bathroom. The room was emptied and clean, and the door was open. Wilf went over to Stan's and grabbed his kitbag and shaving gear. "I'm going to stretch out for a bit," he said, to which Stan nodded and said, "Me too."

Wilf brushed his teeth and shaved, and putting his shaving gear on the dresser, his kitbag on the corner, took off his shoes and flopped onto the bed. It was a small bed, but it was all he needed...his own for the first time in a while. He was deeply content. He soon drifted off to sleep...fully dressed, and into a dead sleep.

He awoke a few hours later. He sat up and rubbed his face. He could hear the noises from the street. He raised the blind on his window. It was still sunny and warm. He'd get out and have a coffee. He took his towel to the bathroom and found it vacant. Having splashed some cold water on his face, he dried it off, brushed his teeth, and took a leak. That done, he put his things away in his room, locked his door, and headed for Sinclair's.

He was pleased to see Serena still there and Stan at the counter on a stool, having a coffee and a cigarette. "Up early, eh?" he said, taking the stool beside him.

"No use wasting good daylight....," said Stan. "I don't sleep that much on Graveyards, actually."

Serena brought Wilf a coffee and asked. "Anything else, Wilf?"

"No thanks, not right now." Wilf replied. He would have liked to have said more, but at least he wasn't blushing. He loved her smile, and had to bend over backwards to seem casual.

As he turned to Stan, he asked "Gus says he's playing the fiddle somewhere tonight."

"Yup...he plays at the 'Hoot'n'Holler Hall' most Saturdays."

"You going?"

"Been there. Good music," exclaimed Stan. "But I don't dance and I don't drink; so not much point. How 'bout you?"

""I think I'd better wait for payday. Got no dancing shoes anyways, and I don't want to drink."

"Tell you what Wilf. Your payday's a few weeks away. I'll go down to the bank and get you a drag for a hundred...how 'bout that?"

"Thanks....but no. You've helped me out enough. I'll wait till payday, and make it on what I've got. Bill Harrison said he'll let me run a tab at the restaurant here till payday. I'm OK. The dancing shoes can wait."

Stan eyed his canvas runners, but made no comment.

Wilf got up suddenly, and said, "I'm going take a good look around town, Stan....take some air...you know...catch you later, partner." Stan nodded; staying put, he accepted another coffee. Wilf paid for his coffee and left.

He'd been to the hospital, in the area he was told was 'Don Park', so he went in another direction, following the bus route across the O'Brien Street Bridge, and then turned right on to Maple Crescent, immediately on the other side of the bridge. He was told this area was called 'Dunbar Heights.' He was enjoying a good day. He felt good with every breath. The sun was warm on his back, and there was a bit of a breeze. The leaves were nicely out now, and people passing would give a nod or a greeting. People were friendly and mostly young. Boom towns had a special energy; young people with little kids and babies... pregnant women were a common sight. Lots of work...lots of money...lots going on. There were houses being built on every street.

Before the mine opened up, Atikokan was a railroad community of a little over three hundred souls. It had been, and still was a divisional point on the C.N.R., with a roundhouse for servicing the steam engines, also coal docks and a water tank to keep up their steam. The station, the Beanery, the telegraph office, and a bunkhouse for out of town railway employees completed the picture.

The Errington open pit had started producing iron ore in 1943, housing the mine workers first in bunkhouses, gradually building a town site. By 1948 the population had risen to 1,500. Now, in 1957, it was 8,000, and still growing. For the new employee at the mine, accommodation was hard to find. Many with houses took in boarders at one hundred dollars a month, and if the house served poor cooking, it was just tough luck for the boarder; there weren't too many choices. He would have to make the best of it.

He continued in the same direction, eventually coming to a Catholic Church. There were no vehicles in the parking lot. He stopped and reflected. He had been raised a Catholic, his father Ottawa Valley Irish, his mother French, from Ville Marie, Quebec. Both were devout Catholics. They were in church every Sunday when he was growing up. Their farm was close to Corning, a tiny place with a general store/ coffee hang out, which was near Bryson in the Pontiac County on the Quebec side of the Ottawa River. Where Wilf grew up was predominantly Irish and Father Shea, the priest of the local church, gave the service in English. His mother, Therese spoke broken English, but got by. She came to the same church every Sunday with Wilf's father, Tim, who spoke only a few words of French. They went as a family every Sunday, Therese and Tim, his little sister Denise, and his two brothers, Patrick and Clarence. Those were good days. Wilf had not seen the inside of a church in many years.

He reflected on where his life was headed only a week ago and how blessed he felt today. He was overwhelmed by a sense of gratitude, but in his whole life, he'd never felt any strong connection with God. Standing in front of the church, he felt an instinctive urge to consider that possibility, but felt at a loss as to where to begin. And then he thought of the way he was dressed....faded grey khaki pants and shirt, wool socks and canvass running shoes...not the way to go to church.

He felt drawn, nevertheless, and went up the steps to the front door. There seemed to be no one around. He tried the door. It wasn't locked. He opened the door. It was quiet inside. He ventured in. The sunlight shone through the stained glass windows, casting a colorful spectrum across the wooden pews. There was a raised altar at the far end of the church, and behind the altar and against the back wall, almost to the ceiling, was a figure of Christ on the cross. To either side of the raised area, and slightly behind the altar, were two rows of wooden benches, undoubtedly to seat the choir.

Wilf took in the quiet of it all, and felt the urge to venture a little further. He went up the aisle passed a few rows, and then sat down on one of the hard wooden pews, which to his surprise, he found quite comfortable. Sitting there in the quiet of the empty church, he thought about his life.

A week ago he was out of it. He'd been on a drunk for months; finally homeless broke and totally lost. How many times in recent months he'd told himself it was time to quit drinking. It never happened....and now finally it did. He'd slipped through a small crack in the wall. He knew the old habit was only one drink away. He wanted to keep the good feeling he now had. He wanted never to drink again.

He heard the entrance door of the church open, and he turned to see a priest quietly closing the door behind him. He was a big man, seemingly not old, with a full head of wavy auburn hair. He started up the aisle. Wilf turned back towards the front and didn't move. When the priest came abreast of him, he greeted him in a gentle voice, "Good afternoon son, I'm Father Grant."

Wilf stood up and shook his extended hand. "I'm Wilf Baker, Father. I hope I don't offend you....I mean I just walked in."

"No problem. This is God's house, and we are God's children. Be at peace, Son."

"Well to be honest, Father, I haven't set foot in a church in years. I'm not even sure why I did this."

"I'm sure it was no mistake. You're most welcome here. You're new in town?'

Wilf liked his manner.....not pious...just friendly. "Well yes," he came back," just got to town a few days ago. Got on at the mine, got me a room....I'm sorry...I'm not really dressed to be here."

"Not at all Mr. Baker."

"Just call me Wilf."

"OK, Wilf. Maybe you need to be here."

Wilf didn't answer that, but felt maybe he did.

"Sit down a moment, Wilf. Maybe we should talk."

"Thanks, Father, but I think I'll be on my way"

"Maybe come back on Sunday. I'm here every Sunday."

"Maybe I will. Nice to meet you Father."

The priest extended his hand again. "Nice to meet you too Wilf."

Wilf shook his hand again, and turned to leave. "Thanks," he said, and went back into the sunshine of the day. He checked his pocket watch. I t was getting near 5:00 pm. By the time he walked downtown, it would be time to eat. He would leave Stan alone. He wouldn't want to spoil a good friendship being too much in his face.

He got back to the restaurant a little past 5:30, and took a stool at the counter. Serena was gone, and the big blonde girl was in her place. She made eye contact with him, and raised the coffee pot. Wilf nodded, and she brought him a coffee.

"What's your name?" he asked.

"Barbara....What's yours?"

"Wilf."

"Nice to meet you, Wilf...I see you around here. What'll you have?"

"I'll have a cheeseburger deluxe....but no gravy, Please."

"OK...got it." She wrote it down, and clipped it to the order wheel above the open window to the kitchen gallery. Wilf lit a cigarette, and sipped his coffee. He liked their coffee. It was a good strength, and he drank it black. He thought about the priest. Nice guy...not pushy...not important....friendly. Didn't overdo it. 'Might even go to that church some day' he thought. It wouldn't be this Sunday, though. He would wait till he was dressed a little better first.

He knew it made no difference to Father Grant, but it did to him. Anyways, going to church was just a thought. Barbara put his food down. He butted his cigarette, downed the rest of his coffee, and thanked Barbara. She nodded acknowledgement. She had a nice smile.

"More coffee?"

"No thanks...maybe when I'm done."

She took the pot and made her rounds, and Wilf got into his food. He splashed a good dose of vinegar on his chips, salted them, and got into his burger. They made a good one, nice and thick. He was just finishing the last of his chips, when Stan walked in. He sat next to Wilf.

"Just about done, eh?"

"Yup. Good enough. I'll have another coffee." He raised his cup, and Barbara obliged him."And what are you up to?"

"Me, I just got up. Slept a couple of hours. What you been doing?"

"Had a walk around town." He didn't mention the church. Stan was not a churchgoer either, and Wilf wasn't going to leave himself open for comment. He finished his coffee. "Nice day out there," he said, finally, and got up to leave.

"Heading out?"

"Yeah...I'll take some air....walk around a bit. Catch you later."

"See you..."

He walked by the theater, and checked out the movie. ...a movie called 'Shane', starring Alan Ladd. It would be on at 7:00 pm. He had about half an hour to kill before showtime. There was a convenience store two doors from the theater. He went inside. There was a book rack in one corner. He browsed for a moment, and then spotted a book by Louis L'Amour....a duster. There was more than one. He bought a couple of them, crossed the street, took them up to his room, and then went back down to the street, and across to the theatre. There was a lineup already formed, although it was still early. "Must be a good movie," he thought. It was a great movie. It was about a gunslinger....a loner who tried to go straight. Wilf could identify.

When it was over, he just went back to his room. There was still life on the street, but he had a place of his own and books to read.....good enough for now. He stretched out on his bed, turned on the bedside lamp, and started into one of his books. He soon felt his eyes getting heavy. He got undressed, got into the bed, and turned off the light. It was quiet in the rooming house with Basil gone. He was asleep in no time.

He'd been thinking about Gus as he'd drifted off to sleep. He would love to hear him play his fiddle someday soon. How he loved that good fiddle music...that good old two step...He fell into a deep sleep. He began to dream...

He was a boy at the old General Store back home, before his brother Patrick had gone off to the war. How he idolized his brother Patrick. Patrick always took him around with him. They fished, they hunted, they trapped, and they worked their father's farm. And then there was Clarence, his younger brother, who Wilf never got on with. Lastly was his little sister Denise, and Wilf was her hero.

The General Store was more than just a store. It was the hangout for the locals. There was an open porch, where people could gather around a couple of tables in the warm weather, and a table inside, when the weather was not so warm. Winters came hard around Corning. There was always a coffee pot on. Coffee was a nickel, and Bill Crofton would be usually at the table. He was a First World War veteran, who'd lost his right leg just below the hip, at the battle for Vimy Ridge in 1917. He survived on a small pension, and lived with his family. He got around on crutches, and Bill would play the fiddle like no one else could. That fiddle went everywhere with him, hanging from a sling made from a piece of rope. When he was on the move, the fiddle hung from his back in its case, and stayed with him.

Sometimes Ben Aubrey would join him at the table with his guitar, a plain old flat top, and they would make the best music Wilf ever heard. His brother Patrick could never resist good two step music, and would step dance to no end. There was an open space in the middle of the floor, and the table was over to one side. If the music was happening, and Patrick was there, he'd be dancing.

Patrick was not an exhibitionist. He just didn't like to see good music go to waste and he liked to show the fiddler proper respect. Wilf was shy to try it but Patrick got him going. Wilf was very proud when he could do it finally and do it well while standing opposite his brother right in step. His father Tim played the fiddle tolerably well but he was a little reserved. He would play mostly at home, alone or for his family. Patrick who could also play the guitar would cord with him.

Those were some of the best moments of Wilf's life, when the music was happening in the old store, and Wilf came by with his brother Patrick. There would always be an audience of avid onlookers, and at least a couple of people playing the spoons. His brother Clarence took no interest in dancing, or music, for that matter, and when he appeared in Wilf's dream the magic of the dream faded, and Wilf was soon awake.

Pay periods ran from the first of the month to the 15th and from the 16th of the month to the end of the month. Paydays were on the 10th and 25th of each month. The rate for an underground miner at Steep Rock was $2.45 an hour, the highest in the country at the time. Wilf had received a cheque of $53.61 on the 10th of June for the two days he'd worked at the end of May. One day, the day of his induction tour, was paid at straight time, and one day in the drift on contract with Stan and Gus, paid his wage plus $20.00 bonus. For the small cheque, there was very little income tax to pay. It was the first money he'd earned in a good while.

Now it was the 25th of June, and with 11 days paid, and a good bonus period in the drift ($21.44 per shift), Wilf had cleared $365.23. His crew had better than doubled their wages with their bonus. Now he had some money. Amazing to Wilf, he didn't even think of drinking. He would give $100.00 to Stan.... $50.00 for the room and the rest for the extras Stan had put his way. He headed over to Sinclair's to pay Bill Harrison for his past month's tab. Bill Harrison was at the till.

"Have a coffee, Wilf. I don't have a bill prepared, but I'll get to it... I'll be with you soon."

Serena was on, and brought him a coffee to the counter. He thanked her as casually as he could, and she smiled like always. Bill got back to him.

"You owe me $64.70," he said quietly, putting the bill in front of him. Wilf gave him three twenties and a ten.

"That's good," he said. Bill brought him his change anyways.

"No, now we're good," he said.

"Well, thanks a lot, Bill," he said putting the change away, "You sure helped me out." Bill just gave him a wave, and went back to the till. Wilf had one more coffee and a cigarette, paid and left. It was still early Thursday afternoon. He had one more graveyard shift to work. It was too early to eat supper, so he thought he'd look at some shoes. There was a men's wear shop right next to the hardware store on the corner. He went in, but didn't see a great selection.

There was a Hudson Bay store on the corner of the next block, across the street from the hardware store. He went in there. He found their shoe department in a section by itself, and a nicely dressed woman approached him. "May I help you," she asked.

"Well, I need a good pair of shoes," he said.

She nodded, as her eyes fell on his runners. "What kind of shoes do you have in mind?"

"Something good...maybe something a little dressy."

She showed him a pair of Oxfords. He shook his head. "Maybe not something so plain."

She showed him a pair of loafers, in soft leather. "Yes something more like that."

"What size are you?"

"Eleven."

She brought out a pair of size elevens, in the same model. "You might need a lighter pair of socks to try them on," she suggested tactfully.

"I'd say so," he said. The shoes were mahogany in colour, with a webbed design on top. They had a good shape to them. She helped him choose a lighter pair of socks, and gave him a shoehorn. He pushed his right foot into the right shoe, and stood up. It was a little tight.

"Let's try a half size bigger, and a little more width," she suggested, pulling out another box. This one fit. He put on the other shoe, and tried walking around. He would take them.

"I'll take them.....and the socks, of course. How much?"

"It would be $28.95 for the shoes," she said, handing him a can of shoe polish. "You're just over $30.00 with the socks,' she went on, "the shoe polish is on us."

"Thanks," he said, accepting the shoe polish. I'd better get a couple more pairs of socks while I'm at it."

By the time he'd left the store, he'd a good dress shirt with metal snaps, a new pair of jeans as well as the shoes and three pairs of socks. He didn't put anything on, but dropped the goods on the chair in his room, and went to check on Stan. He could hear him moving around, so he knew he was up. He knocked on his door.

"Stan," he said, "Wilf here."

Stan opened the door. "Just ready to go for a bite, how 'bout you?"

"Yup, I'm all for that. Here's a hundred bucks, Stan. Fifty for the room and fifty for the extras." He handed him five twenties. Stan handed him a twenty back. "I think that's a little too much for the extras." He said.

"No, you take it. I owe you, Stan."

"Not that much, partner," he said, and stuffed the twenty in Stan's shirt pocket.

"OK then....I'll get supper."

"Fair enough."

Serena was still on. She brought them coffee and a clean ashtray. "I'll have a nice T-bone steak. And Wilf's buying," Stan said grinning.

"Seriously?" she asked.

"Yup seriously," said Wilf, "and I'll have one too, medium rare, chips, and no gravy."

"Same," said Stan.

"So, a good payday, partner, eh?" said Stan.

"Yup...this one's a full cheque. Bills are all paid, and I got me a new pair of shoes."

"You're about due for some. Going dancing?"

"Oh, I don't know about that."

"Gus will be playing Saturday night at the Hoot 'n' Holler hall. You should take a look there."

"Well, it's a ways out of town, isn't it?"

"Yeah, it's out at Eva Lake. Gus would take you."

"Maybe next payday."

Work went smoothly that night. They were told at the wicket that they'd be needing track. There was a pile of rails to one side of the layby, just past the station, and just past a pile of 2"and 4" pipe. In between the pile were a barrel of track spikes, and a supply of fishplates and bolts for the track. (Fishplates were the metal straps bolted to the end of the rails to join them together). They placed two twenty foot rails, four fishplates, and an empty grease pail full of a good number of track spikes along with nuts and bolts for the fishplates atop the motor.

The drift had advanced 300 feet in the time that Wilf had been with the crew, and they were getting too far from their switching layby. It was taking a little longer every shift to switch cars. They hadn't asked the question, and nothing had yet been said, but the problem was obvious; they were still making their cycle, but it was taking longer and longer to get mucked out. They came into the heading with their supplies. Stan brought the train to a stop just behind the mucker. Gus and Wilf laid the rails, fishplates, and grease pail to the side of the drift, and Stan pulled the train back out of the way. Then the three of them went up to check out the face.

It was a clean face with a good clean break. The crew on the cross- shift always left them good. They always broke their rounds well (or as Gus would put it, "right to the nuts"). The cross-shift had even left them set up. The three jacklegs stood at the face, the air and water hoses connected to the machines, oil in the lubricators, the drill ladders placed against the bucket of the mucker, and the face was already marked up. They had only to turn on their air and water, and they were good to go.

"Gotta love a cross-shift like that," commented Gus, placing a fresh wad of snoose under his lip.

"Yup," said Stan, and without further adieu, the three men opened the air and water to their machines, and started drilling their round. Stan's machine started sputtering as he was pulling out of his center lifter, and stalled completely before he could collar his cut. There was a spare machine handy, a little ways back of the face. Wilf and Gus continued drilling. Stan unhooked the B.O. machine, and dumped it atop the motor, then hooked up the spare, re-opened the air and water, and continued with Gus and Wilf on the round.

The rest of the drilling cycle went well. Stan, being a little behind, had just started reaming the cut when Gus and Wilf had drilled off their sides of the round, so they went ahead and tore down their jacklegs, and packed them back. The shift-boss showed up, as they were pulling back their hoses, and spoke with Gus, as Stan continued drilling.

"Getting to be a long haul to switch cars, Gus," he said.

"Yes it is," Gus answered, waiting to hear what was coming.

"You're putting in track today, right."

"Yup."

"I'm told they want to put in a transfer switch...not sure what that is, or how it works. Maybe you know".

"Ya, I've used them. They're what we call a California switch. Better than switching so far from the face. You just ramp up an empty car, and roll it sideways. Pull the train back, and then roll your empty in front of the train, and you've always got an empty ahead of the train."

The shift boss wasn't exactly sure what he meant, but he didn't let on. "Oh I see", he said...."that would solve the problem."

"Well, it works. Just takes a strong bull for a switch man," Gus came back, slapping Wilf on the back. Wilf nodded. He'd used them. It was doable, and it would be faster.

"Well, don't set up dayshift once you've mucked out. The survey crew will be in on dayshift to mark up for the cut-out on the wall some place closer to the face for the switch."

By this time Stan was done reaming his cut and flashed them his light. At his signal, Wilf shut off his air and water. The shift boss waited for Stan, and ran it all past him. Stan just nodded. "OK," he said, and started dragging his hoses back. The shift boss left.

The nipper, a young fellow in his late teens, who did their service runs, had brought their powder and fuses. Gus and Wilf took the blowpipe, blew out the lifters, and started loading the round. Stan joined them to finish loading the round, after he'd packed back his machine, steel and drill ladder, and pulled back his hoses. Once Stan had the round wired with the Thermalite he lit it up, yelling "FIRE". He watched the Thermalite burn, as it ignited the cut and helpers, until it was burning four ways from the cut, then walked quickly back to the cockpit of the motor. Gus had already cracked the air header, pushing a strong gust of air. He joined Wilf on the back end of the motor, and the three men headed for the station.

They stopped at the switch going into the other drift crew's heading, to guard their blast. When the last of the shots went off, they continued on to the station. Once they were comfortably seated on the bench at the station, Gus scooped the used snoose out of his lower lip, and took a thick sandwich out of his lunch pail.

"How 'bout coming to the 'Hoot n' Holler' Saturday night, Wilf? Maybe chase the light fantastic...?"

"I think maybe I ought to wait another payday or two."

"Well, I heard you got yourself a new pair of dancing shoes...what's your problem?"

"I got a new pair of shoes, all right, but I don't know about dancing. That's a ways out of town, isn't it?"

"Not to worry. Just me and the wife going unless Stan here wants to come. Lots of room for all of us."

Stan was negative, but Wilf hadn't exactly said no. "Tell you what," Gus continued, swallowing his last mouthful of sandwich, "You think about it. I always leave about eight o'clock. I'll come by the restaurant about eight. Just be out in front if you're coming. I don't mind saying, I play a good fiddle."

Done with lunch and well into the mucking cycle, they had run the end of their slide rail, halfway through their third train. Stan pulled the train back out of the way, and Wilf and Stan brought one of the rails up for Gus, who had already pulled the spikes from the slides, and pried them loose from the standing rails. All the ties were in place...Gus always dug them in as he mucked. He had a good eye for grade, and was always careful never to let his slides climb.

Stan and Wilf placed the old slides upright, flush to the end of the standing rails. Gus took the fishplates, and started bolting them on, while Wilf and Stan went back and brought up the remaining rail. They laid it down along with the other one they'd brought in between the old side rails, which were now to be standing rails, and began spiking down one of the rails that Gus had just bolted on. Once it was spiked to the last tie, they put the track gauge on the end of it and moved the other rail to gauge just as Gus had finished bolting it. In a few minutes they had that one spiked down. The new rails were now to become the slides. They laid them on their sides with their crown against the sides of the freshly spiked standing rails. Then pounding on their base, popped the crowns tightly into the side of standing rails and spiked them in place tight in against them.

Gus was mucking within twenty five minutes after they'd started on the track. There was no time wasted with those three. The rest of the shift went straight ahead, and they were mucked out half an hour before cage call. The other drift crew was only ten minutes behind them, and the raise crew came out about the same time. Another week well done!

It was a bright warm day when Wilf got off the bus in town. Gus said "Maybe see you tomorrow?"

"Maybe," said Wilf. He hadn't said no.

Saturday evening at 8:00 o'clock, Wilf was in front of the restaurant. Stan, not a dancer (he'd said), had decided to come anyways. He wouldn't say so, but he was a little worried about Wilf. He knew it was a drinking event. Gus pulled up right on time with his wife Molly beside him.

"You're coming too eh Stan? Good on you."

Stan and Wilf climbed in the back, and Gus introduced them to his wife, who acknowledged them both amicably. A pleasant woman, with thick, curly auburn hair, green eyes, and a round face, she was easily as big as Gus, though not so tall.

The car was a '51 Chevy hatchback, dark green in color with overtones of red iron ore dust, like everything else in Atikokan. Gus pulled away, and headed the car out of town for the highway, and Eva Lake. Late June, it was still good daylight. In half an hour they arrived at their destination, The Hoot 'n Holler Hall. It was a big empty, barn-like building, faced by a big gravel parking lot. The double doors on the front of the building were propped wide-open. There were a few people just outside the door talking over cigarettes, and just inside the door was a card table. A man and his wife were seated behind the table. On the table were an ashtray, a cashbox, and a stamp pad with a rubber stamp beside it.

Admission was two dollars, and apparently free for Gus and his wife. Gus had his fiddle in its case in his right hand. He and his wife went in, and Stan and Wilf followed them, stopping at the table to pay the two dollars. The wife of the cashier stamped them each on the back of their left hand, and wished them both an enjoyable evening.

Being early, there were not many people there yet. There were ten or eleven cars in the parking lot, and about two dozen people inside the building, seated around a few of the tables. There was a row of these tables up the right side of the hall from the entrance at one end, to the stage at the far end, with four chairs placed around each of the tables. The row up the other side of the hall began behind the cashiers table to the left of the entrance, and continued up the left side of the hall, to just before the bar, which was set up in left the corner, just below the stage. The stage area was elevated a few feet above the main area, with a few steps leading up it over to the right of the stage. There were a few chairs placed front and center of the stage, and Wilf assumed rightly that this was the area for the musicians.

The 'bar' was three rough 2"x10" twelve foot planks placed across a couple of saw horses. So far there was only one bartender on duty, a tall man in jeans and a T-shirt, and wearing an apron. On the bar in front of him were bottles of rye, rum, gin, and vodka (only one kind of each). There was no wine. There was also a galvanized pail full of crushed ice beside some racks of glasses on the bar, and a metal cash box. Just behind the bar were two large galvanized washtubs full of crushed ice, both full of beer, and a large cooler full of crushed ice and pop. Against the stage, cases of beer were piled in three rows. There was only one brand of beer, Carling's Black Label. There were twenty four long-necked glass bottles to a case.

Gus and Molly took the last table on the right, just by the steps leading up to the stage, and Wilf and Stan came and joined them. Gus had brought a large thermos, and Molly produced a couple of plastic glasses from her purse. As soon as Gus loosened the lid of the thermos, the smell of rum hit Wilf. He could feel the saliva spurt under his tongue, and although Gus was across the table, it seemed to Wilf like it was right under his nose.

"Brought us some rum," Gus commented. Wilf was transfixed.

"Let's go get us some pop, Wilf," suggested Stan, taking up the slack.

Wilf nodded blandly, rising to follow him to the bar. "I better get us some too," said Molly, getting up. "We'll need some coke."

"Relax Molly....we'll get it."

"Oh would you, Stan? You're a dear," she said, already sitting again.

Stan turned to Wilf at the bar, "You goina be all right partner? Your tongue was hanging out about a foot back there."

"I'm OK. Thought it was coffee in that thermos."

"No ....not Gus, not at dance, Wilf." He turned to the bartender, "Got any Pepsi?"

"Nope. We got Coca Cola and 7UP. That's it. What'll it be?"

Stan looked at Wilf. "I guess two 7UP and two cokes." Wilf nodded.

The bartender pulled the requested beverages out of the cooler, set them up on the bar and opened them. They came in six once bottles. "Need glasses?" Stan shook his head. "That'll be one dollar." He stared a moment at the dollar bill Stan put in front of him, looked back at Stan, then put it in the cashbox without comment. Stan and Wilf headed back to the table with the pop.

"Thanks Stan. Don't get much for a buck, do you"

"No, and I think he was waiting for a tip," he said eyeing the little bottles. "I think we'll need more of these."

"No doubt. Next rounds on me, Stan." They rejoined Molly and Gus at the table.

"Thanks, boys," said Gus, raising his glass in acknowledgement of the courtesy. His glass was already half full of rum, and he'd been sipping it straight (to save time.) Molly's glass was only a quarter full of rum, and she had waited for the mix. She took Gus' glass, and topped it off with coca cola, and poured the rest of the bottle to mix her own drink.

"I got two more glasses in my purse, if you boys want a drink. We got lots." Stan and Wilf graciously declined, watching Gus almost empty his glass in one gulp.

"They don't bother you bringing your own?" asked Wilf.

Gus just laughed, his eyes already lit up. "Hell no...let's face it....I'm the fiddler. " He tossed back the rest of his drink, and passed his glass to Molly, who promptly mixed him another, half and half.

"Besides," he continued, "They want too much at the bar, and they're too slow." He immediately took a huge gulp from his next drink, already in his hand. "Anyways," he explained, "I gotta get primed for the show." Wilf nodded understandingly, thinking 'this is a guy I could drink with.'

"He needs to get primed," Molly affirmed. She only sipped at her own drink. She was in no hurry to get drunk. Then looking toward the entrance, she smiled. "Well, here comes Rod," she said.

A tall slim man of about thirty walked in with a guitar case in his hand. "Evening Gus, Molly," he said, approaching their table.

"Hi Rod....these here are my partners in the drift. Stan Rooster and Wilf Baker. Stan and Wilf....Rod Hicks. Rod's driving raise on the other shift."

They shook hands all around. Rod took his guitar out of its case, a Fender electric. There was an amplifier on stage and he plugged his guitar cable into it. "Be having one to get started?" Gus asked, raising his glass.

"That'd be good," said Rod. He then took the offered glass and drank it down but not so quickly. Gus took his fiddle out of the case, checked the tuning (which he knew was on), and then joined Rod on the stage. It was a little past nine now. More people had come in and the tables were filling up. Rod struck a chord on his guitar, adjusted a couple of strings, and then nodded to Gus, who stood beside him, his fiddle in the crook of his neck. At Rod's nod, Gus swept the strings with his bow.

The effect was electrifying. The sound of his fiddle cut the air like a rifle. Gus needed no amp. He broke into 'Silver Bells', and Rod corded in perfect time. Molly was playing the spoons she'd extracted from her purse, beating out the time against her thigh and Wilf could not remember feeling so happy in recent years, He was smiling happy, and close to tears.

Gus was going strong now. He went right from 'Silver Bells' to 'Maple Sugar', and onto 'Rubber Dolly'. Rod's accompaniment was excellent. The sweat ran down Gus' face, lit up in joyful countenance, his eyes like two lanterns, and his right foot beating out the time. A few couples got up and started dancing right from the start, and now more joined in. It was dark outside by this time, and the crowd from the parking lot was coming in.

Wilf could hardly stand to sit in his chair. He began to see the odd one step-dancing alone, and couldn't resist the music any more. He got up and started step-dancing ....alone. In no time he forgot himself, and was just going for it. The old feelings came back, the magic returned, and he was just going flat out. His feet found the old step like it was yesterday in the Corning General Store, dancing face to face with his brother Pat. There were several people playing the spoons now, and almost everyone else was up dancing, as Rod and Gus got into 'The Devil's Dream', into 'The Mockingbird', and on and on. Wilf kept dancing, lost in the magic of good music, and good friends.

A woman joined him on the floor, and she was good. She was a good looking brunette, well built, who might have been thirty, and obviously in good shape. She looked right at Wilf, and never stopped smiling. Finally Gus and Rod stopped for a break. Wilf stood for a moment with her then shook her hand. "I'm Wilf," he said.

"Lucy," she came back, shaking his hand.

"You sure got that step dancing figured out, Lucy."

"Thanks. You're not so bad yourself." she came back.

"Used to do it back home."

"Back home?" she asked

"Ottawa Valley." he replied.

"Cowshit Valley eh?"

"Yup."

"I'm from Pembroke." She said

"I'm from the Pontiac County on the Quebec side, a tiny little place called Corning, near Bryson. Where are you sitting? I'm with the fiddler and his wife. Would you care to join us?" he asked.

"I'm with some friends here, but yes, I could join you for a bit" she said

Wilf brought over to the table, and introduced her around, then gave her his chair, and got himself another from the pile at the back of the stage. She was greeted cordially by everyone at the table.

"I'm pleased to meet you Lucy. I can see good music's not wasted on you," said Gus, extending his sweaty hand.

She shook his offered hand graciously. "No, can't be wasting good music," she came back.

"Care for a little rum, maybe?" He asked, raising his thermos.

"I'd love some." She turned to Wilf. "You're not having any?"

He blushed, "No. Better I don't."

"Well, looks like you dance just fine without it."

Molly held the glass, while Gus poured a good two inches into it, and then asked Lucy if she'd like some coke with it. She did, and Molly added the coke.

"Boy, I came to the right table," she said, taking a good sip.

After the break, Rod and Gus got going again with the music. This time they started slowly, with the Tennessee Waltz. Molly got up and sang the number. She had a good clear voice, right on key. Wilf got up with Lucy for the waltz and stayed for a couple more. When they returned to the table, they found Stan was gone. Molly was still up on the stage with Gus and Rod, so Wilf decided to go and take a look for Stan. Lucy followed him out. They found him just outside the entrance, leaning against the side of the building, having a smoke.

"How're you doing Stan?" he asked.

"Oh, just getting some air."

"Good music, eh?'

"Yeah, they're good."

It was a little cooler now, which Wilf found refreshing. There was a small group behind some of the cars in the parking lot, passing a bottle around, and conversing loudly, the only distraction to an otherwise good evening of fun. Their conversation got louder, then some cursing, and suddenly two of the group started swinging at each other. A few of the others in the group lamely tried to pacify them, but to no avail. The two adversaries were shouting at each other now, both taking some solid punches, and neither of them seemed to be ducking much.

"Brown and Hancock," commented Stan. "Those two aren't happy unless they got a scrap going"

"All in a night's fun, I guess," said Wilf. They went back inside. The band played on. Lucy thanked Wilf, and went back to join her friends at another table. Molly was done singing for the moment, and Stan and Wilf sat down with her at the table. It was past midnight now, and one o'clock was roughly considered closing time. A hat was passed around for a collection for the band; the money from the booze and admission went toward the cost of the hall and management expenses. Stan and Wilf each put in five dollars. There was mostly ones, twos, and small change, with the odd other five thrown in. Eighty eight dollars and some change were collected, which Gus and Rod would split later. They did one more step dance, which joined by only a dozen or so dancing, and the finally a waltz for closing.

Gus got Stan to drive back home, no doubt a good idea. The big thermos empty now, and Gus and Molly were feeling fine. A good time was had by all. Stan dropped Wilf off by the rooming house then drove the car to Gus and Molly's. Parking the car in their driveway, he gave Gus back his keys. Gus thanked him, and Molly gave him a hug with her thank you. Stan walked the half hour walk back to the rooming house. It was nice and fresh in the small hours of that Sunday morning, and the walk felt good. Gus and Molly unlocked their front door, went into their bedroom, got undressed and crawled into their bed, Gus in his under shorts, and Molly in her flannelette nightie.

Molly cuddled close to Gus. They talked awhile going over the joy of their evening. As they talked, Molly pulled her left breast free taking it through the broad neck of her nightie, pulling Gus' hand onto it in a deft but casual motion. Gus stroked it gently and lovingly and as they continued to talk, more fondly and more urgently.

"I think you're in the mood sweetheart,' he said finally. Leaning over her now, he reached for that hairy mound under her nightie. She laid back and giggled as his fingers found their way. He could feel her juice in abundance, and she gasped with pleasure as his mid finger found its way into her opening, warm and slippery, and wet. She threw her arms around his neck pulling him to her warm sensuous mouth, and they kissed a long passionate kiss, their tongues entwined in a familiar duet. At length, Gus gently withdrew from Molly's embrace, and fully erect now entered her. He took his weight on his elbows, wrapping his hands around her shoulders, his face buried in her thick auburn hair as they fucked, both groaning with pleasure.

And then they came, and as from good practice, Molly a little before Gus. Gus laid over her for a few moments, gasping for air, and then rolled over beside her, both speechless for a moment as they struggled to catch their breath. Finally recovered now, Gus reached over to her, lovingly stroking her sweaty, matted hair back from her forehead.

"Good as ever sweetheart. You're the best," he said. She cuddled close to Gus, and managed to say, "I love you, Gus," upon which, and so entwined, they both fell into a sound and dreamless sleep. It had been a great evening all around.

Wilf loved good fiddle music. He was in bed now, reading a few pages of Louis L'Amour's 'Shelako' when he heard Stan come in. Stan went straight to his room. It was a little before 2:00 am. Wilf went on reading his book. He didn't read too many pages when he felt his eyes getting heavy. He turned off the light, rolled over, and fell asleep. He began to dream, and the dream became so vivid and real, he thought he was there on the porch of the old General Store in Corning. Everything was as clear as day. Bill Crofton sat on the veranda bench playing his fiddle, and Ben Aubrey sat beside him playing his flat top guitar in perfect time to 'Maple Sugar'.

His brother Pat came by, and started doing his jig....and he could step dance like nobody Wilf knew. He hadn't seen Pat since he'd gone off to the war. It was so good to see him. He gestured to Wilf to join him, and he did. Wilf was up now facing him, and dancing the step dance, and over to the right he could see his little sister Denise, smiling and playing the spoons. It was a warm sunny day, and such a perfect moment.

Then his brother Clarence appeared, with his usual sour looking presence, and everyone vanished, the magic of the moment gone. There was just Clarence, and Wilf woke up. It wasn't quite four o'clock, still dark, but Wilf was wide awake now, and he knew he wasn't going to get back to sleep. He sat on the edge off the bed in his shorts. There was a little light coming in from the street around the edges of the blind. He lit a cigarette and said out loud, "That fucking asshole can sure fuck up a good dream."

Wilf was the second oldest of the four children in the Baker family. Patrick, the oldest was his hero. Patrick was two years his senior, and took him everywhere with him. There was lots of work to be done on the farm, but they always made time for some fun. Patrick had made himself a boat, and Wilf had helped him. He was game to do anything with Pat. Patrick got himself a pair of oars and off they'd go fishing. Patrick knew where to go, and how to catch them. His favourite was Pickerel. The Americans would call them Walleye, but to Stan and Wilf they were always Pickerel, and Pickerel were the best.

There were always a lot of Jack fish, sometimes called Northern Pike. They were the easiest to catch; they were so aggressive. They would hit on almost any kind of hook, with or without bait. They were often quite big, sometimes ten or twelve pounds, and occasionally, but not often, even bigger. Pat would always keep the Jackfish. They were boney, still eatable, but not nearly as good as the Pickerel. Some of the larger ones Pat would smoke. The rest he would feed to the mink, which he kept in some raised pens behind the barn.

Pickerel were not so eager to take the hook. They had to be coaxed. Patrick kept a minnow trap in the little creek coming into the lake, and would always pull up a couple dozen chub minnows to bring along. Live bait was the way to go to catch Pickerel. They would thread a live minnow onto a plain straight hook, weight it down with a lead sinker, and let it sink to the lake bottom. Once on bottom, they would raise it up a foot or two, and work it slowly up and down. Patrick knew the best spots to fish, and they never came home skunked. Pat had also taught Wilf how to box. Pat was no slouch at that, and found no problems in passing on his skill to Wilf. Wilf was a natural. He had a good reach, and he was quick.

Pat had joined the army in January of 1944. He had just turned eighteen. His father reluctantly gave his blessing, as Pat was determined to go. Pat was bilingual and chose to join the Royal 22e Regiment, (les Vingt Deux), or as the English called them the Ving Doos. He did his basic training in Valcartier, Quebec. Two month later he was shipped over to England aboard the Queen Mary, and was killed during the battle for the Carpiquet airfield in Caen, France, one month after D Day.

It was a terrible blow to the Baker family. Tim Baker, his wife Therese, and little Denise were devastated. Wilf at sixteen had lost his brother, his hero, and best friend. Clarence did not seem affected in the least. When Clarence got the news, it was like someone had given him information. He was strangely unaffected. Clarence was a year and a half younger than Wilf, but in no way close. Wilf disliked him innately, and mostly ignored him. That didn't seem to bother Clarence either.

Clarence was a strange one. He didn't have any friends, and didn't seem to want any. When he wasn't at school, he would follow his father around. Tim seemed to like that. Clarence would do whatever he could for his father. He'd be first up to milk the cows, there to slop the pigs, cut fire wood with his dad. Wilf couldn't stand to work with him, and would always do the wood cutting with his brother Pat. Tim was not a talker. He never had much to say, and Clarence didn't mind; but when Tim did speak to him, Clarence gave him full attention.

His little sister Denise was the last of the children. She was four years younger than Wilf, and she adored Wilf and Patrick. She was a pretty girl, dark hair like her mother, with big brown eyes, always smiling. Pat had given her a flat top guitar for her tenth birthday, and she would practice whenever she could. She would come to the General Store whenever her dad or Pat would bring her along hoping old Ben Aubrey might show up with his guitar, and show her a cord or two. She was coming along with it. She had a good sense of rhythm, a great voice, and loved to sing.

She was definitely her mother's daughter. She preferred speaking French, and though she spoke English well enough, she spoke it with an unmistakable French accent, and had all the mannerisms of her mother. She would be totally animated when spoke, saying as much with her hands, her eyes, and her face as her words.

She loved her brother Patrick. She was so proud of him in his uniform. He looked so handsome in it. She hugged and kissed him the day he got on the train and went off to the war. She was never to see him again. She was crushed when she got the news he wasn't coming home. To Clarence, it was just another day at the office, and Wilf hated him for his indifference.

He put out his cigarette and got dressed. It was raining now, but not heavily. He didn't wear his new clothes, but got into his faded khakis, his canvas runners, and headed for the Beanery. Jean Guy was there, his wife Marie in the kitchen, and five or six night owls, perched on the stools. Wilf took a stool, and Jean Guy approached him with a glint of recognition.

"Oui monsieur, qu'est qu'on peut faire pour vous aider? Un café peut-etre? Et quoi d'autre?" (Yes sir, how can I help you? A coffee, perhaps, and what else?)

"Un café, s'il vous plait, Jean Guy." (A coffee, please, Jean Guy).

"Ah, tu me souviens, eh?" (Ah, you remember me, eh?)

"On n'oublie jamais un bon ami." (We should never forget a good friend.)

Jean Guy offered his hand, and Wilf shook it, then said in English, "Thanks for helping me out, Jean Guy. I'm doing fine now." He pushed a five dollar bill at him.

Jean Guy raised his hand in protest. "We good Wilf. You good now...I'm happy. You come to my place. We're good," he said, pouring him a coffee.

"Well thanks again, Jean Guy. I'll have a cheeseburger deluxe....no gravy. I guess you can tell I'm losing my French."

"Non, tu parle bien, Wilf, mais ce te fait du bien a practiquer, mon ami. Parle Francais quand que c'est possible. Il se reviendra." (No, you speak well, Wilf, but it does you good to practice whenever it's possible. It will come back.)

Marie was soon at the wicket with his order. She gave Wilf a smile and a nod through the wicket, and Wilf smiled and waved back. Jean Guy gave him a refill of coffee, as he placed his order in front of him. Wilf gave him a nod of thanks, bathed his chips in vinegar, and dug in. The bill was eighty five cents as usual. Wilf left a two dollar bill by his plate, and headed for the door. Jean Guy picked up the bill and called out in French, *"Minute, Wilf. C'est trop." (Just a minute, Wilf. That's too much.)*

Wilf stopped by the door. "We're good Jean Guy. Got work, got a place, got a paycheque....life is good."

"Dat's for sure, and t'anks Wilf," he said raising the deuce, and smiling.

Wilf left the beanery and started for home. It was raining harder now, but Wilf didn't mind. He was feeling refreshed, and didn't have all that far to go. He checked his watch when he got in. It was a little past 5:00 am and still dark. He got undressed and into bed; lighting one last cigarette, he reflected on the day. He felt good about catching up with Jean Guy, and thanking him. The food had settled his nerves. He put out the cigarette; only half smoked, turned out the light, and went to sleep, a sound dreamless sleep. It was just breaking day.

A Miner's Story – Chapter 7

A few paydays went by. Work was a good routine beside Stan and Gus in the drift. Gus was always grinning, always sweating. Stan was like a truck. Nothing stopped him. He was all business once that hard hat was on. They were a good team, and Wilf was happy to be there. He hadn't felt so good since he was a teenager on the farm. He'd had some good paycheques now, and had started a bank account.

He'd gotten into running lately, and it felt good. He used to run with his brother Patrick, back in the day when Patrick was teaching him how to box. There was always work to be done on the farm, but Pat would make time for running. They would run for miles together, and it seemed like nothing. Wilf was getting that good feeling back. He'd found a stretch of road that wasn't too busy, and would do his run at least three or four times a week. The road ran past the cemetery and on to a place on the river called Little Falls.

Little Falls was so named because the Atikokan River took a sudden drop of a good twenty feet there. It was a beautiful spot where the river came over the falls and formed a large lake-like pool at the bottom of it. At the end of the road, right by the side of the pool, was a pump house that supplied the town with drinking water. The attendant, a friendly guy, would always give Wilf a wave, if he happened to be outside. Wilf was doing the return trip to town in forty minutes in the beginning, but now had it down to half an hour; he was finding it was easy, and knew he could run almost any distance

He began to think he should quit smoking. After a few weeks of thinking about it, he did quit. When the day came, it came about without any struggle at all. It wasn't as hard as he'd thought, once he did it. The craving only last a few weeks, and then he didn't even think about it. In past years he'd tried to quit smoking, and every time he'd light up again, usually over a drink. The longer he was sober now, the better he felt.

He'd put on a good thirty pounds since he'd come to town, and it was good solid weight. He was at one hundred and ninety five pounds now, and couldn't remember having felt any better. He knew it all came down to the fact he wasn't drinking. Someone had once told him, that when you get run over by a train, it's not the caboose that kills you. All he had to do was just not take that first drink. He had steeled his mind to that.

He had gotten to know the other driftcrew on the level; Joe Kilgannon, Dave Chambers and Ivan Gagnon, a Frenchman from Timmins. He would shoot the shit with them, waiting for the cage in the station at shift's end, or would run across them downtown. Joe and Dave hung out together. Neither one of them were boozers. Dave didn't drink at all, and Joe would have a beer, but Wilf had never seen him drunk. One day at the end of the last afternoon shift, Dave asked Wilf if he'd like to go fishing with him. Wilf said he wouldn't mind at all, but said he would have to get himself a rod. Dave said that wouldn't be any problem. He had a boat and all the gear; they could all head out in the morning.

"We could pick you up at the restaurant in the morning," he said.

"What time, Dave?"

"Say seven, if you could manage that."

"I'll be there."

"And how 'bout you, Stan," Dave went on, "you into a little fishing?"

"Could do. See what happens tomorrow. If I'm coming, I'll be there."

The next morning Wilf was at the restaurant for breakfast at six, and Stan joined him shortly after.

"Guess I'll come too," he announced.

"That's good, Stan. Need a license?"

"No. Not this Indian."

"Hmmm, I think I'm part Indian too, you know."

"But I got papers," he came back, grinning, giving Wilf a playful punch on the shoulder.

Wilf thought his shoulder was broke. "Sure glad were friends, Stan," he said holding his shoulder.

Stan smiled, enjoying his little moment of fun. They had their breakfast, picked up lunches to go, and stood in front of the restaurant to wait for Joe and Dave. It was a beautiful day near the end of July, and it was already warm. The sky was a cloudless blue and the sun felt good. They weren't long waiting for their ride. Wilf asked where they might be going.

"Called 'the floodwaters'," said Dave. "It's actually Marmion Lake, but they call it 'the flood waters'. They had to dam off Steep Rock Lake to get at the ore body on the lake bottom, so they did a water diversion, and Marmion lake was flooded. You'll see a lot of dead trees sticking out of the water. They didn't bother to clear the land before they flooded the lake. It is great Pickerel fishing. You'll see it when we get there. Good day for fishing."

And it was. It was a beautiful warm day. There was a slight breeze, which would help keep the flies away. Joe was driving. He had a '54 Ford Fairlane he'd bought new. They drove through the mine property. The security at the gatehouse saw their sticker, and waved them through. A few miles past the mine and some other buildings which were the mine office buildings the road continued on in a narrower path. Finally Joe stopped on the side of the road where a creek ran under the road, through a culvert. There was a sign by the creek which said 'Hansen's landing'. Dave got out of the car, filled a bucket with water from the creek, and then pulled up on a rope tied to an Alder sapling, pulling a minnow trap out of the creek, filled with dozens of minnows. He emptied the minnows into the pail, put the lid down, and put it into the trunk of the car.

"That's our bait," he explained.

"Figured so," said Stan.

Shortly they came to a fork in the road, took the turn to the right, and in a few miles they came to a Lake. Joe parked his car over to the right side of the road, just before the lake. There were several boats pulled up on the shore. Dave's turned out to be a 'Peterborough Skip'. A cedar strip model, nicely varnished, it was a sixteen footer with a comfortable width. They grabbed their gear out of the trunk, the four rods, their minnows, two tackle boxes, a gas tank and extra gas, and the food. Joe and Dave pushed the boat afloat, and Dave said, "Hop in boys". He got in himself, giving the boat one final shove, as he hopped in. Joe took a paddle, and pushed them out a little farther, while Dave made his way to the stern, and tipped the motor down for action.

The motor was a twenty five horse Johnson. He snapped the fuel line on to it and pumped on the priming bubble, then pulled the cord. Nothing happened. He pulled out the choke and advanced the speed setting on the handle, and tried it again. Two more pulls and it fired. He pushed the choke back in, put the motor into reverse, and gave it a little throttle. When the boat was well clear of the shore, he put it in forward, turned it toward the open lake, and opened it up.

The boat moved well in the water. It was a great feeling for Wilf, the warmth of the sun, the wind of their movement, the smell of gas, and a good day to be out with good friends. He sometimes had a hard time to realize all this was really happening, and when he'd get his mind around it, he'd be more determined than ever to keep it happening. Just don't drink….

They travelled at full speed for a good half hour. Along the way they passed a shaft sinking headframe on the south side of the lake, set up on a rock hump jutting out a ways into the lake. Farther back from the shore were some tents set up for accommodation. A couple of miners stood near the head fame, watching them go by, with envious looks, no doubt thinking they'd rather be fishing than living and working on a bald rock so far from town. One waved as Dave sped by. They both looked more dismal than friendly. Dave waved back, but stayed his course.

Finally Dave cut the throttle to a slow pitch, nosing the boat to his left, towards a grove of dead trees sticking out of the lake. He cut the engine completely at last, letting the boat drift toward one of the dead snags which stood by itself a good twenty feet from the other dead heads, and tied up to its trunk. With the noise of the motor gone now, he explained to Stan and Wilf, "That head frame you saw back there….that's the Plater Grey Louise Mine".

"Doesn't look like much of a mine."

"Well that's just a sinking headframe. It' just a small two and a half compartment shaft they're sinking, and I think they're only down a few hundred feet so far. It's just for exploration right now. Might be just promotion…might never get going"

"What a fucking way to live. I'm glad they're doing it. Long ways from town. Hope they're well paid."

"Not likely. Looks like a hard luck proposition to me. I'd say those boys are down on their luck; they need that paycheque real bad or they wouldn't be there. Anyways, let's get fishing. I've had good luck around this stump patch," he went on, "let's see what we can do here." He handed Stan and Wilf each a rod. The reels were the open-faced type casting reels with level winders. Joe took a rod and sat up on the bow, Dave was in the stern so Wilf and Stan would fish, one from either side of the boat. There were already leaders on the end of the lines, with a lead sinker affixed just above the leader.

"What we do here is called 'still fishing', and this is how Joe and I've been doing it", Dave explained to Stan and Wilf, handing them each a plain straight hook. Joe already knew the drill as he and Dave were frequent fishing buddies. He was baiting his hook as he spoke, threading the point of the hook through the minnow's mouth, out the gill, and then sticking it through the side of the minnow, about half way down its body. Stan and Wilf followed suit. Joe was already fishing.

"You just drop your line over the side, till your weight hits bottom, and then pull your on line up a bit till your hook is about one to one and a half feet off bottom. Then just raise it up and down a little, but very gently." Stan and Wilf nodded politely; they'd done this often before. By the time Dave finished explaining things Joe already had one on his line.

"Looks like we might be doing OK here", he commented, scooping up a nice Pickerel with the net. It was a classic Pickerel. It had the coarse scales, dark on its back and sides, and as well as some smaller fins, it had the prominent spiked dorsal fin down the center of its back. Its head, nicely shaped, came smoothly curved off its body, and it had glassy, bulging eyes, which is likely why the Americans called them 'Walleye'. The fish had to be good three pounds. He pulled the hook from its mouth, hooked it onto the stringer which was tied to the gunwale, and let it hang in the water. The fish was able to swim again, but it was on a short leash. They were off to a good start.

Wilf got the next one. He felt his line jerk a little, at first, and then when he felt it again, he jerked back, setting the hook. He knew he had him. The fish struck hard, diving, pulling away with a powerful lunge and fighting for all its worth against the hold of the line. It wasn't Wilf's first time fishing. He knew how to play a fish. When his rod bent sharply, he let it run, letting out line, but holding a good tension. When the fish slowed down, Wilf locked his thumb on the reel, holding the line taut, and pulling back hard, then relaxing again, but quickly reeling in what he gained.

At last he had the fish near the boat, and he could see it plainly now as it turned, flashing its white belly, that it was a Pickerel, and it had to be a good five pounds. It was a beauty. He had it next to the boat, and Stan was just getting ready with net, when the fish made a power dive, making one more strong effort. Wilf played it again; hoping to God the line wouldn't break. That would usually happen right near the boat. Just to be on the safe side, he kept playing the fish, and let it fight, until he knew it was played right out, and then reeled him in. This time the fish was done, and Stan was able to net it easily.

Once in the boat, the fish suddenly flopped around in strong protest, tangling the net with the hook in its gaping mouth. Stan squeezed its two eyes together firmly with his thumb and forefinger, paralyzing the fish. It became quite still as he did that, with only a slight curve in its tail. He was able to unravel the net now and remove the hook. He didn't trust the loop on the stringer to hold the big fish, so he threaded a length of stout cord through the fish's mouth and out the gill, and let it over the side, into the lake, tying off the cord to the gunwale of the boat.

It was about nine in the morning when Joe got a second fish, a little smaller than his first; nevertheless, a nice fish. By eleven am, they had caught six more, all Pickerel, for a total of nine fish of varying sizes, Wilf's being the biggest. Eight of them were hooked onto the stringer, swimming in captivity beside Wilf's five pounder roped with a stout cord to the gunwales by itself. By eleven, the fish quit biting.

"Pretty quiet here", commented Stan finally biting into his lunch.

"Ya, it seems to go like that", said Dave. "They'll do a morning feed, and then maybe nothing till late afternoon. You boys wanta call it a day? "

"No, I'm for staying. It's nice day to be out here", Stan came back. Joe and Wilf agreed. They were all into their lunch, not talking so much as eating. They all had their shirts off now, taking advantage of the warm sunshine. The black flies were few now; most of them were gone by the end of June. The sand flies could bite, and for such a tiny insect they left a vexing, itchy lump, but they didn't come out in numbers until early evening. It was a good time to get some sun.

Lunches eaten now and with their minds off fishing for the moment, the four of them got into a little small talk. "How's your love life going, Wilf? Getting any?"

"Wouldn't tell you if I was, Joe. No...nothing to tell you anyway.....and how are you doing?"

"I do OK....it's you I'm worried about. You ought a try that Serena over at Sinclair's. She's always got a smile for you I've noticed."

"She's just being friendly, I'd say. I don't let that go to my head. Why don't you try her?"

"I did my best, but got the cold shoulder."

"I'm sure I'd get the same if I pushed things."

"You never know, Wilf,"Joe said, jiggling his line slowly. "Never hurts to be friendly. You never know what's in a girl's mind....."

Wilf let the conversation fade, and worked his own line gently. He was not one to discuss his love life if he had one, not that he wouldn't mind a girl friend like Serena, and he sure did enjoy her smiles. She was a lovely girl, and plainly quite reticent. She had class, in his estimation. The fact was though, she was much younger than Wilf, he had no car, and home for him was his room at Cross's rooming house. He didn't feel in any way ready for courtship.

His first love had been a girl who lived on a neighboring farm. He was fifteen at the time. It was the summer before Patrick had joined the army, and family life was like it had always been. One sunny spring day Patrick and Wilf came to the General Store, in need of a few things, to find Bill Crofton playing his fiddle on the store's veranda, and Ben Aubrey cording along on his flat top guitar. A French couple sat there playing the spoons, and Colleen Arnold, from a neighboring farm stood back, taking in the show. Wilf knew her from school. She was a good looking, full figured brunette, of medium height, about Wilf's age, and not hard to look at all. She waved to Patrick and Wilf as they came up the few steps to the veranda. Patrick waved back and pulled her in front of Wilf, saying, "He can do this, Colleen," and then went into the store. Wilf blushed deeply, feeling awkward in his overalls and ankle boots, but she took him by the shoulders, smiled at him, and started step dancing. He stood opposite her for a moment, not moving at all, but shortly began a few clumsy steps, then quickly relaxed, and got into it, doing it right.

She was energetic, and good at it, and never took her eyes off him. Wilf completely forgot his shyness and smiled back. Bill and Ben played on, and then finally took a break. Colleen thanked Wilf. "You dance pretty good Wilf."

"You too, Colleen," Wilf managed.

"And what else can you do?" Colleen asked.

"Farming, mostly."

She burst out laughing, and hugged him hard. He was blushing all over again. "I mean for fun," she said, pulling back and eyeing him. "You and I should have some fun; you know I don't live too far". (The Arnold property was two farms down Baker's farm.) "I think Dad's calling me," she said finally, and gave him a wink as she left. Patrick was just coming out of the store about then.

"Looks like you've made a friend," he commented. Wilf nodded a little dazed. Patrick sensed his unease. "Don't worry about it, Wilf. If a woman likes you, she'll take you any way you come….work boots and all. Trust me…you haven't seen the last of her, and let me tell you; a guy could do worse." Pat had never been shy. He was a handsome buck, with an easy friendliness, and got lucky without having to try too hard. He'd come to the store for some 4" nails and a roll of haywire. Business taken care of, he and Wilf climbed into Tim Baker's old pickup, and headed for home.

Tom Arnold's farm was a couple of properties down the road from the Baker farm, and Pat and Wilf would walk past it on their way to their fishing hole, which wasn't much farther; just a nice walk for the two brothers. One day, soon after Wilf's step dancing experience with Colleen, Wilf and Pat were on their way there to do some fishing, when Colleen appeared by her fence, just as they were coming down the road. It was a lovely warm spring day; the daisies were up, and the birds were singing, building their nests. She waved and called them over as they came by.

"Got a minute, guys?" she asked. There's something in the barn I'd like you to see."

Pat could see the game. He'd spent some time with her sister Doreen. "Wilf, you go have a look with Colleen....I'll go on ahead and get us our good spot before somebody else takes it."

Wilf hesitated, looking a little confused, but Pat said, "You can catch up later. You know where to find me".

He gave Pat his rod and followed Colleen to the barn, almost in a trance. She was not hard to look at. Wilf couldn't take his eyes off her well rounded behind, as he followed her up to the barn. Once inside the barn, she turned to him as she stood by the ladder up to the loft. "It's up here, Wilf." She said, starting up the ladder. He was beginning to get the idea. He climbed up the ladder behind her, but once he was up on the loft, all he could see was a pile of hay with a canvass tarp laid over it. She grinned at his innocence. As his eyes met hers, she put her arms around his neck, and kissed him on the mouth. His eyes were like golf balls at first, staring at her as she kissed him.

"Just relax," she said, pulling back for a second and then kissed him again, this time sticking her tongue into his gaping mouth. Suddenly his shyness was forgotten, and he responded passionately, rolling his tongue around hers inside her mouth, like a thirsty dog, hugging and squeezing her in a surge of horniness, and coming stiffly erect. Finally she broke for air. "Now that's better", she said.

She stripped her dress, a simple cotton shift and threw herself backside first upon the tarp lying over the pile of hay. She wore no bra, no panties; she laid there naked, silently beckoning with her hands for him to join her. He gazed at her nakedness transfixed for the moment. Her breasts were firm and plentiful, with large nipples fully erect; her legs were spread invitingly, and came together at her nicely clefted mound clothed in a lush thatch of black pubic hair.

"Well?" she asked.

By now he could feel the ants crawling through his veins, and tore his boots and clothes off in a matter of seconds. "I think this is going to work," she said, laughing as she eyed his throbbing erection. Naked now, he dove upon her, kissing her passionately. She pulled his hand onto her breast, and he squeezed it enthusiastically as they kissed. She then pushed his head down, bringing his mouth to her nipple, which he sucked on instinctively, raking it gently with his teeth.

"Ya, ya" she gasped, "like that...just like that...." As he did so, she moved his hand down to her pubic cleft. As he continued with her breast, his hand on her mound seemed to have a mind of its own, stroking and massaging it with unconscious dexterity, his mid finger finding its way into her wet slippery vagina.

"Now," she gasped, "Now Wilf....stick it in...stick it to me...."

It was Wilf's first time, but he seemed to understand the request. He positioned himself accordingly between her waiting thighs, and as he raised himself from his knees, she took his thick, quivering organ into her eager hands, and guided it in. Once thus started in, he pushed it carefully, yet easily in right to the hilt, and then they fucked in wild embrace. They fucked hard, faster and faster, screaming in ecstasy, lost in lust. All too quickly, Wilf felt himself on the verge of coming. He tried for all he was worth to hold it back, holding his breath, fucking harder and faster, experiencing euphoric sensation like he'd never known, as he plunged into her vagina, so warm, and wet, trying vainly to disappear into that slippery vortex. But come he did. He could hear her screams of ecstasy as he pumped vigorously, gasping, gushing and spurting, their sweated bellies making loud sucking noises as he climaxed and caved onto her, panting like a horse at the finish line.

When he'd recovered his breath, he raised himself slowly taking his weight off her and rolling over gently to her side. Colleen lay back smiling with her head against his shoulder. It was Wilf's first time. He looked at her in amazement. She eyed him, grinning broadly, and finally said, "You fuck like you dance...you do it right", she said, and finally, "maybe you better catch up with your brother, Wilf. We can do this again sometime."

"Sure thing Colleen." And they did just that.... and quite often.

Dave's line jerked. "I think they're back," he said. They continued to fish for another couple of hours, pulling in seven more nice Pickerel. These they'd hung on a second stringer, as the first one was near full. It was getting on to early evening, and the sand flies were starting to show, when Dave said, "What do you think, boys? Time to call it a day?" Everyone was agreed. They pulled their fish into the boat, and untied the boat from the deadhead. They were already into their shirts when Dave started the motor and headed for home. It had been a good day's fishing.

They filleted the fish on an outdoor table near the landing, fashioned from a couple of 2"x10" planks about ten feet long, and nailed down onto two saw horses. The four of them filleted the fish in short order, and also removed the cheeks which they placed in a small plastic bag separate from the fillets which they laid on some ice in Dave's cooler. The fish heads, skins and guts were dumped into a burning barrel close to the table along with some split wood. They then poured some gas over the contents and set it ablaze. Wilf put his big fish fillets and another half dozen fillets into a separate plastic bag which he placed on top of the others in the cooler. "I think these will do for me and Stan," he said. Stan nodded in agreement. "You boys keep the rest. Been a great day."

Back in town, Dave dropped Stan and Wilf off at the restaurant. Wilf grabbed his bag of fish, and he and Stan went in. Bill Harrison was at the till asking "What's in the bag, Wilf?"

"Some dead fish," Wilf replied. "How's the chance of cooking us up a couple of fresh Pickerel fillets?"

"I guess we could, Wilf."

"That'd be great Bill. There are two real big ones here," he said, holding the bag open for Bill to see. "If you don't mind cooking them up for me and Stan, you can keep the rest."

"That's a deal."

The waitress on duty was the big blonde girl, Barbara. She brought them some coffee, and Stan had a cigarette while waiting for their fish.

Finally Wilf asked Stan "So no Serena, today?"

"You forgot we had her this morning?"

"Yeah...so we did..."

Stan continued on saying "Maybe Joe's got it right. Maybe you should give her a try."

"That'd be wishful thinking."

"Ya, maybe better to go for the sure thing....maybe big Mabel."

Stan saw Wilf go white faced. He glared at Stan for a moment...then relaxed again and said. "Well maybe not."

They both smiled a little, but Stan knew better than to pursue this. About this time Barbara showed up with their fish, which covered the best half of their wide oval plates; the rest of the plate was heaped with a generous pile of French fries, and each plate was accompanied with a small bowl of coleslaw. Barbara also gave them some lemon wedges for the fish, and white vinegar for their chips.

"Thank you Barbara," Stan said, "You've saved my life!"

Wilf nodded affirmation, and they fell upon their food, eating in silence, like two hungry men.

It was dusk when they'd finished with eating and left the restaurant. They went to their separate rooms. Wilf lay back in his bed and had just started into a fresh Louis L'Amour duster. He did not want to be reminded of 'Big Mabel', even in fun. The fact of the matter, his love life in recent years came nowhere near to the intimacy he'd know with Colleen Arnold. That had continued for well over a year, even for a few months after hearing the news of Patrick's demise. They enjoyed their love affair immensely, and Colleen began providing Wilf with condoms, something that Wilf hadn't thought of; so on it went with no danger of pregnancy. They would find a hiding place, and have their fun, whenever chance permitted. One day, however, things changed.

Wilf would come by to see Colleen at her place whenever it worked, but if he didn't come by soon enough to her liking, she would drop by the Baker farm, as though to visit Denise. Denise was on to her, but kept her own consul, partly because she liked Colleen, but mostly because whatever they were doing together seemed to make Wilf very happy.

There was a copse of trees on the back end of the Baker farm and a small stream wandered through it. Closer to the creek on Baker's side was a thicket of diamond willow, with a little grassy patch behind it. If Colleen came by Denise would distract her mother, and Wilf and Colleen would quietly sneak away to that little hidden patch of grass. If Therese Baker ever suspected anything, she never let on, and she never was a problem.

The problem came one day, when Clarence came around the corner of the barn and saw Wilf and Colleen headed toward the creek. He got closer, very quietly to find them already naked, and well into their foreplay. Without giving himself away, he went back to get his father, Tim, who was sharpening his axe on his grindstone, a homemade apparatus made from a sandstone wheel mounted on a wooden frame. The wheel turned through a wooden trough filled with water. A crank was part of the axel and spun the grindstone by Tim working a foot pedal attached to the crank by a length of stout cord.

With his mind completely on his task, Tim didn't notice Clarence at first. Suddenly Clarence was in front of him, wide-eyed. Tim put the axe aside; having felt the blade, he was satisfied it was sharp enough.

"Well, what is it, son?" he asked.

"I think you better come with me, Pa."

Clarence led his father down toward the creek. Before they could see Wilf and Colleen, they could hear them already in rut, gasping and groaning in their ecstasy, and as they came around the thicket, Tim and Clarence beheld them, both buck naked, in full fledged fornication.....and Wilf and Colleen saw them!

Tim was speechless, but it was Clarence who piped up, "See Pa....I told you better come."

Wilf did not finish that piece of tail. He extracted himself from Colleen's embrace in a flash and still naked, struck Clarence full force to the point of his jaw, cold cocking him. His eyes were wild with rage, and what pissed Wilf off more than anything, was that Tim seemed more upset that Clarence lay stretched out cold on the ground, than anything else. Tim didn't even seem to notice that Colleen and Wilf were naked. Wilf hated Clarence, and hated him all the more for Tim's favoritism; that he seemed only concerned for Clarence. Wilf and Colleen were dressed now, and Clarence was finally starting to move. Tim looked at Wilf and said, "I think maybe you should pack up now, son."

Wilf replied, "Yes, I think you're right".

It was the end of family life for Wilf. Patrick was gone now, and he hated Clarence. Tim was to regret his rejection of Wilf, and regret it deeply. What got Wilf was that Tim didn't really have a problem so much catching him and Colleen fucking. He was embarrassed by it more than anything. What galled Wilf the most was Tim's concern for Clarence, whom Wilf hated, and hated all the more for his indifference to the loss of Patrick. Tim was never to see Wilf again.

Back at the house, Wilf snatched some clothes and his shaving gear, stuffed everything into a kit bag, slung it over his shoulder, and made for the door. Clarence looked on impassively, as though viewing a curious but vaguely interesting event. Wilf's mother hugged him passionately and tearfully in the doorway, pleading with him in French not to leave. He hugged her back, and kissing her forehead, said in French, *"Je vais t'aimer toujours, ma mere, mais il faut que je m'en pars," (I will always love you mom, but I have to leave,)* and turned his face so she wouldn't see his tears.

He had no idea where he was going. Denise ran down the driveway after him, pleading with him, sobbing, *"Non Wilf, je t'en prie....restez,"* (No Wilf, I beg you....please stay), but he just walked faster, and never looked back. He was to find work in the mines, and simultaneously an affinity for booze. He was never able to find again that feeling of intimacy he'd know with Colleen Arnold. He became a good miner. He made good money and blew it. As drinking became a problem his sex partners became a series of acquaintances, one-nighters along with the odd hooker.

A night with 'Big Mabel' was an experience that was to sober him up for a good two months. It happened during his time in Red Lake, when he worked in the drift with Stan. One Saturday off, having spent most of the day in the bar of the Red Lake Inn (locally known as the 'snake pit'), he drank on into the evening and found company with a hefty local barfly. Her name was Mabel, and she confided to Wilf that she was actually an Indian princess. They drank together till the bar closed, and Wilf hardly remembered going home with her; home being a shack in McDougall'sville, a shanty town right next to Red Lake. The next recollection he had, was waking up in the morning beside her in her bed. The shack was a one room affair, which extended into a kitchen and cooking area from the end of the bed to the far end of the shack. On the far wall was a wood burning cook stove, with a table and chairs to the right of it in one corner, and to the left of the stove was coal bucket right next to the entrance.

Being a warm summer's morning, the inside door was open; the screen door, although closed, was torn, and flies were buzzing around him as he awoke. His mouth was dry. His head ached, and he felt totally nauseated; he was hungover. Two little native children peered at him over the end of the bed inn wide-eyed innocence. The evening started to come back to him now. He turned to his left to find the ' princess' had become an enormous toothless squaw, mouth agape, and snoring loudly beside him. To his great relief, he realized he was still fully clothed, and even still had his runners on. At least they hadn't had sex he reasoned.

He eased himself out of the bed, careful not to awake her, and rose unsteadily to his feet, his head pounding. He made his way to the door. Just by the doorway he felt dizzy. He put his hand to the wall to steady himself. As he leaned against the wall he found he was looking down into the coal bucket. A stink rose from it, and as looked down into it, he could see a rotting fish head partly immersed in some brackish water, with one eye of the fish head staring vacantly toward him, peering through a film of soot. The stench hit him as he realized what he was seeing. Overcome now with nausea, he stumbled out of the shack, and grabbed at a nearby Poplar for support. He leaned against it, and wretched, and wretched, and wrenched.

He cursed his drinking, and swore he'd never drink again (and he never did for a couple of months.) There were no secrets in Red Lake, and Wilf's evening with Big Mabel was a source of local amusement for months to come.

Wilf had never again found the comfort in intimacy he'd known with Colleen Arnold. What he missed the most about Colleen more than anything else was that relaxed, warm feeling of closeness they shared while laying back together after some good sex. He'd never felt that closeness with any woman since. Now that he was sober, he realized it wasn't about finding a piece of tail anymore; he would wait for the day he could find a good woman who would have him. He put his book down, got undressed and into bed, and turned off the light. He was soon asleep. That day was to come sooner than he ever thought.

Sunday midnight Wilf was back to work starting his first graveyard shift. Work went along smoothly enough. During the course of his third shift, in the small hours of that Wednesday morning, his shift boss Garth Young came by making his rounds, to find Gus, Stan and Wilf near the end of their mucking cycle. They'd run out of slide rail, so they had already stood the rails, and were just about to spike the new slide rails in place, then finish mucking out, with only a few cars to go.

"Hi guys," said Garth as he approached them. Stan lit a cigarette as Wilf and Gus spiked in the slide rails. Garth could see the face showed a nice clean break from the cross shift, and commented, "Still getting good breaks here I see." He was oblivious to the fact that the ground had changed from the hard brittle granite to the softer, spongier green limestone.

"Ya, but it's a little trickier now," said Stan. "We're out of that granite now and into limestone so we have to load the cut real light. We're still breaking good and so are the cross shift. They seem to have it figured out."

Garth's only mining experience had been driving scrans in the soft ground on 700, and he didn't want to betray his ignorance of the problem between breaking limestone and granite. He simply said, "Yes, it looks like you've got it right." With that left them. They finished mucking out, then set up and drilled off the next round. This round had to be loaded differently.

Out of the hard granite, which broke like glass, they were now in limestone which was a softer, spongier ground, and not so easy to break. There was no more loading the cut solid with 70% Cilgel (dynamite), and then tamping the blast holes. Stan drilled a fourth reamer hole into the cut now, giving the first blast hole an extra hole to break into. This blast hole he loaded very lightly, using only 40% Cilgel instead of 70%. He did not load the hole solid with powder either, but loaded it with a half stick and then a spacer, half stick and a spacer right to within a foot of the collar of the hole, and left the hole untamped. The next blast hole in the cut he used a full stick of 40%, then a spacer, full stick and then a spacer, also leaving a foot of collar, and left this hole untamped. The last blast hole of the cut, he didn't use any spacers, filling the hole with 40% cilgel, and leaving a foot of collar; this time he broke the last stick, and tamped it gently. The rest of the round they loaded with 70% cilgel and tamped the holes. It was a little more trouble than blasting their way through granite, but they were still getting good clean breaks, breaking their rounds right to the nuts.

The week went and Friday morning they were finished till Monday afternoon shift. It was their long change. Stan had decided to pass on breakfast but Wilf went straight to the restaurant. He was pleased to Serena on duty. He took a stool at the counter and Serena brought him a coffee. He thanked her; then she hesitated a moment, and finally spoke. "You go to the 'Hoot'n'Holler' sometimes," she said, more like a statement of fact, than a question.

"Yes, sometimes I do."

"Would you be going this Saturday? Because if you do I was wondering if I could catch a ride in with you. I won't need a ride back because my sister and brother-in-law will be coming in from Sapawe, and I'll leave with them and stay with Mom for the weekend. She lives in Sapawe."

Suddenly Wilf thought it would be a good idea to go to the dance. "No problem, Serena. Yes, I was thinking of going. Gus picks us up around eight in front of the restaurant here, if that works for you?"

"I'll be there," she said, "So, are you having breakfast?"

"For sure. I'll have my usual, ham with eggs over easy, hash browns, and brown toast."

"Got it". She smiled at him for a moment, and then passed on his order to the cook.

The restaurant was fairly busy, so there wasn't time to talk, but Wilf was happy that enough was said. He ate his breakfast at the counter. Bill Harrison had come into the restaurant and stood by the till. Wilf looked up from his food to see Bill give him a wave, and he gave him a wave back. Having finished his breakfast, he had one more coffee before leaving. Serena smiled again at him as she poured the coffee.

"See you tomorrow then," she confirmed.

"For sure Serena, see you then." He left a tip on the counter and went to the till.

"And how are you, Wilf?" Bill asked, accepting his money.

"All done graveyards.....life is good."

He went back to his room in good spirits. He was excited at the prospect of being at the Hoot'n Holler Hall with Serena. So far their relationship amounted to a few pleasantries over the counter. He had no idea if this was going anywhere, but if there was any chance there was, he would certainly give it every chance to happen. He went to the washroom, brushed his teeth, went to his room, and got undressed and climbed into bed. He wasn't sure if he could sleep, so he thought he'd read for a bit, but he was soon asleep.

And while Wilf went to Sinclairs for breakfast the following Saturday morning, Vince Jamieson was just nicely into his second cup of coffee, having breakfast at home with Margo. She was a cashier at Wright's Store, and Vince had come across her when he was in the lineup to her till waiting to pay for some lunchmeats. He'd shown up clean shaven after that and always lined up at Margo's till. Finally he was able to get around to dating her, and soon after made her a proposition; he would cover the rent and groceries if they could co-habit.

"I'll have to talk to my son about this," she said

"Of course you do," he'd agreed tactfully.

"Well, you haven't met my son," she went on.

"No not yet." When he did meet Jimmy, he shook his hand, and was very polite, affecting some cordial interest, and very careful not to laugh as Jimmy stuttered hopelessly, doing his best to reciprocate the greeting.

"P-p-p-l-l-eased t-t-to m-m-meet yoooou, V-V-V-Vince."

Vince had wanted to laugh in his face, but managed to contain himself. The introduction went all right in Margo's estimation. Jimmy was lukewarm to the idea of Vince moving in, but made no strong objection. She had explained to Jimmy as best she could that she needed a man in her life, and suggested it might be good for Jimmy, having lost his father, who was killed on the Juno beachhead at the Normandy invasion before he was even born. She was pregnant with Jimmy when his father was killed in France. The fact of the matter was that on her own, she was just making ends meet. A little help wouldn't hurt at all.

"We could give it a try, Vince," she said finally, after a few short days of deliberation. He packed up and moved in the same day. A year and a half later now, Vince was quite comfortable in the relationship. He was back to shaving once or twice a week, and sat alone now at the breakfast table, his dressing gown open, exposing his hairy chest. Margo, having eaten earlier made him his favorite breakfast of pancakes and sausages. Done with breakfast now, Vince got into the newspaper and raised his empty cup as a signal to Margo to bring him another coffee. She dutifully complied. As she poured he looked up at her briefly, and pointing to the newspaper explained, "Gotta know what goes on in the world."

"Yes Vince, we should know these things," she replied. He went back to reading the paper. Shortly afterwards, her son Jimmy came to the door. Vince liked to open a conversation with Jimmy, just to hear him stutter, then laugh about it. Jimmy knew the game, so did his best to avoid Vince, but on this occasion he had to speak with his mother. Vince looked up from his paper and saw Jimmy as he came through the door, and Jimmy knew Vince had him.

"Well, how are things with you today, Jimmy?" he began.

"Ohhhhhhhhhhhhk-k-k-ayyyy," he said.

Vince laughed till he cried. "Glad to hear that," he said finally, and went back to his newspaper. A tormented Jimmy fled.

"You're being very unkind to Jimmy," Margo said.

"I know. I'm sorry," he said without looking up from his paper, and then started to laugh all over again. She went outside after Jimmy.

Wilf and Serena met in front of Sinclair's a little before eight. Stan had declined to come at first, but said he'd think about it; if he was coming he'd be there at eight. To Wilf, Serena looked more beautiful than ever. She was wearing a low cut cotton summer dress in a floral red and pink print, exposing her tanned, firm shoulders, and showing the top of her cleavage nicely. She wore a pair of oxblood slipper like shoes that went well with her dress, and looked to Wilf like good shoes for dancing. Her hair, always in a pony-tail at work, hung loose, nicely spread over her shoulders.

"You're sure looking good Serena!" Wilf commented without thinking.

"You clean up pretty good yourself, Wilf," she came back.

"Well thank you," he said. He was sure he blushed. He was wearing his new shoes and jeans, and also a new western shirt with metal snaps, he'd just bought for the occasion. Just about then, he was glad to see Stan coming down the street to join them. Serena greeted him as he approached.

"You're coming to the dance Stan?" Serena asked.

"Ya ... might as well". The words were scarcely out of his mouth when Gus and Molly pulled up. They climbed into the back seat, with Serena in the middle.

"You goina introduce us to this lovely lady?" asked Gus.

"I'm Serena," she jumped in.

"I'm Gus, and this is my wife Molly."

"Pleased to meet you both. I hear you play a mean fiddle, Gus."

"Well, you heard right Serena." Serena had just made a friend and off they went to the Hoot'n'Holler.

Arriving at the dance hall, Gus and Molly went on in, and Wilf paid for Stan, Serena and himself at the door. Wilf asked Serena if she'd care to join them inside, but she declined, saying she'd like to wait by the door until her sister and her brother-in -law arrived. Stan went ahead to join Gus and Molly. Wilf wasn't sure of what his status as a date was, but didn't want to leave her alone by the door either, with the odd rowdy already showing up. He offered to wait with her at least until her company arrived.

"Thanks Wilf," she said, "they shouldn't be too long." They made some small talk as they waited. It was warm August evening and just getting dusk. As they talked, a red pickup was pulling up into the gravel parking area.

"That's them now," Serena said. The couple got out of the truck, and made their way to the entrance where Wilf and Serena stood waiting. To Wilf's surprise it was Toivo, the big Finlander he'd met on the train on his way into town, who gave him a huge gulp of whisky which took him nicely out of the torture of one horrible hangover, one which Wilf would always like to remember as his last. He'd also bought Wilf a Coke, when his tongue was hanging out a foot, and the newsie wouldn't allow him three cents credit to cover his shortage. Upon leaving the train, Toivo had given Wilf five dollars.

Serena began to introduce them to Wilf as they got to the door.

"This is my sister Helen," she began, and Wilf shook her hand.

"Wilf Baker," he said, shaking her hand.

"And this is her husband Toivo,"she continued.

"Toivo and I have met," Wilf said, shaking his hand and eyeing him with a smile.

"We met on the train last May, Toivo; you sure helped me out....and I owe you five dollars at least."

"No 'roblem Vilf, you owe me nothing," he said smiling, as he looked him in the eye, shaking his hand. "You lookin' good now."

"Nothing doing Toivo," Wilf came back, handing him five dollars and under protest he paid their admission. They came in with Wilf and Serena and joined up with Stan at Gus and Molly's table. Introductions were made appropriately and extra chairs were pulled over by Stan and Wilf to get everyone seated. That done Gus and Molly offered to share their rum with the new guests, but they both graciously declined. Helen and Serena didn't drink, and Toivo had thought to bring a mickey of whiskey for himself, which Helen had stashed in her purse. Wilf and Stan went to the bar and came back with six bottles of coke and two 7up for their table, and the party was on.

Gus got right into his rum. He'd already had one good shot straight before the mix arrived. Molly waited for the mix, and passed one of her plastic glasses to Toivo, who filled it half full of whiskey and then added a little coke to it. He did this very discretely, looking carefully around before he poured his whiskey. Gus was quite nonchalant about pouring his; he was the fiddler. Toivo offered Wilf and Stan to share his whiskey, but they politely refused.

Toivo was impressed with this. "You not 'rink Vilf?" he asked.

"Not lately, no."

"Maybe good thing, Vilf."

"Yes Toivo, that's a good thing."

Gus raised his glass, and made a toast, "To good times and good music." They all joined him in his toast, raising their drinks simultaneously, Helen and Serena with their 7up, Stan and Wilf with their coke, and Toivo, Molly and Gus with their drinks. Toivo had almost downed his drink already, and finished it with their toast to good times and good music. About that time Rod Hicks, came in with his instrument, and having laid it on the stage came and joined the group. Gus immediately poured him some rum in one of Molly's glasses and Molly mixed it for him. Further introductions were made, and Toivo, Helen and Serena were already feeling quite at home with the group; that special magic of Gus and Molly was upon them all. Toivo poured himself another whiskey; not so strong this time, as he was already comfortably primed.

Once Rod had his drink down, and Gus had one more with him, they rose together and climbed up the short step to the stage. "Excuse us please, good people," he'd said upon rising (slightly in the glow,) "it's time we made some music now."

A general applause swept the dance hall, now nicely filled, as they picked up their instruments, and bowed to the people. Gus swept the strings of his fiddle with a well rosined bow, hitting the hall with the full effect of his fiddler's magic. As he continued into 'Big John McNeil', Rod joined in with his electric fender guitar in perfect accompaniment. Before they were finished people were up dancing, and Gus and Rod went from one number to the next with hardly a moment's hesitation in between.

Wilf asked Serena if she danced a two step. She had been watching the dancers, and said she'd never done that, but she said she'd give it a try. They stepped out on the floor and faced each other. Wilf started it off, and she just stood and watched him for a few minutes. She began to get the feel of it, and once she started to do a few steps, she got into it; a little clumsy at first, but into the next number, 'Silver Bells', she got right into it and once she got the feel of it, she didn't want to sit down. Wilf couldn't stop smiling. Toivo and Helen sat with Molly and Stan, watching the show, and at the end of their first set, Gus and Rod played, 'Life in the Finland Woods'. Toivo couldn't resist that one, and feeling his whiskey now, pulled Helen up on the floor and danced enthusiastically.

Serena's sister Helen was a good looking woman, a little taller than Serena, and darker with high cheek bones. They didn't look like sisters so much by appearance, but in the way they connected at the table, they were unmistakably sisters. They locked eyes as they talked, they laughed together as one, and poked each other playfully. Toivo was not a talker but was greatly enjoying himself. He loved the music and the fellowship. Done with his mickey now, he wasn't looking for more. He was in the groove. Every so often he would shake hands with Wilf as though for the first time.

Gus and Rod finished their set and joined the company back at their table. Gus was by now in a steady sweat, though Rod, a moderate drinker, looked no worse for the wear. Gus poured another drink for Rod and offered some to Molly and Toivo. Molly passed, and Toivo accepted a small amount, indicating as such between his thumb and forefinger a half inch gap. Gus emptied the balance of the contents of the big thermos into his own glass, filling it slightly over half full, and Molly added a little coca cola to it. He then took a good hit off it, letting out a gasp of approval, and kicking out his right leg at the same time.

Done with their drinks, Gus and Rod got up for their last set. It was well past midnight now, and almost everyone was up dancing. Molly got up with Gus and Rod, and sang a couple of waltzes in her strong clear voice, which Gus and Rod followed up for a second time with 'Life in the Finland Woods', by Toivo's request, and again Toivo pulled Helen up to dance. Gus and Rod did a few more two step numbers, and Molly got up one more time to sing for the last waltz of the evening; her favorite....'The Tennessee Waltz"

Serena was up for almost every dance with Wilf. In one brief break, Lucy, whom Wilf had danced with on a previous evening, got into a step dance with Wilf, but Serena was quick to join them, and shortly managed to butt

Lucy out of the way. She left the floor pissed off, (not to Serena's displeasure), and Wilf had continued with Serena, quite amazed. They were still on the floor when Molly was singing the Tennessee Waltz. Serena wrapped herself around Wilf ignoring their sweat and spoke to him as they danced. "Would you care to have a visit with me and Mom for the weekend? She lives in Sapawe. There's a school bus leaves every week day morning for town, so you'd be OK for afternoon shift come Monday. Toivo and my sister will take us home, if that's good with you."

Wilf could hardly believe his ears, but didn't second guess the offer. "Well sure Serena, I'd like to meet your mom," he said, with no idea where this was going. "I didn't even bring a toothbrush," he went on, in an effort to seem nonchalant.

"Don't worry about that" she said as the dance finished, "I've got a spare that's never been used."

He had to laugh, blushing through his sweat, and they both laughed. The dance over, they returned to the table, and without sitting down again, Serena thanked Gus and Molly for a wonderful evening, and said to Helen and Toivo that Wilf would be coming home to Sapawe to meet their mother and stay the weekend, if could they squeeze him into Toivo's truck.

Toivo rose from his chair, and responded, "No 'roblem, Serena."

Helen got up and immediately said how nice it was to meet them all. Stan got up to shake Toivo's hand and Gus and Molly got up, Gus shaking hands and Molly hugging everyone from the table. The vehicles were beginning to leave the parking lot now as Toivo, Helen, Serena and Wilf made their way to Toivo's pickup. Toivo got in, then Helen in the middle, then Wilf, and finally Serena got on Wilf's lap, and off they went for Sapawe.

They went down the highway towards Atikokan for about ten miles, and then Toivo made a right turn at a junction just past Niobe Lake, turning onto a gravel road. The road was a little bumpy, in need of a grading, having the odd pothole. In spite of his best efforts not to, Wilf began to get a strong erection. He hoped Serena wouldn't notice; but she did, and didn't seem to mind at all. Toivo and Helen were either oblivious or indifferent to this, and made small talk as they continued up the road. It was about seven or eight miles from the junction into Sapawe.

A Miner's Story – Chapter 8

Wilf had seen Sapawe, a small sawmill village, just in passing on his train ride from the Lakehead to Atikokan. Sapawe was where Toivo had gotten off the train. He had given Wilf five dollars as he was leaving. Wilf had watched him through the coach window, and Helen was the native woman who'd come out to meet him, along with her little girl. There were a few street lights on in the village. Toivo pulled up at log building that had a smaller out building close by.

"This is it Wilf", Serena said, pulling the door handle. She climbed off Wilf, got out, and then Wilf climbed out behind her. Helen and Toivo followed them to the door, which was unlocked, and Serena let everyone in. The door opened in the middle of the front wall of the cabin. The front room was the width of the cabin. To the right of the entrance was the kitchen area with a wood burning cook stove immediately to the right of the doorway. Near the stove, and a little farther to the left of it, in the front corner of the cabin was a refrigerator. Some counter space ran along the far side of the kitchen, and in the middle of the counter was a sink, just below a window, with a pump fixed to the counter beside it. There was a table and chairs in the middle of the kitchen.

A couch was placed against the end wall of the left side of the room with a rocking chair in the right corner beside it. Helen's little girl Madeleine lay asleep on the couch, and Serena's mother was asleep in her bedroom. There was no hallway in the cabin; the two bedrooms came straight off the main room, one on either side, with a small alcove in between, containing a vanity on which held a sink with a drain, but no taps. There was a mirror in front of the sink. A curtain served as a door.

Toivo bent over to scoop the sleeping Madeleine up in his arms and took her to the truck. Helen opened the door of the truck, and Toivo placed her gently in the middle of the seat. She was still asleep when Helen and Toivo got in and headed for home. "Wish I could sleep like that," Wilf commented. He assumed he'd be sleeping on the couch. Serena sensed his intention and directed him instead to her bedroom. She turned on a small lamp on the beside side table, illuminating a tidy bedroom. The bed was a doublewide she'd once shared with her sister Helen, and now had it to herself. There was a dresser off the end of the bed, with a closet to the right of it, and a straight-backed chair on the other side in the corner.

Wilf stood for a moment, uncertain as to what he should do next. Serena started to undress, piling her clothes neatly on the chair. When she was down to her panties and bra she looked up at Wilf and said, "Well?" Naked now, she lay on the bed, waiting. Wilf quickly got undressed and joined her. He was already in full erection. She wrapped her arms around him as he moved in beside her, pulling him to her open mouth. He reciprocated her invitation bringing his mouth to hers, feeling her tongue sliding against his own. As they kissed, he put his free hand onto her breast. Serena pushed it down to her crotch. She was already wet. He pulled back from their kiss for a moment, to stare at her in amazement.

She spread her legs and said, "Come on, let's do it".

He placed himself between her spread legs, taking the weight of his body on his elbows. She already had her hand wrapped around his stiff, quivering penis, and was guiding it effectively home. Entranced, Wilf responded, entering her gently but obediently, easing himself into her warm, wet orifice until he was completely immersed in her. She gasped with pleasure immediately as he began to fuck her; gently and slowly at first, but he was soon lost in euphoric magic, letting his body lay against hers. Pulling down on her shoulders, he had his head beside hers now as he began to pump harder and faster, pushing upwards into her vagina as far as he could reach, lost in lust.

It was mindless, uncontrolled, and seemingly timeless. Serena was screaming in ecstasy, lost in multiple climaxes; their sweated bellies sucking, as he fucked her now in shorter and faster strokes. Wilf could feel himself close to coming, and was holding his breath now, fucking furiously, until he just couldn't keep it any more. Helpless to hold it back, he let it come, feeling the delicious ecstasy of ejaculation in longer, slower strokes now, until he was spent; he then collapsed upon her, his head against hers, his face in the pillow, gasping for air.

Serena lay there in a sweat, but her breathing was coming back, as Wilf was catching his. His erection was gone now, but he could still feel himself inside her; feeling a little embarrassed, he raised himself on his elbows, intending to extract himself. Serena wrapped her arm around his neck, pulling him close.

"No, not so fast," she said, "leave it there a minute," and kissed his sweated temple. "Boy, you do it right," she went on.

"So do you," he managed. He was amazed beyond anything he could have imagined at what he had just experienced with Serena. It was such a special happening, and for Wilf, so totally unexpected. He was feeling comfortable with her now; relaxed in nature's very special way. He finally eased himself off her, slowly and gently extracting his limp penis from the comfort and warmth of her wet slippery vagina, and lay beside her in a wonderful feeling of calmness. Serena lay next to him, taking hold of his hand. They laid there together in the dark of the room, talking quietly.

"Well, you sure surprised me, Serena," he was saying.

"What were you expecting, a virgin?"

"Well, I never did think about you... I mean not in this way.... I mean I never thought I'd ever be doing this with you.... not in a million years. I think you could have just about anyone you want. I'm a lot older than you, and I'd think it bad manners to be coming on to you. You're real nice, Serena, and I really appreciate seeing you around."

She started to laugh. "You are a gentleman, Wilf! I knew I liked you right from the start. I loved the way you blushed. You were just getting on your feet then. You were always so polite, always sober. I haven't been with a man in a good while, but I always thought you'd be a nice guy to know." He passed on the thought of saying, 'Nice to know you' and as the thought passed he felt her hand around his penis, already stiff again.

"Hmmm, look who is back," she commented as she moved over him, kissing him briefly on the mouth. "Don't move." She went on to straddle him, and slid her wet vagina down and around his stiff, quivering gland. Without another word she proceeded to fuck him, slowly and rhythmically at first, laying her head upon him, spilling her hair over his body. He could feel her erect nipples against his chest; then, getting caught in the lust of the moment, she raised herself on her hands, and arching her back, fucked him ever harder and faster. Wilf lay back pushing upwards against her thrusts, gripping her buttocks as she fucked him until, unable to hold it back any longer, he gushed into her. She collapsed over him, having reached her own climax, the two of them sweated, gasping for air.

They lay together so entwined; and that was how they fell asleep. Wilf was the first to come awake the next morning. Serena was still close against him, snoring gently. The sunlight shining past the edge of the curtain was bright, and birds were singing, so he knew it was well past dawn. He felt totally comfortable, and really didn't feel like moving, except for the need to relieve himself. He could smell the coffee brewing, and could hear gentle noises coming from the kitchen, so he knew Serena's mother was up. He didn't want to meet her on his own; he would wait till Serena was awake. He would visit nature after proper introductions were made.

He didn't have to wait too long, when Serena began to stir. She pressed against him first, and then opened her eyes. She looked into his eyes, smiled, and then closed her eyes again, hugging him close. After a moment she came wide awake. She yawned and stretched.

"Good morning," she said.

"Morning."

"Sleep OK?"

"Very well."

She stood up now, naked, and stretched again, then took her dressing gown from a nail, put on some slippers, and went out to the kitchen. Wilf got up and got dressed. He heard her say, "Good morning mom, I've got some company," and then, "Come out and meet my mom, Wilf."

He came out, and beheld a native woman. She was a tidy woman, about 5'6", in jeans and a T-shirt. She could have been 50, graying a little. With high cheek bones, dark eyes, and a sharp nose, she had a pleasant look.

"Mom, this is my friend Wilf, and Wilf, this is my mother Rachel", Serena said.

Rachel stuck out her hand, smiling, never taking her eyes off his. "I am pleased to meet you Wilf. My daughter has told me about you....many good things."

Wilf knew he was blushing. Shaking her hand, he noticed it was fairly big for a woman, and strong. He was very touched by her welcome.

Serena went to the pump beside the kitchen sink, filled a pail with water and handed it to Wilf, pointing to the alcove behind the curtain between the two bedrooms.

"Here's some water if you want to wash up a bit. I'll get you a towel." The water was crystal clear he noticed, and mentioned it.

"Dad dug our well over a spring," she said, "most places here have running water, but we never did get hooked up. I'll get you a coffee?" He nodded setting the bucket down at the sink in the alcove.

"There's something I gotta do first," he said. She knew. "The outhouse is out back," she said. The outhouse was a two seater, a feature that had always puzzled Wilf, and was placed about fifty feet behind the cabin. He was fairly bursting to go. He reflected on the warmth of his welcome, as he was passing his water. It was like he'd stepped into another dimension. Rachel was as cordial as polite, and didn't betray the slightest inkling that he'd just slept with her daughter. Her friendliness was unconditional.

When he came back, Rachel was making pancakes and Serena was washing up. There was a coffee on the table for him. Rachel mentioned there was canned milk and sugar on the table, but Wilf declined.

"Thanks, but no....I take it black," he said.

"My husband used to drink his black, but he liked to put sugar cubes in his mouth, and drink his coffee from the saucer through the sugar cubes in his mouth." She was a full-blooded Ojibwa Indian. Her English was good, but she spoke with an unmistakable native accent. Wilf loved hearing her talk.

"Was he Swedish?" he asked.

"Yes.....how did you know?"

"Well, I knew a guy that drank his coffee like that, and he was Swedish."

"Yes, he was Swedish. His people came from Minnesota, but he was born in Canada. They could all speak Swedish.....all his people."

"What was his name?" he asked, watching her turning the pancakes.

"His name was Axel.....Axel Carlson."

"He built this cabin?"

She nodded, putting the pancakes onto a plate. "Yes....he was a hard working man, but he drank too much. In the Sawmill he worked on the trim-saws in the planer....but he lost his job. He didn't seem to understand you're supposed to go to work every day."

"That's too bad. What happened to him?"

"Well he stayed drunk for three months after that, and then one night his heart stopped and he died," she explained, placing the pancakes on the table.

"I'm sorry."

"You don't drink?" Rachel asked.

"No...I gave that up," he said with conviction.

"That's good. Drinking is a bad thing."

Serena reappeared from washing up, and pumped another bucket for Wilf. "There's a clean towel in there for you," she said handing him the fresh bucket of water.

"Thanks," he said. He drained his coffee, and went into the alcove to wash up. While he was washing up, Toivo arrived with Helen and Madeleine. They were all at the table having coffee when Wilf was done washing up, and there was a big stack of pancakes with some ham on a plate at Wilf's place.

"You're not eating?" Wilf asked, as he sat down.

"No....ve eat already....yust like to visit."

"Good seeing you," Wilf said, pleased to see them. Serena took a couple pancakes, and a little ham, and Rachel, all done with her cooking, joined them at the table, taking pancakes and ham.

Wilf sure had an appetite. Serena passed him the butter and syrup, which he quickly applied, and dove into his food. Rachel was quite pleased with his enthusiasm for her breakfast. He wolfed it all down without a word of conversation. Rachel poured him a fresh coffee, just as he finished.

"Would you like some more pancakes, Wilf?" she asked, impressed with his appetite.

He blushed with embarrassment. "No, I'm fine. That was lots."She smiled at him, and poured more coffee for the others.

"Vilf....how 'bout ve take it sauna," suggested Toivo.

"Sure....love a sauna."

Toivo drained his coffee and got up. "Take easy, Vilf.....I fix it sauna."

Wilf got up to join him, when Serena said, "There are only two pancakes left, Wilf, and a little bit of ham. You might as well finish them up." Wilf didn't say no to that. He finished off the pancakes, the last of the ham, and downing his coffee, thanked Rachel and Serena for a lovely breakfast, excused himself, and went out to join Toivo.

The sauna structure from the outside looked to be about 10'x14'. The exterior walls were shiplap and unpainted. The roof was a shanty styled roof done in asphalt shingles. The entrance was at one end of the longer wall. The entrance door was hung on metal hinges, but had an improvised wooden latch to close it. Outside the building, there was a neat pile of split firewood covering most of the wall from the entrance to the end of the building. Smoke was already coming from the chimney.

He opened the door of the building to find Toivo filling a five gallon pail with water from a pump mounted near the front corner of the sitting room to the right of entrance. The sitting room was about 6'x10'. At the opposite end of the room from the entrance was an L-shaped sitting bench. Along the upper wall near the bench was a row of nails driven into the studs, to hang towels and clothing. The door coming into the sauna from the change room was open; Toivo had just filled the last pail needed to top off the 45 gallon drum, which stood on end by the door coming into the sauna.

Wilf followed him into the sauna room to have a look. The sauna itself was the larger of the two rooms, about 8'x10'. The doorway was cut in the middle of the wall separating the sauna from the change room. The floor of the sauna was a solid slab of cement, which filled the room from wall to wall, and sloped gently to a drain hole in the middle of it. Along the length of the back wall, opposite the doorway were two wooden benches; one just above the floor, and a second one just above, and a little bit back from the lower one. There were a couple of enamel basins placed on the upper bench, a couple of bars of soap, and a galvanized pail on the lower bench.

Next to the drum filled with water, and in the far right corner, was the heater, which was also made from a 45 gallon drum. It was placed on its side. It was a heavy wall drum, whose front end came flush to the wall separating the sauna and the change room. Its door opened into the change room, so the fire could be stoked from the change room. The top of the heater was covered in rocks, cemented in place, over top of the barrel, and around the chimney, which went up through the roof.

"I build it sauna for Helen nine years ago," said Toivo. "Axel help me. ....He dead now. Now I need build new sauna for my place. We have running water and good shower...but you can take it shower or you can go to church, but you never get it clean like sauna."

"You did a great job, Toivo. I'm going to like this."

Toivo smiled at this. Wilf followed him back into the change room, and closed the door behind him. Toivo put the five gallon pail back beside the pump. "Come, we go have coffee now. Let ladies go first." Wilf followed him back to the cabin.

Toivo opened the cabin door. "OK ladies.....sauna hot now,"" he announced. Rachel, Serena, Helen, and Madeleine all filed past him out the door with their towels and face cloths. Toivo closed the door behind them, and offered Wilf a cigarette.

"Smoke time, Vilf."

"No thanks, Toivo....I quit."

"No booze, no smoke," said Toivo surprised. "Good for you, Vilf." He shook his hand, and passed him a coffee. Then he said, "You like Serena, eh?"

"Yup!"

"I think you got lucky."

"I think so too."

They both laughed

"Good for you, Vilf. You good guy for her."

"Hope so."

Wilf passed a good hour with Toivo while the girls took their turn in the sauna. The time just seemed to fly by, just having a coffee and shooting the shit with Toivo. Before he knew it, the girls were back with their towels and wet hair, chatting amicably.

"OK Vilf....we go now," said Toivo.

When they got to the sauna, Toivo threw another big chunk of birch into the fire. They stripped down in the change room, hanging their clothes on the nails, and stepped into the sauna. Wilf almost choked on the heat, and let out a yelp when he put his bare ass on the bench. Toivo saw the problem, and slopped a pail of cool water from the tank over the bench. "There Vilf....not so hot now."

They sat back for ten or fifteen minutes, just feeling the heat. They were soon dripping in sweat like they'd just stepped out of a shower. Wilf was just nicely getting used to it when Toivo took a half pail of water, and threw it over the rocks. The water hit the rocks with a whoosh, instantly sending off a thick cloud of steam, making Wilf cough.

"Coming good now," Toivo commented, as he took a handful of fresh cut birch branches, and started beating his back. There were more branches on the bench. Toivo suggested Wilf try it. He did, and found it quite stimulating. Toivo grinned. "Old Finnish thing," he said. Wilf nodded.

They were both in a good sweat now. Toivo handed Wilf a clean face cloth and a bar of soap, and took the same for himself. They started scrubbing themselves. When they had their upper bodies soaped and scrubbed, Toivo rinsed himself with a pail of cool water from the tank, and then handed Wilf a pail full to do the same. The coolness of the water felt good.

They stood up now, washing their groin, hips and thighs, then rinsed again. Lastly, seated, they scrubbed their calves and feet, then rinsed. The water in the barrel was down to less than half now. "OK Vilf....ve go cool off now." Wilf followed him out the door into the change room, and the two men sat naked on the bench. Toivo took a beer from his knapsack, and offered one to Wilf, who declined.

Toivo came back again with, "You can take it shower or go to church, but never get it clean like sauna."Wilf had to agree. He was quite pleased with himself that he'd refused the offer of a beer without the slightest hesitation. Man, if there was ever a time for a beer, it was right then after a sauna! "I might be getting OK," he thought to himself, "....if I can say no to that one, I can say no to the rest."

Toivo drained his beer almost in one gulp, and then opened a second one. He drank the second one a little more slowly, and when he was finished it said "Come on....ve go one more time, Vilf." Wilf followed him back into the sauna. He waited till Toivo threw a pail of water over the bench, before he sat down. No sooner had he sat down, than Toivo threw a good half pail on the rocks. The whoosh of steam choked Wilf; he breathed slowly through his wet face cloth till the heat settled.

"Need to get used to little bit," Toivo commented, observing Wilf's reaction. Wilf nodded agreement. They both laughed. Toivo sat back as the sweat came on. "No need vash it this time," he stated, "already clean." They stayed as long as they could take it; then rinsing off their bodies with buckets of cool water from the tank, they left the sauna to dry in the change room and get dressed. Toivo had one more beer before they picked up their towels and face cloths and returned to meet the girls in the cabin. Wilf kept his aside for the morning; Rachel gathered up Toivo's with the others for the wash, and offered Wilf a razor with a fresh blade.

"Best time to shave," she said, "right after a sauna." She had already placed a basin of water for him in the alcove. Wilf excused himself, and took the razor and his face cloth into the alcove. There was a mug of shaving cream there with a brush (no doubt from her deceased husband) beside the basin. He took off his shirt, and lathered his face generously; his face was still warm from the sauna, his whiskers soft. He shaved, and the beard came off with no resistance at all, leaving his face as smooth as a baby's behind. He couldn't help smiling at his face in the mirror. He wiped his face clean with his cloth, put on his shirt, and rejoined the company.

"Have good shave, Wilf?" Toivo said more as a statement than a question. Smiling, Wilf caressed his face and nodded. "See, need it sauna, Vilf....make it nice shave." He was with his wife and Madeleine by the door now, preparing to leave. He and Helen paused briefly to confer privately, and then Toivo said, "You people come to our place for dinner tonight, OK?" Everyone agreed, and Toivo and his family left for home.

Wilf had noticed a scrub board hanging from the cabin wall. He knew how things were getting washed around here, the same way his mother did it. Rachel got it done. She kept things clean, like her cabin. She kept a nice place. After the company had gone, Serena steered Wilf into the bedroom; Rachel seemed to take no notice. Serena lay back on her bed, fully clothed, except for her shoes. "Let's just relax for a bit," she suggested. Wilf joined her. Within a few minutes of lying down beside Serena, the impact of the past twelve hours came over him....a night of good sex, a hearty breakfast, and a great sauna....within minutes he was fast asleep, and slept for a good few hours. Serena immediately fell asleep too, but was the first to awake. When he opened his eyes, he found her smiling at him.

"Good sleep?" she asked.

"That's for sure."

She kissed him, stretched, and then got up. Wilf felt so comfortable he didn't feel like moving, but finally he did. He felt good with every breath; so relaxed and rested he couldn't remember ever having felt so good. When they came out of the bedroom, they found Rachel kneeling down in front a galvanized washtub filled with warm soapy water, scrubbing the soiled face cloths and towels over her scrub board. As she wrung them out, she placed them in a cylindrical wicker basket fitted with shoulder straps. As she was wringing out the last towel, Serena began emptying the wash tub with a pail, pouring the used water down the drain of the kitchen sink. When she had it nearly empty, Wilf picked up the tub, and poured the remainder down the drain.

"We rinse them out down by the lake when it's not frozen over," Serena said. "Let's you and I go and do that for Mom. I'll show you around Sapawe….not that there's much to see," she added with a grin. Wilf happily nodded agreement. He picked up the basket, but found the straps too tight for his broad shoulders; he simply slung it over one shoulder by one of its straps, and followed Serena out the door.

Rachel's cabin was at the edge of the village, which in daylight now, Wilf could see would only house a few hundred people. There were a few blocks of assorted dwellings laid out along a gravel road. Most of the places were tidy. A few had lawns; some had flowers and grew a garden. There was a good flat area in the middle of the village, which held a baseball diamond with some bleachers. A couple of young fellows were playing catch there.

There was a hump in the road as it passed the field, and atop the rise was a general store and restaurant. Serena pointed it out as 'downtown Sapawe'. He looked into the restaurant. Up the middle were stools by a counter which ran opposite the grill where the cook was frying up a couple of burgers. There were some booths along the far wall by the windows, and down at the end was a jukebox. A couple sat in one of the booths, no doubt waiting for their burgers. Other than that, the place was empty. The building also served as a Post Office. The general store had a separate entrance.

"This is where we'll catch the school bus tomorrow morning," Serena explained. Wilf nodded.

They walked past the Sawmill near the shore of the lake. Being Sunday, it was not running so it was totally quiet. Right down on the lake opposite the mill was a boom of logs which enclosed a good supply of logs for the mill. (A log boom is a series of large logs chained end for end to form a 'bag' containing a large amount of logs afloat in a body of water. Thus contained, the logs can then be towed from across the lake by a tugboat)

. A catwalk ran from the shore into the midst of the logs so that a man working from the catwalk with a pike pole could pull the logs in bunches over to another man feeding the jack ladder. The jack ladder drew the logs out of the pond and into the mill where they'd be turned into lumber.

The founder of the mill was J.A.Mathieu, who had previously owned and operated a mill in Fort Frances, Ontario. He had his Sapawe mill up and going, long before there was any road in. The spot was well chosen because it was on a lake which was close to the railroad. There was also an abundance of good timber close by to feed the mill. He had hired mostly local natives Indians, who turned out for the most part to be good workers. Axel Carlson, Serena's father was a white man, as were about a third of the payroll. He used to operate the trim saws in the planer, till booze got the best of him.

"My dad worked here for a long time," Serena said, "but he got drinking too much and too often, and started missing shifts. Finally they let him go. I'm glad you don't drink, Wilf."

"Me too....so far, so good," he thought.

"Ever work in a Sawmill?"

"Yes, I did once for a few months. Thought I'd try to get out of mining. No, it's not my thing, saw milling. Went back mining. I've heard it said, and it seems to be true.....'once a miner; always a miner'."

"Do you like mining?"

"I'm not sure that I do. I keep doing it. Seems to be in my blood. I always come back to it."

"Will you stay at Steep Rock?"

"I don't want to leave that place. We're told they have an ore body that would last a hundred years. I'm making good money with two of the best partners you could ask for. No.....I'm not about to walk away from that. It's a good go, Steep rock."

"I'm glad, Wilf. I hope you'll come to visit again soon."

They walked a little ways down the shore of the lake past the mill to where the rock shore sloped gently to the lake, when Serena indicated that this would be a good place to rinse out the towels. Wilf was still a little overwhelmed by her last comment, to which he'd made no reply. The fact of the matter was that he couldn't imagine anything he'd rather do than visit Serena. Almost in a trance, he carefully emptied the contents of the basket on the shore of the lake. Serena placed the towels and face cloths in the water by the shore of the lake, moving them back and forth in the water, until she was satisfied all the soap was rinsed out; then one by one she and Wilf wrung them out together, placing each one back in the basket as they did them.

It was getting to late afternoon when they made their way back to the cabin. There was a clothesline there strung between two trees, and some clothespins hung in a cloth bag from a limb of one of the trees. Serena hung the towels and face cloths out to dry, as Wilf handed them to her, one by one. When they went back into the cabin they found Rachel just pulling out a batch of fresh dinner rolls from the oven. She offered one each to Wilf and Serena, who took them eagerly, buttered them, and ate them immediately; the rest she placed in a wicker basket, and covered them with a white linen tea towel.

"I guess we might as well get going now", she said, opening the door.

Wilf and Serena waited for her outside the front of the cabin, as Rachel pulled the door closed and locked it. Rachel had a few flowers growing in front of her cabin. There was no lawn, but no weeds either. It was mostly shaded by trees, with a pathway leading to the gravel road a short distance away. The three of them headed off to Toivo and Helens, Rachel with her basket of buns, and Wilf and Serena beside her.

When they arrived for dinner, Toivo greeted them at the door, and told Wilf to leave his shoes on. Helen had the table set for six, and bid them to sit at the table, as dinner was almost ready. The dining area which was also part of the kitchen came off their entrance on the side of the building. There was a front entrance which came through a screened porch, which ran along the front of their cabin facing the lake. A counter ran along the length of the far wall of the kitchen, with a sink and taps in the middle, and a window in front of the sink. Along the wall at right angles to the counter were the electric stove and fridge, side by side.

The cabin was larger by half than Rachel's, being about thirty feet by thirty. At the far end of the cabin from the kitchen area was a sitting room, with a large sofa placed against the far wall, and a coffee table in front of it. There were two matching armchairs, facing each other; one at either end of the sofa. There was also a rocking chair, placed beside the armchair on the right. A hallway met the right wall of the sitting room. There were two bedrooms, one on each side of the far end of the hallway, and a bathroom that came straight off the end of the hallway. The bathroom had running water, with a toilet, a sink, and a large porcelain bathtub, complete with a shower head and curtain.

Wilf took a seat beside Serena on one side of the table, and Rachel and Madeleine sat together on the opposite side, facing them. As Helen was bringing the vegetables to the table, Toivo, seated at the far end, was carving generous slices from a huge haunch of venison cut from tender two point buck, which had been marinated for twenty four hours in a game marinade before cooking it. It was nicely done to a juicy medium rare. Helen had made rich, thick gravy; and setting it down in the middle of the table, sat down at the end of the table opposite Toivo. She offered a brief prayer of grace and finished by saying, "OK everybody….Let's eat!"

There was a lot of good food; a large bowl of new potatoes, along with bowls of carrots and beets, and a salad made from fresh lettuce, cucumbers, tomatoes, onions, and radishes…..all from their garden. With Rachel's buns, the roasted venison and gravy, there was lots to eat. There was little conversation throughout the meal, no doubt due to the good food, and the good appetite of hungry people. When everyone had eaten, Helen served up a blueberry pie, from blueberries just picked.

Done with dinner, Wilf felt like a sausage. He rose from the table, thanking Helen and Toivo. 'Thank you so much," he said, "you sure know how to feed people!"

"You're welcome anytime, Wilf," Helen came back, "Good food's not wasted on you!" Toivo confirmed the comment with a nod. "You come again, Vilf."

Helen and Serena set about clearing off the table and doing the dishes, and Madeleine helped to dry. Toivo and Wilf retired to the sitting room, Toivo on the couch, Wilf on the adjacent chair. Rachel joined them, taking the rocker. Wilf was feeling totally content.

"You sure know how to live, Toivo," he commented.

"Ya sure, ve live good. Life is good, ya?"

""You cut pulp, eh?"

"Ya, I cut pulp. I work for a contractor Morris lePoint. He pays six dollars a cord. I cut four cords for my day, and then go home. Take me six, maybe seven hours. Sometimes cut logs for mill here. That pays different. I have chain saw now. Before used Swede saw."

"I worked in the bush when I first left home. That's hard work, Toivo."

"Yes....hard work, but nobody bother you. You all by yourself. Yust me and my horse. I make twice money they make in Sawmill, and no boss. I get paid for what I do, not for hours I work. You miner. You work contract too."

Toivo had a cigarette, and they talked over coffee, as Rachel rocked in her chair with her eyes closed. When they were done in the kitchen, Serena stood next to her mother, now asleep, and said, "Let's go home, Mom."Rachel's eyes popped open, awakened from her reverie.

"Oh....is it time to go already?"

"Yes.....it's already dark out there Mom," she said, taking her hand and helping her out of the chair. With a good dinner under his belt, and a relaxing day, Wilf was feeling he could have dozed off himself. He pulled himself out of his place of comfort to join Serena and her mother for the walk back to Rachel's, thanked his hosts for a fine meal and a good visit, and good acknowledgements were made all around. Toivo shook Wilf's hand as they were leaving and said, "Next time you come to visit, I show you my horse."

"I'll look forward to that, Toivo," Wilf said, and he left with Rachel and Serena for the walk home. It was late summer now, and there was coolness to the air, which Wilf found pleasantly refreshing. Wilf smiled at the offer of Toivo's to show him his horse. He knew it wasn't about the horse so much. Toivo, in his best way, was saying they had more things to do together, more to talk about. He just wanted to extend a welcome for another visit. Wilf felt privileged.

He thought about Toivo going to work by himself in the bush, just the man and his horse. Toivo was a young and powerful man, granted; but for all that it took a lot of discipline to work that hard, and work alone. On the upside, he could see that Toivo loved his independence, loved to work, loved his family, and loved his life. These were not people Wilf would meet in the bar. Yes, he would like to spend more time with Toivo. They were soon at Rachel's door.

Rachel brushed her teeth, bid Wilf and Serena good night, and went to bed. It was only a little past nine, but Wilf and Serena did the same. They lay naked together, and talked for awhile, going over their day together. Wilf told her he'd never had a better one. Serena smiled at this, and bent over him and kissed him. She could feel his erection as she did so, and as he returned her kiss, he could feel her warmth. They went with the feeling, and made love. There was no more guessing now, no uncertainty; only two friends enjoying their lust, and making love.

Wilf didn't have to worry about coming too soon, because Serena started to climax minutes after they started to fuck, and continued to with loud enthusiasm throughout his efforts. He stayed in that special zone of ecstasy, fucking ever harder and faster, until he came....and came, and came...and so did Serena.

They lay together still entwined, still in a sweat and panting, until finally they got their breath; then Wilf slowly extracted his lost erection from the lovely warmth of her vagina. They talked a little further into the night, enjoying their naked closeness, until finally the feeling came over them again, and they made love one more time before going to sleep.

They awoke early that Monday morning. It was just breaking day. A crow was squawking, perched on a limb just outside their bed room window.

Serena snuggled against Wilf. "Noisy brat," she commented. Wilf just squeezed her tighter. He loved the morning scent of her body after a night of good sex. Any time he had sex with a hooker, and her scent would be on him, his first impulse was to take a shower. With Serena, he just wanted it to last.

Before long, they could hear Rachel in the kitchen, so they finally bestirred themselves from the comfort of their bed. Serena got into her housecoat, Wilf into his clothes, and they came out to join Rachel in the kitchen. She bid them good morning, and asked them had they slept well. Both Wilf and Serena assured her that they had. Rachel had coffee on and was making porridge. Serena pumped some water for herself to wash up, and Wilf went out to relieve himself. They joined Rachel shortly after for coffee and porridge. Done with breakfast, Wilf had another coffee with Rachel while Serena went to her room and got dressed. He raised his cup to her and said, "Thank you so much for having me in your place, Rachel. It's been a pleasure to meet you and your family. It's been a great visit."

She blushed in her beautiful modesty and said to Wilf, "I am pleased to meet you Wilf. You are a good friend for my daughter and you're welcome in my place any time."

Serena appeared from the bedroom, dressed now, with her night bag in her hand. "I guess were good to go now, Mom," she said, "Thanks for having us."

'This is your place too, Serena, and Wilf is welcome anytime."

Serena kissed her, and said to Wilf, "We better get going now. The bus is leaving in fifteen minutes."

Wilf got up to follow her out. "See you Rachel," he said, and she waved back. "Come again," she said.

Wilf went his first afternoon shift in a very good mood. Gus eyed him changing in the Dry, and grinned. "I see somebody put a smile on your face, by the looks." he said. Wilf nodded and Gus laughed. "Good on you," he went on. Wilf made no comment, but couldn't stop smiling. He finished getting into his diggers, and caught up with Stan and Gus at the wicket. The shift boss was already giving Stan the drill for the shift.

"You're coming into a clean face, Stan," he said. "Day shift put in track and pipe, and you're set up to drill." Stan nodded, accepting his work sheet, and the three of them headed for shaft house to catch the cage.

"Looks like we're off to a good start," said Gus, then added, "don't mind at all." The cage came back to surface; the cage tender rang three bells, and swung open the shaft door. "1100....going down," he bawled, and Stan, Wilf and Gus got on board, along with the other drift crew, and the two raisemen. Dave Chambers, the leader from the other driftcrew asked, "Are you guys drilling or mucking?"

"We've got a clean face," said Stan, "we're set up to drill."

"We got a muck pile."

The cage stopped at 1100'. "Eleven hundred!" The cagetender said almost shouting as he let them out. Stan eyed him as he was walking off the cage. "I know," he said. Gus burst out laughing. The cagetender was looking quite chagrinned. Dave and his crew took the motor in front with its string of cars, and took off for their heading. Gus, Stan and Wilf climbed on the other motor and headed in for their clean face. They used the California switch for switching cars now during the mucking cycle. But when they weren't mucking out, their string of Hudson's was parked in the layby back from the heading out of way.

When they arrived at their heading, they found everything in perfect order, just as they'd been told. The three jacklegs were standing at the face, hooked up to the air and water hoses. The three drill ladders were placed against the bucket of the mucking machine. The drill steel lay beside the ladders, ready with fresh bits. The grade was already taken and the face marked up; even the lubricators were topped with oil. There was not a mark or bootleg on the face; a good clean break. They had only to turn on their air and water, and they were good to go.

Stan lit a cigarette, and Gus took on a fresh wad of snoose. "Great way to start the week," said Gus. Stan nodded, even smiling. Wilf went back to the headers to open the air and water to the machines. Minutes later the three men were drilling. The ground was a little softer now. They were out of the hard granite that broke so well and into a light green limestone. It was a little faster drilling now, but there were some fine mud slips in the ground, so they had to keep their hands on their feed, ready to slack off the pressure the second the water quit returning from the hole they were drilling. Catching it right away, they would just slack off the pressure to let the machine hammer loosely till the steel came unplugged. They were all good with this problem. Not once did they stick a steel or leave a steel plugged. They had the round drilled off in just less than two hours.

The three men finished drilling within minutes of each other. Stan looked at his watch when they shut off their machines. "Not bad," he said. Looking back, he could see the nipper had arrived with their powder and fuses, and was putting it down to the side of the drift a ways behind the mucking machine, and the shift boss was fast approaching.

"How're you doing, Garth," Stan greeted him, over his shoulder, still looking at the face.

"Boy, no flies on you guys, eh? Already drilled off."

"Yep....so far, so good."

Garth looked at the face. "Can't break much better than that, can you?"

"They're good. Always leave us good. Tricky ground to break, this limestone, but they're doing it right."

Garth just nodded and left them to it. Gus and Wilf were done gearing out now and packing the powder and fuses to the face. Stan immediately started loading the cut while Gus and Wilf went to work loading the rest of the round. Once the round was loaded and wired, Stan lit the Thermalite, yelling "FIRE", Gus opened the air header to blow smoke, and the three men climbed on the motor and rode out to safety. They had their lunch in the station, and having waited a good half hour for the smoke to clear from the blast, went back in. On the way back, they picked up the string of Hudsons from the layby and brought them up behind the mucker. Gus went first up to the face, pulling up the water hose, and washing down. The pressure was good, and he kept it on the muckpile first, then the back and walls, and then climbing up on the muck pile, he pulled up some slack, and started washing down the face. It was a clean break. He turned to Wilf and Stan and yelled, "Right to the balls, guys....she broke right to the nuts!"

"Of course," said Stan. Wilf had to laugh.

The mucking out cycle went off smoothly. The other drift crew was already drilling, so nobody was in their way. They were mucked out in good time. They parked the empty Hudsons in the layby, shot grade, marked up the face, set up the cross shift to drill, and were back to the station well before cage call.

The week just flew by for Wilf. They were paid on Friday on their way to their last afternoon shift. They'd made twenty one dollars per shift bonus, which was a little better than double their wage of $2.45 per hour. Stan and Gus were pleased, but as Stan put it, "We earned it; we did the work," to which Gus added drily...."Yes, but it's always nice to get paid for it". Wilf had to grin at that.

On that afternoon they came into a clean face again, and were drilled off without a hitch when Garth showed up, just as Gus and Wilf were tearing down the gear, and Stan was loading the cut. He greeted the three men cordially enough, but it was plain by his face that he had something on his mind.

"So what's up, Garth? You're looking kind of grim," said Stan, opening up the conversation.

Garth looked like he'd been caught naked in a food store. "Well, you guys might not like this, but the word is from upstairs that they're putting in a third shift starting next week." He let that sink in a little before he went on.

"And?"

"Well, the third shift will start graveyards Sunday night, so you boys, being dayshift next week will follow the new crew. We're pretty well done development on 700 now, so we gotta move some of these guys somewhere".

"And who would be in this 'new crew'"?

"There's an Arnold Atchez...."

"Don't know him."

"He's Nova Scotian...one of the boys from Springhill."

"A coal miner eh?"

"Well, he's worked driving scrans on 700."

"So we get one of the mud miners for a cross shift."

"And who else?" Stan continued.

"There's a Hank Loster...."

"I know Hank....know him from Red Lake. He's a good driftman......and who's the third?"

"Vince Jamieson...he'll be leading shift."

Gus, Wilf, and Stan looked at one another like they'd been shot.

"You know Vince?" Garth asked, a little timidly.

"Do I know him? He's a fucking idiot. If they had to put him somewhere why is he with us? They should put him breaking rocks on the grizzly with an eight pound sledge. That's what he'd be good for. He's no miner, and he never will be."

"Sorry Stan. He's got seniority. These orders come from the top. Vince bitched when Wilf got put with you two, but he was told he was already on development, so he had no case. Development's done on 700 now, so he could bump Wilf, but we've made a third shift instead. You'll have the same shift rotation, same days off as before...."

"Only now we follow Vince..."

"Well, maybe Hank will keep him straight."

"I doubt that. Vince Jamieson is a one man band."

"Wish I had better news, boys, but that's how it is. Well I better keep going". He turned and left.

Stan and Gus grumbled as they finished loading the round. Wilf worked in angry, sullen silence, his face set. With the loading done, Stan starting wiring up the round; Gus and Wilf went back and waited for him by the motor. Gus attempted to humour Wilf a little, opening up with, "Not your favourite guy, this Vince fella, eh?"

Wilf finally loosened up a little. The glare left his face. He even smiled grimly. "You can say that again," he said.

Stan was done wiring the round now, and lit the Thermalite, yelling, "FIRE"; Gus opened the air header to blow smoke, and the three of them got on the motor and headed for safety. They stopped and waited by the switch into the other drift crews heading to guard their blast. When the last of the shots went off, they continued on to the station for lunch, and waited for the smoke to clear from their heading. Nothing more was said about Vince Jamieson.

Gus broke the silence with, "Going dancing tomorrow, Wilf?"

"I'd best wait for the next long change."

Gus knew it wasn't just dancing on his mind. "You need to get yourself a car, Wilf."

"There's a thought, Gus. Don't even have a driver's licence at the moment."

"Any time you want to take your road test, you're welcome use to my car."

"Thanks, Gus....I'll get back to you sometime."

A driver's licence was not on the top of Wilf's mind at the moment either; it was Vince Jamieson. Gus knew that, and he was just trying to move him away from it. They'd finished their lunch now, and had given their heading good time to clear of smoke. Stan got into the cockpit of the motor, Wilf and Gus got on the back end of the motor, and the three men headed back in to muck out their round.

As they neared the layby to pick up their cars, Gus said to Wilf, "Don't let this Vince thing bug you too much, Wilf. We'll keep things going here, just like we always do." As Stan came to a stop, Gus hopped off the motor, threw the switch into the layby, and hooked the cars to the motor as Stan pulled up. Once Stan had pulled the cars back clear of the switch, Gus switched him back toward the face, and hopping onto the front bumper of the first car, rode it back to the mucking machine. 'For a big heavy man he sure can move', thought Wilf. Wilf forgot about Vince Jamieson for the moment, and got back into the magic of working with and being on the best crew he'd ever worked with.

Gus had shut off the screaming air header now, and had already wet down all the scattered muck from the mucking machine to the muck pile.

Wilf pulled him some more slack on his water hose, and Gus continued washing down the muckpile, the back, and finally right up to the face. He passed the hose to Wilf, saying, "She broke right to the nuts, partner"; then he jumped on the mucker.

Wilf continued to wash down the muck pile as Gus mucked the first car. Minutes later, the car was filled; Wilf dropped the hose, and jumped on the back end of the loaded car, as Stan pulled the train back to the California switch. Gus grabbed the scaling bar and started scaling; he had the back scaled of 'loose' by the time Stan returned with an empty car in front. Wilf stayed at the switch now.

Within minutes the second car was full. The three of them worked together like clockwork. Soon the eight cars were filled. While Stan and Wilf went to the waste pass to dump, Gus pushed his slide rails ahead into the muck pile, and then continued washing down the pile till Stan and Wilf returned with an empty string of cars.

They were mucked out in good time; thirty cars filled and part of the thirty-first car. They hung the grade chains, shot the grade, and marked up the face for the cross shift, also setting up the machines (jacklegs), and even filling their lubricators with rock drill oil.

"Well boys, good enough...let's get out of here", Stan said jumping back on the motor. Gus and Wilf hopped on end car, and they headed for the waste pass to dump, and then home. They sat on the bench at the station a little early, to wait for the cage. The two raisemen arrived shortly, followed by the other drift crew. It had been a perfect week....except for the news of the coming third shift. The cage was soon there to take them up.

Stan and Wilf got to the restaurant at about 12:35 am. As the restaurant closed at one, this gave them time to order something and get fed before it was time for bed. The big blonde girl Barbara was on, and took their order. To Wilf's disappointment he learned from her that Serena was off for the weekend and had already left for her mother's on the school bus, having finished her day shift. Stan could see Wilf's face drop."I'll have a cheese burger deluxe, no gravy," he managed.

"I'll have the same," said Stan, and then said to Wilf when she was gone with the order, "Maybe Gus got it right Wilf."

Wilf stared at him puzzled "About what?"

"Maybe you need a car."

Monday morning dayshift came, and Wilf, Stan, and Gus got off on their level. They were told at the wicket that Graveyard had just blasted, and had left them a muckpile. It struck them odd that they weren't coming into a clean face, unless Jamieson had not done a full cycle. (Drill off, blast and muck out). They got on the motor at the station, and started down the drift for their heading, already apprehensive something was not right. They dropped Gus off at the headers, where he shut of the air from blowing smoke, and got the water going on the muckpile. The air was still a little smoky.

Stan and Wilf left him to it, and went back to the layby with the motor to pick up the string of Hudsons. When they got back to Gus with the cars, he wasn't on the mucker yet. Usually he'd be waiting with a full bucket, ready to muck the first car. He was still washing down.

"You'd better come and have a look at this," he yelled.

Stan and Wilf squeezed past the train to catch up with Gus, and see what he wanted. "Not much of a muckpile is it?" he said, more as a statement than a question. He had the back and the face washed down, by this time. The round had obviously bootlegged by at least two feet. The center back hole and the two back holes to the right of center were looking up steeply, and the side holes on the right side were noticeably looking out.

There was an 8' steel stuck in the cut which had been blasted with the round; its straightness now become more S-shaped. The two backholes on the left side of the round were drilled nicely flat, and the side holes on the left side of the round were in perfect alignment with the drift.

"Looks like Hank Loster drills the left side," said Gus.

".....with Vince on center, and the coal miner on the right," Stan concluded. "What a fucking mess."

It came as no surprise to Wilf. It confirmed everything he knew about Vince Jamieson. Driving a scran drift in the soft ore body with a chipper was about the extent of Vince Jamieson's talent. "Same old Vince," was all he said, and then added," at least it won't take long to muck out."

Gus began filling the cars, and when the train was filled, Stan and Wilf headed to the waste pass to dump. Garth showed up just as Gus started mucking the second train.

Stan said to Garth, "Take a look at our new cross shift. They came into a clean face, and all they could do was drill and blast a round. They didn't even get it mucked out, and I doubt if they broke six feet. Doesn't take much to keep them busy."

Gus had managed to pull the stuck steel out of the face by hooking it to the mucker with a half inch chain, and backing up hard. When the slack jerked tight on the chain the blasted steel came out looking much like a hockey stick. Gus had left it to the side of the drift. He pointed it out to Garth as he approached. "Looks like Vince left us a calling card," he said. Garth eyed the steel and then the face. For a moment, his mouth formed a round "O". He climbed up on what remained of the muckpile taking a tape measure from his coat, pulled out three feet of tape and stuck it into a bootleg. It went in two and a half feet.

"That won't do," he said, and taking in the irregularity of the right side of the face at a glance, went on to comment, "pretty sloppy drilling, I'd say."

"Yup," agreed Gus, "looks like they shot those holes straight from the hip. We were doing fine till Jamieson showed up."

"Well looks like he doesn't have too much experience.....maybe he'll catch on."

"I don't think so," said Stan, "You can't tell him much; he already knows everything. I knew him in Red Lake. He couldn't even mine a stope. He's just a blowhard with a big mouth." (A stope in a gold mine is the area in the quartz vein between the levels where the ore is being mined.)

Garth left them to it. They mucked out and dumped the second train, and four cars into the third train they were mucked out. On a good break there would have been a good thirty cars; they had mucked only twenty. When Wilf and Stand parked the cars in the layby, and joined Gus at the face; Gus was washing out the bootlegs with a copper blowpipe attached to the end of a water hose. He'd marked two foot square in paint around the area of the frozen ground where the cut had been. "To be avoided," Gus said pointing it out to Stan to which he replied, "Yup."

Stan eyed the red square where he should have been able to drill his cut. "I guess we'll have to move it over to your side Wilf. I'll let you do the honours today." Wilf nodded. They shot grade and marked up the face. Wilf's side was already a foot in the bush due to bad alignment from the cross shift. They set up and started drilling. Wilf brought his holes to where the right side of the face was marked, a foot to the left of the cross shifts bootlegs. He started his cut well to the right of the frozen ground, and used the right side of his square as part of the right side of the round.

Gus had cleaned down to the lifters, washed out the bootlegs, and flagged the remnant holes with pieces of broken drill steel. He had this done before they started drilling. The center lifter and the two lifters on Wilf's side of the face had been looked down far too steeply; Wilf collared his over a foot higher, and looked them down only slightly. On the left side of the face, the lifters side hole and back hole had all been drilled with good alignment; however, because of the frozen ground around the cut, the left side had inevitably bootlegged as well.

In spite of the mess of a face, the three men found their rhythm, and the drilling went smoothly: Wilf drilling the cut helpers, the square (diamonds), and most of the right side of the round, with Stan and Gus slashing over to it. It was a different way of drilling a round from the convenience of drilling on the clean face, and having their cut in the middle, but they were good miners, adept at adjusting to most fuck ups, and still their getting it done with their usual efficiency.

They blasted their round in good time to make the cage. Stan could tell from the sound of the shots going off that it broke well; "Right to the nuts," as he liked to say. Gus wasn't saying much, it was the first time since he's been with Stan and Gus that he'd seen Gus in a bad mood. There wasn't much too to say. They all felt it.

Their drift contract was paid at $16.00 @ foot. An eight foot round, blasted with a perfect break, and then mucked out, would give them an eight foot advance, and pay them $128.00. Dividing that three ways would make forty two dollars and change each. Subtract their wage of $2.45 per hour for eight hours; it still left them with a good $22.00 per shift bonus. Usually their bonus came in at $21.00 to $22.00 per shift, better than doubling their wage.

Two and a half feet of bootleg @$16.00 per foot would cost them a loss of $40.00 off their contract, and this was only the first time. This, in all likelihood, would be a daily occurrence; not only did they have to work around a fucked up mess, they were losing money on it as well... so much for day one with the new cross shift. When cage came down to 1,100; Stan, Gus, and Wilf got on, tired, discouraged and filthy, to joined the other drift crew and the two raisemen for the ride up to surface.

The situation that had put Vince Jamieson on to their shift was that the development of the scran drifts on the 700' level was complete. 700 was in full production now; the development of the hanging wall and footwall drifts, the cross cuts through the ore body, and the development of all the scran drifts, was all complete now. Those who had been on the development went on development on 900 or 1,100, wherever there was a spot. There weren't enough development headings available for all of them to go to, so many of them remained as production miners on the 700' level, operating the big 125 horse power slushers in the scran drifts. Vince had enough seniority to get a development heading.

The floors of these scrans were covered with a good thickness of cement. The walls and backs of the scrans were coated with solid rebarred cement to several inches in thickness, to withstand the pressure that would come when the ore body began to cave, as the slushermen started raking the scrans with the big scrapers, pulling the iron ore into the waiting trains below in the crosscuts, as it poured into the scrans from the boxholes..

There were two trains hauling from the scrans; each had a motorman operating the big Mancha Mule (as the motor was called), and each motor man had a switchman. If one train was dumping, the other train would wait in the cross cut till the hanging wall drift was clear to go. To look at an engineer's map of the level, it looked much like a small underground city. The main drifts were all lit up; no expense had been spared on the development of the 700' level. All the scrans were set up with two way radios, which were wired in to connect to a dispatcher's radio. The dispatcher could coordinate the traffic of the motor crews, so not to jam the hanging wall drift, and let them know which scrans were ready with muck. The footwall drift was used as a supply drift, so not to interfere with moving the muck. With iron ore at a premium price of $23.00 a ton, this was all affordable. Steep Rock was making money.

One day far in the future, when the 700' level had been picked clean, they had only to go down to the next level and do it all over again; and there was another open pit being mined (the Hogarth), and another shaft being sunk, to drift under that pit when it got too deep, and undermine that one. Steep Rock was a huge mine with work estimated for a hundred years.

Wilf had never seen a bizarre setup like this anywhere in all his fourteen years as an underground miner; he'd always worked in 'hard ground' where everything had to be drilled and blasted - not caved into a scran drift and then raked out with a slusher. But he wasn't going to look a gift horse in the mouth, the money was too good, Stan and Gus were the best partners he could wish for, he was off the booze, and he was in love with Serena, the loveliest friend he'd ever met. Too bad about Vince Jamieson, but with all things considered, Wilf thought he'd best put up with him.

On the morning of Wilf's last day shift, Bill Briggs, the underground superintendant was making his rounds through the mine. Lately, Bill would spend the morning touring and inspecting the mine with its various headings. Then spend his afternoons upstairs in the office in staff meetings. This morning found him on the 700' level, very pleased the way the muck was pouring from the scrans, into the waiting trains, and into the ore pass. Sometimes the muck came so fast that the crusher couldn't keep up; the ore pass would be full, and a train would have to wait by the ore pass until there was room to dump. Nobody minded that, especially Bill. That meant production was at 100% capacity.

This particular morning Bill came by the ore pass to find a train waiting to dump; the motorman and the switchman were having lunch, at ease, sitting on the motor. "Got nothing better to do than eat?" he greeted them.

"Nope," came back the reply from the motorman; and then having finished his sandwich, took out his cigarettes, and offered one to Bill. Bill thanked him, but declined the offer, saying he was trying to quit. The trammers both lit up, as Bill eyed the full ore pass, and commented, "I guess when you're marching you're not fighting."

"What do you mean, Bill?"

"Oh, just something Napoleon said".

"Who's Napoleon?"

"Just some Frenchman."

Just as he said that, the muck started going down in the ore pass. "I better let you boys get dumping," he said, and he went on, and left them. The trammers dumped, and Bill went on to visit the 1,100' level. It was a little past ten that morning when he found Stan's drift crew laying track and grumbling loudly.

"How's business?" he greeted them.

"Not worth a shit."

Looking things over, Bill could see that the slides were run right out, and did not even come close to the muck pile. Gus didn't even have enough slide rails to clean up the drift. He had it cleaned up to six feet from the muck pile and then he'd come to the end of slides.

"They've jumped the track," said Gus. "They should have put in track and they didn't even leave a note to say we needed track and pipe. We had to go back out to the station, and get the rails....and pipe. They must have stretched their hoses to get drilled off."

"Well, how'd they get mucked out that short of track?"

"They used a couple of eight foot scaling bars run off the end of the slides." Gus pointed to two eight foot steel scaling bars lying in the drift. "They didn't even bother hiding them," he went on.

"And take a look at that face, Bill," said Stan, "look what we'll be drilling on. They've bootlegged over two feet again. We get this every time."

Bill climbed up on the muckpile to check out the face. He took out his tape measure, and pulling out a good three feet, stuck it the bootleg of the center back hole. It measured thirty one inches. He shook his head coming back down the pile. By this time Stan, Gus and Wilf had stood the rail, spiked in the slides, and were ready to start mucking.

"This is not good boys. I'll be writing them up for jumping the track and pipe. I know you guys are breaking your rounds. Having to follow a mess like this is not only difficult to work around, but could be dangerous."

"Any chance of getting them taken out?"

"Sorry Stan. It's out of my hands. The line up of the crews comes from top management."

"Well one good thing about it though... it sure doesn't take long to get mucked out. We only get about twenty cars from a round like this. Used to get thirty on a good break."

"I'll let you boys get mucking," he said, and started back down the drift. Gus resumed mucking out.

With the track and pipe in, the round mucked out they had the face cleaned up now, and were set up to drill. They didn't bother going to station for lunch; they just had a sandwich sitting down by the side of the drift. Gus opened up with, "Well, so much for going to Briggs."

"No," said Stan. "That didn't go anywhere."

"Jamieson must've caught somebody up there fucking a sheep. He sure doesn't make it on talent," Gus came back. Gus, done with his sandwich, took on a fresh wad of snoose, and got to his feet. "Well, might as well do something once." Stan and Wilf got up and joined him at the face.

As usual the cut had to be moved; this time Gus agreed to do the honours. Stan and Wilf would slash into his square on the left side of the face. They went to work and got it done and, not any too soon. Having had to go back for the track and pipe, put it in, and then working through Jamieson's tangled mess of a bootlegged round , it had put them behind schedule. They just finished in time to make the cage, but they knew by the sound of their shots going off, that they'd broken a good round.

Joe Kilgannon greeted them as they got to the station. "Working overtime?" he razzed them. "Yeah....we're doing Jamieson's work and our own. Who'd they put in your place for a third?"

"Oh, we got real lucky. They put in three good men for our cross shift who've never missed a round, they're always breaking them right out to the nuts, and they always leave us good."

"We got Jamieson."

"Ouch."

The cage came and took them up; and so ended their first week with Jamieson.

A Miner's Story – Chapter 10

Being that Wilf's next scheduled shift would be Graveyards, beginning Sunday at midnight, it didn't work well for a weekend in Sapawe with Serena. On starting his second graveyard shift, still following Vince, who'd just finish his first afternoon shift, Wilf was waiting with Stan and Gus in the shaft house, for the cage to return the afternoon shift to surface, and take graveyard shift to 1,100 to do their shift. The cage came to surface with their cross shift; as they filed off the cage passed Wilf and his crew, Vince walked right passed Wilf with his eyes averted, and not saying a word....not his usual obnoxious self at all. Wilf smiled at this. Once down to the level, he commented on that to Stan and Gus.

"Looks like Jamieson got an earful," he said, "notice he's not saying much."

"Yes, he got told," said Stan, "Briggs wrote him up, and he was given a written reprimand. We'll soon see if it did any good."

It didn't. There had been note in the book from afternoon shift that they'd mucked out, leaving graveyard a clean face, but that they didn't have time to dump their last train of muck. They didn't find the train at the waste pass, so they started walking in, and found the train with the motor derailed at the switch going into Kilgannon's heading. Joe Kilgannon, Dave Chambers and Ivan Gagnon were working on getting the big motor back on the tracks.

"We've got a muck pile, explained Joe, "and we've got to get mucking." He couldn't of course, until they got this train out of their way.

"That's our fucking Jamieson for you. The note left in the book said, 'unable to dump due to shortage of time'," Stan said. He felt like going home in disgust, but he wasn't going to leave the mess for Joe and his crew, and the shift that followed. Before long they had the motor back on the track and going. Stan apologized to Joe for their delay, but Joe just slapped him on the back, saying, "All in a night's fun, Stan."

The rest of the shift went all right. They were able now to dump the train and get the empties into their layby out of Joe's way. There was the usual amount of bootleg on the face, but it was becoming just a routine now; they just worked around the problem, and broke a good round. At least there was enough track and pipe in. They mucked out, set up for day shift, and made the cage call in good time. Joe and his crew were already in the station when they pulled in, and the two raisemen showed up soon behind them.

"Quite the cross shift you've got," commented Joe.

"I'll be glad when I'm rich," said Gus. The cage came and took them up.

One morning about halfway through his week, the thought came to Wilf that maybe Serena could be persuaded to drop by his room at Cross' Rooms, and visit him. Cross' Rooms were at the end of the block, and adjacent to Iron City Cleaners, the local dry cleaner. Serena had her room in town at Burk's Rooming House, which was a flat roofed two storey structure like Cross' and was located on the other side of the dry cleaners. He came straight to the restaurant that Wednesday morning, fresh from his mid week Graveyard shift, and found to his delight, that Serena was dayshift for the week. As she brought him his coffee to the counter, he quietly suggested an offer of dinner, and perhaps a movie afterwards.

"Sure", she agreed, smiling, "that would be fun." She continued making her rounds with the coffee pot, and Wilf took his coffee over to the booth behind him, to join Stan, who'd just arrived.

"Well, I see you're all smiles this morning," Stan began.

"Well, it's a beautiful day out there...."

"Right"

Serena was right by to take their order. Stan was about to speak, but noticed that Serena and Wilf had locked eyes, as she stood by their booth, the pad in her hand. Wilf ordered his usual ham and eggs, with home fries and brown toast. She wrote it down, and finally turned to Stan. "I'll have the same," he said. Stan waited till she left and then commented quietly, "You look like a guy in rut." Wilf blushed, looking carefully around to see if anybody noticed. Stan chuckled quietly, as he lit a cigarette. Wilf ignored his mirth. The food came, and they ate in silence.

Done with breakfast, Wilf went to his room and slept for a few hours. Upon awakening he decided it was a still a little early in the day....he and Serena had agreed to meet at the Steep Rock Hotel lobby at six o'clock; it was only one thirty. He decided it was a nice day; a good time to go for a run to Little Falls and back. He was really in good shape for it now. He would time himself, and try to beat his left effort. Sometimes he would do that. Today was a good one. He was back in just over a half hour by two minutes, soaked in sweat. He went upstairs to his room and stripped, and then down the hall for a bath.

He shaved for the second time that day, as the tub was filling. The whiskers came off so easily, being so warm and sweated. The tub was full now and he eased himself into the hot water. He liked a shower for the efficiency and convenience, and always showered at the end of the shift in the mine dry, but this was better for his date. That shower didn't get rid of that red iron ore dust like a good bath. He didn't need a shave that badly either, but just to make sure.....

At six o'clock he was at the Steep Rock hotel lobby. Serena showed up right on time, looking great, and he told her so. "You clean up pretty good yourself," she came back, giving him a hug, and the two of them went into the Walnut Room to dine together. 'The Walnut Room', as it was called, was the dining room of the hotel. It was a nice place to go to. The hotel itself, was fairly new, having been only been built a couple of years previously. The Walnut Room came off to the right of the lobby, and overlooked O'Brien Street. It had a nice decor, accented by a walnut stained finish, which gave it its name. Its windows faced the East, so the evening sun did not shine directly into the room, giving it a nice shaded effect, and an elevated view of the street.

The dining room was only about half full, when they arrived, so the hostess was able to offer them some choice as to where they might want to sit. Wilf and Serena were agreed on a small table on the far side of the room near the window. Once seated, the hostess asked them what they might care to drink. They both spoke for a coffee. The hostess handed them each a menu, and sent a waitress over with some coffee. "Cream and sugar?" she asked. They both said black.

There was fresh Pickerel on the menu, and they both decided on that. The waitress took their order when she returned with their coffee, and left them to themselves.

"You like Pickerel?" Serena asked.

"It's my favourite of any fish. My brother Patrick and I used to go fishing Pickerel together. We had a dog named Buster, and that was one smart dog. If I went to the barn for my rifle, he'd bring me my hunting bag, but if we were going fishing, he'd stare at my fishing rod. Couldn't fool old Buster. Great dog."

She smiled at this. "You never mentioned your brother Patrick...."

"No... Patrick's gone now. We lost him in France during the war."

"I'm sorry. I guess you miss him a lot."

"Sure do...." She could see he was getting a little choked, and mercifully, the waitress arrived with their order.

They thanked the waitress, and Serena moved to a better topic. "I could take you fishing Pickerel," she said. "Come visit me at Mom's your next long change, and I can take you to a good spot right on the lake. We still have Dad's boat, and we keep his motor and all the fishing gear locked up in that little shed behind Mom's cabin."

"I'd love to go fishing with you, Serena. Matter of fact we're coming to our long change pretty quick. I've got two more graveyards to go, and we're there."

"Great. I'll ask for this Saturday off, and we can go in on the school bus on Friday afternoon."

"You know," he said squeezing some lemon onto his Pickerel fillet, "you're my first date in a long, long time."

"Been a good while for me too," she said, "what kept you waiting?"

"A lot of foolishness....used to drink a lot."

"I've never seen you drunk."

"I hope you never do. I've got better things to do now."

She smiled it this. "I'm glad, Wilf."

They finished off a lovely Pickerel dinner with some ice cream and another coffee, and agreed to take in a movie. The movie playing at the theater was entitled, "From Here to Eternity". They took in the earlier show at seven. It was a great cast. Burt Lancaster, Deborah Kerr, Montgomery Clift, Ernest Borgnine and Frank Sinatra were among them. It was done in black and white, which seemed to enhance the mood of the film; it was about the time coming up to Pearl harbour and the subsequent Japanese attack, which precipitated the American entry into World War II.

After the movie he walked her to her place, which was only two doors down from his own, and right across the street from the theater. They paused for a moment in front of her entrance, when he quietly asked her, "Would you care to see my place?"

Serena was reticent. "Let's wait for the weekend," she came back, and gave him a hug. "Thanks for a lovely evening," and seeing him blush said with a little grin, "It never does hurts to ask." She kissed him lightly, and went in. He went to his room, a little more embarrassed that he'd asked than he was disappointed with her answer. Then he thought about it; "No, it never hurts to ask," and he smiled at the thought. He would be seeing her for the weekend. Much better like that.

The next two shifts just flew by for Wilf. He went to work that night and to the amazement of Gus, Stan and himself, they came into a clean face. The jacklegs set up and good to go, grade was shot and the face marked up. AND.....there wasn't an inch of boot leg!!! The back holes had been drilled nice and flat and the side holes straight with the drift. They were all agape.

Stan was able to put his cut in the middle. "Just like old times" Gus commented. They were drilled off in no time. Gus and Wilf were just pulling the gear back, and Stan had started to load the round, when Garth showed up.

"You boys are making good time tonight," Garth began.

"Well, we just can't believe it. Jamieson must've turned a new leaf. Just look at that face. Broke right to the nuts," said Gus

"Well actually Vince was away. He sprained his ankle badly, and won't be back the rest of the week," replied Garth.

"Well, I guess that explains it. Who was in his place?" asked Stan.

"They put Hank Loster leading and brought in Al Wasney for a third."

"I know Al. He's a good driftman," said Stan. "Looks like Hank got that Atchez lining up his back holes and side holes properly. I hope Vince stays gone. This is how it should be. Hank should be leading shift."

Garth plainly saw the difference, but was reluctant to step into that conversation. He looked at his watch, and said, "Well, Vince has seniority, so what can you do? Carry on guys. Vince should be back by next week."

"Ouch."

That shift and the next one went by like a dream, and then Wilf was off for his long change, all done with graveyards. Gus asked had him as they were stepping out of the cage, if he might make it to the 'Hoot 'n Holler Hall' come Saturday night, but Wilf was vague. "I'm not sure what I'm doing...have to wait and see," he said.

"Maybe you might have something better to do," Gus came back, smiling.

"Well, anyway I got a ride to Sapawe this afternoon."

"Just play it by ear, Wilf. If I see you, I see you. Me and Molly will be glad to see you if you make it."

Wilf got to town and was having Friday morning breakfast with Stan in Sinclair's Restaurant, and with Serena serving. He was in a great mood. Serena got the weekend off; she would be done at three o'clock and the two of them would take the school bus to Sapawe. They could board the bus from where it was parked, in the next block to where they lived. It was getting late September now, but they were into a beautiful Indian summer. The days were getting shorter, but still sunny and warm.

"Catch you later," he said to her at the till.

"I'll see you on the bus," she confirmed.

Stan caught their drift, but made no comment. He paid his bill and followed Wilf to the rooming house. They went to their separate rooms, and got some sleep. By two o'clock Wilf was wide awake; he was not a great sleeper on graveyards. He would usually get about four or five hours, and he'd get by on that. Today it was four hours and he was up and going, feeling fine, anticipating a good weekend with Serena. He looked at his watch; it was two.

He got up and pulled his pants on, and went to the bathroom to wash up and shave, then finished getting dressed. Putting his shaving kit, toothbrush, a change of clothes, and his dancing shoes into his knapsack, he brought it along with him as he left for the restaurant to have coffee. Serena was still there. It was two thirty; she would be off at three. He had his coffee at the counter. At three she told him she was going home to change and clean up; that the bus would be leaving at three thirty. She poured him another coffee just before she left.

"I'll see you on the bus," he said.

He drank his coffee, picked up his knapsack, paid his bill, and went straight to the bus. Serena was already there. "I got us a couple of steaks from the restaurant," she said, "thanks to Bill Harrison. I told him you were coming to Mom's for dinner. Bill likes you."

"That's great, Serena, but what's your mom going to eat?"

"These are two nice, big T-bones. Mom and I will be doing good to finish one between us. Don't worry; we'll be fine."

They got on the bus. Serena knew the driver who said 'Hi' as they got on. "Carl", she said, "this is my friend Wilf." Wilf shook his hand. Because it was a school bus there was no fare to pay. They took a seat near the back. Carl pulled out of the lot, and headed for the high school to pick up the students and return them to Sapawe.

It was still sunny and warm when the bus pulled up and parked at the General Store in Sapawe a little before five. When they got to the cabin, they found Rachel doing some bead work on pair of moccasin slippers she'd made from a deerskin that Toivo had given her. She greeted them both with a hug. "So nice to see you again, Wilf," she said."Nice to see you, too, Mom." He realized he'd just called her 'Mom', without thinking. She smiled at this, and Serena caught Wilf blushing, and grinned.

"What's for supper, Mom?"

It was Rachel's turn to blush. "Oh, I'm so sorry...you got my completely by surprise...."

"No problems, Mom....I've got a couple of nice T-bone steaks from the restaurant," Serena said as she pulled the package out of her bag.

Rachel looked horrified for a moment. "Serena....you didn't just take them, did you?"

"Of course not, Mom.....they're a gift from Bill Harrison."

As Serena opened the package on the counter, Rachel beheld two thick T-bones, a good pound or more each. "Oh Serena, those are lovely. I've got some nice new potatoes and fresh carrots from Helen's garden," she said.

"Well we're good then, Mom. ......why don't you just relax, Mom? I can make supper. Wilf you having a coffee? Tea?"

"Well maybe a tea, if that's no bother," he said.

"No...no bother. Mom...how 'bout you? Tea?"

"That would be fine, Serena," she said. There was hot water ready in the kettle. Serena poured the tea pot full, and added two tea bags. She put the pot on the coffee table for them, along with two mugs. "We use Salada tea....Mom's favourite," she explained as she set it down, "and she likes it strong if you're good with that.

"I am," Wilf said, "I like it strong."

"Milk or sugar?"

"No thanks....I like it straight."

"So does Mom," she said, and left them to returned to the kitchen to cook supper.

Rachel sat in her rocker, and continued with her beadwork while the tea steeped and Wilf relaxed on the couch. "That's a fine pair of slippers you're making," he commented.

"Oh thank you," she acknowledged, "these are for Toivo, but it's a surprise", she confided. Wilf nodded in solemn understanding. "Yes," she continued, "He's a great hunter. He brought me a lovely skin he'd shaved and tanned himself from a deer he got last fall. I'd like to give him something back," she explained. She was working on the top part of the front of the slippers; one was done, the other one on which she was working was almost done. The one completed showed the figure of a hunter pointing a rifle at a deer; it was an amazing piece of mosaic for such a small area. Rachel used tiny black beads to show the figures of the hunter and the deer, and white beads a little bit larger to fill in the background. The outside of the scene was bordered in a double row of red beads, bringing a striking definition to her art.

"You do beautiful work, Rachel," he said as he poured the two mugs full of the tea, now nicely steeped, "Toivo's going to like those."

Rachel smiled. "Thank you Wilf", she said modestly, "I learned these things from my mother."

When Rachel and Wilf had drunk their tea, Serena announced that dinner was ready, and they joined her at the table. Serena had put out large bowls of new potatoes, fresh carrots and a bowl of gravy she had made from the steaks. Serena knew how Wilf liked his steak, (medium rare), and she had it done exactly right. She'd split her steak with Rachel, giving her the tenderloin, plus a little more. Wilf could see by the cut it was a medium rare as well.

"Mom and I both like it red and juicy the way you do," she explained.

"I don't like things cooked too hard," Rachel confirmed.

Serena had cooked lots of potatoes and carrots. Wilf helped himself to a good amount of both, and poured some of the rich gravy over his potatoes. He hadn't eaten since breakfast and he had an appetite. They were all hungry, and ate quietly, totally into their food. It was a simple meal, but a very good one. When they were all done with dinner, Serena rose from the table, and began to gather up the dishes. Rachel got up to help, but Wilf interrupted her. "You go and relax, Rachel; I'll help Serena clean up here." Rachel protested, but Wilf took her gently by the shoulders, and steered her toward her rocker. She accepted the hint, and having seated herself again in her favourite chair, resumed the work on Toivo's slippers. Serena rewarded Wilf's good intentions with peck on his cheek; he beamed with pleasure from her gesture, and got to work with Serena on the cleanup and dishes. Serena washed and Wilf dried.

Over dishes, they discussed that it would be a good evening for a nice walk when they were done; it would do them well, after such a big meal. They could drop by Helen and Toivo's, which was near the lake on the far side of the village and say 'hello' for a minute. When they were all done with the dishes, they found Rachel was fast asleep in her rocker, her mouth agape and the last slipper lying on her lap; the needle was hanging by a thread from her work. They decided to let her rest, and make the visit without her.

Stepping outside they found it a little cooler now, but still warm. The days were shorter now, being just passed equinox, but it was still good daylight at six thirty, and the black flies and mosquitoes were done for the year. It felt good to be out and moving in the cool of a nice evening. Wilf felt moved to speak of Rachel's talent.

"Your Mom's sure making a beautiful pair of slippers for Toivo," he began.

"Yes, that's a craft passed on for generations by my mother's people. My mother's pure Ojibwa. It was her first language. She didn't speak any English till she was placed in the residential school."

"Did you learn her language?"

"No. I wish I had, now. Dad spoke Swedish and English, so we always spoke English at home. Mom married a white man because she was determined that no children of hers would ever be put in a residential school."

When they arrived at Toivo and Helen's, they found Toivo feeding his mink, which he kept in stilted chicken wire pens a good forty feet back from the house. He had a full acre of land, which came right to the edge of the lake. He'd built his log house a ways back from the lake, where it was shaded amongst some lovely pine trees. Like Rachel's place there was no lawn, but the yard was neat, and Helen maintained a few nice flowers along the front of the house. They kept their garden closer to the lake, where it was open to good sunshine. On the shoreline they had a dock, which extended out a good fifty feet from the shore. The 2"x10" planking was spaced an inch apart, and nailed cross ways to two stout stringers of peeled spruce logs, which came to rest at the far end upon a crib set sunk to the lake bottom with rocks, and rose about three feet above the surface of the water. There was a 16' cedar strip boat tied to it, with a 10 horse Evinrude outboard motor affixed to its stern.

Near the shore, a little ways past the dock, Toivo had built an ice house. It was 12' by 16' in area. He had it filled with ice which he cut from lake when it was frozen to a thickness of 20". He would cut it in chunks about 2' square with his chain saw. The slide which started from the front ice house came down to the lake. When the ice on the lake was frozen in the winter to the thickness that he wanted, Toivo would cut a hole in the ice near the slide, and cut the 2'x2' chunks of ice with his chain saw, lift them out of the lake with a set of tongs, and set them on a sleigh fashioned with steel runners.

He had a six inch pulley hanging above and a little back from the front opening of the icehouse, with a stout rope running through the pulley. His horse (who he called Barney) would pull his load of ice up into the ice house. The house was filled from wall to wall with the chunks of ice, evenly placed. The floor had been covered first with a good four inches of sawdust; then the first layer of ice. On top of the first layer he would place a cover of another good few inches of sawdust and then the second layer of ice. The second layer of ice he would cover with more sawdust as well. Set up in this way, the ice never melted.

The walls were of shiplap; the roof was peeked at a 45 degree angle. There were no windows but there was an open space from the top of the walls to the overhanging eves, so it was well ventilated and shaded.

He didn't have a deep freeze, but anything he wanted kept fresh or frozen he'd take to the ice house, pull back the sawdust, and lay whatever item it might be next to the ice, then bury it with sawdust. Although he had running water in his house, and people in Sapawe would drink it with no adverse effects, Toivo preferred to take his drinking water from the ice house. The lake water, once frozen, was totally clean. Any bloom or bugs normally found in the lake water would not be found in the ice, once frozen. The freezing expelled any impurities. When he wanted drinking water, he would take a heavy ice chisel and cut a good chunk from a block in the icehouse, hold it with his tongs under his garden hose to rinse off the sawdust, and then place the chunk in a clean galvanized pail. The pail he would place on the kitchen floor in the corner near the fridge, and he would take his drinking water from the pail, as it melted. The water would always be cool and fresh, and the ice would last a long time.

Toivo greeted them both warmly as they approached. "Hi Vilf," he said, "ve shake hands later, maybe," he went on, by way of apology for the mess on his hands. "For sure, Toivo," Wilf came back. Serena gave Toivo a friendly pat on the back. Helen and Madeleine came out of the house to join them.

"You people want a coffee?" she asked.

"No hurry for that," Serena said, "but what do you think, Wilf?

"Sure....whenever..."

"I'll put some on," Helen said, and went back into the house.

Wilf was watching with great interest as Toivo dished out the food to the mink from an enamel hand basin now about half full with raw ground meat. There were four or five mink in each pen. Toivo would pull back an opening in the screen on the top of the pen, and scooping a good amount from the bowl with a large mixing spoon, he would shake it off the spoon into the pen. The mink would dart like lightning to their meal, their beady little eyes transfixed in carnal appetite. Toivo would be quick to close the hatch again.

"What are you feeding them, Toivo?" Wilf asked.

"Today, porcupine," Toivo answered. "I shoot two porcupines today, when I work in the bush. Vatch this Vilf."

His bowl was empty now, but there was the second dead porcupine lying on the ground near a burning barrel. He splashed some gasoline into the barrel and when the fire came up strong, he held the porcupine over the fire with a pitchfork until the quills and fur were scorched away, leaving only the singed carcass.

He had a huge meat grinder bolted to the top of a large stump about chest high; in front of and just below the spout of the meat grinder was a small stand. He placed his now emptied bowl on the stand, and with the pitchfork, dumped the carcass of the porcupine whole into the meat grinder. Using both hands, he turned the handle of the meat grinder, grinding up the porcupine, bones, guts, hide, and all into burger for the mink. The bowl was almost full again, and Toivo finished dishing out supper to the mink. Wilf was quite impressed with Toivo's setup.

"They eat everything," said Toivo.

"I know," said Wilf, "my brother Patrick and I used to keep some mink back on the farm when I was growing up."

"You have brother?"

"Not any more....we lost Patrick during the war."

Toivo rinsed off the bowl with the hose. "I'm sorry, Vilf. Var is very bad. You have any more brothers?"

"There is one still on the farm. Clarence. I can't stand the guy. Mom and dad are both gone now, so I haven't been back there in years. I've got a good sister, Denise. She still lives back there in the country. She's married to a Frenchman, and they've got their own farm. Good guy, that Frenchman."

"My family all in Finland," said Toivo..."like to see them, one day."

Serena sensed Wilf he was getting a little choked as he mentioned his sister. Toivo laid the empty bowl upside down to cover the meat grinder and covered them both over with a tarp. As if to ease the tension, he said, "Come on, now...ve go in for some coffee." They all agreed that was a good idea.

Serena and Wilf spent a good hour with Toivo, Helen and Madeleine over coffee. Toivo relaxed with a few beers, and Madeleine played with her cat. Serena got around to mentioning that she and Wilf would be going fishing in the morning, and might like to drop by on the way to get some minnows.

"No 'roblem (problem)," said Toivo, "you know where ve keep it minnows." He kept a tank for minnows set into the lake, just back of the dock. He would put out a trap for them in a small creek that came into the lake a little farther up the shore from his place, and always kept a good stock of them in his tank, for fresh bait. He would sell them for six bits a dozen for anyone who came looking, but for Serena they would be free.

"Anybody wants to join us?" asked Serena.

"Thanks," replied Helen. "But tomorrow we're going into town; we gotta get some shopping done, and we promised Madeleine she could go to the movie of 'Treasure Island' for the Saturday matinee. I might even join her. Maybe see you when we get back. Bring us over some fish, if you get lucky, and we'll cook some up."

"Well, we'll see how it goes. Never can tell. We might get skunked!"

"Well, drop over anyways, and bring Mom; if there's nothing else, we can pull some moose meat out of the ice house."

"Well OK then; we'll see what we can do about that. Anyways, Wilf, we better catch up to Mom, and see what she's doing." Wilf got up, and they thanked the family for their coffee and company, and started for Rachel's cabin. It was dark now but the main road had street lamps. Once back they found Rachel had already gone to bed. So Serena and Wilf decided to make it an early night and do the same. They made love and were soon asleep.

Rachel was already up when they awoke and they could smell the coffee. Wilf got up and got dressed first, feeling a keen urgency to relieve him. He greeted Rachel as he emerged from the bedroom and she poured him a coffee which he accepted with thanks, but immediately put it down on the table, saying, "Excuse me Rachel; I'll be right back". She nodded and smiled in quiet understanding, as he bolted out the cabin door for the outhouse had just as Serena entered the kitchen in her house coat.

Wilf came back to find Rachel and Serena seated at the table, each with coffee and bowl of porridge in front of them. There was a bowl of porridge put out for Wilf beside his coffee as well, so he pulled up a chair and joined them.

"Looks like you will have a good day for fishing," commented Rachel, looking towards the window. It was just past 6:30 am, but because of the lateness of the season, it was just nicely breaking day. There was a mist over the lake due to the morning coolness, but there was not a cloud in the sky; the sun was already beginning to show itself; very soon that mist would burn off. The leaves were already beginning to turn to their autumn colours now in shades of orange, yellow and red, and the rising sun shining on them made them look even more beautiful.

"I made you a lunch," Rachel said.

"Oh, what'd you make us, Mom?"

"I had some bannock. I cut you some thick slices from that. They're buttered and wrapped in waxed paper. I put them in that paper bag on the counter, with a couple of apples. There should be lots of coffee left in the pot to fill your thermos." (She always made coffee in a large enamel Dixie percolator, and she always made lots.)

"Thanks Mom," Serena said, getting up. She poured them all another coffee and filled the thermos. There was still some coffee left in the pot so she put it back on the stove then rejoined them at the table. "Maybe we should let Wilf try a piece of your bannock now, Mom."

Rachel nodded and brought her loaf of bannock on a cutting board with a bread knife to the table. She cut three slices from the loaf, very neatly, and a good half an inch thick.

Serena took a slice and while buttering it she continued "Help yourself Wilf. It goes great with just butter."

Wilf had had bannock before but done by the camp fire method - wrapped around the end of a stick and cooked over a fire or eaten from slabs cooked on a frying pan. Rachel's bannock was much different. Rachel put her dough in a 12"x18" pan and baked it in the oven. It came out a good 3" thick, the full size of the pan. Wilf took a slice and buttered it, and took a mouthful. It was like heavy unleavened bread, of a very fine texture, very dense, but still soft in his mouth. It was plainly delicious. He ate the whole slice without a word. After he had eaten it all he turned to Rachel, who'd been watching him devour her bannock with a very pleased interest. "Rachel," he said, wiping his mouth, "that's the best bannock I ever ate!"

Rachel modestly thanked him for his compliment. "Have some more," she said.

"Well maybe I'll split one with Serena."

"You go ahead on it," Serena said, as pleased as her Mom with Wilf's enthusiasm for the bannock. He did take the remaining slice, and promptly ate it, well buttered. Rachel offered to cut some more, but Wilf raised a hand in protest. "No thanks, Rachel. I'm full. That was great. Thank you."

Serena poured them the last of the coffee, and said, "Well, I guess I better get dressed to go fishing," and left them to their coffee. She emerged shortly after from her bedroom ready to go, drained the last of her coffee, and put the thermos and their lunch into a wicker picnic basket. She took the basket, and a water jug from the counter, and said, "OK, Wilf, let's go fishing." Wilf followed her out the door, giving Rachel a courteous wave as they left. Rachel waved back, wishing them luck.

The sun has risen and they could already feel the warmth of it coming on. The mist was gone from the lake, and they could feel a slight breeze with a gentle freshness to it, as they came around to the shed in back of the cabin to pick up the motor, the gas and fishing gear. It was going to be a nice day.

Serena unlocked the shed. Inside was a five gallon gas can about half full of mixed gas, (more than they would need), and a four and a half horse power Champion motor. Wilf took the motor on his right shoulder and took the gas can in his left hand, and stepped back to let Serena get at the fishing gear. She put the gas funnel in the dip net, and moved the rods, tackle box, an axe, a gaff hook, paddle and minnow pail outside the door, before closing it, and locking it. Between them they were able to make it to the boat in one trip, with all their gear.

The boat was a homemade job about fourteen feet long, a little weathered, but still usable. It was upside down and only five or six feet from the water's edge. Without a word being spoken, Wilf went to one side of the boat, and tipped it on edge, and Serena went to the other side to ease it down onto its bottom. The two of them slid the boat into the lake. There was a set of oars which had been lying under the boat. Wilf put them into the boat, placing the oar pins into the oar locks, then went back for the motor and clamped it onto the stern, while Serena placed the paddle and the rods into the boat. When everything else was in the boat, Wilf asked Serena, "Are you the skipper?"

"I am," she said, and waited in the back end of the boat while Wilf pushed off. As the boat went adrift, he jumped in the bow. Serena attempted to start the motor while Wilf paddled them into deeper water. Placing the knot at the end of her starting cord into the slot on the plate above the flywheel, she wrapped the cord around, and around the groove of the plate, and then pulled hard. Nothing happened. She opened the choke and tried again. It sputtered, and then died. She tried once more; this time it fired and then died. Wilf was coming toward her to see if he could help, but she told him, "It's OK. It just hasn't been used in over a year; it'll start." She gave it one more pull; this time it started and kept running. She closed off the choke, once the motor was running smoothly. There was no reverse on the old Champion so she just spun it around backwards, until they were a good distance from shore; then turned it back to the front, and opened it up.

Before crossing the lake, she headed for Toivo's dock to get some minnows. The family at the house were up but not gone to town yet as Toivo's pickup was still in the driveway. Serena saw Helen wave from the window, and waved back, but didn't go up to the house; she stayed focused on her agenda. She filled the minnow pail with water from the lake, and with the sieve-like net that lay beside the tank, scooped a good two dozen of the minnows from the tank into their pail; then Wilf and Serena climbed back into the boat. This time Serena got it started on the first pull, and aimed the boat for the other side of the lake.

Across the lake Wilf could see they were approaching a small island. As they neared the island, she cut their speed down to half throttle, and brought the boat around the island, then killed the motor, letting the boat drift in the middle of the channel between the island and the far shore of the lake.

"You can drop the anchor here Wilf. I've always had good luck right in the middle of this channel. We'll give it a try."

The 'anchor' was an old galvanized pail, about ¾ full of hardened cement; certainly heavy enough. Wilf let over the side. It seemed about thirty feet to the bottom. He drew the rope taut, and tied the slack end around a thwart, next to the gunwale. He commented to Serena about the depth. "The Pickerel seem to like the cooler water," she said, "deep is good." Wilf had always known that was true.

There was a bit of a current there, because the river from Crooked Pine Lake came into the end of the bay, not far up the shore from the island. Without further discussion, they baited their hooks with minnows, and then let them sink to the bottom. Once on bottom, they raised their lines a foot and a half, and started jigging them up and down, gently but steadily.

It was Serena who caught the first one. She felt her line jerk a little, then felt it again. This time she jerked back hard, and felt the fish; it was hooked. She kept the tension on the line, pulling back on her rod; then letting it run; then pulling back hard again. Finally the fish was played out, and she was able to pull it up beside the boat where Wilf scooped it up in the net and dumped it into the boat.

It was well hooked; the hook came through the hard surface on the top of its mouth. Wilf squeezed its eyes together with his thumb and forefinger, paralyzing the fish to remove the hook and hook the fish onto the stringer; that done, he fixed one end of the stringer to the gunwale of the boat, and dropped the other end with the fish attached, over the side of the boat into the lake. It was a nice size of a Pickerel, a good three pounds.

Serena caught one more before Wilf caught his first one. This one was a good size, easily between four and five pounds. Then Wilf caught another. They soon had eight fish on the stringer. By late morning, they'd quit biting. "It's always like this with Pickerel," Serena said. "They'll start to feed again in the late afternoon. Want to stick around for awhile?"

"Sure, why not? It's nice out here." And it was; it was a warm Indian summer day. The sun felt good on them now. They had their jackets off, and were down to their T-shirts. It was a beautiful time of the year. The black flies and mosquitoes were all done now. It was a great day to be out on the lake fishing. There wouldn't be too many days like this. Once the Indian summer passed, things would start to cool off very quickly. They got into their lunch now, and continued to fish; a bannock sandwich in one hand; a rod in the other.

"Well, I can't show you much about fishing," said Wilf after a bit; he admired her innate practicality in everything she did. His sister Denise was much the same, being raised on a farm.

"Well, I learned a lot from my Dad and Mom. Dad and I used to fish lots together before he got too haywire, and lost interest in everything but the booze. I had some good years with him as a little girl. We still don't have an indoor toilet, but you know it's sometimes what you don't have that makes life good; I mean look at Mom. She's a pretty special kind of a person, and she's never seen a city in her life. She's always busy and always happy."

"She sure makes a great bannock," commented Wilf. Serena had to laugh at that. "She can do a lot more than that," she came back.

"I know Serena..." he didn't finish that sentence; his rod almost jerked right out of his hand. He dropped the last piece of his bannock on the seat of the boat, and got both hands on his rod, his thumb pressing down hard on his line, trying to stop it from flying out of the reel. He knew just the way it hit; it had to be a big Jackfish (Americans called them Northern Pike.)

He couldn't slow the loss of his line no matter how hard he pressed down on it with his thumb. He grabbed hard on the handle of the reel, but it spun painfully in his hand. He had to let it run; he kept trying his best to slow it down. Finally just before it seemed like the fish would strip his reel of line, he managed to get it stopped. Holding the handle of his reel taut, he pulled back hard on his rod, almost bending the steel rod in two; then relaxing the rod, he quickly reeled in the hard won slack. He continued in this way, pulling back hard, then relaxing and quickly reeling in his gain, when the fish jumped clear of the lake some forty or fifty feet from the boat. It was one huge Jackfish; it had to be a good twenty pounds.

No sooner had it hit the water again that it dove deep, and took off with fresh energy. Again the line flew from his reel, and Wilf fought to regain control. Serena reeled in her line so as to avoid a tangle as the big fish headed under their boat; it seemed to have a strategy. Wilf had lost them before when they dove deep like that. He had regained some slack when the line went straight down, but the fight was soon on again, when the fish took off on the wrong side of the boat. His rod was doubled again, and he was vainly trying to pull slack against the bottom of the boat. Serena tilted the motor out of the water, lest the fish managed to wrap the line around the prop, which would end Wilf's chance of ever landing this monster.

Finally the fish began to tire, and pulling back hard, and then reeling in, Wilf was able to gain back his lost line, a yard at a time. He had it near the boat now. It made one more plunge, but Wilf was ready. He wasn't taking any chances. This round didn't last long, and he got it pulled up beside the boat, resting quite still. He carefully passed his rod to Serena, crossing his fingers and winking as he did so; then he picked up the gaff hook, and passing the point of it gently into the fish's gills, he reefed hard on the gaff, and heaved the fish into the boat.

The fish protested violently, flopping boisterously, upsetting the tackle box, and tangling his line as it tossed and squirmed, pounding on the boat's bottom. "This won't do," said Wilf. He waited till the fish lay a still for a moment, then put his foot on it. Leaning hard with his weight against it he said, "Could you pass me the axe, Serena?" He took the axe from her, and bearing down, with his foot on the fish's side, gave a sharp blow to the back of the fish, just behind its head, with the back end of the axe head. The fish stiffened and quivered for a moment, then lay still, quite dead now.

"Boy, that's some fish," Serena said. She handed Wilf a spring loaded fish scale from the tackle box. He put the hook of it under the fish's gills, and lifted it clear of the boat. It showed eighteen and a half pounds. "Well, almost twenty," he said. "That might explain why the Pickerel left us."

He laid the fish down on the boat's bottom again, and set about extracting his line. Unlike the Pickerel which were a smaller family of fish, the Jackfish had a huge mouth. The Pickerel's head compared to its body was relatively small. It had big glassy protruding eyes, which is no doubt why Americans called them 'Walleyes '. Its head came rounded to its mouth, which was much smaller than the Jack's. Pickerel had a spiked dorsal fin the length of its back; its body was dark grey to black in colour, and their scales were coarser than the Jackfish.

The Jackfish had no dorsal fin and its scales were smoother; it was a green colour, usually, with white spots, but could also be brown. Both the Pickerel and Jackfish had a white underbelly. The biggest difference was the head. A Jackfish had to be a close cousin to the Barracuda. It looked identical. The head came right off the body, and it was all mouth. Its eyes were much smaller than the Pickerel, more beady than glassy. They were also a much more aggressive fish than the Pickerel. You didn't need to use any bait to catch a Jackfish. Any kind of a flashy spoon or plug would do. Where the Pickerel was fussy, required that live bait, and wouldn't bite all that hard, the Jackfish was more aggressive and would bite on anything; it would strike hard, and fight harder.

Wilf set about retrieving his hook from the fish. Only the end of the leader could be seen protruding for that massive mouth; the fish had swallowed the hook right into its gullet. Wilf tried putting his foot against the fish; then wrapping the line around his hand for a grip, and pulling hard. The line bit into his hand, but the hook stuck fast; then he tried forcing the end of the axe handle into its mouth, which was lined with rows and rows of needle like teeth, as sharp as razors. He took the pliers from the tackle box and with his shoulder against the head of the axe, got a purchase on the leader with the pliers, and jerked hard. The hook came out finally, along with a good part of the fish's gullet, left hanging out of its mouth.

"Boy when those Jackfish bite, they bite!" he exclaimed. That was one fish that didn't go on the stringer; they left it lie dead on the boat's bottom. "Now maybe we can catch some Pickerel." Serena nodded in agreement and let down her line again. Wilf put a fresh minnow his hook and let down his line. His piece of bannock he'd put on the seat was on the floor now, near the fishes head. He picked it up and threw it in the lake saying "Thanks asshole."

Serena looked up and said, "What?"

"Oh, I was just talking to the fish." Serena shrugged. Wilf smiled. He still had his apple. He started into that. He had just nicely finished his apple when Serena got a hit. It was a nice size, a good three pounds. They hooked it onto the stringer, and soon had a few more, rounding out their limit of six Pickerel each. The Jackfish didn't count. There was no limit on Jack, and it was another species anyway. They decided it was time to pull up the anchor and head back. It had been a good days fishing.

Their first stop, coming back, was Toivo's wharf. They tied up at the dock; first Serena emptied their remaining minnows back into Toivo's tank.

"What about the fish?" Wilf asked.

"You can put the Jackfish in the ice house for now till we see what Toivo wants to do with it. It doesn't look like they're back yet. He'll probably feed it to the mink. I don't want it anyways. Bring the Pickerel up to the house. There's a good place to clean the fish just back of the house".

Wilf laid the Jackfish under some sawdust in the ice house; then followed Serena up to the house. She led him to a table in back of the house near the meat grinder by the mink pens. The table was solid enough; it was composed of two 2"x10" planks eight feet long nailed tightly to a couple of sturdy saw horses.

"We can clean the fish here," she said. She'd brought a sharp knife from the tackle box that had a long, thin blade. Wilf laid the stringer of Pickerel on one end of the table; Serena took one of the fish from the stringer and went to work on it. She cut through the flesh behind the gills on both sides of the fish, just up to the spine, and then slit the belly from the anus to the gills. That done, she ran the knife from the incision behind the gills along the spine all the way through to the tail of the fish, cutting through the ribs, neatly stripping a fillet from the side of the fish. She rolled the remaining half of the fish over, and stripped the fillet from the other side in the same way. Lastly, she cut the cheeks out of the Pickerel, and put them aside to be kept with the cleaned fillets.

She dropped the naked carcass into a plastic pail near the table. "Toivo will want to feed these to the mink," she said. "Of course," Wilf said, then commenting on filleting effort said, "looks like you've done this before."

"Yes, a couple of times," she said, and without slowing down, she placed one of the fillets skin side down on the table, and skinned it, by pressing down with her thumb of her left hand on the tail end of the fillet, and sliding the knife blade with her right hand along the length of the fillet close to the skin, neatly separating the flesh from the skin; she then did the same thing which the other fillet, and threw the skins into the plastic pail. The whole process of cleaning the fish was done in a matter of minutes, with no wasted time or flesh.

As a finishing touch, she pushed the sharp point of the knife just underneath the ribs, which were still with the fillets, and deftly sliced them away from the fillets. Except for the fine lateral bones, the fillets were bone free. Without any hesitation, she started on the next fish, and continued until half the fish were cleaned. About that time, Rachel showed up, having walked over from her cabin; she brought with her a blueberry pie she'd made.

"Looks like the fishing was good today, "she commented, eyeing the pile of fillets, and the remaining fish.

"Yes Mom, it sure was, and you should see the Jackfish that Wilf caught, almost twenty pounds! We left it in the ice house."

"Here Serena," Wilf said, taking the knife, "let me give you a break." She nodded compliance; Rachel dropped the pie off at the house and followed Serena to the ice house to look at the Jackfish, while Wilf continued filleting the remaining fish.

Wilf was having a great day. He was even enjoying cleaning the fish. He did it a little differently than Serena. Instead of slicing through the ribs, and removing them later he would cut around them, so they remained with the spine. They both would start with slicing the belly from the anus to the gills. He would then cut behind the gills like Serena had and then run the tip of the knife through the flesh of the fishes back, cutting along the dorsal fin from the back of the head to the tail. Then he would cut around ribs to complete the separation of the fillet. That done he would skin them the same as Serena did. She did seem to be a little bit faster doing her way.

Alone, cleaning the fish, he got to reflecting on his life to date. This was living like he knew it as a boy growing up. With the exception of Clarence, he had a family he loved and enjoyed. Growing up on the farm he'd been close to nature. There was hard work to be done, but it was good work. They grew their own vegetables, raised their own meat; he hunted and fished with his brother Patrick. It was a life he'd greatly missed. Lost in the mining game, the camps, the booze, the barflies and the hookers, his life had become a shell and he despaired of not ever getting that good feeling back.

He was finding it now. He was finding good people in his life. Serena was a gift. He loved everything about her. At times he thought he was dreaming. She was so down to earth, so beautiful; so practical and capable, so good to be with, and he was sober.

Bunkhouses and camps had been his life for a good few years until lately; bunkhouses were warehouses of packsack miners and dysfunction. He'd felt the magic of that first drink in his first camp at the Levack Mine in Sudbury; in that magic euphoria he was no longer a farm boy, but a man of the world, a man among men who'd been around (some to the war, but mostly to other mines...other bunkhouses.) Looking at it now, he realized it was a form of being institutionalized.

His mining mentor in Levack was a case in point; Long John was good miner, but a hopeless drunk. He was the one, who broke Wilf in on the machine (jackleg); who taught him to mine. The company loved John's work, but when he drank, it got so he could no longer make it to work; he would try to keep his drinking down to periodic binges, and the company would turn a blind eye when he'd be absent, sometimes days at a time, because he was always good when he worked.

Wilf had once seen a doctor come into the bunkhouse, sent by the company to revive Long John, after one of his binges; they had to give him injections, just to keep him alive. By this time Wilf had acquired a constant appetite for the booze, but also had discipline to make it to work the next day. He was young and strong, he was resilient, and he loved to drink. He reasoned that if he ever got like Long John, he would just quit drinking.

One day, the doctor came to revive Long John, but John didn't make it; he was packed out of the bunkhouse in a body bag; and one day, a year or two later, Wilf lost his job for absenteeism. He went on to other mines and other camps, always trying to find that magic balance of working and drinking; he would sober up for sometimes weeks or even months at a time, but inevitably the booze would win, and he'd be back on the tramp. He came to realize if quitting drinking was so simple, it wouldn't be called a problem.

But the obsession to drink was gone now. He had good things in his life. And it was all so simple. Just don't take the first drink, and the rest would never happen. ('When you get run over by a train, it's not the caboose that kills you,' he'd heard some place.) It was just that simple; don't start.

Toivo had pulled up in his pickup with his family, just as Wilf finished cleaning the last fish. Serena and Rachel came over to greet them and show them Wilf's Jackfish in the ice house. Wilf set the knife down and went over to join them. Toivo was appropriately impressed. He did have a smokehouse, but preferred smoking Lake Trout. "Ve feed it to the mink," he said, "enough there for three days."

Rachel and Helen went into the house with the groceries, and Toivo picked up the fish with one hand under the gills and headed to the meat grinder; Madeleine and Wilf followed him. On the way, Wilf asked Madeleine how she enjoyed the movie.

"Oh, it was pretty good," she said. "Mom and I watched it, and Dad went for a beer. The bad guys didn't get their way. I like a story like that."

"Treasure Island, eh? I think I read the book years ago; maybe I should go see the movie."

"Sure. Take Serena. You'd really like it."

They were interrupted by Toivo. He'd taken in the pile of fillets in a glance, as well as the pail of fish remains, and commented enthusiastically, "Good fishing, eh, Vilf?" Wilf nodded agreement. Toivo had taken the tarp from the meat grinder, with his free hand, and had put the enamel bowl underneath the mouth of it. Wilf took the fish from him to feed it into the meat grinder, so Toivo could put both hands to turning the handle of the grinder. As Toivo turned the handle, Wilf fed the big fish into the grinder, and watched it disappear into the bowl as ground fish meat. Madeleine looked on, wide eyed.

The bowl was heaping full, before they'd ground up half the fish. Wilf set the truncated remains of the fish down to help Toivo dish out the mink feed. Madeleine stood by in awe, and then said to Wilf, "Are you going to marry my aunt?"

That caught Wilf by surprise. "Well I don't know, Madeleine. Do you think she'd have me?"

"I'll go ask her," Madeleine said, and ran to the house. Toivo was laughing so hard he had to set the bowl down. Wilf didn't think it so funny.

"Madeleine thinks you a good guy," Toivo explained, and continued grinding the fish when he was able to quit laughing. They had finished dishing out the contents of the bowl, and this time Toivo emptied the Pickerel remains from the pail into the empty bowl, as the mink were well fed now and the bowl was too small to accommodate the rest of the fish plus the Pickerel remains; he would use the pail now to contain the remaining ground fish. Toivo had just started grinding up the rest of the fish and Pickerel leavings, when Madeleine reappeared with a cooler to gather up the Pickerel fillets. She came up to Wilf, and said, "Aunt Serena said if you want to marry her, you'll have to ask her yourself." Having picked up the fillets she went back to the house, leaving Wilf speechless. Toivo had to laugh again.

"You in 'rouble now, Vilf," he said, and continued to chuckle as he turned the crank on the grinder. Wilf was quiet, as he fed the last of the fish, and the Pickerel remains into the grinder. Toivo, done grinding and done laughing now, pulled over a garden hose with strong jet on the nozzle, and hosed out the grinder. "Vonce in awhile need it clean," he explained. He picked up the pail of ground fish, and said, "You go in house and vash up, Vilf. I take it mink food to ice house, and then come in too".

Wilf saw Serena sitting on the couch having a coffee, as soon as he entered the house, and immediately blushed; Serena burst out laughing, to add to his embarrassment. She'd set her coffee down and collapsed in silent mirth, her shoulders involuntarily going up and down, her contorted face covered in her hands.

"I need to wash up," he said simply, and headed for the bathroom.

Serena met him by the bathroom door, just as he emerged, and hugged him. "It's OK Wilf. I know it was Madeleine's idea. She really likes you, you know." Wilf finally found the whole thing funny. Just about then, Toivo was back, and Wilf stepped out of the way, to let him into the bathroom. Toivo made no further comment.

Dinner was nicely ready when Toivo came out of the bathroom and everyone took a seat at the table. Helen had done up ten of the fillets, rolled in bread crumbs, then fried in butter, to a perfect golden brown. There was a big bowl of new potatoes, along with beets and carrots from her garden, and even slices of bannock from Rachel's loaf. There was little conversation over dinner, except for some appropriate comments about the good food and good fishing.

With the main course done with, and the dishes removed, Helen brought out Rachel's pie and a quart of vanilla ice cream. Madeleine's eyes grew wide at the sight of the ice cream. She sat in rapt attention as Helen served up the pie in soup bowls, adding a share of ice cream to each serving. As she watched, she turned to Wilf, seated beside her, and whispered quietly, "Did you talk to Aunt Serena yet?"

Wilf could only see the humour in this now. "No, not yet," he whispered back. To his relief, Madeleine received her dessert just then, and her attention moved to her pie and ice cream in front of her. Coffee was served with the pie, with good compliments given to Rachel on the delicious dessert, and she humbly thanked people for their gracious comments; apart from that their time was spent in quiet enjoyment of the lovely pie and ice cream.

Once they were done at the table, Toivo, to everyone's surprise, suggested they take in the evening at the 'Hoot 'n' Holler' Hall. Wilf had vaguely thought of it, but had made no mention of it to Serena. Helen was looking bland, so Wilf turned to Serena, and asked her what she thought. She in turn spoke to Helen and asked her how she felt.

"I'll go if you go ", she said, and Serena turned to Wilf and said, "Well, how 'bout it?"

"Well sure then, might be fun. I did bring my dancing shoes but they're over at your Mom's."

"We can drop by and pick them up on the way," said Serena.

Madeleine asked, "Can I come too?"

"No Madeleine," Helen interjected, you need to stay home and look after Gramma." Madeleine seemed to accept her responsibility graciously.

Once the dishes were done, Toivo offered to drive Rachel and Madeleine over to Rachel's cabin. Serena Interrupted, saying, "We should be taking our boat back."

"Couldn't that wait for good daylight?" said Rachel.

"It's a full moon tonight, Mom. There's not a cloud in the sky. We won't have any trouble finding our way. I'd like things put away before we go to the dance." Before anything further was said, she asked Madeleine, "Would you like to go for a boat ride in the moonlight with me and Wilf?"

Madeleine shrieked with delight, shouting, "Yes, yes, yes!"

"Well, I guess that settles it," said Helen. "Mom, you and I can get a ride over with Toivo, and we can meet up when they get to your place."

Wilf took Madeleine's hand, and they followed Serena down to Toivo's dock. Serena climbed aboard first, and after getting Madeleine placed in the middle seat, went to the stern and waited for Wilf to cast off. Wilf untied the boat, and climbing into the bow, gave it a push from the dock. The lake was as still as glass and the moon was full and bright, casting its golden path across the lake. It was a late Indian summer. The air was cool, but not uncomfortable. Serena started the motor on her first pull, and headed the boat for home.

The rush of air as the boat sped back to Serena's landing felt refreshing. Wilf turned back to see Madeleine staring ahead, wide-eyed in rapt enjoyment of their little voyage. He turned back, smiling, and shortly they arrived, to see Toivo and Helen on the shore, waiting with a flashlight in hand. Rachel had gone into her cabin and turned on the lights.

As the boat neared shore, Serena killed the motor and let it drift in. Toivo grabbed the bow as it touched the shore, to steady the boat as Madeleine climbed out. Wilf went to the stern, and undid the motor. He brought the motor and the gas can with him as he left the boat. Serena had gathered up the rods and the remaining gear. Once she was out of the boat, Toivo and Wilf dragged it back up on land, and laying down the oars, turned the boat over to cover them. The five of them walked back to Rachel's with the motor, the gas can, and all the fishing gear in hand. Madeleine led the way with the flashlight.

Wilf and Serena took a few minutes to stow the motor, gas can, and fishing gear in the shed behind the cabin as Madeleine proudly held a light for them. Once done they joined the group in the cabin. Madeleine got settled in with Rachel for the night, Wilf got into his dancing shoes, and along with Toivo, Helen and Serena, they bid Rachel and Madeleine a good evening. As they were leaving, Helen said, "Watch out for Gramma, now, Madeleine." Madeleine nodded gravely. Rachel had to smile. They closed the door behind them, and went to Toivo's pickup. Helen got into the middle, and Serena climbed in on top of Wilf by the door. Toivo got in, started the truck, and off they went to the 'Hoot 'n Holler Hall'.

They arrived in good time. It was quite dark now, but the parking lot was well lit up. There were a number of vehicles already there, but it wasn't crowded. A small group of people near the edge of the lot were passing around a bottle, but all the other arrivals were already inside. Toivo parked the truck and the four of them went straight to the entrance. Wilf got their tickets. They were happy to see Gus and Molly already there in their usual spot and they went directly to their table.

It was still half an hour before showtime. Gus and Molly were just settled into some of their rum and coke. They were delighted to see Wilf and his group. Stan hadn't come in this time, and Rod Hicks, the guitarist hadn't arrived yet. Wilf and Toivo got Helen and Serena seated at the table with Gus and Molly, and went over to the bar for a half dozen 7up and coca cola. This time Toivo took a turn to buy. By the time they'd returned to the table, Rod Hicks had arrived, and Gus and Molly had set him up with a good stiff drink. Wilf and Toivo pulled over an extra table and a couple more chairs, and joined the group.

The hall was nicely filling up now. Wilf was getting to know a lot of the crowd from the mine, and looking around, he recognized quite a few. "Ever see Jamieson here, Gus?"

"No, never have. Don't think he's much for dancing. I've never seen him here."

"Well, that's a good thing, I guess." He took a sip of his coke, and then said, "I hope that ankle of his stays sprained."

Gus was already getting a nice glow and didn't pursue Wilf's comment. He downed the rest of his drink and as he poured himself another said, "Well, I better finished getting primed. Ten minutes till show time." He'd filled his plastic glass two thirds full of rum, then added a little coke for colour and immediately took a huge gulp from his glass, letting out a gasp of pleasure; his eyes were already getting wet and glazed. Toivo was into his mickey of whisky which Helen had brought in her purse. He'd mixed a drink in one of Molly's plastic glasses with some 7-Up. (Unlike Gus, he put only a third of a glass with whisky, adding mostly 7-Up.) Molly was nursing a shot of rum and coke, but unlike Gus' drink it was a less potent concoction.

Wilf, Serena and Helen were all having either Coke or 7-Up. Rod was near done his drink when Gus asked him if he wouldn't have a drop more. Rod declined with thanks whereupon Gus looked at his watch, exclaiming, "Hey, look. Its show time!" and downed the rest of his drink in a gulp. Rod finished his, and joined Gus on the stage. The hall was filled nicely now, and applause broke out from the audience as their got their fiddle and guitar in tune. Once Gus was satisfied they had it right, he hollered, "OK everybody.....its SHOWTIME!!!!"

A huge applause swept the hall on the first stroke of his fiddle, as he got into a flawless rendition of the "Orange Blossom Special," Rod stepped up in perfect accompaniment.

Many, including Serena and Wilf, unable to resist the magic of good music, got right into it. Gus went on with several good step dancing numbers, going to 'Maple Sugar', then 'Rubber Dolly', and five or six more, before slowing down to a waltz. By the time Gus and Rod took their first beak, there were a number of people up on the floor dancing.

Gus and Rod didn't take too long for a break before they were up playing again. Right after the third break Molly surprised Wilf by dragging him out onto the floor just as Gus and Rod started into 'Silver Bells'. She got right into the step dance, and Wilf was amazed that such a big woman could be so light on her feet. She was good at it and kept Wilf going right into the next number, which was 'Big John McNeil'. The sweat was running down her cheeks now, but she just kept right on dancing. At the end of that one she gave Wilf a pat on the back in thanks, and took her seat, breathing hard for a few minutes, but pleased with her effort. Gus was laughing as he played on with his fiddle.

"Boy, you surprised me all to hell, Molly," Wilf said, "looks like you done this before."

"Yeah, been awhile, but thanks Wilf. That was fun."

"You still got the moves Molly."

Toivo got up with Helen to try a step dance, but soon gave up. He did get Helen up for a waltz though, as soon as Gus started into 'Life in the Finland Woods'. It was past midnight now, and Gus and Rod took one last break before their last set. Toivo was just at the end of his mickey, and Gus poured out the last of his rum from his big steel thermos.....a drink for Rod...a drink for Molly.....and the rest (a big drink for Gus). Gus wasn't greedy, just a little more thirsty than most. Once they had their drinks, they got up and played through their last set, which they carried on till one in the morning.

They finished off in the usual way with Molly singing 'The Tennessee Waltz' in her beautiful strong, clear voice, followed by Gus thanking everyone over the mike for coming out, and making such a great evening possible. On that note, a round of applause spread through the audience. A hat was passed around to take up a collection for the band. Gus and Rod did all right; people gave in a generosity which was heartfelt, and somewhat influenced by the evening's drinking.

When the hat came back to Gus and Rod, there was lots of money in it. It was heavy with coins, and there were bills as well. Gus held the hat up high, and thanked everyone over the mike for their generosity. Another round of applause went through the room, and Gus bowed graciously.

Wilf, Serena, Helen and Toivo said their goodbyes and thanks to Gus, Molly and Rod. There were hugs and handshakes all around. Rod and Gus packed up their instruments as Toivo and his party parted with a wave, to return to Sapawe, and home in Toivo's pickup, with Toivo at the wheel, Helen in the middle, and Serena on Wilf's lap.

They arrived at Rachel's cabin to find Rachel asleep in her bedroom, and Madeleine asleep on the couch, covered with a quilted blanket. Toivo scooped her up in his arms still sleeping, and placed her gently into the front seat of his pickup, as Helen held open the door; then Toivo and Helen climbed in, and they headed for home. Serena folded up the blanket and put it away; then she and Wilf went to her bedroom, got undressed, and went to bed. They lay together naked and relaxed, and talked quietly in the dark. Wilf felt inspired to comment on their evening at the 'Hoot 'n' Holler Hall'.

"Gus and Rod, they sure put on a show for us," he said, "They make that thing happen."

"They sure do," Serena agreed, "I don't think it would ever be the same without them."

"Gus has got something nobody else has got," continued Wilf. "It isn't just his music that's great. Its, how could I put it....the magic of his spirit that comes across."

"Yes," agreed Serena, "He's one of a kind. He's got a big heart, and we all feel it."

"Yes," said Wilf, "I think that's what it is."

"Anyway, to change the subject, when are you going to ask me to marry you?" She could feel Wilf blushing in the dark, and giggled.

"Well, I thought we agreed that was Madeleine's idea," he said.

Serena rolled over top of him, and kissed him long and hard on his mouth. "Maybe it was, but what do you think of that for an idea?" Wilf made no immediate comment. "Well, if you ever do get around to asking, my answer will be yes," she said, as her hand found its way to his stiff erection. "Anyway," she continued, "enough of this talking. Let's make love."

And without another word spoken, that's just what they did. Wilf entered her gently at first, as she guided him in; Serena was already wet and gasping with pleasure. He fucked her gently at first but soon fucked her hard and fast, matching Serena's enthusiasm. They were getting to be well acquainted lovers now, enjoying their magic of their lust. A long and wonderful day, and fun filled evening together culminated in a drenching orgasm, had left them both exhausted. They remained entwined for some good moments, catching their breath, and then shortly fell asleep in fond embrace.

Wilf awoke before dawn, with a pressing need to relieve himself. He was still wrapped around Serena. He managed to extract himself without waking her as she continued to snore gently and quietly. Rachel, though always the early bird, was not up yet. He quietly got into his shorts, and found his way to the outhouse. It was a cool, late September morning, but still Indian summer, and still no frost. The sky was a cloudless, predawn grey on the Eastern horizon. Against the darkness of the sky, the stars were plainly visible. The fresh coolness of the early morning felt good on his bare skin, as he passed his water, and that felt best of all. Back inside, he stripped off his shorts and quietly returned to Serena's bed. She did not wake up, and he was soon fast asleep himself.

He awoke much later, to find Serena nestled comfortably against him, wide-eyed and smiling. The brightness of the morning sun poked through the gap in the curtains, and he knew Rachel had to be up because he could already smell fresh coffee. He made a move to get up but Serena straddled him saying "Not so fast!" She carefully eased herself onto his erect penis and started to fuck him. In spite of the delicious erotic feeling it gave him, his eyes belied his alarm and her indiscretion. He pointed to the door to convey uneasy concern. She put her finger to her lips and continued to fuck him with mounting enthusiasm.

It was soon beyond Wilf to feel or show any objection to the experience; he became her willing accomplice in lust, clinging to her now and thrusting up against her, as she bent over him, fucking him harder and faster, until at last, she sat up rigid, in a gasping quivering climax. Wilf pulled hard on her buttocks, and pumped into her a spasmodic gush of seminal fluid.

Done, she lay over him now, out of breath and panting. When they had both recovered normal breathing, she could sense his embarrassment, and started laughing; quietly at first, but soon quite audibly. She got out of bed and threw him a towel. "Here,'" she said, "wipe it up with this." She got into her housecoat and joined her mother in the kitchen. Wilf joined her, fully clothed, a few minutes later, and looking a little sheepish, as he said good morning to Rachel. She wished him the same, and poured him a coffee, showing no notice of anything amiss. He thanked for the coffee, and excused himself to go to the outhouse. He was almost back to the front door of the cabin when Toivo pulled up in his pickup, with Helen and Madeleine.

"Good morning Vilf," he said, climbing out of the truck, "ve bring it you nice breakfast."

Helen joined him, with a bowl of pancake batter mixed with blueberries, and Madeleine with a platter of the Pickerel fillets still uncooked from yesterdays catch.

"You no eat yet, eh?" Toivo asked, hopefully.

"No, not yet, Toivo."

"Good."

It was Helen who opened the door. "You've got company, Mom," she said, coming in with Madeleine and the food. Rachel was just about to make some porridge. "I see we got here just in time," she continued, "you just sit down and relax, Mom, we'll take care of breakfast, won't we Madeleine?"

"Yes Mom," Madeleine confirmed, "you sit down, Gramma. Mom and I will cook breakfast." Wilf had to smile at this; Madeleine could barely see over the counter.

And cook breakfast they did, while Wilf and Rachel relaxed over coffee. Serena had gotten dressed by now, and was turning the pancakes while Helen fried up the Pickerel fillets. Just before dinner was served, Toivo had kindled a fire in the sauna, and had returned just as the food arrived on the table.

"Ve take it nice Sauna after eat," he explained.

Wilf put away a huge breakfast, as did Serena. They even outdid Toivo for food consumed. "I see you hungry, Vilf," he commented favourably.

"I think it was because those two did most of the dancing," said Helen.

"Yes, it had to be the dancing," Serena confirmed, without raising her eyes from her plate.

Everyone was done eating now. The blueberry pancakes were all eaten except for two still sitting on the serving platter, and one fillet of Pickerel. Everyone was stuffed. No one could eat any more. Madeleine suggested they take the remaining fillet home for her cat; Rachel agreed, and wrapped it up for her in some waxed paper. The pancakes Rachel could warm up for tomorrow's breakfast.

"Vilf, you and me, ve go first for sauna; ve let the ladies clean it up here. After you and me, ve go hunt some birds. Make it nice partridge supper tonight." Wilf looked to Serena in question. "You go ahead, Wilf; Helen and I will clean up here," and Madeleine said, "I'm helping, too."

Wilf and Toivo took towels and went to the sauna. It was already giving off a good heat. Wilf helped Toivo top off the water in the forty five gallon drum, and the two of them got undressed, hung up their clothes, and got into the sauna, closing the door behind them. After a hard night's dancing, and some good sex, Wilf due for a cleansing; he was getting pretty ripe. Toivo splashed a basin of water onto the hot rocks, and steam erupted in a whoosh. Wilf choked on the first impact of the hot vapour, but quickly settled into the relaxing cleansing effect of a good sauna.

"You can go to church, or take it shower, but never you get it clean like sauna," Toivo reiterated, as the two of them, now in rivers of sweat, started soaping themselves down, and scrubbing their bodies. Wilf had to agree; nothing could clean you like a sauna.

Once they were both well soaped and scrubbed, they rinsed off with pails of water from the tank; then they stepped out of the sauna into the sitting room for a cool down. Toivo took a beer for himself from his knapsack and handed Wilf a large bottle of Club Soda. "Here Vilf, this no hurt you," he said.

Wilf felt the coolness of the quart bottle in his hand as he took the opener from Toivo, saying, "Thanks, Toivo." Toivo toasted him in Finnish touching his beer to Wilf's club soda saying*, "Kippis, mino hoeveri." (Cheers, partner).* Wilf clinked glasses back with a *"Kippis!"* He knew that much Finnish.

He took a long hard pull, draining almost half the bottle. After a good, hard sweat, it hit the spot. Toivo finished his beer and said, "Might as well we do it one more time, eh Vilf?" Wilf set the remainder of the bottle down on the bench, and followed Toivo back into the sauna. They did one more hard sweat, followed by a good rinse, and then went back into the sitting room, closing the sauna door behind them. Having dried themselves off with their towels, they sat naked on the bench, to cool off a little more before getting dressed. Toivo had another beer and Wilf finished off his bottle of Club Soda.

"That no hurt you," Toivo explained, "yust vater".

"Well, it sure hit the spot, Toivo; sauna makes me thirsty." Toivo nodded agreement. He stoked the fire again with a couple of good chunks of Birch; then the two them got dressed, picked up their towels and face cloths, and rejoined the ladies, who by now had the dishes cleaned up and put away.

"Sauna all ready for you now," Toivo told them, "Me and Vilf, ve go hunting. See you later at the house, OK?" The ladies, along with Madeleine picked up their towels and headed for the sauna and Wilf and Toivo left for hunting.

They stopped at Toivo's first, where Toivo brought to the pickup a couple of .22 caliber rifles, and a box of .22 shells. One was a bolt action Cooie .22, and the other a Remington pump action .22. Wilf noticed he had a couple of bales of hay in the box of his pickup. "For my horse," Toivo explained. It was just into early afternoon now, the day had nicely warmed, and there was no wind, just right for hunting birds. Toivo took them down a road just outside the village that went off into the bush, a little ways past his property.

"Good time to hunt birds," Toivo explained. "They come out now to the road to eat some 'ravel (gravel)."

The 'birds' he was referring to were Partridge, commonly referred to as Grouse in Western Canada. They liked to feed on clover when they could find it. He was also including Spruce Hens which fed almost exclusively on Spruce needles. They had a darker breast meat and a sharper taste. Once the birds had fed and their crops were full, they would come out onto the road to peck gravel for their gizzard to digest their meal. Both species of 'birds' would do very well in a stew.

"Yes, we used to hunt the birds back home when I was growing up. Mom used to make a great stew."

"That's what ve do, Vilf. Ve make it nice stew for supper."

Before long they came to a gate; it was simply a long steel bar across the road locked to a post. Without a word, he handed Wilf a key. Wilf opened the lock and let him through, then locked it again, and got back in the pickup.

"I have key, because I v'urk up this road. Sometimes cut logs for Sawmill on this company road. I have 'rapper's licence, too; no need licence to hunt. Pretty soon I show you my horse."

Before long he pulled up by a clearing. It was a logging landing; there were logs along the side of the landing, skidded into a pile, and the open ground was riddled with stumps of trees already cut down. A big Clydesdale horse stood in the middle of the clearing and lifted his head as Toivo came to a stop.

"That's my horse, Barney," Toivo explained, "Good horse. No need it tie him up. Yust feed him," and so saying brought one of the bales of hay from his truck and cut away the binder twine, putting it carefully into his pocket. The horse nudged Toivo's shoulder, and Toivo drew a nice Mackintosh apple from his other pocket, and held it up for the horse. The horse took a bite, quite mindful of Toivo's fingers; then Toivo let him have the whole thing.

"See how smart is that horse," commented Toivo. Wilf had to smile. They had an obvious relationship. Toivo went to the truck and came back with a paper shopping bag half full of oats. He spread the oats over Barney's hay, and left him to it.

"Come Vilf," he said, "now find some birds. Sunday a good day for hunting on this road; nobody working, no 'raffic ... nobody here"

Before long they came across three Partridge pecking the gravel by the side of the road. Toivo stopped the truck and they quietly got out, Toivo with the Cooie, Wilf with the pump-action Remington. Toivo took aim on the left one and Wilf on the one to the far right. They both fired together. The two birds they shot immediately went into flapping convulsions; then lay still. The third bird flew. Both birds were hit right in the neck.

"Good shooting, Vilf," Toivo commented; Wilf nodded agreement, then picked up the birds and threw them into the back of the pickup. They continued further up the road and came upon five Spruce hens perched in a Poplar tree near the road. Again Toivo parked the truck, and the two of them took out their rifles and took aim. Toivo's shot went first, then Wilf's, both on target. The two Spruce hens fell flapping to the ground. The other three didn't flush, but remained perched in the tree, while Wilf and Toivo shot them all.

"Not very smart, those birds", commented Toivo, as he gathered them up and threw them into the pickup.

"No. Not very smart Toivo. Back home we called those Spruce hens 'fools hens'. They'll just sit there and let you shoot them. Partridge are a little more wary."

"What you mean, vary?"

"Like more nervous."

"Ya, ya. More vary. I see."

Before long, they came across four more Partridge, pecking gravel along the road. This time they weren't so 'wary', and Toivo and Wilf shot all four of them without any of them flushing; the first two weren't done flapping their death dance, when the remaining two were shot and killed. Toivo and Wilf gathered them up and threw them into the pickup.

"Well, I think ve got enough birds for supper," he said.

"I would think so" said Wilf. They headed back for home three hours after they'd began.

They arrived home to find Helen, Madeleine, and Rachel, all at the house. Before even putting the rifles away, Toivo and Wilf gathered up the eleven dead birds, and laid them out on the cleaning table outside. Helen brought a couple of sharp knives from the kitchen, and a large mixing bowl. They immediately went to work cleaning the birds. Wilf joined them at the table as Toivo returned the rifles to the house. Madeleine stood next to Wilf, watching the process in rapt attention. It didn't take long with the three of them at it, and Toivo came in as a fourth, as soon as he had the rifles put away. Toivo and Wilf each had a sharp pocket knife.

The cleaning of the birds began first with tearing off the skin, which separated easily from the birds, eliminating the need for plucking. The next step was to nip off the head, the feet at the ankle joint, and the wing tips at the last joint of the wings; then they cut open the abdomen, cutting across just below the bird's breast. Once that was done, and the guts were removed, they sliced open the gizzards, to remove the sack of gravel it contained.

Wilf was pleased to see that Helen and Rachel were going to the trouble of saving the gizzards, and he followed suit. A lot of hunters didn't. Many would just rip the breast free of the bird, and throw the rest away. They did cut the breast free cutting across the back and boned the breast meat from the carcass; the legs, livers, gizzards, and even the little hearts were all saved. As the birds were cleaned, they were piled into the mixing bowl. In less than an hour, it was all done. Helen took the bowl of cleaned bird flesh into the house and immediately started on her stew.

She would make it out of the breast meat. She began by rolling the breasts in flour, then browning them in a hot frying pan sizzling in melted bear grease. Once the meat was nicely browned, she put it all into a large stew pot, and covered them in water. When the water came to a boil, she turned down the heat, and let the birds simmer. After a good hour of slowly simmering, she added the dumplings to the pot, and left it simmer for another half hour. The remaining pieces of the bird (legs, livers, hearts, backs and wings) all went into a soup pot. She did start the soup, but they wouldn't be having any soup for supper. This would take some time.

Toivo put all the entrails into his gut bucket, and dumped the whole works into the burning barrel. He then poured a good splash of gasoline into the barrel, and tossed in a lighted match. It came to flame with a big whoosh, as he looked on with satisfaction.

"Nothing there for the mink," he explained to Wilf, "and ve don't leave it food for the bears."

Wilf nodded agreement. "Ve vill have nice supper Vilf. Come, ve go in and vash up now." Wilf went to follow him in, but Madeleine, who hadn't left his side, held him back.

"Did you talk to Aunt Serena yet? She asked.

"Yes Madeleine. We talked a little bit."

"What did she say?"

"Well, she seems to think that might be a good idea, but why do you think so?"

She took his hand in both of hers, looking up to him and said, "Cause I'd like you to be my uncle."

Wilf almost choked on hearing that. He finally managed to say, "Let's keep this our little secret for now OK?" he gave her a pat on her back and said, "Let's go in and wash up Madeleine." She hugged his leg, and said, "OK", and followed him into the house.

The gamey smell of the stewing birds was already pleasingly strong. Toivo was sitting back with a beer, Helen and Serena were preparing vegetables for supper, and Rachel was in the rocker, rocking gently with her eyes closed. Wilf went into the bathroom and washed up. There was coffee made, and when he came out of the bathroom, he poured himself a cup, and joined Toivo on the couch. Madeleine sat down beside him. He commented to Toivo on Helen's use of bear grease for cooking, saying his mother did that too.

"I shoot a nice big black bear last fall. I shoot the male. Cubs need their mother bear. Best time of the year to shoot bear. Nice and fat, ready for winter. Lots of meat for the mink. Ve keep the fat for cooking; good for baking pies...anything." He went to the fridge for another beer.

"We used it all the time back home when I was on the farm. Patrick and I would always get a bear late in the fall. Mom would use the fat for cooking, and we used the meat for mink food too. I've tried eating bear meat, but I didn't like it much."

"No," agreed Toivo. "Good mink feed, but not so good for eating."

Helen announced that dinner was ready, and they all came to the table. There were piles of food. There was a bowl of dumplings, a huge bowl of Partridge and Spruce Hen breasts, and a bowl of wild rice. There were also carrots and beets from the garden, and a bowl of gravy for the rice. Madeleine sat next to Wilf, so Wilf offered to serve her. She chose the lighter meat, so he forked her a Partridge breast. She accepted some wild rice with some gravy. He gave her some beets, carrots and a couple of dumplings. "How's that, Madeleine?" he asked handing her the plate.

"That should be lots," she replied politely.

Dinner went well, and a lot of good food was eaten. A third of the bird breasts remained, but those would never go to waste. There was no pie for dessert this time, but everyone was stuffed anyway. Helen and Serena started on the cleanup. Rachel made a move to help, but Helen wouldn't hear of it. "You just sit and relax with Wilf and Toivo", she said. Rachel complied reluctantly. Madeleine stayed to help, carefully bringing one plate at a time to the kitchen sink.

While they were doing the dishes, Toivo went into his bedroom, and returned, showing Wilf the deer hide beaded slippers, now completed, that Rachel had made for him. Wilf betrayed no previous knowledge, and was appropriately impressed. Rachel was beaming with pride. "I yust keep these for Sunday," said Toivo putting them carefully on. They were a perfect fit. He smiled, and stood once he had them on, saying, "Thank you so much, Mama," as he kissed her, then went on, "I very lucky man."

It was getting dark when they'd sat down for their supper, as the days were getting shorter, and with the time involved for making the stew they were a little late in eating. Now that they were done with the dishes, it was quite dark, and Rachel's eyes were getting heavy.

"We should get going now," suggested Serena. Wilf got up, and offered his hand to Rachel, who let him help her out of her chair. Toivo offered to drive them, but Rachel declined, protesting it was a nice evening for a walk, and the fresh air would do them good. Thanks and hugs were given all around, and Toivo, Helen, and Madeleine saw them to the door.

"Come back soon, Vilf; maybe ve shoot some duck next time, eh?"

"OK, Toivo," Wilf replied. "We'll think about that."

The evening was considerably cooler for the walk home, but not uncomfortable. The coolness brought on a mist over the lake, but the air was clear and well lit along the road to Rachel's. It was well past nine when they got to her place. Serena went in first and turned on a light. She had a package of the breast meat that Helen had given her, and she put that in the fridge. Rachel bid them good night and went straight to bed. Serena and Wilf were not far behind. They brushed their teeth, got undressed, and climbed naked into bed.

They lay close together for awhile, talking quietly over the events of the day. It certainly wasn't the day Wilf expected, starting with a huge breakfast of blueberry pancakes and Pickerel fillets followed by a cleansing, relaxing sauna; then there was Toivo's horse Barney and an excellent hunt for birds. And what a meal those birds made! Serena's family were just great people to be around. They lived a pretty simple life, but it was a very full life, a good life.

"It's been a wonderful day, Serena," Wilf acknowledged, holding her close. Her hand had found its way to his stiff erection.

"Looks like it's not over yet," she said. She leaned over and kissed him long and hard, her tongue sliding eagerly into his mouth. He rolled her back, returning her kiss. They were horny for each other, and didn't need to bother with a lot of elaborate foreplay. They seemed to of one mind about that; he was hard and she was already wet. She guided him into her opening and they began making love, first gently, and slowly; finally from the depth of their lust they climaxed, Serena lost in multiple orgasms, Wilf completely spent.

As his breathing restored, he raise himself on his elbows, to take his weight off of Serena. Looking down on her, she was smiling contently. "Boy, that was a good one," he managed.

"As good as it gets," she said. They lay together and talked, feeling totally relaxed and at peace. They had been well rested when the day began, and though it had been a very eventful day, it had been by no means strenuous. They were enjoying the moment, and were not overcome by sleep. In due course, the urge came upon them again, and without discussion, or any foreplay, they proceeded to copulate again, and once again culminated in a strong and mutual climax.

Finally, as they were both relaxed again, Wilf surprised Serena, as he stared peacefully at the ceiling in the darkness of the room. "You know Serena," he said, "maybe we should get married."

"Yes," she agreed, "I think maybe we should." She waited a moment for him to continue the discussion, but he'd rolled over and fell asleep. She had to laugh, and shortly fell asleep herself.

It was breaking day when they awoke, which was closer to seven now, being the end of September. Rachel, always the early bird, was already up, and they could smell the coffee. Wilf got dressed quickly, in need to relieve his bladder. Upon emerging from the bedroom he greeted Rachel with, "Good morning Rachel", and she returned the courtesy, handing him a fresh coffee, as she did so.

"Did you sleep well, Wilf?" she continued.

"Like a log," he said, accepting the coffee with thanks, and immediately setting it down on the table.

"I'll be right back," he added, as he bolted for the door. Rachel smiled understandingly.

When he returned from the outhouse, Serena was up and in her jeans, stripped to her waste, washing up in the alcove. She shortly got into her bra and T-shirt and joined Wilf at the table. "I could use a wash myself", he said, and taking the emptied basin, pumped into it some fresh water. He took it into the alcove, striped off his shirt, and washed away the fragrance of Serena's love, and then shaved himself. He returned to the table feeling refreshed.

Rachel had made porridge, and asked, "Is porridge OK this morning?"

"Porridge is fine," Serena said.

"I have some bannock and jam," Rachel added, putting out a plate of neatly sliced bannock, and a jar of her own homemade strawberry jam. She poured them both a fresh coffee before sitting down to join them for porridge. They had a quiet breakfast. Wilf couldn't resist having a couple of good slices of bannock with his porridge; he liked it better than any bread he'd ever tasted, with the possible exception of his mother's homemade bread, but that was a long time ago and this was now.

He spread a thick layer of Rachel's jam over a slice and bit into it. She smiled at the effect that showed on his face. "You sure make great jam, Rachel," he commented emphatically through his mouthful of bannock. She thanked him modestly for his compliment.

Done with eating, they all had another coffee, before Wilf and Serena packed up to leave. Afterwards, they gathered up their things for the bus ride back to Atikokan. Wilf was into his runners again, his dancing shoes put away in his knapsack, along with yesterday's shirt, socks, and undershorts. Serena had her night bag packed, and the two of them hugged Rachel, thanking her for a lovely weekend.

"Come back soon, Wilf," she said as they stepped into the day.

It was cooler now, and there was a hint of frost; the Indian summer was wearing off. The sky was clear, and the brightness of the morning sun was coming on. It was nice and fresh, but it was getting well into fall. They were soon at the Restaurant/General Store/Post Office. The school kids were waiting for the bus, standing together, talking amongst themselves when the bus arrived. To Wilf's surprise they remembered him from his last visit, and one of them even greeted him by name.

He took a seat beside Serena near the back of the bus and quietly went over the events of the weekend, as they rode together. It was living at its best. Life was good to him!

The bus was back in Atikokan now. The driver pulled up at the High School and let the school kids off, then drove the bus back to the parking bay, one block down the street from Cross' Rooming House. Wilf and Serena thanked the driver as they got off the bus. Wilf walked her to the restaurant. She hugged him at the door, and said, "Can I buy you a coffee?"

"Sure, why not," he said, coming in. He took a stool at the counter, setting his knapsack down beside him as he sat down to a coffee.

On his last afternoon shift, Wilf was back to work along with Gus and Stan, as usual. They were told at the wicket that dayshift had just blasted; the track and pipes were in, and they had only to go in and start mucking out. They got off on their level, and pushed in their string of Hudsons, with Stan on the motor, and Wilf and Gus riding the back end of it. Stan bought the cars up behind the mucking machine. Gus shut off the air header from blowing smoke, turned on the water, and pulled the hose up to wash down the muck pile.

He started first by washing down the scattered muck between the mucking machine and the muckpile. The smoke had mostly cleared from the blast, and as he pulled the hose ahead and got right up to the muckpile, he could see a twisted eight foot steel sticking out of the middle of the face, and that the muckpile wasn't as big as it should be.

"Looks like Jamieson's back on the job," he said to Wilf. Wilf gave a disgusted nod. It had been such a nice weekend, and afternoons had started so well. Gus handed the hose to Wilf, and started mucking out; first cleaning up the scattered muck in front of the mucker, then getting into the muckpile. Wilf continued washing down till Gus had filled the first car, then Wilf dropped the hose, rode the train back to the California switch, and switched an empty to the front of the train for Gus to fill. Wilf stayed at the California switch now, switching the next empty ahead of the train for Gus, and Gus continued washing down the muckpile in between cars.

When all eight of the cars were full, Wilf rode the tail end car to the waste dump with Stan. Once all eight cars were dumped, Garth showed up, just fresh off the cage.

"How's it going, guys," he greeted them as he approached.

"Jump on and we'll show you," said Stan. Garth jumped onto the back end of the motor beside Wilf, and the three of them headed back to catch up with Gus. Stan stopped short of the mucking machine, and flashed his light at Gus not to muck; Wilf and Stan went up with Garth to join Gus in front of the mucking machine. Garth immediately noticed the stuck steel sticking out of the face. By this time Gus had the face and muckpile well washed down, and the frozen ground and bootlegs were plainly visible.

"Looks like Jamieson is back," said Stan. Garth stared at the mess wide-eyed, taking it in, but not saying anything. It was Gus who spoke up next, Gus, easy going Gus, the last one to ever complain.

"I did my best to jerk that steel loose with a chain on the mucker. It won't come. Now I've got to muck around the fucking thing, and we've got it right in our way when we go to drill off. What is so hard about lining up your cut? The idea is to drill the holes parallel; not connect them. He's run that eight foot steel right into the hole beside it and jammed it right in. No wonder he doesn't break his rounds. Can't you put Hank Loster leading? He's a miner, Jamieson never will be; we'll be lucky if he doesn't get us killed."

Garth measured the boot legs with his tape; they were over three feet. "I'll write this up," said Garth, "Unfortunately Vince has seniority and insists on leading. Briggs even made the suggestion he be moved, but management doesn't want any conflict with the union."

"What about ability?" said Stan, "shouldn't that count for something?"

"Technically, Vince has the ability," Garth said, "he was on development on 700 driving those scran drifts; so he had experience."

"Any fool could break a round on 700. They were taking five foot rounds with just a V-cut, and when the ground was too soft for drilling a five foot hole, they were using chippers. A mud miner, that's what he is." There was a big difference between driving a scran drift through the soft ground of the ore body, and driving a drift through the hard ground on the 1100' level. Some skill was required to break a good round in the hard ground, and it took a good crew to make a complete cycle; to drill off, blast, then get it mucked out, all in the same shift.

Garth knew that. He didn't want to be in this conversation. He tried to move to an irrelevant comment on the good weather they were having, but found him ignored. "Well do your best boys," said Garth. Turning to leave he added "I'll make a strong suggestion in the log."

"Maybe you could suggest these stupid pricks be taken out," said Stan but Garth just kept on walking.

Gus managed to get mucked out in spite of the eight foot steel protruding from the face. In all, he had only mucked nineteen cars, where there should have been a good thirty. By the time Stan and Wilf had dumped the train, parked the empties in the layby, and came back with the motor, Gus had cleaned down to the lifters, and carefully flagged each of the five bootlegged lifters with a piece of broken drill steel. He was washing out all the remaining bootlegs with a copper blowpipe, and painting a circle around each one with the yellow paint can.

Stan hung the grade chains, and gave him line. Gus marked center, and then marked off the face; the three of them pulled up the jacklegs, the hoses, the ladders, the steel and bits, and set up to drill. Once the oil was in the lubricators, and they were set up to drill, they paused for a sandwich, sitting down on the side of the drift.

"Well, we said it out loud and clear," said Gus.

"I'm afraid that's not going anywhere," said Stan. Wilf was silent; his face was set, not liking this more than anyone. Gus made an attempt to lighten things up, and turning to Wilf said, "You know this Jamieson a little?"

"I know him a lot," said Wilf testily, "and for two cents, I'd beat his face off."

Stan was done his cigarette and Gus was nicely into a fresh wad of Copenhagen. Finally Stan, feeling enough had been said, got up. "Well, might as well do something once."

Wilf and Gus joined him, opened their air and water and started drilling the lifters. Stan with one in the center had to move over a foot to avoid the bootlegged lifter. Wilf and Gus couldn't drill their corner lifters right in the bottom corners of the round like they should. They could only collar theirs a foot to the inside of the bootlegged corner lifters. The bootlegs were tight to the wall and so they could look their lifters out gently to come out right at the end of their holes.

Now Stan had his lifter in four feet and slid in his eight to deepen it. When he put his machine on his eight, Gus and Wilf had their corners in four feet. As Stan finished his eight, Gus and Wilf had their inside lifters drilled the four feet, and had slid their eight foot steels into the corner lifters to deepen them to eight feet.

Done with the center lifter, Stan moved up to drill the first hole in the cut. He collared it well over to Wilf's side of the face in order to distance himself a good two feet from the frozen cut in the middle of the face. As he started his hole, Gus and Wilf started to deepen their corner lifters to eight feet. Stan and Wilf both had their backs to Gus, when suddenly there was a loud BOOM like a cannon going off behind them. Stan was knocked over top of Wilf who was knocked flat on his face with his machine still running. The noise of the explosion was so near and so loud that they were deafened by the blast.

Dazed, the two men slowly got up and put their hats back on. Stan was trying to say something to Wilf. He might have been shouting, but Wilf could only see his lips moving; and there was Gus, sprawled flat on his back, not moving. His machine, though it had been blown back a good twelve feet from the face, was still running full throttle, with a short remnant of the blasted eight foot steel still in its chuck.

"Wilf, you stay with Gus; I'm going for help." Stan was shouting, but Wilf could barely hear him, so great was the ringing in his ears from the blast. Numbly, Wilf nodded understanding. Stan climbed on the motor and went for the station, full throttle.

At least Gus was breathing. His face was a horribly cut up, swollen mess. At last he started to move a little, and began moaning softly. Wilf took one of his hands, and shouted, "I'm here Gus, can you hear me?", but Gus couldn't hear. Wilf tried again, shouting at the top of his lungs, "Can you hear me, Gus?"

"Yes, I can hear you, Wilf," he said very softly. Wilf could only see his lips moving; then he said more loudly, "Wilf, I can't see." and then shrieking, "Wilf, I can't see!"

Wilf couldn't stop his tears; he tried not to make a sound as he wept, not that Gus could hear him. He squeezed his hand gently and yelled through his tears, "I'm right here, Gus. Stan is coming."

Gus stared vacantly with sightless eyes said nothing. Down the drift Wilf could see the light of the motor returning. They were pushing a flat car in front. Wilf could see three lights on the motor. When the motor drew up behind the mucker, Wilf could see the basket stretcher on top of the motor.

Stan had returned with two of the drift crew, Dave Chambers and Joe Kilgannon from the other heading. Their third man, Ivan Gagnon, had gone to surface to get an ambulance called. Wilf, not moving from his side, continued to hold Gus' hand. Wilf's body shook as he wept. The two men from the other crew looked at Gus in horror as they laid the stretcher down beside him.

Stan pulled Wilf to his feet and to his surprise Wilf threw his arms around him, knocking his hat off, hugging and clinging to him while weeping uncontrollably. Stan held him for only a moment then pushed him loose. Gripping him by the front of his shirt with his left hand slapped him hard to his face with his open handed right. Wilf was then able to compose himself somewhat. His hearing was coming back a little now, as he heard Stan say, "Sorry, partner."

Wilf nodded in understanding, finally shouted in Stan's ear, "He's blind, Stan!"

Stan nodded. "Give us a hand here, Wilf." They laid a blanket down full length beside Gus on the opposite side of the stretcher. Turning Gus gently on his side pulled the blanket tight against him and rolled him carefully back onto it.

The four of them each took a corner of the blanket. With one hand grasping the middle they carefully lifted him onto the well-padded stretcher and then eased the stretcher onto the flatcar. Joe and Dave got onto the back end of the motor and with Wilf on the flatcar next to Gus, the five of them headed for the station.

The ambulance was waiting in the shafthouse when they got to surface. The driver had backed the ambulance into the headframe and was ten feet from the cage door when they got there. The driver had an attendant with him, and as soon as Gus was in the ambulance and the door was closed, they drove away with Gus to the hospital, their lights flashing, and their siren going.

"I'm going home," said Stan.

"Me too," said Wilf.

Garth nodded understandingly. "Your heading will be shut down for a week at least," he said, "The mines inspector will need to do his investigation." Garth himself was visibly shaken, trying hard to be composed. "We'll find you both a good spot in the meantime," he added.

Stan nodded vacantly, and without voicing a reply, turned and left him. Garth had offered them a taxi ride home, compliments of the mine, but they'd declined; it was close to a bright full moon; they would walk the four miles to town. Even in the dark, they knew the road well enough. They needed some air.

For a mile and a half they walked in silence, each in their own thoughts. The mood was heavy. Finally Wilf broke the silence. "I'm going to kill that stupid fucking prick," he stated matter-of –factly. Stan knew he meant it, and knew enough to let him talk.

"And how would you kill him, Wilf?"

"I'd pound his face into the ground, and if he's still breathing, then maybe I'll choke him to death."

Stan was encouraged some by the word 'maybe', and thought he might get it of his system if he'd keep talking. It was a cool evening in late September, but not freezing at night yet. The air was crisp and clear, and it felt good to be walking. Another mile went by and Wilf had not said another word. His face was set, and Stan knew he could be dangerous. Maybe Serena could help; a good piece of tail would certainly take the edge off, but the next long change was three weeks away, and it didn't look like Wilf was in the mood for love. Stan was trying to get Wilf's mind off of Vince Jamieson; finally he said, "You need to see Serena, Wilf."

"Who?"

Now Stan was worried. He took himself a cigarette, and just out of courtesy, offered one to Wilf. To his complete surprise, Wilf accepted the offer.

"Sure, what the hell," he said. Stan lit Wilf's, then his own, eying Wilf as he took a long deep drag, and then inhaled. He did seem noticeably more relaxed.

"I hope I haven't fucked you up, Wilf. I mean you had quit."

"Yeah, well fuck it anyways."

They were coming down the last hill on the mine road now, just coming into 'Lone Pine' as was called that part of Atikokan, just on the edge of town.

They walked in silence the rest of the way home. As Stan went to his room, Wilf asked him for one more cigarette. Stan gave him the rest of his package. Wilf protested he only needed one.

"No problem, Wilf," Stan said. "I've got almost a whole carton in the room."

Wilf accepted the offer and without another word, went to his own room. He took his runners off, and lay upon the bed in the dark, revisiting the disastrous event of the hours before. He couldn't sleep, so he turned the light on and tried to read, but couldn't concentrate. He stared at the ceiling finally lighting another cigarette. He felt a great sadness for Gus, whom he knew was never going to be the same, and felt enraged that it had to happen at all. But it did happen.

It was breaking day before he finally could feel sleep coming on. He turned off the light, and let himself fall asleep, still fully clothed, on top of his blankets, the bed still made. He awoke in the late morning, still in a rage, and went to the restaurant, not bothering to shave. Stan was alone in a booth, reading a newspaper over a coffee. Wilf sat at the counter nearby, and Serena handed him a coffee without being asked. "I'm sorry about Gus," she offered

"Thanks," he said. The ringing was finally gone from his ears, and his hearing was close to normal again. She smiled at him, and reached down and touched his hand. He felt embarrassed for a moment, looking carefully around to see if anyone had noticed. There was only Stan, who broke the silence, looking up from his paper.

"Care to join me, partner?" he asked.

Wilf came over to the booth, seemingly to extract himself from Serena's intimate touch. Stan folded the paper and put it aside. "What we need is a good breakfast," he said. Wilf nodded vacantly, seemingly transfixed.

"Serena, bring us a good breakfast, would you? Ham and eggs, lots of good homefries, and some brown toast with it, please."

Serena scribbled out the order, relieved that Stan had broken the silence. Stan didn't push him for conversation, and when the food arrived, they ate in silence. Wilf was right into the food in spite of his mood, and cleaned off his plate in no time at all. Serena came with more coffee, and took their plates.

Stan offered Wilf a cigarette, took one himself, and lit them up. Wilf drew deeply on his cigarette, and then exhaled. Serena saw he was smoking, but was careful not to betray any notice.

"Feeling any better now?" Stan began.

"Ya, a little thanks."

"Let's take a hike up to the hospital, and see what's going on with Gus."

"Ya, let's do that."

Off they went to the hospital, and when they got there, they found out Gus had been taken by ambulance early that morning to St. Joseph's Hospital in Port Arthur. One eye was gone they were told, and the other on was damaged badly. There was some hope for that eye, but not much. On their way back to Cross' rooming house, it was Wilf who broke the silence. "You knew him before, Stan?" he asked.

"Yeah, I sure did Wilf. We worked partners driving an 8x8 drift at the Celebrity Mine out of Watson Lake up in the Yukon; that was a few years back. He was as big as ever then, but boy, that man was tough. We were in camp for over four months without coming to town. He never touched a drink in camp, but he sure hit 'er when we got to town. We were in this restaurant and bar just out Watson Lake a ways on the Alaskan Highway; 'The Last Chance' I think it was. The waitress was crossed eyed, and he was fat. She'd walk by him, and had to laugh because he was fat; then he'd laugh at her because she was cross eyed. You had to be there; every time they looked at each other they'd burst out laughing. They'd never seen each other before, but they were having a great time of it laughing at each other. They had everyone in the place laughing too. I have to laugh when I think about it. Gus used to say, "There's nothing like fun."

"Let's hope he's not done yet," said Wilf. They were back at Cross' now.

"Well, I think I'm going to go up to my room and stretch out for awhile," said Stan, as they reached the door.

"Me, I think I'll go for a walk. I need to keep moving. Catch you later." And Wilf went walking; he wasn't paying much attention to where he was going, but before too long he found himself at the church where he'd met Father Grant. He went to the church door and found it unlocked, and quietly went in. He saw Father Grant, who was stooped near the altar, bent over, arranging some flowers. He came up fairly close to him and made a sound as if clearing his throat, to let the good priest know he was there. Father Grant turned to him, quite composed and smiling, not startled in the least.

"Yes my son, what brings you here?" he asked, "What can I do for you?"

"I haven't been to church in years, Father, at least not since I last saw you, and that was only once. Maybe you don't remember me."

"No my son, I do remember you. Your name is Wilf Baker, and we talked. That was last spring, I believe."

"You have a good memory, Father."

"You are not someone I would easily forget, son."

"Well I'm here Father, and I do need to talk."

"Do you need to confess?"

"Could we just talk?"

"Of course we can, Wilf. Let's talk. Sit down here and we'll talk."

They sat together on a pew in the quiet of the empty church. Wilf told him of the terrible event of his last shift with Gus. "I'm sure his mining days are over," he went on.

'I'm sorry."

"What's eating me up is it shouldn't have happened, it didn't have to happen, and it happened to one of the best men I ever worked with or ever knew."

"We must pray for him, Wilf: let us pray now."

And pray they did; but at the end of their prayers Wilf finally said, "I want to kill the son of a bitch that did this to him."

The priest could see with some alarm that he meant it; his eyes were tight, his face set, and his words came out in a growl through clenched teeth. He put his hand over Wilf's and said, "Vengeance is mine sayeth the Lord; I will repay."

"I'd like to help him," said Wilf.

"No Wilf; this is God's business. Vince Jamieson will have to live with what he has done."

Wilf got up slowly and thanked Father Grant. "I'm sorry Father; I guess I'm upset," he said.

"Of course you are."

"I am feeling a little better now."

"That's good Wilf. May you come and see us on Sunday."

"Thanks Father, maybe see you Sunday," he said, as he was leaving. He left as quietly as he came in without looking back. His rage had subsided considerably; he no longer thought of killing Vince, but he certainly wasn't going to pray for him, as Father Grant had suggested. He made his way back to the restaurant. It was past five, and he was feeling hungry. Serena had finished her shift, and was gone.

The big blonde girl, Barbara, was on now. He ordered a cheeseburger deluxe. Stan wasn't around, but he wasn't feeling sociable anyway. He ate his cheeseburger and chips seated on a stool at the counter; then went back to his room. Stan was just getting up, and he passed him in the hallway.

"Eat yet?" he asked.

"Just finished; I'm going to stretch out now."

"Catch you later."

"Yup."

That was Saturday. Sunday went by and then it was Monday dayshift. Stan and Wilf showed up at the wicket to get their instructions for the shift. They already knew their heading was shut down for the week, pending the investigation of the mines inspector, and a possible inquest. Garth looked up. Seeing them he said "You boys will be on the 700' level for the week or so till we get your heading going again. Tom will give you the lineup for the shift." Garth pointed to Tom Cruikshank in the adjacent wicket so they moved over to Tom's side.

"Hi guys," said Tom, "I guess you two will be with me for this week at least. I'll keep you both together. I'm putting you in Scran 5-3. Get on the manhaul car at the station on the 700' level. That'll take you in. You get off at crosscut #5 and keep right on that crosscut till you come to the third scran. That'll be your spot. Just keep filling a train whenever you can get one."

They got off the manhaul at the fifth crosscut, and finding their way to their allotted scran, climbed up the manway into it. They set their lunch pails down behind the big electric 125 horse-powered slusher anchored behind the mill hole. The scrans on 700 were right above and at right angles to the crosscuts. The mill hole was quite large (6'x6') and over it had a grizzly of heavy rails spaced two feet apart. It was placed in line with the scran to prevent the big scraper from falling through the mill hole as the muck was raked in from the boxholes. The rails of the grizzly were cemented in flush with the floor of the scran so that the scraper wouldn't catch on them as it raked the muck into the waiting cars below.

Stan and Wilf walked past the mill hole to check out the scran. The boxholes had been cut alternately from the left side to the right side of the scran, every twenty feet, running the length of the 100' scran drift. Every one of the boxholes had its pile of muck spilling out into the scran. They were all running as they should. What stopped them in their tracks were the cracks throughout the thick cement that coated the walls and back of the scran drift.

"I don't like the looks of this, partner," said Stan.

Wilf nodded in agreement. "Not good, partner," he said.

They got to the end of the scran, and noticed that the walls and back were not only cracked, but squeezing in somewhat. The tail block at the end of the scran was a grooved wheel, two feet in diameter whose heavy axle was anchored between two heavy I-beams cemented between the floor and the back of the scran. The heavy inch and a quarter back cable would run over around it, as the slushermen drew the scraper back and forth, up and down the scran. Although the walls and back were showing cracks, and squeezing in, nothing was caving, and the tail block remained solidly in place.

"I'm wondering if that big scraper could pass all the way to the end here. It's getting pretty tight," commented Stan finally.

They turned to see a light emerging from the manway. It was Tom Cruikshank, their shifter for the week.

"Having a look, eh, boys?" he began.

"Ya not so good eh?" commented Stan.

"Well, it's cracking up a bit: it's hard to hold against pressure. But don't worry.... nothing's going to fall on you; this cement is thick, and it's all rebarred. Once we started pulling the muck from these boxholes the ore body started to cave into them. That was the plan; block cave."

"Looks like you're caving more than the ore body here," said Stan, eying some of the cracks.

"Well, once the caving began, the ground around the scrans didn't seem to support itself so well; but these walls and back are coated in thick, rebarred cement, and lots of steel sets in between. Nothing's going to fall on you."

"I am sorry about Gus, "Tom went on. "They may be able to save his right eye. I sure hope so. I'll be paying you two the same bonus you made in your drift contract (the miners slushing in the scrans were normally not on contract and worked alone.) Oh, I think I just heard the trammers pull up to your mill hole. I'll get out of your way, and let you get slushing." He left for the manway, and Wilf and Stan got behind the slusher. The slusher was a pretty simple machine. Wilf slushed and Stan watched.... a pretty slack shift for two highball driftmen. The usual thing on 700 was to have one miner per scran, but Tom Cruikshank had been told to keep Stan and Wilf together for the week.

The switchman of the train crew poked his head through the manway, and at the flash of his light Wilf started filling the train. The switchman stayed where he was in the manway, where the motor man could see him to spot the next car, and where the slushermen could see him, when he flashed his light for them to stop while they moved the next empty car in place and to start again when it was ready.

Wilf ran the slusher first. The bench behind it was wide enough for both of them and Stan sat beside him having a smoke as Wilf slushed. The blade of the scraper was hinged on the two arms of the scraper, so that as he drew it back towards the tail block it would fold up, giving less resistance. As he dragged it back toward the mill hole, it would open up, catching the muck from the boxholes.

Wilf only pulled from the two boxholes closest the mill hole at first, and filled five of the twelve 10 ton cars before they quit running. Once they'd hung up, he pulled the scraper back farther to the next two, and pulled from them till they quit. Finally, to fill the last two cars of the train, he was dragging the scraper all the way back to the tail block, pulling the muck from the last three boxholes. They were still running, when he'd filled the last car. He left he scraper near the mill hole, and shut off the slusher. The switchman climbed down the manway, and rode the train to the ore pass on the back end of the last car, to empty their load.

Wilf and Stan took a walk up the scran, with a scaling bar in hand, to see about getting the boxholes running again. Stan poked at the first one. There was a chunk near the collar of the boxholet that seemed to have gotten it plugged. Stan put the tip of the bar against it and pried against the top of the boxhole. The chunk came free and the muck again spilled into the scran. The next boxhole would not let go even with Stan's best effort with the scaling bar; for that one they would place a shot at quitting time, and blast it loose.

"I feel badly about Gus," said Wilf, "we had such a good go, the three of us."

Stan nodded in silent agreement, as he prodded the hangup in the next boxhole. That one and the next one came down easily, but on the last one they heard an unwelcome sound, as the freed muck came spilling out of the boxhole into the scran. There was an audible groaning, grinding kind of sound which seemed to settle against the wall of the scran drift. Steep Rock was a good go, but it was starting to crumble.

They didn't get another train to fill for the rest of the shift. There were only two traincrews hauling the muck from the scrans, and there were a good number of scran drifts. The traincrews were on contract, and never stopped unless the ore pass was full, and they couldn't dump; otherwise they were never short of places to pull. They would take the scrans in order, so the miners in the scrans would have to wait their turn. Sometimes that meant a lot of waiting. Stan and Wilf had nothing to do for the rest of the shift, except to place a charge for the one hangup they couldn't bar down, and blast it down at quitting time. Miners working the scrans were paid company time; they were not on contract, no bonus was paid. Stan and Wolf knew they were being given special treatment to be left together and on contract.

Stan and Wilf sat on their bench, having a cigarette, as they waited.

"It's no wonder there's no bonus paid for the scrans," commented Stan.

"Yes," agreed Wilf. "It was good of them to pay us our drift contract while we're here."

"Maybe they figure they owe us," said Stan," I mean they were warned about Jamieson; they've got egg on their face."

"Maybe, but that's not helping Gus much."

Quitting time rolled around and they lit the fuse on their boxhole shot, and then guarded their blast from the bottom of their manway. Once it blew, they went home. The rest of week went by much the same, usually filling one train per shift. Once they got started on a second train, but their boxholes plugged up before it was filled, so the trammers moved onto the next scran. They did get the muck moving again, but the train crew never got back to them.

"Sure don't get overworked doing these scrans," commented Wilf.

"No, not much," agreed Stan.

On the Friday after shift, they decided to drop by Molly's to see how she was doing with everything. They found her weeding her flower beds along the front of her house. She invited them in for a coffee. She seemed herself as she prepared the coffee and served them, but started to cry as soon as she sat down at the table to join them. She got a hold of herself quickly however, apologizing for her outburst.

"Poor Gus," she began. "He's lost the sight of his left eye completely.....and the right eye? Well I don't know. He can see light, and shapes, and such like. They're keeping him in St. Joseph's Hospital for now, but I don't think he'll ever be right again."

She cried again, and composed herself, again apologizing. "Hank Loster offered to take me into the Lakehead tomorrow to see Gus. Maybe you'd like to come," and then cursed Vince; "that fucking Jamieson....."

Stan and Wilf did join them the next day for the ride in to the Lakehead to visit Gus. Molly had brought sandwiches for the trip along with some MacIntosh apples. Hank was able to give Stan and Wilf the update on the mining inspector's report. What the inspector had surmised was what Wilf had suspected right from the start. The inspector along with a cohort had determined that the lifter that had missholed shouldn't have been drilled in the first place. (A 'misshole' or missed hole is a loaded hole which didn't detonate).

There were the five lifters which were in keeping with the pattern of the round. The missholed lifter didn't belong there. Normally the leader, Vince, would only be drilling the center lifter, leaving the corner lifters and the two inside lifters to the wingmen on either side of center. It was determined by the angle of the bootleg that it had been drilled by the center machine from the same leg that was positioned to drill the center lifter; and as it was looking down more steeply, did not connect with the inside lifter drilled by the miner on the left, namely Hank Loster. A tattered remnant of tape fuse about three feet long had been found after the incident, the remaining piece apparently unburned. The copper end had not ignited; seemingly it had not been hooked into the round, or at any rate the copper end had not been snapped onto the Thermalite properly. The end of it was unbent, so likely it was not hooked up to the Thermalite at all; and thus although the hole was loaded, it did not go off. Vince Jamieson was quizzed by the inspector, and was asked had he drilled that lifter, which he vehemently denied. "It's not my job to drill anybody's lifter except my own," he maintained, "I only drilled the center lifter."

The miner to Vince's left, Hank Loster, was questioned separately by the inspector. He was no fan of Vince Jamieson in the first place, and he had a different story to tell.

"Vince drilled his center lifter, then swung his machine over and drilled that missholed lifter from the same leg. It wasn't helping me any. It was looking to the left, right out of alignment and looking down too much. Vince drills everything way too heavy. I waited till he was out of the way; then drilled the lifter in the right place and lined it up properly. I didn't load his misplaced hole either. It should've been left unloaded. Vince must've loaded it, and it's always Vince who hooks up the round. He must have forgotten to hook that one in."

When Gus had carefully checked out the face, washed out the bootlegs, and flagged them. It was understandable how he would miss that one. He had not allowed for stupidity. He had found the expected five bootlegged lifters; that other hole should never have been there.

"Vince was a bull head to work with," said Hank. "Couldn't line up his holes...he was all over the place... no system. He had no business drilling that lifter; he was only supposed to drill the center lifter, but he swung his machine over my way, and drills my inside lifter from the same leg he'd drilled his center lifter it a way out of line, and looking down too much." Hank, in his passion, was repeating himself.

"I drilled the lifter properly, and loaded my own holes. That haywire lifter should have never been loaded, but Vince loads it anyway; and he keeps loading his cut heavy in that soft limestone ground, bootlegging every round. I told him to blast it light, but no...this is how Vince does it.

Vince always insisted on being the one to wire up the round, and I'm sure he missed hooking that fuse into the Thermalite, and that's why it missholed. Anyway, we'll be back in our heading come Monday. We'll see then how this all plays out."

They arrived shortly at the hospital, and went up to Gus' room. Gus was asleep when they came into the room. His eyes were bandaged and he was snoring quietly. Molly took his hand gently, and said, "It's me Gus."

"That you honey?"

She squeezed his hand, and said, "I'm here Gus."

Wilf could see the tears rolling down Gus' cheeks through the bandages. Gus squeezed back on Molly's hand, and said, "Thanks for coming to see me, dear." Molly collapsed on his chest, sobbing uncontrollably.

Gus stroked her head lovingly. "We'll keep going sweetheart. I can still play, can't I?"

Molly had brought his fiddle, but thought it best maybe not to leave it with him. "I'm sure you'll be doing that Gus," she managed, "but maybe not just yet."

"No, I'm pretty flattened out right now; they don't even want me sitting up. They'll keep my eyes covered for now. They said I've lost the sight of my left eye, but there's some hope the right one might come back. They keep putting drops and gook into it, so for no infection, you know. Maybe I'll be OK."

"Gus, Stan and Wilf are here to see you," Molly said.

Gus stuck out his hand, and the tears started again; these were tears of joy. He shook their hands, each in turn. "Welcome aboard," he said, and the three of them could feel lumps in their throats, but managed to keep it light.

"We miss you at work, partner," Stan said.

"Ya, we had a great time."

"Let's hope we do it again," Stan came back, "remember One-eyed Jack McMasters?"

"Ya, did know him. He was up on that Yukon job; good man, but nuts when he drank, like most of us, I guess." Gus was laughing now, and Molly had brightened up. "We'll get past this, honey," he said, squeezing her hand.

"Yes we will, Gus. I brought you your fiddle, but maybe I should leave it with the nurse for now."

"No, just put it in the closet."

"OK, but I'll tell the nurse."

"OK, do that."

"I brought you some clothes too, and I'll hang them up in the closet."

"Good enough. With any luck, I'll be into them soon."

Finally she said, "Gus, Hank is here too. He's the one who brought us in."

Gus was quiet for a moment. There was an awkward silence; then finally Gus asked, "Hank, who put that hole there?"

"Vince."

"I figured so. Is he still leading shift?"

"I don't think so. The heading's been shut down for the last week, pending the mines inspector's report, so we've all been put on 700 for the week. He's made his report now so we're back in our heading after the weekend, except for Vince maybe. I'm hoping he'll be kept on 700, slushing in a scran drift."

At his point Wilf interrupted, "Remember how the rounds broke when Vince had a sprained ankle?"

"Right to the nuts," said Gus. "Well it looks like something good may come of this." He stuck out his hand, "Put 'er there Hank." Hank's eyes were wet as he shook Gus' hand. "We're good, Hank," he continued, "you done a good thing, bringing my partners and the missus out."

He paused. "Now you boys run along for now; me and the missus got some catching up to do. And thank you so much for coming." It was just Gus' way of being considerate. Molly had elected to stay in town for a few days, and thanked Hank for bringing them in. They had nothing more they wanted to do in the Lakehead, so the three of them left Molly with her mate, and headed back to Atikokan.

They were quiet for a ways coming back when finally Hank broke the silence with "Doesn't look so good for Gus, does it?"

"No, it doesn't," said Stan. "It is what it is, I guess. Too bad."

As they pulled into town, Wilf was quiet, but Stan said, "For what it's worth, I am feeling a little better for the visit. Thanks for bringing us in, Hank."

"You're welcome. Where you boys want off? Sinclair's OK?"

"That'll be fine."

Work went well again in the drift for Stan and Wilf. Tom Higgins, a good driftman, was brought in as a third, to fill in for Gus. Wilf did the mucking now, and Tom did the switching. They went in for Sunday graveyard for their first shift back. They were the first shift back in the heading following the disastrous shift that put Gus in the hospital. They had to finish the round they'd started that fateful day, as they were the first shift back since the incident; it was the last time they had to follow one of Vince Jamieson's fuckups. Once they'd drilled and blasted the round, it was clear sailing.

From then on they followed Hank Loster. Hank came in on afternoon shift as leader now, replacing Vince Jamieson, who was left on 700, to operate a slusher. Al Wasney, a good driftman, was brought in as Hank's third man. Things went very smoothly for Stan, Wilf, and their new partner. Hank's rounds broke 'right to the nuts', and left Stan's crew good every time. The week of graveyards passed uneventfully. Production on the 700' level was good. The muck raked from the scrans continued to fill the trains nonstop. The conveyor from the crusher station below the loading pocket never waited for the iron ore to load the railway cars on surface, bound for the docks in Port Arthur.

Some of the scrans, however, were showing more and more the effects of pressure, as the ore body continued to cave. Some cracks were getting worse now, as the relentless pressure of an ore body that had lost its structure, pressed ever downwards on the scrans below. One scran became so tight, that the big scraper could no longer pass through; so it was replaced with a smaller one. A heavy I-beam was installed near the end of that scran, to restrain the crushing pressure. It was placed from wall to wall just below the back near the tail end of the scran; but the squeeze continued in spite of the I-beam, and the walls bulged in below the I-beam, finally making it impossible for even the small scraper to pass. That scran had to be abandoned. The big slusher was removed, and the manway and millhole closed off. A good flow of muck continued from the other scrans, although they were all getting squeezed.

Friday morning came, and Wilf was invited again by Serena to come to her mother's for the weekend. He hadn't as yet bought a car, or for that matter an engagement ring for Serena. He had more money in the bank than he'd ever be able to accumulate in recent years. He had a bank balance of $2,304.26 plus an emergency fund under his mattress of $300 in twenties, as well as a hundred or so in his wallet for walking around money. Money wasn't the problem. He was upset about Gus and was beginning to have his doubts about his future at Steep Rock. Apart from the problems of caving ground, the price of iron ore had dropped from over $23.00 @ ton down to $11.00 @ ton. Serena was considerate and didn't push it.

He had breakfast with Stan at the restaurant once back in town from his last graveyard. Serena served them. She told Wilf that she'd be off at three, and had Saturday off. She said if he'd care to come, they could catch the school bus for Sapawe. He went to his room after breakfast and slept a few hours, then arose and packed his knapsack for the weekend. He wouldn't be bringing his dancing shoes this time. The 'Hoot' 'n Holler' would never be the same without Gus, who had been the heart and soul of that hall. He was so much more than a great fiddler; he was warm and animated, effortlessly and infectiously friendly. People loved him. People who couldn't dance came for the music, or just to be there.

Rod Hicks declined any further engagements; without Gus, his heart wasn't in it any more. A musician was found who played an accordion quite well, accompanied by a rhythm guitar and a drummer. The accordionist seemed to want to play a lot of polkas with some waltzes thrown in, but the magic of Gus' fiddle was gone. People just weren't into coming anymore; they'd come to see Gus. The crowds dwindled. As the large building was unheated, and it was getting cool being late in the fall, management decided to close it down for the season. It never reopened.

Wilf got back to the restaurant shortly before three with his knapsack in hand, and Serena served him a coffee at the counter just before her shift ended at three, then left to go home to change, and pack her bag for the weekend. Wilf had his coffee and a cigarette, then left to join her at the bus bay for 3:30. It occurred to him now that the smoking habit was back to stay. For months he'd been free of it when he lit up that cigarette Stan had offered him, walking home that night from the mine after Gus' disastrous accident. He was in a rage at the time, and Stan meant well. It did help to settle him down; that cigarette hit the spot at the time, but he soon realized that once you light up again... you're smoking.

Of course he would quit again. Now just wasn't the time; he would wait till he felt a little more settled again. He knew too, that drinking would be the same; if he had one drink, he'd be drinking. He wouldn't do that one. Serena was at the bus bay ready to go when he got there. The driver hadn't shown up yet, so he lit another cigarette. The driver showed up before he was half finished. He stepped on his butt and boarded the bus behind Serena. It was past mid October now. The Indian summer was fading. There were colorful leaves still on the trees, but it was much cooler now. There was heavy frost in the mornings, and the leaves were beginning to fall.

The afternoon sun was bright and warm when they arrived at Sapawe. Serena had brought some steaks again from the restaurant, and Serena, Wilf and Rachel had a quiet dinner together. After dinner, the three of them walked over to Helen and Toivo's for an evening visit. The days were much shorter now, and it was already getting dark as they made their way. When they got there, they found Helen had just made their supper, and Toivo was washing his hands in the bathroom. Madeleine was helping to bring the food to the table.

Toivo greeted them through the open bathroom door, and Helen offered them dinner, but they declined graciously, having already eaten. She explained they were eating a little later than usual, because Toivo had shot a bear that came near where he was working in the bush that day. He had skinned it out in the bush, cut off the head, the paws, and removed the guts, before hauling the carcass home in the back of his pickup. Wilf, Serena and Rachel sat back with a coffee in the front room, and let Helen and her family have their supper. Once dinner was done with, and Helen started the cleanup, Wilf went with Toivo out to the pickup to have a look at his bear.

The carcass of the bear, minus its head, paws, hide, and guts, looked very much like the body of a man, nude and decapitated. Toivo had salvaged a copious amount of the bear's winter fat from its belly, and it lay in a large blob on the tarp, next to the carcass. The fat Helen would use for cooking. It made an excellent shortening, good for frying anything, and would keep well in the ice house. Toivo would strip the carcass of its flesh, and grind it up for mink feed for the winter. It was a male bear that he'd shot. He knew better than to take a mother bear from her cubs.

Wilf and Toivo looked at the carcass together for a moment, when Toivo broke in with, "How'bout ve shoot some ducks in the morning, Vilf?"

"What about this guy?" Wilf asked, indicating the carcass.

"Ve leave it here for now, Vilf; you yust vatch." With that, he backed his pickup as close as he could to the meat grinder and burning barrel. "OK, Vilf," he continued, "you help me now." Toivo took a front corner of the tarp, Wilf followed suit, and took the other front corner, and the two of them dragged the carcass and the fat off the pickup, onto the ground; then Toivo pulled the edges of the tarp over the bear, and said, "Ve leave it for now. I come get you early; ve shoot some ducks."

The dishes were put away, and Rachel and Serena were waiting for Wilf outside, by the doorstep of the house, ready for the walk back home. Wilf joined them. They said their goodbyes and headed back to Rachel's. Wilf didn't seem to share anyone's enthusiasm much. He was in a somber mood, and had been since the accident. He tried not to seem moody, but Serena didn't try to humour him either. She just let him be with it.

Rachel bid them good night after returning home. Serena and Wilf were in bed soon after. They made little attempt at conversation, simply laying quietly together for awhile. Finally they got around to sex, and then slept the night through. When they awoke, it was still dark, but Rachel was up, and they could hear Toivo at the door, early as he had promised. Rachel let him in. The coffee was already made, and she had a large batch of porridge on the go. Wilf quickly got dressed, and joined them in the kitchen. A sleepy Serena in her housecoat joined them a few minutes later at the table.

"You're up early," she commented to Toivo.

"Ya, ve shoot some ducks today," he replied simply. Serena nodded vacantly. Something Wilf had come to appreciate about Toivo was that he was not much of a talker. He said what he had to, but not much more. He accepted a bowl of porridge when it was ready, and ate it quietly. Done with that, he said, "OK, ve go now, Vilf."

Serena said, "Just a minute Toivo," and poured Wilf a thermos full of coffee. "What about some lunch," she asked.

"No need it lunch; soon back."

"Well, I'll get you dad's shotgun at least," she said to Wilf; then went around to the shed in the back in her housecoat, and came back with her father's double barrel twelve gauge shotgun. "You got shells?' she asked. Toivo nodded.

"You come for supper tonight," he said in parting, "Ve cook some ducks." Wilf followed him out the door and got in his pickup. Toivo also had a double barreled 12 gauge, already in the pickup. Toivo drove back to his place, where Wilf followed him down to his dock with the two shotguns, and into Toivo's boat. Toivo had Wilf sit in the stern seat, and having cast off; he took the seat in the middle. He placed the oar lock pins in the oar locks, and placing the two shotguns carefully on the seat between them, he cautioned Wilf, "No smoke and no talk, Vilf," and quietly began to row the boat toward the island across the lake.

It was more than half a mile to the island. There was a mist over the lake with a frost that morning, and the air was quite cool. Toivo rowed on quietly, and it was just breaking day when he rounded the end of the island. He was carefully moving up to where the Crooked Pine River came into the bay at the end of the lake. The water was shallow there and there was an abundance of wild rice along the shore. They were close now; he set the oars down quietly, and let the boat drift putting his finger to his lips, pointing toward the rice patch.

Wilf nodded understanding, and looking in that direction Wilf could see the object of Toivo's stealth. A flock of Mallard ducks were quietly gorging themselves on the ripened rice. The fog was lifting nicely now, and dawn was slowly coming on. Toivo passed Wilf a couple of shells. They loaded their shotguns and slowly and carefully stood up. They were nicely within range. The ducks continued to feed, taking no notice of them as they took aim. They fired together, getting two ducks sitting, and two more, just as they started to move; then the ducks were gone.

Toivo rowed into the rice patch to gather up the four dead ducks. "Ve have lots for good supper now," he said.

Wilf had to smile. "I would think so," he agreed.

Toivo didn't worry about the noise now. He started up the motor and headed the boat back to his dock. Once he'd tied up the boat, the two of them took their guns and the ducks up to the house. Helen and Madeleine we already up having their breakfast and Serena and Rachel were there too, having a coffee with them. Toivo showed them the ducks. "Ducks for supper OK Helen?"

"OK" came Helen's reply.

Toivo then turned to Wilf. "Vilf, can you help me now clean up bear meat?"

"No problem, Toivo."

"First, maybe one coffee, ya?"

Once that was done, Wilf followed Toivo to the bear carcass, and they left the women to pluck and clean the ducks. Toivo brought along two good boning knives, a meat cleaver, and an extra good sized tarp, neatly rolled up. That tarp he opened up and laid it over a wheelbarrow. Wilf would soon understand the purpose. First Toivo opened up the tarp that covered the bear carcass. A few horse flies buzzed around the carcass, but being late in the season, there weren't many, and they were getting pretty slow. Toivo just ignored them, and got to work stripping the meat from the bones, Wilf followed suit immediately. The knives were sharp, and the blades were strong; they cut away the flesh in big chunks, and it didn't take them long before they had the bones stripped bare of meat.

Toivo threw the bones into the burning barrel, smashing the longer bones into shorter pieces with the meat cleaver until there was a compact pile of bones in the bottom of the barrel; then he poured a good splash of gasoline into the barrel and put a match to it. It ignited in a whoosh, as Toivo looked on approvingly. "Now let's grind up the meat," he said. He didn't bother with the enamel basin this time, but put a small wash tub under the meat grinder, to catch the discharge. Wilf fed the grinder with the chunks of bear meat, and Toivo, as strong as an ox, kept grinding it up.

When the tub was near full, Wilf took hold of it with Toivo, and together, they dumped it onto the tarp on the wheelbarrow. Wilf offered to 'spell Toivo off on the grinder'. Toivo declined and thanked him saying "good exercise." Wilf had a hard time not to laugh. They continued in this way until all the meat was ground up and in the wheelbarrow, which was nicely heaped now with ground bear meat. The grinding went a lot slower than the stripping, but from start to finish it took them less than three hours. It amazed Wilf that such a large animal could be reduced to a compact pile of ground meat in a wheelbarrow.

The fire in the barrel had burned itself out now; Toivo looked into the barrel and was satisfied the fire had done its job. He turned on the water hose, and adjusting the nozzle to a strong jet, rinsed out the grinder and the small wash tub, and having covered the grinder again, shut off the hose and stretched it out downhill to let it drain, as it would soon be freezing. Taking hold of the wheelbarrow Toivo coasted down the sloping ground to the ice house. There, he took a scoop shovel and cleared an area about ten feet square of sawdust; once the ice was laid bare, he began putting the bear meat onto the ice.

Wilf lit a cigarette and watched him work. He took a spade, and started placing shovelfuls of bear meat, each about five or six pounds, on the bare ice, in neat rows, each pile being two inches from the next one. Once he had emptied the wheelbarrow, there were several rows of little piles; he then laid the tarp from the wheel barrow over all the little piles as well as the bear fat, which also made a few more little piles, and with the scoop shovel began to heap sawdust over everything. Wilf took the shovel saying, "Take a break, partner."

Toivo lit a smoke and let him shovel. "Lots of meat for the mink this vinter," he explained to Wilf.

"I would think so," said Wilf, as he shovelled, trying not to laugh.

When it was well heaped in sawdust, Toivo said, "Good enough now Vilf; ve go now have it lunch and after make sauna, get clean. Tonight, nice dinner."

With that, they went up to the house and had some lunch. Helen, Rachel, and Serena had worked together plucking and cleaning the ducks and Helen was putting the stuffing in them now, which she'd made with wild rice and onions from the garden. Asked if anyone was into a sauna, the women declined; they would stick around and do supper. Serena said she would just take a shower at the house. Toivo and Wilf left for Rachel's to have their sauna.

They fired the sauna up, and once it was hot, they indulged themselves with a few good sessions in and out of the heat; Toivo had his beer in between heats, and had provided Wilf with a large bottle of club soda. A couple of hours after they had left the house, they were back, with supper just on the verge. The smell of those roasted duck was most pleasant. Toivo sat back with another beer and Wilf a coffee, as they waited for dinner. They were nicely done their drinks when dinner was served.

All four ducks were placed on the table. Two each on separate platters placed on opposite ends of the table. The potatoes, beets, and carrots were laid out in bowls in between. Toivo served the duck from one end of the table, and Helen from the other. Toivo carved off a good chunk of one duck for Wilf, giving him a leg, a thigh, half a breast, and dug a generous scoop of the wild rice and onion dressing for him from the ducks cavity. No gravy had been made, but there was butter for the vegetables. All in all, Wilf had a pretty good plateful of food.

He waited until everyone was served before he started on his food. He noticed that the skin on the duck was quite black, and having eaten roasted wild ducks many times before in his life, had never ever seen them come out like that. He bit into the breast that came with a covering of skin, and found the skin delicious.

"How do you get the skin to come out like that, Helen?" he asked.

"I sprinkle sugar over it, before I put them in the oven. I put them in on a high temperature for about twenty minutes, to give them a good singe and keep in the juice; and then I turn it down and let them cook slowly."

"Well it sure tastes good," he said. "I've never had better."

"Thank you Wilf. I love watching you eat!"

It was a most enjoyable dinner for everyone there. There was no pie for dessert this time, but it wasn't really necessary; everyone was stuffed. With dinner done, Wilf sat back in the front room with Rachel and Toivo having a coffee, while Serena, Helen and Madeleine cleaned up on the dishes. When the dishes were done, Serena gathered up her mother, who had dozed off in the rocker, and Wilf, who joined them for the walk back to Rachel's cabin. As they were leaving Helen said, "If you come by tomorrow, we've got roast venison on the menu." They were all in agreement with that, and had hardly started back, when Wilf burst out laughing.

"What's so funny?" Serena asked.

Wilf told her the story of the grinding up of bear meat, and how Toivo had laid it out to keep in the icehouse. He concluded with saying, "He's quite the boy, that Toivo; I mean who would have ever thought of doing something like that?"

"Toivo would have. He's a Finlander."

And that to Wilf pretty well explained it. He'd spent some good time around Port Arthur in the past year, and there were a lot of Finns there. They were a unique culture to themselves. Finland was next to Sweden, but their language was totally different; in fact there was no other language similar, except with the possibility of Estonian, which was somewhat similar, but not completely. The Finns had their own bookstore and newspaper in Port Arthur, published in Finnish. There was a Finnish restaurant called the 'Hoito' that served excellent Finnish pancakes, and the restaurant was always jammed full of customers at breakfast time with a lineup at the door of people waiting to get in.

Traditionally great woodsmen, many of them worked in the bush cutting pulpwood for the pulp and paper mills in town. Hard working people, these Finlanders would spend their winters in their camps in the bush cutting pulp, and building up their stake till spring breakup, when the bush would be shut done till the snow was gone. At spring breakup they'd come to town with their hard earned money, and a good many would go on a prolonged binge, drinking as hard as they worked, till their money ran out.

Every spring there would be a few of them, depressed from the fallout from their bouts of extreme binging and the resultant empty bank account, hanging themselves. It was a joke around Port Arthur, that if you were a Finlander, you needed a license to buy a rope. There was a story going around, (perhaps unfounded) that one spring seven Finlanders were found hanging from the same tree. True or not, Finlanders in many cases went to extremes; when they worked, they worked hard; when they drank, they drank hard; if two Finlanders fought, one was liable to pull out a knife; and if they had a bath, it had to be a steam bath.

Toivo was a reasonably balanced family man. He loved his beer, but drank moderately. Oddly, Wilf had noticed he seemed to prefer rye whisky to Finnish vodka. He was a hard working man, but loved the time he spent with his family. The dock by the lake, the ice house, his passion for hunting and his little mink ranch were all in keeping with his Finnish roots; and the obsession with feeding the mink was not out of context. The wonderful thing about it was that bizarre session of grinding up Toivo's bear meat that had pulled Wilf right out of the heavy mood that had hung on him ever since Gus was blasted. Every time he thought about his afternoon with Toivo, he'd start laughing again. What was life but living, and sometimes it was fun.

They were back at Rachel's cabin now. She unlocked the door and let Serena and Wilf in. Serena turned on a light, and everything was just as they'd left it. Rachel bid them good night, went to her bed, and was soon asleep. Wilf and Serena went to bed and did not sleep. Wilf was happy now. He and Serena were right in the mood for some fun sex, and made love a good few times before finally giving into sleep. Every time in between sessions, Wilf would think about Toivo, and start laughing again.

"Was it that funny?" Serena asked.

"You had to be there," Wilf explained.

"Toivo is nuts," she said.

"I think we're all nuts, Serena, but he's one hell of a guy! He's one of a kind."

"Yup, he is," she agreed then rolled over and fell asleep. It took a little longer for Wilf as he was enjoying reliving his afternoon with Toivo.

They both slept in the following morning. It was already daylight when they awoke. Rachel had been up for awhile. She had coffee made, but waited on them to start her porridge. Wilf was first out of the bedroom, eager to relieve him. He wished Rachel a good morning as he made for the cabin door. Rachel smiled at this. On his way to the outhouse, he saw there was a heavy frost on the ground. Winter was not too far away. He reflected on Toivo as he passed his water, and still felt the giddy mirth. His mood was further enhanced by a night of good lovemaking. Serena was up in her house coat and passed him on his way back from the outhouse; she was on her way there. Rachel had the porridge on the go now, and a coffee on the table for him. Thanking her, he sat done to a coffee and a cigarette. She made no comment that he'd started smoking again; she simply brought him an ashtray.

"Did you sleep well," she asked.

"Like a log," he said. She could see he was all smiles this morning and was happy for him. "It was sure a great dinner we had," he went on.

"Yes, it was a very good visit," she agreed. The porridge was ready when Serena was back, and the three of them had their breakfast. Rachel had also sliced up some of her bannock, and put out some of her homemade raspberry jam. They ate quietly, enjoying their food, followed by another coffee; then Wilf took a coffee to the sitting room, to get out of their way and let them clean up. He brought the ashtray with him, sat down on the couch and had a cigarette with his coffee.

Just as he was nicely finished his coffee and cigarette, Toivo showed up at the door with Helen and Madeleine. He'd brought with him the leftovers from last night's dinner. Wilf and Toivo had eaten one duck along with its dressing between them. The ladies, including Madeleine, had only managed to eat a duck and a half amongst the four of them. Toivo handed them the bag containing the remaining duck and a half.

"Make it nice lunch for later," he explained; "how 'bout ve take it sauna now," he went on. Wilf and Serena were in instant agreement; they needed a bath. "Good. Come on Vilf. You and me, ve make it sauna." Wilf followed him to the sauna. Toivo was all business, getting the fire kindled in the heater. Once he had it going, Wilf helped fill the tank in the sauna with water. Wilf filled the buckets from the pump and passed them to Toivo, who emptied them and passed the empty buckets back to Wilf. Soon they had the tank filled, and closed the sauna door to let the heat build up. The fire in the heater was going strong. Toivo threw another good chunk of birch into it, closed its door and took a seat on the bench.

"Sit down now Vilf. Relax." He took out his cigarettes and said, "You smoke now, eh?" Wilf nodded, sitting down, and accepted the offer of a cigarette. Toivo had one, too. "Good to visit with you, Vilf," he said, sticking out his hand. Wilf shook his hand and said without thinking, *"D'accord,"*

"D'accord?"

"Wups, that's French. It means I feel the same."

Toivo shook his hand again. "It's good to be friends, Vilf. You Frenchman, eh?"

"Well, half French. Mom was French but my dad was Irish."

"I see."

The sauna was heated nicely. They went back to the cabin, to let the ladies go first. Once they were all done with the sauna, the six of them lunched on the remains of the ducks and dressing, and some of Rachel's bannock as well. After, Toivo left for home with Helen and Madeleine, Serena and Wilf worked with Rachel to wash the towels. When they were all washed, Wilf went down with Serena to rinse the towels in the lake, wring them out and hung them out to dry on Rachel's clothesline. Going back into the cabin they found Rachel had gone to her bedroom to take a nap. It was not yet mid-afternoon so Serena and Wilf decided to stretch out and relax as well. A good night's lovemaking, a good sauna, and a good lunch had taken its toll. They were both soon fast asleep themselves.

They awoke a couple of hours later feeling rested. Rachel was already up and had made coffee. Wilf went to the pump by the sink, and splashed cold water on his face. Serena handed him a towel and did the same. The morning's heavy frost was long gone now, and the afternoon had warmed considerably. There was also a good gentle breeze so the towels would soon be dry. They sat down for a coffee with Rachel. She had put together a blueberry pie, made from a jar of blueberry preserves she'd put aside from the summer's bounty. Her pie was cooking in the oven, soon to be ready.

When they were done their coffee, she checked the pie and found it to be cooked. Using hot mats, she put it to cool and poured everyone another coffee. Wilf had a cigarette with the second cup. When they were done with that coffee, Rachel put the still warm pie in a shallow cardboard box. The three of them, along with the pie, headed over to Toivo and Helen's for a venison dinner.

It was another good feast which was followed by the blueberry pie with vanilla ice cream. Madeleine eyes came wide with the appearance of dessert. She put away a full share of it. Again, once the cleanup was done, and all the goodbyes were said, Wilf, with Serena and Rachel, went back to Rachel's. Being the end of October, it was by now quite dark, though there were street lights to brighten their way. The air had cooled considerably, and another good frost was certainly coming on. When they arrived at Rachel's they found the towels on the line dried. While Wilf and Serena gathered them up, Rachel opened up the cabin and turned on some lights.

Serena folded up the towels for her mother and put them away. Rachel went straight to bed while Serena and Wilf weren't far behind. They lay together naked and talked for a good while before making any moves toward sex. Wilf's mood had totally changed now since he first arrived. Whether it was Toivo's bear meat that did the trick or Serena's good lovemaking, he couldn't be sure. One thing was for sure. He knew he'd been very blessed to have good people in his life now. As he lay relaxed and warm next to Serena, he felt tremendous peace.

Wilf from the beginning felt the difference in age with Serena but she plainly didn't. Serena was in no way promiscuous, but young, healthy and in love with Wilf. She would ignore his hesitancy to initiate sex as she knew he loved it and it was good. Serena was not in the least reserved to get things started and loved Wilf for the gentleman he was.

As they talked on, in due course her hand came over his penis. Finding it quite stiff, she suggested they get on with some good lovemaking. Already wet and without further ado, Wilf obligingly mounted her and began the copulation; the magic of good lovemaking was right there. For Wilf, it had to be Serena. It was a lot more than just plain sex. It was ecstasy beyond anything he'd ever known. The climax was something very special but what he enjoyed as much or more was just laying with her so relaxed after coming; just being with her. He enjoyed everything he did with her. He loved her mother, and Toivo's family. He sometimes wondered if this was really him, if this was all a dream. But Serena was real, she loved him, and that was plain to see. From being a seemingly incorrigible haywire, he at last was finding balance in his life.

The bitterness of his lost family; his hatred for his brother Clarence; his wasted years of dissipation and self-loathing were all gone now, as though it didn't matter anymore and it never did. Wilf was happy now. Yesterday was yesterday. He knew Serena was the one. He had to have her in his life. However there were some uncertainties that bothered him. Serena made it plain to him that she was there for him whenever he was ready. She made no ultimatum and just put it out there. He as much as agreed that was what he wanted but was reluctant to actually make it happen.

He had some money now but hadn't looked for a place nor bought a car let alone buy a ring. There was a nagging feeling of uncertainty about the future of the mine. Production was good and steady from the underground but it was slowly falling apart. The magic of his partnership at work had faded with the loss of Gus from the team. He had no doubt that he'd struck gold with Serena but so far had made no real move to commit.

They'd gone to bed just past nine that evening and had made love three times by midnight. Through all that, Serena never tried to open the discussion on marriage or any form of living arrangement. Finally, tired from a long happy day, they slept. Again Rachel was first up in the morning with the coffee made, and porridge on the go. Wilf and Serena had their breakfast with Rachel, and then got packed up for the road. They kissed her good bye and caught the school bus back to town. Serena went back to the restaurant for the late shift while Wilf went back to work at the mine to start his week of afternoon shifts.

It was now the 8th of November. The days were getting shorter and much cooler. Snow hadn't got there yet but wouldn't be far away. Wilf was in the Dry getting changed for another shift, his last graveyard. He'd had a good visit with Serena for a weekend two weeks previously but now he was right back into the routine of work. Stan and Tom Higgins were there changing for work as well. Once changed, the three of them strapped on their lamps and went to the wicket to get their lineup for the shift. Pipe and track were in, they were told, and they were coming into a clean face. Off they went for a good end to a good week.

Tom Higgins, who was replacing Gus, had worked out all right. Mercifully, with Hank Loster replacing Vince Jamieson as lead miner on their cross shift, and Al Wasney, a good driftman brought in as a third, things went smoothly for Wilf's drift heading on the 1,100' level.

Vince had been put on the production level, operating a slusher on 700 in a scran drift. There wasn't too much he could botch up there. No great skill was required to be a slusherman. The slusher had two handles. Push down on the left handle, the back cable would tighten and pull the scraper back to the tail block. Push down on the right handle, the pull cable would tighten and draw the scraper with the muck in front of it into the mill hole. It was a job that suited Vince Jamieson right down to the ground.

Production on the 700' level went on steadily. The muck from the scrans went nonstop, although some of the scrans were showing more and more the effects of crushing pressure as the ore body above them crumbled and caved into the boxholes. The cracks were getting worse on the cement walls and backs of the scrans as relentless pressure on them pushed and squeezed. But still good flow of muck continued from most of the scrans in spite of this.

On that same graveyard shift, a miner named Duff Dick came to work his last shift. He had given his notice and planned to return to Scotland with his wife and children once he was done with work at the mine. As it was to be his last shift, he'd spent a good few hours in the pub before showing up for shift. Tom Cruikshank, his shifter, could smell the beer on him at the wicket but let it pass. 'What the hell. It's his last shift,' he thought.

Duff Dick went to his usual work place slushing a scran drift. He was working alone operating the slusher. The train crew had pulled up and needed seven more cars to fill the train. The muck in the scran was coming freely through the boxholes and he soon had their train filled for them. Duff Dick was quite sure, that even if the train crew made it back to his scran, it would be very late in the shift. He took a walk up the scran to see how the muck was coming. Every boxhole except one were running. The one that wasn't running was empty and vacant. No sign of a hangup and no muck in sight. Being his last shift, he thought 'why bother', and went back to the slusher. Cruikshank had made his rounds while he was filling the train so Duff knew he wouldn't be back till much later in the shift. A long day and night in the pub were taking their toll so Duff took the bench from behind the slusher and put it against the end wall of the scran. He then got comfortable and went to sleep. He was never to awake from that sleep.

There was a rumbling sound unheard by Duff Dick in his deep sleep. He might have heeded the warning had he been awake. He would have fled down the manway and then run to safety. But that was not to happen. Within minutes the rumbling sound became a powerful whoosh. A thick stream of red mud poured out that empty boxhole, down the scran and out the millhole filling the crosscut below right to the back. The mud continued to pour into the scran. With the crosscut plugged now, it pushed back past the millhole over and behind the slusher neatly filling the end of the scran right to the back, burying poor Duff Dick alive! It was indeed Duff Dick's last shift.

The mud coming from the millhole flowed both ways down the crosscut until it finally ran out. The train crew was the first to come upon the problem. They came to a stop just in front of the bank of oozing mud. "Holy shit, would you look at that," one of them said. His partner stared, his mouth agape.

"We'd better get some help," the other said, and they took off for the station on the motor, leaving the cars behind in the cross cut. On their way, they came across the production shifter, Tom Cruikshank, who was walking towards them up the hanging wall drift.

"What's up, boys?" He asked. The two train men were interrupting each other in their excitement.

"The whole crosscut is buried in mud," they yelled not in unison.

"Let's go have a look," said Tom calmly as he jumped on the end of the motor beside the switchman. Back they went. Tom was aghast at the sight of it. "Holy fuck, isn't Duff Dick in that scran?" The thought had just occurred to all three in horror.

"Get your cars out of the crosscut boys," he said. "I've got to get a mucking machine in here and start cleaning this up. The Eimco 21 is too small for this job. Leave the cars in the hanging wall drift for now and bring in the Eimco 40 from the layby. Can either of you boys run a mucking machine?" They both shook their heads.

"No worries. Just bring in the Eimco 40, and then bring in the cars behind it. I'll get us a mucker. When you get the train back here, I'd like one of you to go around by the footwall drift to the other end of this crosscut, and see if there's any sign of Duff Dick. Then stay with the train. I'll be back with a mucker."

Tom went down to the 1,100' level. He found Wilf, Stan and Tom Higgins eating their lunch at the station after having just mucked out their cross shift's round. "I'm going to have to leave you boys shorthanded," he said, "I need a good mucker for the Eimco 40." He explained the emergency. "Who can I ask?" he went on.

"Never run one," said Tom, "I just know the Eimco 21."

"Me neither," said Stan.

Wilf had never run one either but he was sure he could do it. It was a much bigger machine than the Eimco 21. It had a broader bucket that dumped into a hopper right behind it which channeled the muck onto a conveyor extending fifteen feet behind and was raised so that it had the clearance to load the ten ton cars. He'd seen one of these machines before. To him, mucking was mucking, and other than that, it was just a matter of figuring out the conveyor.

"I think I can do it," Wilf offered.

"Good," said Tom and then turning to Stan and Tom Higgins, he said "You two are on your own now unless I can find you a third."

"We'll manage," said Stan.

Wilf was concerned when he got to where the mudrun was in the crosscut. Nobody had thought of this happening and nobody had heard from Duff Dick. He could see at a glance that there were more problems with this block cave method than just pressure and squeezing....maybe this was one problem too many.

He hooked up the bullhose to the mucker, opened up the air to the machine and was quickly able to find the valve that activated the conveyor. The bucket and traction levers were much the same as a 21, except the bucket was not mounted on a rocker but on a pivot. It dumped directly into a hopper and fed the conveyor that loaded the cars. He tested the functions moving the machine ahead and back a few feet and dumping the empty bucket against the hopper.

He was glad he'd brought his slickers. He still had the pants on from the drift on 1,100. He put on the coat, as well; this job was going to be messy. He also wore safety glasses now; he'd started wearing them ever since Gus' accident. He dropped the bucket, and hit the traction lever, pushing the machine into the slimy mud. It was a soupy, sloppy mass, without much solid form to it at all. He filled the bucket and dumped it, and continued doing that. He'd filled a 10 ton car with the slop and could see little difference in the crosscut. He hadn't moved ahead at all as the mud just kept running.

There was a kind of solid consistency to it, though the loaded car looked more like a small pond of mud than anything. It slopped over the sides of the conveyor as he mucked, and the mass jiggled and shook in the car as the trammers pulled the car back to switch. By the time he'd mucked out half the train, he could see he was actually moving ahead on the stream of mud, and by the time he'd mucked all twelve cars full, the mud had quit pouring out of the millhole. Halfway through the next train, the millhole was open and the manway was clear. By this time the shifter was back.

Doesn't look good for Duff Dick," he said to Wilf, "I was around from the footwall drift. The crosscut was plugged with mud just like this end, and nobody's seen Duff Dick. Better not muck any more from this end. I wouldn't want to see it to run again, and get you caught from behind. Best you move your machine over and work from the footwall end."

Wilf agreed but pointed to the manway. "Let's take a look and see if we can see Duff," he said.

Tom agreed, and went up the manway first, and was able to stand on the edge of the millhole. Wilf came up behind and found Tom Cruikshank speechless, his eyes agog. Wilf looked in the direction of his stare to see the head of Dull Dick protruding from a bank of mud; he was still buried to his shoulders, but the mud had slid from his head and neck. His hard hat had been knocked loose, and his hair was matted in the red mud; he was quite dead.

The shifter was transfixed and speechless. Wilf broke the silence, shaking him gently. "Maybe we should get him out of here before we do anything else," he said to Tom. Tom came around.

"Yes," said Tom. "We better get poor Duff out of here."

There were four miners from the mine rescue squad waiting down below in the crosscut. The mud that had poured out of the boxhole had run out now, and the boxhole was again open and empty. The scran drift was still covered with the thick mud from the tail block at the far end of the scran to the front end, where it came to a tapered to a finish by the drop at the mill hole's edge.

"Take a break now, if you like, Wilf," said Tom, "I can get these guys to dig him out. It's getting near quitting time actually; you can go now if you want."

"No, I'll stay. I want to see this thing through."

"Good enough."

Two of the mine rescue boys start digging Duff Dick out of the bank of mud, scooping the sloppy mud away from its hapless victim toward the open millhole. As they scooped, the mud gradually slid away from Duff Dick's slumped over seated posture. As it finally showed his knees and then half of his shins, his body fell forward landing him face first in the mud. Before the two mine rescue workers could lift his body free, one of the workers got sick to his stomach. The worker went for the manway trying to restrain his vomit, but he couldn't. As he climbed down the manway his eyes were streaming with tears while he wretched, and wretched, and wretched.

Wilf climbed up in his place, and he and the other worker were able to pull the body free of the mud. Another worker brought up the basket stretcher; they strapped in the lifeless body, and lowered it down through the millhole to the crosscut below, where it was placed on the hood of the waiting motor and conveyed to the station. Wilf and the shifter went out with the motor. The rest of them followed out to the station on foot. At the station, the shift boss took a water hose, and with a gentle pressure, rinsed the mud from Duff Dick's face. His face, once washed clean, was as black as his boots, in a horrid death mask. Tom dropped the running water, and wept uncontrollably.

"I shouldn't have let him go to work tonight," he finally managed; then said very quietly to Wilf, "I knew he'd been drinking. I should have sent him home."

Wilf shut the water off; then put his hand on Tom's shoulder, and said, "He's OK now, Tom. His problems are over."

By the end of the day the company had made an analysis of the problem and had filed a report. They had realized by now that this block caving method was not caving en bloc as they thought it would. Instead of the ore body crumbling and caving evenly it had funneled straight up from the boxholes like so many smokestacks. One of them unfortunately caved right into the old Errington pit bottom, right into a lake of red mud. It was diluted by rain water to its soupy consistency sitting there in a massive volume at the bottom of the pit. Once the pit bottom had been perforated, the slimy mud ran freely down the crater, out the boxhole into the scran, out the millhole, and both ways down the crosscut.

It had become apparent that this grandiose plan of block caving was a bad idea. They were not recovering the orebody below the pit bottom as they'd hoped. The boxholes had funneled straight up through the orebody instead of drawing evenly from it. Although the orebody didn't cave as planned, the craters so created had broken the structure of the orebody. The weight of it now unsupported came to rest fully on the scran drifts. Those scran drifts that they'd worked so hard to prevent from caving, were steadily getting squeezed, and crumbling more and more every day. They could not continue to mine by this method. The scrans could not hold up against the pressure, and it was now becoming dangerous.

It was now into the second week of November; Wilf had come to show up for his first day afternoon shift. The air was chilled and the sky was grey. Any precipitation now would be snow. He hadn't taken Serena up on her offer for a visit for the long change just passed; he just wasn't in the mood, with what had just gone down with the mud run and subsequent death of Duff Dick. He'd made the trip into Port Arthur again with Hank Loster to visit Gus instead. Molly and Stan had also come along. Gus was sitting up when they got there. The bandages were off his eyes, but all those present were soon to realize that Gus was virtually blind.

Molly came to him right away with a hug, and Gus hugged her back. She had to tell him that Stan, Hank, and Wilf were in the room; he couldn't see them. He stood up to welcome them, sticking out his hand in the wrong direction. His face was healed now, but the left eye had had to be removed. He was waiting for its amputation to heal completely, and would then be fitted for a glass eye. With his right eye he could tell light from dark, some colours, and shadows, but he hadn't much sight at all and no hope of improvement. Stan, Hank, and Wilf all gave him a hand shake, hugging him as they did so; they were stuck for conversation, but managed to say a few words in greeting him. When Gus sat down again, Molly told him about the mud run and the demise of Duff Dick.

"You know," Gus said finally, "that is not a good mine, at all."

"No, not so good," affirmed Stan.

Stan, Hank, and Wilf didn't stay long, but left Molly to be with her mate. She would be staying on a few days. Molly and Gus thanked them for coming, and with that they headed back to Atikokan. It was a quiet ride home; they were all with their thoughts of the grimness of Gus' condition, and the recent demise of Duff Dick. It was a somber weekend for Wilf. He went to church that Sunday for the first time since he'd come to town. Father Grant greeted him at the door with a strong hand shake, and was most pleased to see him.

"I'd like to see you again father, "said Wilf as he was leaving. "Then don't leave Wilf. Stay behind, and I can see you very shortly."

Father Grant made time for him soon after the service and Wilf brought him up to date on the recent sad events. Gus, who was to all purposes now blind and would remain so, had bothered him the most. Gus' mining days were over and life for him and Molly would never be the same. Wilf loved them both and felt a crushing sadness. Father Grant listened attentively and then prayed with Wilf.

"Life will be different for them son but with God's help Gus and Molly will find their way."

Wilf had left him feeling much better than when he had come to church that day; perhaps more for the good priest's compassion than his prayers. But that was yesterday and it was now Monday. He was starting his first afternoon shift which was his first shift back after last week's disaster. He approached the shifter's wicket with Tom Higgins and Stan. Before they received any instruction for the shift, they were all given two weeks' notice of layoff from the mine. Of the 400 miners employed in the underground, 300 were to be laid off as November the 25th, Wilf, Stan and Higgins included.

The three of them were told that they were to continue in the drift on 1,100 until their layoff became effective. This particular shift they would be coming into a clean face. They went to work that afternoon none too surprised about their news. Garth came by their heading just as they were drilled off. He made a lame attempt at levity as he approached.

"Hi guys," he began. "They say 'if you don't like the news, shoot the messenger'."

Stan ignored the humour of it saying, "It's nothing personal, I'm sure, it just is what it is, that's all; I was looking for a job when I found this one."

"What do you think you might do?"

"Elliot Lake's going strong. There are a number of mines there always looking for miners. Its uranium but the money's good. I'll likely go there but I'll finish this one first." Higgins agreed with him.

"How 'bout you, Wilf?"

"I don't know just now....I'll cross that bridge when I come to it, I guess. What's happening here?"

"Well, they're giving up on the block cave method; it's not working...." Garth went on to tell them of what was in store. Production from the underground would be put on hold. They were going to try a different approach. They planned to slash out an broad area above the 900' level and cover the exposed area using old electrical cables from the open pit and old hoist cables from the underground criss-crossed to form a huge matt. They would then try to cave the ground below this matt and pull it out on the 900' level. The matt spread out over this wide area would ensure that the ground would cave evenly unlike on the 700' level; at least this was the hope. This of course was experimental and would not involve a great number of miners. Garth would stay on as he was a development shifter. But the production shifters, including Tom Cruikshank, would all be laid off on the 25th. The development on 1100 would be halted. All development would go towards creating and setting up the matt method.

"Doesn't sound like I'll be missing out on too much here," commented Stan. He knew work of that nature would most likely be on company time. It would be tedious and not done on contract, so no bonus would be paid. "Well, it's been good here while it lasted," he concluded.

Garth was about to leave them when Wilf asked, "What about Jamieson? Did he get laid off?"

"No. Vince was hired in '56 and all those hired on or before '56 get to stay on. He'll be doing the matt," Garth replied.

Wilf had to smile at this."From the sounds of that, it should be just the right job for a man of Vince Jamieson's talent... dragging around old cables, I mean. That'll suit him just fine." Garth simply left while Stan and Tom Higgins had to laugh.

For the two weeks that remained, work went on without a hitch for the miners on 1100. Toward the end of the last week it had finally began to snow. Not a lot at first but the weather was freezing now and any snow that came now would remain for the duration of the winter. Their last shift was a Friday, the last Friday of day shift. At the end of their shift, they came up to surface for the last time and took their shower in the Dry as usual. However, this time they gathered up their gear, put it in their kit bags as this time they'd be leaving the mine for the last time. As Stan had put it, 'It was good while it lasted'. It was over now.

Wilf had considered the idea of following Stan to Elliot Lake, which was still into a boom, but was reluctant to leave town. He didn't want to walk away from a good friendship with Serena and was trying to get his mind around how he could get things to work. Steep Rock was the main employer in town but with the mine in recession now, most spin off work like building construction was on hold as well. There was the possibility of work in the Sawmill in Sapawe but that wouldn't even come to half the money he'd been making. On the other hand, he had money now, well over three thousand in the bank, three hundred cash in his room, and over a hundred dollars in his pocket. He had enough without making big money. If he took a job in the Sawmill, he could be with Serena. They could work something out.

He got off the mine bus with Stan, took his mining gear up to his room and then headed over to Sinclair's. Happily Serena was there. Wilf took a stool at the counter and when she brought him a coffee, he asked her when she might be finished.

"I'm not done till eight o'clock," she said. "What's up?"

"Could we go for some dinner, say over at the Steep Rock when you're done here? I need to talk to you."

"Sure we can," Serena answered. "I'll just need to go to my room and clean up a bit first."

"I'll be here when you're ready," said Wilf.

About then Stan walked in, took a booth and asked "Goina join me for some food partner?"

"I'll join you for some company but I'm going out for dinner a bit later."

Stan noticed Serena smiling and responded. "Oh, I see."

Wilf sat just having a coffee, through Stan's dinner. He waited until Stan had finished eating and had been served a coffee, before lighting a smoke. They talked of their immediate plans now that they were both laid off. Stan was talking strongly of leaving by month's end for Elliot Lake. There was lots of work available there with good money to be made and huge bonuses being paid for good driftmen. It was the place to go.

"So what about you, partner? What you think about that?" asked Stan in closing.

"Sounds like the place to go all right Stan. Sounds good for sure, but I think I might just stay around for a bit. I need some time to think about this."

Stan glanced over to see Serena listening closely. "Right, well best of luck to you partner. Keep in touch,"he said shaking his hand, and got up to leave.

Wilf stepped out of the restaurant into the freshness of the early evening. It was just past six thirty but already dark. There was a skiff of snow on the ground. The weather was freezing but not uncomfortable. Serena would not be ready for a good hour and a half so he had some time to kill. He thought that maybe he should take a walk over to the Steep Rock Hotel and see about reserving a table at the Walnut Room for an eight thirty dinner. He'd better make sure they'd be still open at that time. Once that was taken care of, he would still have plenty of time to get changed and meet up with Serena to go for dinner.

It wasn't all that far to the Steep Rock Hotel. Three blocks straight passed Sinclair's, one block to the left and across the street would put him right in front of the hotel. He enjoyed the walk. The fresh air hit the spot and his mind was full of the possibilities of a life with Serena. As he approached the front entrance to the hotel he noticed a group of men who were forced out of the bar due to the six thirty to eight pm closure. (This 6:30 to 8:00 pm closure was in effect in Ontario pubs at the time. The idea was to get the drunks home for dinner. The law was changed in 1965 leaving pubs open right through to 1:00 am.) The group was mostly drunk, stood around talking noisily in the parking lot adjacent to the bar's exit. Among them was Vince Jamieson who was scheduled to work a graveyard shift. His eye caught Wilf approaching the front entrance.

Vince had felt slighted when he had been taken out of the drift and replaced by Hank Loster. But he was feeling good about the fact that Wilf had been laid off while he himself still had a job. Vince had had a few beers and felt like letting Wilf know just how good he felt about that. "How's it going haywire," Vince began. "Heading back to the Kimberley, eh? Maybe see how things are doing on Cumberland Street?"

Wilf stared him up and down ignoring his comments but Vince went on.

"Or maybe you'd just like to hang around, and shack up with your squaw in Sapawe? Maybe try the Sawmill..."

Vince never finished what he'd started to say. Wilf nailed him with a short left jab knocking him off balance and then connected with a hard right to the jaw knocking him to the ground. Vince was obviously drunk but would have been no match for Wilf even if he was sober. Wilf would have left things go at that but Vince got back on his feet. He was unwilling to let it go.

"A good job is wasted on a tramp like you," he said. "They're keeping the right people."

Wilf could see the fight was over even if Vince couldn't. But Vince was asking for more. Every grudge he ever felt on Vince took over. At first he toyed with Vince. He was in no hurry now. Wilf knew he had him and he was enjoying this. Vince finally came in with a huge roundhouse swing, but Wilf stepped inside his wild effort and pounded him hard in the guts. Then he let him recover...almost.

"This is for Gus, asshole," he said, as he booted him hard in the groin.

Vince doubled over for a bit but slowly managed to regain his posture and his breathing. He stumbled toward Wilf again mouthing obscenities while attempting another wild swing. He missed Wilf completely, almost falling on his face. The crowd from the bar had closed in around them now. A couple of the drunks were cheering Wilf on but a few were trying to get Wilf to stop.

"Leave him be, Wilf," one shouted. "He's drunk. He's no man to fight with you."

Wilf wasn't hearing anything now. He saw red only as his eyes were tight and transfixed as though in a trance; his face a mask of fiendish delight. He was overcome with the satisfaction of beating on this mindless prick, and was powerless to stop himself. He let Vince recover his balance then nailed him again. Vince was getting shaken now and realized this was a no win. Looking puzzled and confused, that obnoxious look of his was gone. Vince attempted one last abortive swing and missed again. Wilf pounded him several times in the gut. Vince doubled over, winded and barely able to stand. Wilf by this time had lost any sense of self control and went berserk.

He punched Vince hard on the jaw straightening him up. Then hit him three more times in the face so hard and fast his hands were a blur. Vince fell back, sliding to a sitting position against the fender of a parked car. Wilf continued pounding his face in as Vince was sprawled backwards against the car. Vince's nose and jaw were broken, eyes blackened, teeth knocked out, and his face an unrecognizable swollen mess. Vince slid down the side of the car crying till he was sitting on the ground. Wilf took him by the throat with both hands, and squeezed, and squeezed, and squeezed until Vince passed out.....he wasn't crying any more.

Two of the men present who had the sense to intervene, took ahold of Wilf from behind taking an arm on either side to pull him off. At first they were lifting Vince with him but two more men stepped in and broke his grasp. Someone took Vince's pulse and found he was still alive. Vince began to breathe again finally. He was crying, still slumped against the car where he fell.

"Wilf, you could have killed him!" It was Joe Kilgannon who spoke.

"I intended to," was Wilf's response with no change of expression.

Joe passed him a mickey of rye, almost full, hoping to settle him down. "Better have a drink, Wilf." Joe suggested.

Without a word, while still staring at Vince's beaten face, he took the bottle, and putting it to his mouth, Wilf upended it and emptied half of it. Joe watched in awe as the bubbles rolled up the neck of the bottle. The air displaced the liquid flowing down Wilf's throat, as though it was a straight drop from his mouth to his gullet. Wilf could feel the burn of good whisky warming in his stomach and that old familiar euphoria spread through him like magic. Joe reached for his bottle in vain. Wilf wasn't letting go of it. He upended the bottle one more time but this time emptying it completely. He then let out a very satisfied gasp as he handed the empty bottle back to his gaping friend. "Thanks, partner!" Wilf proclaimed "That was just what I needed." Joe accepted the empty bottle more amazed than disappointed.

Just then a police cruiser showed up with an ambulance. The police constable looked at Wilf's bloody knuckles and then at Vince's pulverized face and asked Wilf, "Friend of yours?"

Wilf answered "Not really."

"You were drinking?"

"I wasn't. But I am now."

Vince was loaded onto a stretcher and into the ambulance. The constable waited until the ambulance left and when he proceeded to ask Wilf what started the fight. A few from the group spoke on Wilf's behalf assuring the constable it was a fair fight and totally provoked by the other party. The constable then asked Wilf if he worked at the mine.

"No, not any more. I worked my last shift today. I've just been laid off."

"Then you'd best leave town. If you're gone by tomorrow, we'll let this pass." Wilf nodded in agreement. The constable then got in his cruiser and left.

Joe offered a ride but Wilf declined the offer. "Thanks, I'd like to walk," he said. From the wild look in Wilf's eyes, Joe was relieved to be done with him. The crowd outside the bar had dispersed by now so Joe went his way. Needless to say, Vince didn't make it to work that night.

Wilf was no longer thinking about dinner with Serena. His reality had suddenly changed. The old familiar thirst was upon him now and more whisky was what he needed. He started back for Cross' but instead of turning right at the corner, he turned to the left. Half way down the block, he crossed the street which put himself in front of Vet's Taxi stand. It was a mindless detour he'd made as though in a trance. He stepped inside the taxi shack. The dispatcher looked up from his paper asking, "Need a cab?"

"No. I need a bottle. Got any whisky?"

The dispatcher got up, went to the door, and looked both ways down the street. Satisfied Wilf was alone said, "I can give you a twenty six of Gold Stripe for ten bucks."

"Good enough." Wilf gave held out a twenty. The dispatcher reached for his twenty but Wilf held onto it "Whisky first!"

The dispatcher eyed his knuckles and nodded in agreement. He momentarily left Wilf, went outside to a boot locker around the back of the shack and pulled out a bottle. When he came back with the bottle and ten dollars change, Wilf gave him the twenty. About then a call came in for a cab. The dispatcher handed Wilf a brown paper bag as he took the call. Wilf took a long hard pull from the bottle then put it in the bag and left.

On the way back to his rooming house, he passed Serena on the street. She was just in front of Sinclair's about to enter the restaurant to meet up with Wilf when she saw him coming down the street. Serena was aghast when she saw him close to her. He was obviously drunk. Her eyes fell on his cut up knuckles, and his hand wrapped around the brown paper bag. Wilf, reeking of rye whiskey, walked passed her transfixed like she wasn't there. Serena couldn't believe the change. Two hours previously he was having a coffee in the restaurant with Stan waiting for a dinner date with her. Nobody had to explain it to her, it was over!

Wilf climbed the stairs into the rooming house. After taking another huge gulp of whisky, he pounded on Stan's door. Stan opened the door and just shook his head. "We need to talk, partner," Wilf attempted. "I think you're right. We should go to Elliot Lake, and drive a drift. Whaddaya say, Stan."

"No fucking chance, Wilf. You find your own way now," he said as he slammed the door in his face.

Wilf stared at the closed door for a moment, then muttered, "OK then....fuck you too!" and went to his own room. Not having drunk for six months he'd lost his tolerance for booze. He was quite drunk now. He gathered up his clothes, stuffed them into his empty kit bag and stuck in his shaving kit. After taking another good gulp of whisky, he carefully put the bottle in the top of the bag and closed it. The last thing he did was to take the three hundred dollars out from under his mattress and put the money into his wallet.

Wilf took his two kitbags, his mining gear in one and his street clothes in the other threw them over his shoulder and went downstairs to say good bye to Sadie Cross. It was well past nine now. She answered his knock, coming to the door in her housecoat, her hair in curlers. She took in his condition in a glance and asked "Yes, Wilf?"

Wilf said nothing for a moment as he dug in his pocket for the key. Finding it, he handed it to her with his cut up left hand. "Checking out, Sadie," he said simply rocking on his feet.

"Right," she said accepting the key. "And good luck to you, Wilf." She made no further attempt at conversation and started to close the door.

Before it was completely closed, Wilf managed to say, "Thank you, Sadie." Then he turned and left.

Packing his two kit bags over his shoulder, he headed back to Vet's Taxi. When he got to the stand he told the dispatcher, "I want a cab for the Kimberley Hotel."

The dispatcher looked at him for a moment. "In Port Arthur, you mean?"

"Yup"

"That'll cost you a hundred dollars. You got that kind of money?"

"I got it"

The dispatcher called in a cab. Then Wilf said, "Maybe get me one more bottle, partner.....I better take one for the road, eh?" The dispatcher obliged him, getting him one more twenty six of Gold Stripe and took another ten dollars. The cab pulled up, Wilf put his kit bags in the trunk and carefully removed his now half empty first bottle. He then got into the cab for his ride to his old stomping ground, the Kimberley Hotel.

In a sober moment much later and flat broke again, Wilf would reflect on his seemingly inevitable pattern and would ask himself why it should happen like this. It certainly wasn't the first time. Did he really ever have a plan? Or had he been saving all this time and just banking money for his next drunk? Did he really have a choice? Was he a victim or did he volunteer? Was he pushed or did he jump? And did any of this really matter now? He had given up the offer of a good life for another ride on the merry-go-round. He did it. He had a drink and now he was drinking.

THE END

About the author and this story:

Reid Youngberg was born in Malartic, a gold mining town in northern Quebec, 14th of August, 1943. Reid's father was in the mining industry all his working life supporting his family. In 1948 after having taken employment at Steep Rock Iron Mines, he moved his family to Atikokan, Ontario where Reid grew up. He graduated from Atikokan High School and at the age of 18 went off to Thompson, Manitoba and started working as an underground miner with Inco (International Nickel Company).

He worked all across Canada in the mining industry for almost thirty years including Atikokan for two of those years. Reid worked underground at Steep Rock Iron Mines in the mid sixties. Although A Miner's Story took place at that same mine, the story is based on facts and events occurring from the end of May to the end of November in 1957. The characters are fictitious but based on people that Reid knew and worked with.

42882272R00143

Made in the USA
Lexington, KY
21 June 2019